The Rectory

Rebecca Guy

Purple Stag Creatives

Also by Rebecca Guy

Ruin

Shattered

Haunted

Lost

Ivy Cottage

About Author

Rebecca Guy was first introduced to all things paranormal at the tender age of ten when she received Hans Holzer's 'Ghosts-True Encounters with the World Beyond' from Father Christmas. She tortured herself with the stories late into every night, after which she was too terrified to sleep.

Thanks Santa. The trauma started a love affair with all things horror and supernatural and she now like to write her own novels to torture herself and others with until they can't sleep. After all, sharing is caring. Rebecca was born and raised in Staffordshire. She still lives there with her three children and a beagle called Rosie.

a amazon.com/Rebecca-Guy/e/B07YZJ2G6T

f facebook.com/rebeccaguyauthor

⊙ instagram.com/rebeccaguyauthor

𝓟 pinterest.com/rebeccaguyauthor

Contents

Prologue

Prologue

T HE WOMAN STOOD IN the dining room, tears rolling down her cheeks as she wrung her hands. She stared at the pile of photographs scattered on the table. Her heart felt like it had been wrenched out of her chest and hung out to dry, each memory in front of her part of the idyllic family life she had always wished for. Everything had been perfect until this point. Perfect until it wasn't.

She put a shaking hand to her mouth and forced back a sob as the front door opened and her husband called out. His voice was unusually hoarse and as he appeared in the dining room doorway she saw his eyes were red, and bags sagged the skin underneath, although no tears fell now. It was many hours later. Many hours after the event that would change their world forever.

'It's done,' he said, his voice cracking. 'They have all the information they need. It's over.'

'Do the police need another statement? Because I'm not sure I can take any more questions. I can't go over this again, I don't think I could stand it.'

The man shook his head, 'No, it's over,' he said simply, then he gazed around the mess of photographs on the table as she nodded.

'Thank Goodness.'

He frowned. 'What are you doing with these?'

The woman looked up at him. 'I'm packing her away, I can't look at her any longer. Don't tell me I can't, because I have to do this. My heart, it won't...'

He sighed and placed a hand on her arm. Not loving, but protective. He was always protective, and she would always follow his lead and cover his misdemeanours. That's what family was about, wasn't it?

'Okay, it's okay. We'll get through this together, just as we always do. God will help us, and soon it will all be over.'

'God!' the woman spat through an unexpected burst of anger. 'You think God has a hand in all of this? She's gone, and nothing you or God can do will bring back my little girl. It will never be over.'

She had spoken out of turn and expected words that would shut the situation down immediately, but the man only slumped into a dining chair with a heavy sigh. He fingered his clerical collar, a sheen breaking out over his brow. He looked beaten and washed out, and she was sure that she mirrored his state. Tears rolled down her cheeks and dripped from her chin as she watched him. He was grey when he shifted his gaze to her.

'Our little girl is where she needs to be. There is a plan in all things, my love, you have to believe that, and this plan is perfect, and so is our part in it, as is God and all of his creations.'

The woman had never been less sure of anything in her life, but one thing was clear; her husband always had a plan, even when God must look on helplessly. She swallowed and shook her head, pulling herself together. There was nothing to be done about this now, the wheels were in motion and she simply had to go with the ride, that was the way it was. The way it had always been. He was right about one thing; her daughter was certainly better off where she was, she agreed with that at least.

Tears threatened to engulf her as she moved her gaze to the table and the memories of her perfect little girl, just seven years old. Seven. How had it gone so wrong? The woman sniffed and grabbed a box from the doorway, throwing it on the ground at her husbands feet. When he didn't move, she scooped handfuls of photographs and framed prints and shoved them carelessly into the box, eager to get them out of sight so that the pain would diminish.

It didn't seem fair that she was the child's mother. This sort of thing only happened to other people, other families, why would it happen to this God fearing family? Why the family that stayed on the right side of life and the law. Had she not done enough?

The man sat, rubbing at his mouth, his gaze vacant and sad. He leaned to pick up a photograph that had floated to the floor in the woman's haste to pack the pictures away. The woman swallowed hard, waiting for him to say something. Anything, that would make this better. Anything that would turn this situation around and make the events of the last few hours disappear. A reset. But he didn't. He simply shook his head and placed the photograph into the box with the rest.

'Put her away if you must. We have a life to get on with, and a child to raise.'

A swell of emotion folded the woman to the floor with another sob as she thought of her eldest daughter, who knew nothing of the events of the previous few hours. 'How do we tell her? She's going to get home from school and we have to tell her that her sister is dead. She's just eleven years old. How do we do that?'

The man licked his lips before turning to look at her. His body was heavy, weary, but his eyes had hardened with resolution. 'We'll do it because we have no choice. We'll do it and we'll manage, like we've managed the rest of this tortuous day. We'll do it so that she has a good future and a better chance at life than her sister did, because one day this will be easier, and the next it will all be over. We have to stick together and carry on, my love. That's all we can do. Life goes on. Shall I help you get put these boxes away?'

Chapter 1

'WHY DOES MY KITCHEN look like a murder scene, Joe? Weren't you watching her?... and my new shoes? Really?'

Beau Winters stilled as the shrill voice surged from the kitchen beneath her room. She stared at the keyboard; her hands poised above the keys, and dared to hope it would stop there.

But then there was a series of bangs, and a male voice, low and mumbling, which only led to more bangs and a clatter. Beau sighed and lowered her hands in resignation.

Here we go.

She leaned back in the chair, which sat hard and firm at her back, closed her eyes, and waited; and it came, as she knew it would.

'Are you *fucking* serious, Joe? I have to go to a meeting in the morning - a meeting for which I brought these shoes, by the way - and now they look like they've been involved in something suspicious! What the hell is this?'

There were more bangs, and a child protested. Beau stared at the blank laptop screen and traced the sound of footsteps beneath her as Joe moved from the living area to the kitchen.

'Shoes don't commit murder, honey-'

'These shoes will if they're not clean by morning. See the stiletto?'

The volume was rising, and Beau gave up any thought of working through it. She peered through the bedroom window at the lush green park which sat over the tiny residential road. It looked idyllic in the summer sunshine. Peaceful. Unlike 5 Rosseter Avenue, where a storm was brewing on the lower level of the four-story red brick suburban townhouse. Again.

And fancy that, in an area where everything is smiles and roses - outside of front doors, anyway. An area where neighbours with fixed smiles bring you housewarming cookies peppered with a little arsenic - oh, you got sick? What a shame. Here's a bottle of cyanide Prosecco to help you on the mend.

Beau felt a grin creep onto her lips. Cynical, Hannah called her. Downstairs, Joe was busy calling Hannah something else.

'You're an utter lunatic, Han. I'll clean up here, you see if you can save the shoes-' Joe's voice is calm, but Hannah's shrill screech cuts him off.

'Save the goddamn shoes!' There was a sharp *pah*. 'I'll wrap them around your goddamn neck, Joe. You're a lazy parent, did I ever tell you that?'

Only about a million times, Beau thought, putting her head in her hand as she watched a man throw seed from a paper bag to the mallards and swans on the park lake. Even from her window she could see him smiling from ear to ear, and although she couldn't hear, she could see him gently telling off the greedy swan who chased the other birds away for a snatch of the seed.

'The kid was having fun, Han. She was making prints. I didn't know she'd pick the wrong pair of shoes.'

'That's because you're an idiot.'

There was another bang, and a period of quiet where the only sound was seven-year-old Leila crying. Beau could envisage the scene with clarity. After nine months, she knew how these things went almost beat for beat.

Hannah is standing two inches from Joe's nose, her face red, her lips pinched into a tight line, and poor Leila has her hands over her ears.

And to think I laughed when Hannah told me. I thought it was funny! Why did I think it was funny?

Beau thought back to that clear night last November. The two of them, huddled on the back step of this very house in winter coats and a blanket, each with a glass of wine, and Hannah lighting a cigarette and blowing smoke as she'd said: 'We all need an argument now and then, Beau, or how is there ever anything to make up after? Besides, they're not real arguments, they're non-arguments. Who can come up with the snappiest line, you know? We always laugh about it later.'

Well, you might, but Leila sure doesn't, she thought now as she watched the man in the park empty the bag upside down and gave it a shake before walking away. The swan followed, and downstairs Hannah jibed.

'Maybe, Joe, you should understand that the only pair of shoes suitable for prints are your god-awful running shoes that smell like they've come up from hell and stepped in doggy-doo along the way. Sometimes I wonder what you're actually teaching Leila. I'm working to keep a house over our heads, and you're spraying ketchup around the kitchen.'

'Paint.'

'Paint. Well, of course it is. I was just hoping that for once you would be sensible, and it would be something simple to clean.'

'Sensible is my middle name. It's water based.'

Downstairs, Beau heard Hannah huff. 'Great. Nice one Joe, that makes all the difference, especially where it's dried. If my fuck-ing shoes are wrecked, I'll wreck you... No, I'm serious Joe, this is *not* a game!'

Except it is a game, isn't it, Han?

Beau leaned back and folded her arms across her chest, her eyes falling to the blank screen in front of her.

Sometimes she wished they didn't have to have non-arguments daily. For that matter, she wished she didn't have to hear the making up daily, either. For a couple that had been together for twelve years, they weren't keen on letting go of each other, or taking their eyes off each other, no matter what was said in the heat of the moment.

Maybe it *was* a game.

Maybe all of love was a game, and they'd found the elixir. The magic stone. The key. Good for them. Heaven knows Beau had never found it. Her recent divorce showed her that. The fact that she and Patrick hadn't been sleeping together for the last seven years of her twenty-six-year marriage *should* have shown her. The fact that he had been sleeping with a friend for an entire eight months before she found out absolutely proved it. Love could be grand, and free, and sweet, but love was also greedy and rough, and it could bite. Hard.

There was another bang downstairs and more shouting, and Beau gazed back out of the window. The man by the pond had now gone, and the park suddenly looked gloriously empty. Gloriously *peaceful*.

Just a small break, she thought. She looked back at the blank white page on the screen in front of her and tried to ignore the cursor, which blinked accusingly.

Wow. This is good shit, Beau, great shit. The next bestseller. I can see why you nabbed a sixty-thousand-pound three book contract. You're awesome. Better believe it.

Beau shut the lid with a snap, feeling her cheeks flush as she stopped the cursor's cutting jibes.

I am a bestselling author, you'd better believe it. Even if Beau Winters can't get a crappy story from her crappy head right now, and is possibly about to lose any chance of another contract because she's on, not the first - oh no, not the first - but the **second** *deadline extension and still hasn't written one word of the damn book. Not one.*

Maybe Beau is about to crash and burn. Maybe she's about to become irrelevant and broken - a two-hit wonder. Maybe she will never again have to explain - through clenched teeth and a fixed smile - that it's Beau, as in **bow** *- not* **boo***. And yes, she knows she writes ghost stories. Isn't it ironic? Ha-de-ha, except that it's fucking* **bow***. Not so ironic. So, I'll take a break if that's okay, while I'm still flying high.*

The cursor silenced, Beau squeezed herself between the bed and the chair and heaved a hip to push the chair under the desk against the plush pile of the carpet. Then she left the small bedroom, slamming the door a little louder than necessary, and feeling a small amount of satisfaction at the bang.

See? Not totally defeated. There's still some fire there.

Chapter 2

W ARM AIR PRESSED AROUND Beau as she clipped across the road, her boot heels echoing on the empty street. It was a Wednesday afternoon, and most people living on this street were at work, grinding nine-to-fives to pay for their vast mortgages, two kids, gardeners, cleaners and three cars to go on their three-car drive. (And not over three years old, of course - got those 'Joneses' to keep up with next door).

Feeling an immediate sweat break out on her brow, Beau shrugged out of her brown leather jacket, and wished she could remove her jeans and boots without causing a ruckus because there was no way she was going back to the house to change with a screaming match going on. Besides, she had slipped out unseen and didn't need that fact changing.

She pushed out her bottom lip to blow air up over her face and scanned the park as she entered through the large wrought-iron gates.

Well, there's no-one here to cause a ruckus.

Oh, there would be if you strolled into the park in your knickers. I guarantee it. Bird man would be back with more seed and more of an eyeful than he expected.

Beau snickered while cursing the air con that kept Hannah and Joe's house cool and gave a false impression of the day outside. She stopped at a bench and pulled her long red curls back into a ponytail using the bobble that sat permanently on her wrist. Fanning her face with a hand, she picked up her coat and continued on into the park, heading to the shaded area of trees where the temperature fell a few degrees, and offered mild relief.

She found a bench and dropped onto it, placing her coat next to her with a sigh. She looked towards the central pond, which shimmered in the heat of the day. It should have been tranquil, but the noise of the squabbling ducks was almost worse than the noise in the kitchen at home... well, okay, maybe that was an exaggeration.

How the hell did you get here, Beau? More to the point, how the hell are you going to get yourself out of this mess?

A breeze stirred the air, bringing cool relief, and Beau closed her eyes with a heavy sigh. It felt like heaven... until someone else appeared to join that slice of heaven with her.

'Can't be as bad as all that, pet,' a gravelly male voice said.

Beau opened an eye. Had she looked all that bad? Maybe she had.

'I'd like to contest. It's pretty bad,' she confirmed, closing her eye again.

The man would leave. No-one likes someone who is not fine when passing the time of day, do they? No one really wants to know your problems, just the same way they would never admit they weren't fine either.

Except that appeared not to be the case.

'You should feed the birds.'

Beau took a minute to try to connect that piece of advice to the mess that was her life at the moment.

'Sorry?' she finally offered with a frown as the bench creaked and she felt movement under her thighs.

Great. Who the hell is this guy?

Beau opened her eyes and turned to look fully at the man now sitting next to her. Bird man.

Who else?

He was older than she had thought from her window; his face ingrained with creases, and his hands calloused. His jacket and trousers were shabby – not dirty, but worn – and his shoes looked like they had seen better days. Grey wisps of hair floated above his head like a halo in the faint breeze as his face crinkled into a smile.

'You disconnect, pet. The world falls away. There's a great feeling of peace and wellbeing just being away from the human race for a while. Whatever is bothering you, it disappears when you're feeding the birds. It's a wonderful feeling.'

'I saw you earlier.'

The man moved his lips, mashing them together like he was removing something from his teeth with his tongue. Then he nodded. 'I'm not so alone, eh?'

'Not entirely. I was in the second story of hell, watching the swan try to take the seed all for himself.'

The man chuckled and Beau found herself smiling, catching his radiating warmth and contentment.

'Ah, Priscilla. She's a greedy thing. I have to put her in her place a little so that the smaller ones can get their share. She means no harm, but there's enough for all of them. She doesn't understand, it's not her fault, see?'

'Priscilla?' Beau's face wrinkled into a frown, and the man met her eyes with his own delighted bright blue gaze.

'Priscilla, Queen of the Lake. It's my take on–'

'Priscilla, Queen of the Desert.'

'Well, sort of. Without the rainbow drag and camels, of course.'

Beau laughed and eyed the lake, trying to find the swan.

'More for my wife.' The man pointed a finger at a couple of swans on the far side of the lake. 'She's the one on the left.'

'Ah,' Beau nodded, and then she paused. 'Why your wife? Was that her name? I mean, she is a beauty, the swan, isn't she?'

'She is, she is.' The man's eyes crinkled into a smile. 'But that's not the reason, and my wife's name was Ruth.'

There was a pause and a small huff, and Beau turned to the man, who was now smiling off across the water. She let him have his moment of reflection while she chewed over the information, still not finding a connection.

'I have to admit...'

'You're confused.'

Beau nodded and held her forefinger and thumb apart to show him how much. 'A little.'

'That swan is a prissy miss, just like my Ruth. Ruth was an old battleaxe fighting everything, whether she needed to or not. She'd go in all guns blazing just to buy a loaf of bread. There was drama. So much drama in my life, and Priscilla reminds me of her. Fighting for food as though it's her last feed, although there is plenty to go around and always more tomorrow. There's no need for the hustle and rush, no need for the fight, you understand?'

'I do. Sounds like you come out here for the peace as much as I have today.'

The man smiled. 'Ah, no. Now I come out to remember her. To remember the nonsensical fights and squabbles over nothing. The birds, especially Priscilla, are my comfort and company. They take me out of life for a while. I've had enough human company and drama to last me a lifetime... and now my lifetime is in its last length, I intend to enjoy it on my terms.'

Beau felt her smile slip into sympathy, but there was a contradiction in the man's words, and the apparent loss of his wife, that she was curious about.

'I'm sorry for your loss.' It wasn't enough, but it was all she could find to say.

To her surprise, the man laughed.

'Oh, I'm not, God rest her soul. Love of my life, she was, but it wasn't a peaceful life. Oh, she was tiring. Left this earth over three years ago now. The old bird I used to call her. I wouldn't be surprised if she hadn't returned as that bloody swan, just to keep tabs on me, you know?'

'The old bird,' Beau laughed. 'It would be perfect.'

'It would, it would, and she knew how I loved them.'

The man crossed himself, and Beau saw tears glisten in his eyes. She placed a hand on his forearm and squeezed gently.

'A peaceful life I have now,' he said with a nod, and the tears were gone as quickly as they arrived. 'And long may it last. I have to meet her up there when I go. For now, I keep to myself and my birds, and that's all I need.'

Beau was wishing her life was that simple when her phone pinged. She automatically pulled it from her jacket pocket and checked the notifications. An email. From no one important. She felt a wave of relief and put the phone away with a sigh.

'That'll be half your problem, pet. Phones. Not got one of those, either, they're life stealers. I'm not on call. No one should be.'

'Well, my life is twenty-four hours, seven days a week, I'm afraid. I have to be connected. Something important could come through at any time. I work for myself, and my business colleagues are based worldwide. Who knows what would fall apart if I didn't have this wondrous device?'

Beau laughed, but the man only smiled.

'Nothing would fall apart, pet. Life is twenty-four hours, seven days a week for every one of us, regardless. Life doesn't belong on devices. We should be connected with what's out here.' He swept an arm around the park and for the first time she wondered why he had the jacket on at all. He must be roasting. 'Life is about this. This is what's real. What's on that device isn't real. It's not tangible, and you certainly shouldn't be held by it. One day you will look up from your phone and wonder at the world, but by then you'll be too old to enjoy it.'

Beau felt her cheeks redden at his insinuation.

'Everything is online these days. The world is changing, I'm afraid. I wouldn't have a business without it, and so I really don't have a choice.'

'I won't disagree with you about change, but you *do* have a choice, as do all of us. You don't have to be online all of the time.'

'I'm not-'

'You just said that anyone can contact you, day or night, even if they are on the opposite side of the world.'

'Well, yes, that's effectively true, but I don't look at my phone in the middle of the night!'

Not often, anyway, unless I'm playing Happy Hospital at 2am because I can't sleep.

Beau bit her lip and looked away, expecting a good talking to from this stranger, but it didn't come.

'Then that's what matters, pet. That sigh as you put it down said different, but I'll not argue with you. I'm through arguing with anyone. So, what brings you out here for the peace today? I haven't seen you around the park before.'

Beau heaved a sigh and blew out a long breath.

'Oh, lots of reasons. So many. I split up with my husband nine months ago, and since then I've been living in my friend's spare bedroom - they live across the road. I pay rent, but I feel I'm intruding a little. They have a daughter, and it's their family home.'

'It's noisy?'

'Unbelievably so. My friend and her husband believe in arguing daily so that they can make up daily. It's adorable, but so...'

Beau struggled for the right word, but the man had just the right words on tap.

'Annoyingly needless. I've been there.'

'Right, exactly. I have to work. I have a deadline that has been pushed back twice, I'm coming to the end of my contract, and I need that renewal, especially now that I'm having to support myself. The money won't last forever.'

'You can't write in the noise, pet, it's not conducive to creativity, and nor is feeling uncomfortable. Also, one room must be pretty cramped. They're big houses, but small rooms. My nephew lives on the same row as your friend. Frederick Stephenson?'

Beau was trying to squash her surprise that he must recognise her, when she realised he was waiting for a response. She shook her head.

'I don't know him.'

'Ah, well, he's usually working. Another one with no time for himself or anyone else. If I didn't see his car every now and then as he arrived back from work, I wouldn't know if he was dead or alive. I'm not surprised you don't know him. I'd be surprised if his own son knows him.' He waved a veined hand in dismissal. 'Anyway, can't you use one of the bigger rooms as an office?'

'None free. They have an office, a playroom, a gym, a music room, and a cinema room.'

The man shook his head with a laugh. 'No need to ever go outside again.'

Beau offered a huff of agreement.

'You're right. Hannah works from home, only leaving for meet-ings, and Joe home educates their daughter Leila, who's seven. Their schedules overlap and I'm never there alone. I wish some-times that they could leave together, just an hour or two a day, so that I could work in peace.'

'Headphones are a wonderful invention.'

'I have some, but it's not that. I feel... I don't know, like I'm intruding. I can't really settle, and if I ever do, that's when I get disturbed - every damn time.'

'A guest in your own home.'

'Except that it's not my home, after all. I suppose I'm still reeling, what with the divorce and losing my house and my routine. It's been an upheaval.'

'Mentally and physically.' Beau felt the truth of the statement as the man smiled. 'How far through the new book are you, Ms Winters?'

'Um...' Beau tried to keep her composure. It was par for the course, but still new and very disarming for strangers to know who she was when she hadn't offered the information. It made her feel transparent and vulnerable.

The man chuckled. 'My daughter has read both of your books, multiple times, and she's waved them under my nose more than a handful of times. I have a head for faces, and I recognised you from the picture on the back. I'm sorry if I caught you off guard.'

Beau felt her defenses lower as she shook her head. 'It's no problem, I just didn't expect it out here. I'm glad your daughter enjoyed them both.'

'She raves about them, and she's waiting impatiently for the next one.'

Beau shifted uncomfortably. 'Well, it could be a while yet.'

'Sounds like this situation has you strapped, how far did you say you were through it?'

'I didn't, and nowhere.'

The man raised his eyebrows, his gaze serious. 'You've written nothing, even after two deadline extensions?'

Beau dropped her gaze and picked at her thumbnail with a shake of her head. 'Not a word. I'm stuck.'

'Creative block.' The man mumbled. 'That's a terrible wall to be behind, and worse that when you push it, it only gets stronger.'

Beau felt her stomach drop, because he was right. That was exactly how it felt. It couldn't be pushed through, and she was at a loss for how else to approach it.

'I know it,' he continued. 'I was an artist when I was younger. For a while, I lost the ability to paint.'

Beau felt a faint flicker of hope as she looked up to meet his eyes. Kind eyes, she thought.

'So what did you do?'

'Pulled back. Stopped the painting and stopped worrying about it. Eventually, it came back, I just had to get out of my own way.'

Beau's heart seemed to roll in her chest. 'But I have to write. I have a-'

The man nodded and held up a hand as he cut her off.

'An *extended* deadline. And that makes it tougher to pretend, I agree, but the harder you push, and the more frustrated you get, the worse it will be.'

Beau saw the compassion on the man's face, and her eyes filled with unexpected tears as the hopelessness of the situation hit her.

'So what am I supposed to do? No, don't answer. I already know what you're going to say. Creativity is personal, so I have to figure this out for myself.'

The man scanned the lake ahead.

'Seems obvious to me, pet. Number one, you need to sort your clutter. Number two, you need to move.'

A tear fell onto Beau's cheek, and she swiped it in frustration, glad the man had chosen that moment to look away.

'If I could move, I would have done it by now. I need to have my income steady before I can get another mortgage or take on a rental. I had an advance payment for the books, but I've seen nothing since. I'm living off savings right now, and that means squat in the land of credit and bills.' She sighed and tried to smile. 'At least I don't have any *stuff* left to sort. I'm clutter free.'

Another tear let go, and the man took her hand. Beau felt warmth radiate through her. Not the heat of the day, but an unfamiliar warmth, almost a sense of comfort.

'No, pet, you have a lot of clutter. Up here,' the man points at his temple with a smile. 'The only way to sort that clutter is time and space. You have neither, and until you do, you won't write again. Not for long anyway, and nothing worth writing about. Sometimes these problems are sent to us for a reason.'

'Like I haven't been through enough?'

'That will only become clear when you've been through every-thing and come out the other side.'

The man patted her hand and then let it go as the truth of the statement filled Beau's gut with a swirling dread. It was okay for this old man with no worries to tell her this, but it was a very real predicament for her. An impossible predicament, and after Hannah and Joe had been so nice about her moving into their space. How was she supposed to tell them she couldn't write there? And what choice did she have, anyway? She had no other options, nowhere else to go.

'I don't know what to do,' she whispered, putting her head into her hands as the urgency of the truth hit her. The man was right. She knew it at her core, and yet she was stuck. On top of that, she only had another six and a half months to write the damn book. Her heart pattered against her ribs. 'What the hell am I supposed to do?'

A cloud fell over the sun, plunging the shaded path into apparent darkness after the bright light. A chill swept over Beau, and she shuddered.

There was no reply.

Beau looked up to see the bench next to her empty. The man was gone, almost as if he had never been there. She hadn't even felt him stand up or heard him move away.

And you didn't even thank him, get his name, or offer to sign a book for his daughter.

Her heart fell as her eyes search the path and the lake, but the man was nowhere to be seen.

Beau frowned and shuddered in the breeze. She pulled on her jacket and heard her phone ping twice. Her hand immediately dropped to her pocket and then she paused.

Bird man is right. I don't want to be on call. It's ridiculous.

She drew her hand away and stared at the lake, trying to think her way out of a hopeless situation.

Chapter 3

IT TURNED OUT THAT Beau could have saved herself a ton of tears, stress, and pointless frustration if she had just been 'on call' after all. It had taken her a measly thirty-five minutes to give in and check her phone after the hopeless toiling and spinning of her thoughts, only to come back to the same answer: there was no way out.

Except here is her phone, showing her that there *is* a way out. A way that she would never have thought of.

Her jaw dropped as she stared at the email.

Is this divine intervention?

The sender was unknown, probably got her email from a site or service that she subscribes to. One that didn't 'sell personal information to third-party companies'... except for her email and preferences, obviously. Good job this time she didn't mind, and as she read the email for a second time, she even welcomed it.

Need a break or a change of scenery? The subject declared. Oh, hell yes, she thought, and then took in the beauty of the subject matter below it.

House sitter required.

For winter overstay and maintenance of beautiful Bluebell Cottage, situated three miles from the small village of Hollydale. Set in a secluded clearing among six acres of woodland at the foot of the magnificent Holly Tor and within skipping distance of a private cove.

The quaint, cosy, two bed cottage is double glazed and has central heating. All mod cons and furnishings supplied, food and extra supplies available via village amenities. Direct access to isolated beach and extensive hiking.

Tenant(s) must be sensible, hardy, enjoy isolation, have a good level of fitness, and no children. Maintenance to be upheld in collaboration with the caretaker who does not live on site. The tenant will pay for any breakages or damage during tenancy.

Required September through February.

Please enquire for details and salary.

Salary?

Beau's heart began to thud as she scrolled to the picture of the pretty cottage sitting amongst the backdrop of tall pines. Honeysuckle climbed the whitewashed walls of a two-story cottage which boasted a wooden wraparound deck complete with red Victorian frill. A contrasting a pale blue front door sat half open as if welcoming her inside.

Beau felt a pull of... intuition? Certainty? She didn't know, but she absolutely knew that this was her ticket out. This was her opportunity. Not only that, but they'd pay her for the privilege?

She scanned her eyes over the email for the telephone number, punched it into her phone, and waited as it rang out.

'Hello?'

'Er, hi, my name is Beau Winters. I'm just calling about your advert for the house sitter at, er... the, er... cottage?'

Beau wrinkled her nose and pressed a fist to her forehead.

Why didn't you at least remember the name of the place? Idiot!

'Bluebell Cottage?' the voice clipped. Female, at least eighty-five, but sharp as a tack. Beau felt her cheeks redden and closed her eyes.

'Yes, that's the one. I wonder if the position has been filled yet?'

'No, we've had a few enquiries but no-one that's stood out. It needs a special kind of person, you see? Resilient, trustworthy, and hardworking, sure, but the cottage is extremely isolated, it's not for everybody. Once you're in, it's tough to leave in the depths of winter. I also need to be upfront and tell you there's a clause in the contract that says you stay the duration. It's much harder to get sitters after the winter has begun, you understand. The cottage is *very* remote. Am I making myself clear?'

Nervous anticipation somersaulted in Beau's stomach. 'Yes.'

'This is usually where I lose people. Do you want to make your excuses now? Or would you like me to go on?'

Beau swallowed, thinking about the small, but cosy, room she had just over the street. This park was pretty. She could use it more, maybe even come out here to write...

...and then her thoughts turned to the bird man and the things he said. Things that she knew were true, and her resolve strengthened.

You need this Beau, it's do or die... well, maybe not die, but squirm in mortification as you tell everyone that you're a failed author, that you couldn't cut it. A two-hit wonder.

'Hello?'

'Yes,' Beau said, feeling like she was struggling for breath as her heart tried to break down her rib cage. 'Please go on. I need isolation for my work, and this sounds like the perfect opportunity.'

'Wonderful. Well, Ms Winters, my name is Mrs Locket, and I am the owner of the cottage. If at any time you become unsure, please stop me. I have no time for doubt, and no energy for time wasters. The cottage is a serious business.'

Beau swallowed hard. 'I will, but I'm certain the cottage is just what I need.'

'Good, good.' Mrs. Locket sounded both pleased and relieved as she explained that her family had owned the cottage and land for generations, but now she was simply too infirm to stay there herself, even during the summer. With no siblings or children of her own to take on the cottage, she didn't want it standing empty while she took the time to decide what to do with it. Empty meant damp, she said, and that was bad news. The cottage was also in a small valley, and if the weather blew right, it was at risk of damage.

'Roof tiles had to be replaced three times just last year after heavy storms, and the last thing I need is the cottage becoming a wreck. All weather-related damages and general repairs will be paid for from the family account. I have passion and money, Ms Winters, it's will and energy I no longer have. I can no longer even make the three-mile walk to and from the cottage. It pains me not to be able to see the house I grew up in. A rector's daughter rarely grows up in such a place, I'm sure.'

Beyond the brusque, business-like nature of the conversation, Beau caught a wistful tone in Mrs Locket's voice and used the moment to draw out some history.

'Ah, then the cottage is a rectory?'

'Was. The church atop Holly Tor has long since passed into dereliction after the tithes stopped coming in, but we were self-funded, which meant that we kept the house. My father tried to keep the church going but... well, with a church on the other side of the village with easier access, why would one bother? Especially as it's such a climb. I suppose the church is still ours, but no one wants it either way, it is worth nothing, especially now that the youths have got to it with their nightly defacing. The place is littered with cannisters, condoms, and cigarette ends now, I'm told. Shame really. My father died there. I hope one day his ghost gives them such a scare that they never go back.'

Beau felt her story antenna flicker to attention as she listened. This could be great material...

And that's a lawsuit waiting to happen, Beau.

She shook the thought from her head. 'Well, I certainly hope he doesn't give me a scare while I'm there.'

Mrs Locket let out a huff. 'Well, no-one's seen him up to yet. I'm sure you're safe on that count.'

And on that note, Mrs Locket was back to business, and on to her assessment of Beau - Her work (author -no, Mrs Locket didn't know of her and had never read her work), her current family status (no dependents), marital status (the word single almost didn't come out at all), and her health (no complaints). After what Beau would later call a thorough grilling, Mrs Locket finally seemed happy.

'Well, you fit the bill perfectly. Before I had Gerard, I advertised for men only, but they just don't seem to get on with the place. It has a much more feminine feel. Gerard is a godsend, but-'

'He's the caretaker?'

'Yes, but he can't live on site, mores the pity. That would be ideal, but he has six children, all squashed into a property on the edge of the village. He's not a big talker... he probably never gets a word in edgeways at home, but he's capable and trustworthy and will be on hand whenever you need him. Day or night.'

'Permanently on call,' Beau muttered, thinking about the bird man.

'He's paid well, and for the most part, you won't need him. Things are pretty quiet around the cottage, as you can imagine. Are you still interested, Ms Winters?'

Beau found herself nodding, although a lump sat in her throat.

It's a huge step, Beau, you don't even know where Hollydale is!

I guess I'll find out soon enough.

'Yes. It sounds perfect for my needs.'

'Right, well, the first of September is a few weeks away yet, but I'll send the-'

'Could I start earlier?'

Mrs Locket stalled. 'Er... well, the cottage is empty at present. It's easier to look after in the summer months. I'm afraid the final sum of the salary is non-negotiable...'

'That's no problem. The payment is more than adequate, I could just do with a place to stay as soon as possible. The sooner the better, really.'

Beau knew she had said the wrong thing as Mrs Locket's voice hardened.

'Pardon me? Why the hurry? You must have things to sort before making such a commitment. This isn't a lighthearted decision to make, Ms Winters. It's not a campground, it is a serious job, and there are responsibilities.'

Beau pulled her mouth back in a grimace. 'Yes, of course, I understand that. It's just... I'm living at a friend's house after a messy divorce. My home hasn't long been sold, and this place is far from ideal -it's cramped and noisy. I'm on a deadline with this next book. I need space to... to...'

'Breathe,' Mrs Locket almost breathed down the line, and Beau almost felt her relief. 'Well, that's understandable. How soon do you want to move in?'

'As soon as possible. I could come tomorrow?'

Mrs Locket gave a raspy laugh that sounded like sandpaper. 'Hang on now, I have to sort getting the place cleaned and moving necessary supplies there. You also have to sign the contract, and I recommend you scrutinise it first. Besides, don't you want to see the cottage and its placement, Ms Winters?'

'I'm looking at it,' Beau said, imagining the pictures in the email. 'It's perfect.'

Mrs Locket sighed. 'Okay, well then, how about...' There's a pause, and Beau imagined a grey haired Mrs locket readjusting her glasses as she squinted at the calendar. 'Saturday?'

Beau's stomach fell. Three days too long. But then she grinned.

This means you have a paying job, and a quiet place to work for the next six months! Holy shit, Beau!

'Saturday will be perfect, thank you.'

'Good. I'll organise everything here and send the contract to you via email tonight. Once you sign it and send it back, there will be no backing out without a large lawsuit. I won't be messed about at my age, and I'm willing to pay to make *you* pay if you break the terms. Are we on the same page?'

Beau swallowed hard.

'Understood perfectly.'

There was a pause, and Beau pulled the phone from her ear to check the display. Still connected. She wrinkled her nose as she put it back to her ear.

'Mrs Locket?'

'I'm here. There's a lot of perfection in your life, young lady. I hope Bluebell Cottage can live up to your expectations.'

'Oh, it will, Mrs Locket. I'm absolutely certain it will. It can't fail to. Thank you so much for this opportunity. It's perfect.'

'Hmm. We'll see.'

Chapter 4

I N THE GROUND FLOOR room that functioned as a gym, Hannah gave a last push, panting hard as her feet pounded the treadmill. After thirty seconds of hell, she tapped the speed down from eighteen to five, her eyes rolling with relief, and her body flowing with endorphins. As she slowed to a walk, she pushed her fingers through the wet strings of hair that had fallen from her dark ponytail and clung to her cheeks. Her chest heaved, her skin buzzed, and from the warmth in her cheeks, she knew her face was somewhere between tomato and beetroot on the red marker.

The breeze from the self-standing fan caressed her body, cooling the sweat on her top and leggings. She was blissfully enjoying the cool air when the door opened, and Joe stuck his head inside. It was as far as he liked to enter this room, he always said the weights and machines gave him chills. He'd much rather take Leila to the park and behave like a child instead. It was what made him a great dad, Hannah thought. He couldn't care less what other parents thought of him running races across the grass, hurtling down the slide, or climbing the net.

'I'm sorry about the shoes. Am I off the hit list?' Joe's brown curls flopped into his eyes, and Hannah raised an eyebrow.

'Can't tell if you're serious until you've had a haircut.'

'Not my problem.'

He grinned under his mane before pushing it back with his hand, just as she had with her own hair a few seconds earlier. His deep brown eyes and crow's feet came into view and Hannah couldn't help but grin with him. He was as adorable as a puppy. Give him a guitar - or a playground - and he was happy. He had no ambition at all, but Hannah had no intention of getting down and dirty with Leila, because she *did* care what people thought.

That's exactly why he's the stay-at-home dad, educating Leila in dodgy kitchen crime scenes, and I am the businesswoman.

'Is it my problem?' he enquired, his grin slipping. She gave him a reassuring smile.

'No. Exercise makes everything better. It seems the murderous feeling is all gone, you lucky, lucky, man.'

Joe huffed a laugh, but his grin was again short-lived.

'Good to know, but... well, your good mood is about to be tested. You'd better come into the kitchen.'

Hannah stared at him, waiting for a punchline that didn't come. She sighed and stabbed the stop button, irritation climbing up her spine as the treadmill came to a halt. 'For Christ's sake, Joe, what have you been letting her do now? Can it at least wait until I've had a shower?'

Joe pouted, but his eyes retained humour. 'You'll want to hear this, and we have some making up to do, remember? You said you'd murder me with a stiletto, Han, and showers can be lonely.'

Hannah turned away from him, pretending to mess with the treadmill settings as she fought to keep the smile from her face. She composed herself, turned off the machine, grabbed her towel, and headed toward him, keeping her poker face intact.

'I would never murder you with a stiletto, Joe,' she said, rising to her tiptoes to kiss his lips lightly. 'Because then I'd have to throw away a perfectly good pair of shoes... too much evidence.'

He grinned down at her.

'Good to know, Carry on in. I'll just check on Leila.'

Hannah squeezed past him as he held the door, rubbing the towel over her face and neck as she headed down the hall and into the kitchen.

She had expected to see Leila and a mess, but instead Beau was sitting at the table with a coffee, staring out through the open bifold doors over the freshly cut back lawn, looking deep in thought. Hannah paused in the doorway, assessing her friend with a fond smile.

Despite the heat of the day, Beau was wearing jeans, heeled boots, and a battered brown leather jacket - the one that Hannah had always wanted to steal, but never got chance. She had coiffed her red hair into a perfectly messy ponytail, her snub nose was pretty with freckles, and she possessed huge green eyes that Hannah had once tried - and failed - to copy with lenses that hid her own hardly show stopping blue ones. Beau looked immaculate, as always.

Why Patrick wanted to sleep with anyone else is just beyond me. Fucking idiot.

Beau had been staying with them for almost nine months after the whole fiasco had come out and the divorce had been pushed through, but Hannah had barely seen her. The woman was like a vampire. She only ever seemed to come out at night. Day after day, she shut herself up in her room and wrote. Now Hannah wondered how she was doing. They usually wound down the evening together with a glass of wine, but Beau never seemed to say much about her feelings anymore.

Maybe she got everything out at the beginning when she cried a lot, or maybe the focus on her work helps. Still... up in that room all day?

Possibly feeling Hannah's gaze on her, Beau turned and met her eyes with a smile that Hannah returned as a ripple of love trickled through her. Beau scooted the chair back and stepped into Hannah's open arms as Hannah laughed.

'Beau? You're not a vampire after all? I'm gutted!'

'You were thinking maybe Twilight?'

'Urg. Vampire Diaries for sure. Sorry I'm so sweaty, us non vampires have to keep fit.'

They laughed and Beau pulled back as the door swung open and Joe entered the kitchen. He nodded at Beau's cup.

'More coffee?'

'Please,' Beau answered, moving back to the table, and handing Joe her cup. He took it before fetching two more from the cupboard.

Hannah glanced between the two of them, sensing the void of something they knew that she didn't. Joe whistled as he made the drinks, further altering the new dimension that Hannah found herself in. She moved to the table and pulled out the chair next to Beau.

'Why are we coffee-ing together in the day? As nice as it is, it's not normal. What's going on?'

Beau pursed her lips. 'I'm leaving, Han.'

'You're what?' Hannah's heart stumbled and dropped down into her stomach, where it sat pounding wildly as reality wheeled on its head again. 'Really?'

Beau nodded, her eyes serious, and Hannah shook her head.

'No, Beau! Why? When?'

Beau shrugged. 'I can't stay here forever, and you two have been more than kind, but I'm invading your space. It's time to move on.'

Hannah grasped Beau's warm hands, her eyes wide. 'No, you're not. This house is far too big for the three of us. You're not invading anything. You don't need to leave, Beau. Please don't. We love having you here.'

'She means she loves the extra rent money.' Joe said over his shoulder with a wink.

Hannah felt a pull in her heart and threw him a glare. 'That's not true.'

She saw Beau grin from the corner of her eye.

'It's not? Who wouldn't love the extra cash?'

Hannah turned back to Beau. 'Of course, but I love you more. It's nice to have an extra body in this big old house.'

'Even one you moan you don't see all day,' Joe threw back with a laugh and Hannah rolled her eyes.

What the hell is his problem?

'That's beside the point. I'm working all day too. I love it that the extra body likes to drink wine and talk crap with me into the early hours.'

'You love that she lets you smoke Royals, that you think I don't know you're smoking, while drinking wine and talking crap.'

Joe grinned, but Hannah felt the heat in her cheeks and the white lick of irritation in her gut. 'So, what's the problem? I've never hidden it from you, Joe.'

Joe's smile fell and he looked taken aback. 'Well, you never directly told me, or asked how I feel about it. I only know because I found the packet hidden on top of the cupboard.'

'Well, how *do* you feel about it?' Hannah snapped, folding her arms over her chest. 'Shall we go into this now, be-?'

'I don't like it,' Joe said cutting her off and causing irritation to fire her every nerve, like wicks sparking to life and riding the line down to the explosion that would come if he didn't shut the fuck up.

'Well, we're not all saints like you, Joe. Some of us work hard, some of us need a fucking-'

Joe held up his hands and shook his head as he cut her off. 'Hannah, this is not the time. Beau is trying to talk to you, just leave it.'

It took all of Hannah's resolve not to get up and place her hands around his stupid throat, because as much as she hated Joe right now, he was right.

She bit her tongue and seethed as he brought the coffee over to the table, sliding one to each of them, before picking up his own and heading to the door.

'I'm obviously in the way, I'll leave you to talk. Beau, I'm sorry you feel you have to go. Probably something to do with living in a nuthouse where everything gets blown out of proportion, eh?

I don't blame you, but you're welcome here anytime, for as long as you like, as far as I'm concerned.'

His pious tone sent a strand of Hannah's carefully squashed anger spinning loose. 'Oh, piss off, Joe, before I knock your fucking head off, stuff your mouth with an apple and roast it.'

Joe paused in the doorway, and then with a shake of his head, he left, shutting the door behind him.

Hannah gritted her teeth, her hands curled into shaking fists under the table. 'For fuck's sake,' she muttered.

Beau gave her a small grimace of pity.

'He's a lunatic, Beau. I can't decide if I love him or hate him sometimes, and now you're leaving me here alone with him.'

'You were here alone with him for eleven years before my life went down the pan.'

'It was hell.'

'You love him to death.' Beau reached to take Hannah's shaking hand and warmth radiated through her, pushing down some of the irritation that Joe had left behind. She sighed.

'I do.'

Beau grinned, 'so were you going to roast the apple or his head?'

'What?'

'You said you were going to stuff his mouth with an apple and roast it... just curious whether that was the apple or his head?'

Hannah felt her confusion and the last of the irritation slide away as she laughed.

'Probably both. I love you, Beau, won't you stay?'

Hannah dipped her chin and pushed her mouth into the pout that no one could resist. It was the pout that had led to them becoming fast friends when Hannah had used it to convince Beau to attend the theater with her one evening after work, back when they both worked as legal secretaries. The show had been an assessment of the psychological profile of serial killers – not the sort of thing any of Hannah's previous friends were interested in, but Beau had loved it as much as she had, despite the pout, and Hannah had never had to use it again... until now.

Beau blew softly through her nose and smiled, sending anxious butterflies through Hannah's stomach. 'Don't do that, Han.'

Tears formed in Hannah's eyes. 'I have to,' she managed.

'You don't. It will just make me feel worse than I already do, and I still have to go.'

'Why?' Hannah tried to catch Beau's gaze as it dropped to the table. Missing it, she grabbed her hand instead. 'What's wrong, Beau?'

Beau shook her head. 'I'm sorry, Han. I really appreciate everything you and Joe have done for me since Patrick left. You've held me up in so many ways and I can't thank you enough for having me here...'

'But you don't need to go. Joe was kidding about the rent, we love that you're here. What's the matter?'

'I know, and I'm so grateful, but I can't work here. I've tried, I really have, but I just... the words, they don't seem to come. I haven't written a single thing since I moved in.'

Hannah felt her mouth drop open. 'Nothing? But you're up there all day, every day. I thought you'd be almost done by now; I was waiting for us to crack the champagne open within the next month for sure. What about the deadline?'

Beau shrugged and finally met her eyes. Hannah's stomach lurched at the pain she saw there. 'Oh, Beau. What can we do to help? Surely that's not about location. You've been through so much over the last nine months. I haven't spoken to you much about what happened because you were doing so well. I just presumed...'

'I'm fine, Han, really. I just need to write, and it's not coming here. I need peace, and as lovely as this place is, it's not quiet enough.'

'I can tell Joe and Leila to keep it down in the day. I know they're noisy. Do you have headphones? I can buy you some brilliant noise cancelling ones...'

Hannah trailed off, feeling like the world was spinning on a different axis as Beau gave a sad smile and pulled her bottom lip between her teeth. Then she shook her head. 'It's not Leila, Han. I barely hear her, and anyway, this is your house. You can be as noisy as you like. I shouldn't have to change that. Look, I've made some arrangements, I'll be moving out Saturday.'

Hannah reeled as the world ground to a halt, its gears creaking and clacking, and in the thunderous silence that followed, she wondered if she had heard right. She scrunched her eyes against a threatening headache and placed a thumb and forefinger into each socket, rubbing, before looking back at Beau.

'Saturday? You mean... Saturday? Three days? Oh, God, Beau, I didn't talk to you enough, did I? How did you arrange this without telling me a thing? We're best friends! How did this happen?'

Beau sipped her coffee and swallowed loudly. 'It was a really sudden thing, only today. I had an email advertising for a house sitter in Hollydale. It seemed like the perfect deal to get out of here, out of my head, and into my writing. It's what I need, I can feel it, and so I called and arranged it. I've already signed the contract.'

Hannah blinked as the ground seemed to fall from under her. 'What? Don't we even get to talk about this? You're actually going?'

Beau nodded and swallowed hard. 'It's a done deal. Here, look.'

Hannah watched as she pulled her phone from her pocket and swiped and tapped at the screen. Finally, she showed her an email with an advert and some pictures of an old Victorian house that was quite literally in the middle of nowhere. As she read the email, a new spark of anger lit inside her.

What is this? Who gave Beau the room, the shoulder to cry on, the escape when she needed it? And now it's being thrown back in my face?

Hannah struggled to keep her voice steady.

'How have you thought properly about this, Beau? If you had the email this morning and it's all arranged, then it's been decided on a whim, and it's never a good move to make decisions on a whim. Have you thought about how you'll survive out there alone? It's miles from anywhere. How will you manage?'

Beau looked hurt, and Hannah felt a morsel of satisfaction.

Now she knows how I feel.

'I'll be fine. I know how to take care of myself, I'm not a child.'

'I didn't say you were a child.' Hannah watched Beau's cheeks redden. 'But you realise that you've never lived alone in your whole life... ever.'

Beau shrugged. 'Then now's the time to learn. I don't think I'll notice much anyway, my intention is to throw myself into work, and it's only a six-month contract.'

'I don't think you realise that six months is going to feel like six years on your own, especially when there's no one else around to talk to. I've done it, it's not nice.'

'I think it will be healing, and I need the space-'

Hannah slammed her fist down on the table, causing both cups to jump, and her untouched coffee to spill. Beau drew back, wide eyed.

'Goddamn it, Beau. You left home at twenty-two to move in with Patrick, whom you married within the year and spent the next twenty-two years with, before moving in here with us. You *won't* handle being alone. You'll panic out there and I can't come up to Hollydale to save your ass. Do you know how far away that is?'

Beau leaned forward to pick up her cup and finish her coffee. Hannah's cup remained untouched, aside from the spill on the table. At the moment, she thought her stomach may reject it, anyway.

Beau drank and then stared into her empty cup.

'Well, you don't need to worry. I won't need saving, and no, I don't know where it is, and I don't care. I'll find out on Saturday.'

Beau's nonchalant attitude was beginning to grate on Hannah's last nerve. This house was three miles from anywhere, before she added the distance to civilisation. How could Beau think this was a good idea?

'It's on the West Coast of Scotland. Scotland, Beau, you know, around four hours north, give or take a couple?'

Another snatch of satisfaction filled Hannah as Beau's eyes widened, and she wrinkled her nose.

'Scotland? But the woman I spoke to, Mrs Locket, was English.'

'What does that matter?'

'Well, it doesn't. I've just... I've never been to Scotland.'

Hannah sighed and tilted her head to look at Beau, who was looking a little off balance.

'I told you that you shouldn't do things on a whim. Christ, Beau. Look, it's okay, just call the woman back and tell her you've changed your mind. Stop looking for silly ways out and just stay here. We can work through this.'

Beau shook her head and tucked a freshly loosened red curl behind her ear. 'No, Han. I can't.'

'Of course you can. It only happened this morning. Plead insanity, say you had an argument with your husband, but you've made up now. Say anything, but ring the lady back.'

'I can't. I've already signed the contract.'

Hannah slammed her hands back onto the table.

'Beau don't be ridiculous! Just un-sign it, that must have been all of two hours ago! What difference can it make?'

Beau shook her head. 'Mrs Locket said that once I signed it, it was a done deal, so to think hard. She will sue me if I back out.'

Hannah spat a laugh, unable to help herself. Sometimes Beau was so naïve.

'Of course she won't. That's just a threat.'

'She sounded pretty serious to me.'

Hannah rolled her eyes.

'For fuck's sake, Beau, how are you so fucking naïve? See? That's because you've never had to stand on your own two feet, always fucking held up, always someone to fall back on. Things don't work that way. Tell Mrs Bobbet, or whatever her name is, to stick the contract up her arse, that's all you need to do.'

Beau's face was red, and there were tears in her eyes. She looked hurt, and Hannah knew she was close to breaking. Not much more to do, then they could make up and go back to normal. Friendships were always better with a bit of tension, it made you appreciate the other person so much more, and Beau was sure to thank her for getting her out of this ordeal... except that Beau was now shaking her head, her watery green eyes suddenly hard.

'No, Han. I'm not calling anybody, because I'm leaving. I want to go, I've had enough, and I need to write. I need to secure my future.'

Stunned, Hannah searched for something to say. When had Beau developed such resolve? It was infuriating not to be able to show her what a mistake she was making moving so far away - and alone to boot. How could she make her see that she wouldn't cope?

That's manipulation, Joe's voice said in her head, but it wasn't manipulation, it was care.

'Look, Beau, this is idiocy. You've already made one huge mistake in your life, don't add this to the list.'

Beau blinked and frowned. 'What big mistake?'

Hannah laughed mirthlessly and rolled her eyes. 'Not keeping an eye on what Patrick was doing.'

'I didn't think I had to. He was my husband!'

'Yes, he was, and if you were fulfilling all of his needs, then he wouldn't have had to look elsewhere, would he? You weren't paying attention, you weren't looking at the goddamn details, just like you're not now.'

Hannah waited for the tears, and then the breakdown of confidence that would be the beginning of Beau changing her mind, but it didn't come. Instead, Beau stood, pushing her hands against the table to move the chair back. She paused, breathing hard, as Hannah held her own breath. Then she turned to leave, and confusion passed through Hannah.

'Beau? I only say these things because I'm concerned. You know that, right?'

Beau turned in the doorway, much like Joe had only minutes before. She smiled, but the light didn't reach her eyes.

'You're wrong, Hannah. There's a second mistake I made. It was becoming friends with you.'

Beau left the room and, as the door banged shut, Hannah's heart collapsed.

Too far, you went too far, you stupid, stupid bitch.

She swung out from the table, toppling the chair to the floor with a clatter, and lunged for the door just as Joe walked through it.

'No,' he said, grabbing her arm and twisting her back into the kitchen. 'Don't go after her. The damage is done, Han. Sometimes you take things way too far.'

'I was only trying to help.'

Hannah gritted her teeth as she prised Joe's hand from her forearm.

'Help? You told her Patrick's affair was her fault, Han!' He looked crestfallen, and Hannah sneered.

'It probably was. I was trying to make her see how naïve she is. There's no way she will cope alone out there, she doesn't get it.'

Joe stared at her.

'No, *you* don't get it. Number one, Patrick was the one at fault, don't bring her into it. Number two, Beau can do anything she wants to, including move away. She's a grown woman. Who are you to tell her she can't?'

'She won't manage,' Hannah hissed at him. Sweat trickled from under her running top and down her waist at both her anger and the lack of control over the situation.

'It's not your problem.'

'I love her.'

Joe opened his mouth, seemed to think better of it, and instead shook his head as he looked down at her sadly. Hannah folded her arms across her chest.

'What?' she growled as he moved to the cupboard and ran his hand along the top. He found what he was looking for and threw the packet to Hannah. She flinched as it hit the table.

Now Joe is acting weird... this is the most surreal fucking Wednesday I've ever experienced.

'What's this?'

He stood with his arms folded across his chest, his face a mixture of anger and disappointment. 'Go and smoke your Royals and calm down before you come back inside.'

Hannah felt the craving, and the indignation, as she took a cigarette out of the pack and looked at Joe. 'What was with the pitying shake of the head?'

'You said you loved her.'

Hannah's mouth curled as she put the cigarette between her lips. 'Aw, are you jealous?'

Joe smiled.

'No, it's not that, Hannah. Sometimes I really wonder if you know what love is.' A small laugh left his mouth. 'Sometimes I wonder if you even know what friendship is.'

Chapter 5

T HE FOLLOWING SATURDAY, BEAU was ready early. She had packed her things slowly over the last three days, and it seemed that her pitiful life right now comprised a suitcase and two bags. She wished she could say that the bags were full to bursting with meaningful personal belongings, but one was barely half full, and the other was her laptop.

And actually, if she was being pedantic, 'ready' wasn't quite the word she would have used. Her actual emotions swung between panicked, overwhelmed, and petrified.

'I'm going to be okay, aren't I?'

She was standing in the kitchen, trying to force down the cup of coffee that Joe had insisted she had before she hit the road. Her entire body seemed to be shaking from the inside out, making the kitchen sway, and the coffee in her cup slosh. She put it back on the table before it spilled.

'You'll be fine, Beau. You're going to be absolutely fine.'

Joe slouched against the kitchen counter, His dark hair mussed, and dark rings under his eyes. He smiled, but he looked tired.

Beau couldn't say she was surprised; they had been making up for what felt like more than half the night after two days of weird atmosphere and arguments that Beau knew were more than likely about her.

'You really think so?'

'I know so.' Joe moved to stand next to her at the table, folding his arms across his chest. 'Want to know a secret?'

Beau shrugged. 'Is it relevant? Because I'm not sure I can do small talk right now, Joe.'

Joe nodded, his curls bouncing.

'Yeah, it's on point. The secret is that living on your own really isn't that hard once you get used to the company.'

'What company?'

'How well do you know yourself, Beau? Because I'll tell you right now that there's a neurotic, egotistic, know-it-all living right in there.' He tapped her temple. 'Until you've been alone long enough, that shitty little voice is going to bring you down every chance it gets. It's going to tell you that you can't handle it, that you're going to break, and that you have to leave. It's going to tell you that you're doing a shitty job, that you can't manage, and that your entire existence is pointless.'

Beau wrinkled her nose. 'Thanks, Joe.'

'I'm only telling you what I encountered when I lived alone, at first anyway. It was constant. Like some neurotic, schizophrenic, crazed man was living in my head, and I guarantee there's the same psychotic woman living in yours.'

Beau thought of the cutting remarks from the blinking laptop cursor, which were a daily assault that came on the back of every break from writing she tried to take, and thought he may have a point.

'So what are you saying I should do with her?'

'Listen out - you'll hear things like 'you can't', or 'you won't', or 'you're useless', or the best one I ever had which was 'you're a useless piece of shit. What fucking imbecile can't even fry an egg?' When you hear those things, shut the bitch down. You have to tell her straight and prove her wrong.'

Beau smiled. She thought she had heard worse from the cursor before she had set up the house-sitting job. Since then, it had fallen quiet, possibly waiting to see what would happen when she got there. 'So you heard the voice and learned to fry an egg?'

'Yeah, and guess what? It turned out it wasn't so hard. I mean, man, if I'd have listened to that guy, I'd have thought my life was over. Can't even fry an egg? I learned in two minutes and kicked the psycho back into his cage. That's what you have to do.'

'Right. Sounds fantastic. Maybe I'm lucky, and I don't have a psycho woman in my head.'

Maybe just a psycho cursor. Is that worse?

Joe downed his coffee and looked at her with a grin.

'Oh, she's in there, believe me. Any tough time you have, she'll be riding that pain with hysterical joy, and never failing to kick you while you're down.'

'Why are you telling me this?'

'It's valuable. If you kick her back enough times, one day she gets the message and decides you can manage after all. After that? Living by yourself, and with yourself, becomes bliss. Everything gets easy. That's the secret.'

Beau grinned. It didn't sound like an amazing going away gift, but it was advice she could store away just in case she felt like hanging herself one day and realised the woman was in there egging her on.

'Okay, I'll keep that in mind.'

Joe took his cup back to the sink. 'You do that. Have you finished your coffee? It's ten-twenty.'

Beau blinked at the clock, and then shook her head as nerves swelled in her stomach.

'No, I can't, Joe. I feel sick. I should probably just get on the road. Once I'm there, I'll be fine. Give another kiss to Leila, and will you tell Hannah goodbye for me?'

Beau hadn't joined them for tea yesterday evening, although she had popped her head in to say she would be leaving as close to 10am as she could. Only Joe had answered, and it was only Joe that had risen this morning to see her off. Beau decided she wasn't going to let Hannah spoil this terrifying adventure for her. If they were going to leave on bad terms, so be it, but at least she would have said goodbye, whether Hannah wanted to or not.

Maybe she wouldn't even have phone reception out there, and maybe that wouldn't be a bad thing. Hannah was a force to be reckoned with, and although she had been more than generous over the last nine months, maybe a break from the friendship wouldn't be such a bad thing – especially if Beau had the perfect excuse not to contact.

Joe crossed back to Beau and enveloped her in a brief hug.

'Don't look so scared, you'll be fine, and of course I'll tell Hannah. She'll come round, Beau, she loves you.'

Beau forced a smile as Joe grabbed her bags and she pulled the suitcase out to the car. Joe put them into the boot and slammed it shut, patting the roof of the blue BMW as she got in and started the engine.

'Don't forget to tell her. Bye Joe.'

'Safe journey.'

She raised a shaking hand from the driver's window as she pulled away, and saw Joe raise his in return. Her heart was thundering, her mind was whirling, and she had never felt more like throwing up, but she was on her way, and there would be no turning back now.

Well, not without a lawsuit, anyway.

Chapter 6

C ONTRARY TO HANNAH'S PREDICTION, the journey to Hollydale took almost eight hours, from the built up town of Chester where Beau had lived all of her life, to the tiny village in Scotland which sat on a single-track road on a thin leg of land that sat between a smattering of islands and land in a part of the UK that looked like it had been torn up and scrunched before being thrown back into the sea, like whoever was going to throw it away had a last minute change of heart.

It could have been worse. The views were beautiful and traffic was sparse compared to the city, but honestly? After an eight-hour journey with only two stops Beau thought there had been a beauty in not knowing where the hell she had signed up to be, because if she had known she probably wouldn't have been here at all.

Still, she finally found herself in Hollydale just after 6.30pm, cranky, exhausted, stiff, and completely missing the 5pm meeting she had intended to arrive early for, which would have given her time to explore the village and grab a bite to eat.

How did you get this so wrong? Why the hell didn't you put the place into the sat nav, or at least Maps, before you started out?

*Because Hannah said the trip was four hours, not bloody eight...
and I took her word.*

Beau drove past a handful of stone houses and came to a stop
at a tiny layby outside a small, unkempt, double fronted pub.
Its walls had at one time been whitewashed, but now looked
pale grey. She felt her heart begin to thump as she looked at
the swinging sign above the door - The Stone Bull.

Here it is. Here I am. This is the place, Beau, you're really here.

She felt a shudder run down her spine and licked her dry lips
as she pulled out her phone and checked the name of the place
Mrs Locket had said to meet. The Stone Bull.

Beau turned off the engine, cutting the music, which left an
uneasy silence - or maybe it was just Beau that was uneasy.
Trying to fight the urge to hightail it out of there, she got out
of the car and stretched. A strong breeze blew her hair into
her face, and she caught it with a hand, looking up and down
the lane for another Stone Bull. One that didn't look quite so
ominous.

The village street was eerily quiet. The Village Store and Bakery
looked shut, its windows dark, and a white blind half drawn.
Hollydale Cafe and a small shop named Quills and Feathers appeared just as vacant, and further up and down the street were
whitewashed cottages that looked tired and dreary. The sun
was shining – albeit half-heartedly - as the afternoon dimmed,
but the street looked dull, grey, and desolate.

Above Beau's head, there was a low creak that sent tingles down
her spine, and she looked up to see the pub's iron sign blowing
in a gust of wind. It creaked back again, swung a little, and came
to a halt as the breeze died.

Beau felt her heart drop. Mrs Locket hadn't given her the type
of establishment The Stone Bull was, and despite the name, she
had envisioned a small coffee shop or sandwich bar, bright and
cheery, full of people dining out as she had intended to do when
she arrived.

*You'd have gone hungry here, Beau. The Cafe isn't open, and
there's not a cake to be had from the bakery. What the hell have
you done?*

With the entirety of Hollydale seemingly in view, it was obvious
where she was supposed to be. She turned back to the pub,
whose small dark windows peered back at her suspiciously.

No, not suspiciously. They're just windows. Now let's get inside and get the keys before you're walking to the cottage in the dark.

Before she could talk herself out of it, she moved around the car, grabbed her bag from the passenger seat, and pushed open the door of the pub.

As her eyes adjusted to the dim light, Beau saw she was in a small entryway. The wall ahead was shedding its orange paint and decorated with a row of pins down the right-hand side. Two pieces of paper were pinned to the wall; one offering a reward for a lost dog, and the other offering a 'ladies' night of fun, wine, and mysticism' at Quills and Feathers. At the only sign of life she had seen so far, Beau was disappointed to see the date had long since passed.

She turned her attention to the two green doors on either side of her. One said Lounge in faded gold script, the other said Bar. She chose the bar, grimacing at the loud screech the door emitted as it scraped the tiled floor below.

Inside was dark and wooden, with a dull patterned carpet that matched the curtains and only served to enhance the shadowy corners despite the dull light from the wall sconces. The air was cold, damp, and smelled heavily of spirits and stale smoke.

As her eyes adjusted to the gloom Beau became aware of an elderly man leaning up the bar, his flat cap low over his face. He wore a dark woollen jacket over dark trousers and could have stepped right out of a photograph from the early 1900s. His right hand clasped a pint of ale, his elbow resting on the bar. He didn't move as Beau entered the room, and for a moment she wondered irrationally if he was asleep... and had been since the 1900s. Then he spoke.

'Bart? There's some besom...' The man assessed her with a squint, bushy grey eyebrows so low it was a wonder he could see at all. 'The likes of you doing around here?'

'I...' For a moment Beau lost all words. His accent was strong, his words muffled. She reddened as she realised he'd been watching her while she had been assessing whether he'd been sleeping. She also realised how ridiculously out of place she looked with her floral shirt and leather jacket, designer bag over her shoulder, and heeled boots. She shifted. 'Um, I'm here to see-'

'That would be me. Beau Winters, I presume? You certainly know how to keep a lady waiting.'

Beau turned to see a tall lady step out of the shadows to her right, almost as though she had stepped through the wall. She wore burgundy corduroy trousers over flat shoes, and a cream wool jumper that accented the deep cream of her hair. In her left hand was an ornate walking stick. Beau had assessed that the lady was around eighty-five on the phone, but she realised now that she had been harsh. This lady had to be no more than fifty.

Beau checked herself and moved forward, her hand out-stretched.

'Yes. I'm Beau. You must be Mrs Locket.'

Beau's warm hand met Mrs Locket's, which was thin, bony, and cold. She smiled and then flinched as the man at the bar barked again.

'Dinna fash!'

'Sorry?' she said, swinging back to him.

The man scowled and Mrs Locket gestured toward a small table for two that hid in the shadows next to a tiny window which let in about as much light as a pinhole in a blanket. 'Ignore him. He's talking to Bart. We've wasted enough time. Sit.'

Beau pulled out a wooden chair as Mrs Locket sat down oppo-site and pushed a glass toward her. 'Water?' she asked, her hand on a glass jug.

Beau's mouth dropped open. 'Well, I was hoping to grab a glass of something stronger. It's been one hell of a drive. I could do with a break.'

'I don't doubt that the journey was tiresome, Ms Winters, but being this late is bothersome for both of us. We have some paperwork to go over, and then I have to give you direc-tions to meet Gerard, and that's before you've even begun the three-mile walk to the cottage.'

Mrs Locket looked her up and down, leaning to look under the table, before meeting Beau's gaze.

'Nice to see you've dressed for the walk and the weather.'

Beau felt a flare of indignation. 'I always dress like this, and I'm used to walking in heels. I'll be fine.'

Mrs locket cocked an eyebrow, but dismissed the comment with a small shrug that made Beau feel stupid.

'If you say so. I had Gerard drop a couple of bottles of red, white, and champagne at the cottage for you, along with a week's worth of basic groceries. Anything extra you'll have to pick up yourself. You can have a stronger drink there when I'm sure you won't break an ankle. Time runs short, and the light is quickly lost now. So, back to my original question. Water?'

Beau watched the lady's bony hand reach for the jug handle.

'Please.'

With a tight smile, Mrs Locket filled two cups and pushed one back to Beau, who took a polite sip.

'Thank you. So, you're not meeting Gerard with me?'

'I was.' Mrs Locket sipped from her own glass before she continued. 'But time runs short, as I said. I have my nurse coming over at seven, and she appreciates good timekeeping... as do I.'

Beau's felt her cheeks flush again. 'I'm sorry,' she mumbled.

Mrs Locket waved a hand elegantly. 'What's done is done.' She pulled a file from a bag under the table and placed the yellow docket on the table between them.

'I understand that you have signed the contract already. I have the printed copy here, but there have been a couple of addendums. Nothing major, but I'd like you to sign the fresh copy if you don't mind, then we'll go over the terms of the arrangement.'

'Okay,' Beau straightened in her chair, expecting Mrs Locket to point out the extras that she would be signing for, but she didn't. She simply turned to the back page and handed her a pen. She gestured to where Beau should sign and date, and against her better judgement, Beau signed without question. She didn't want to annoy Mrs Locket further, and her lateness was obviously a problem. She supposed she should have called, but the Bluetooth in the car simply refused to acknowledge the existence of her phone and Beau had surmised that by stopping to make the call, she would just have wasted more time. Better to get there as fast as she could instead.

The best decision isn't always the wisest, obviously.

'...through the terms, then,' Mrs Locket said, forcing Beau's attention back to her. Beau nodded, and Mrs Locket slipped on a pair of thin framed glasses and began to read.

'You will cover all living expenses from now until the end of the term of your stay, which is March 31st next year. Any problems or repairs will be reported to Gerard in a prompt and *timely* manner.'

The emphasis on timely, Mrs Locket caught Beau's eyes with her own, which Beau noticed were sharp and pale blue, before her gaze dropped back to the paper in front of her.

'You will be liable for any damages or breakages that are not general repairs or weather related. You will not leave the cottage for three consecutive nights at any time unless permission is requested. There are to be no parties, get togethers, or similar group arrangements at the house. The furniture is old, as is the house, and I'd like its condition respected.'

Beau swallowed hard.

What the hell have you got yourself in to? Maybe Hannah was right...

Then she remembered that Hannah - her self-proclaimed best friend - hadn't got up to see her off or say goodbye and hadn't been in contact all day up to yet, either.

Hannah will never be right. Even if she is.

'Agreed?'

'Yes, that sounds fine.'

Would it make a difference if it didn't? I've just signed the contract anyway, and without even looking. Excellent job, Beau.

Mrs Locket seemed content with her answer. She took off her glasses and shut the file, placing a hand on top.

'Okay, that's the hard stuff out of the way. The easy stuff now. Everything you need except food and clothes will be provided. You are to treat the place like your own while you are there. The surrounding natural landscape is beautiful. Explore it, or you'll go mad holed up inside. When I lived in Bluebell Cottage I used to be out daily before this damned disease set in the hips. Now we're here in this unfortunate position where I can't stay any longer. Too hard, and too painful.' She waved a hand. 'In any case, that's beside the point. A walk up the tor and to my father's old church is well worth the climb. The views across the ocean to Jura and Islay are spectacular. On that note, there is a small motorboat moored high up on the beach. It is seaworthy if you fancy a trip out and the weather is accommodating. Gerard will tell you everything you need to know and show you anything you need help with. He has his phone by his side at all times. You can call him day or night. That is part of his remit.'

Beau chewed her lip as Mrs Locket pulled up a sleeve and looked at a gold watch on her arm.

'Right, well, unless there are questions, I'll direct you to Gerard. I'm almost out of time. Questions?'

Beau shook her head, which was completely empty of questions now that she had been asked. She couldn't think of a damn thing.

'Well, if you think of anything, you can call me on my mobile. I'm available most afternoons between one and three. If I don't answer, leave a message and I'll get back to you when I can. Please don't keep ringing. If I haven't got back to you, it's because I haven't had time. In an emergency call Gerard. Clear?'

'Yes.'

'Good. Now you'll want to continue down the lane two miles or so.' Mrs Locket pointed an arm the way Beau's car was already pointing. 'You'll come to a small track on your left. Follow it until the end. It's about a mile and not well kept, although I had Gerard fill some of the bigger holes last year, so take care. At the end, you'll meet Gerard, who will guide you over the land to the house. As I said, the walk is around three miles. If you have some better boots, I suggest you put them on and use them. Heels are no good for carrying luggage or shopping to Bluebell Cottage.'

Mrs locket rose, extending her hand, and Beau imitated the movement, grasping the icy fingers in hers.

'Lovely to meet you, Ms Winters. I hope your stay at my cottage will be comfortable.'

With that, she walked out, pausing at the door to look back as Beau stared after her.

'Don't forget to change the boots.'

Then she was gone, and the door screeched slowly shut.

Chapter 7

B EAU FOUND THE ENTRANCE to the track - which was little more
than ruts with a stream of grass and weeds rising from the
middle - and bumped her way down it slowly as the sun lowered
before her. The bushes on either side had recently been hacked
back, although they offered no view, and new branches were
already forcing their way back into the middle, brushing the car
with their delicate fingers. It seemed to Beau that it would be
a constant fight, and as the wheels found another pothole, she
wondered why Mrs Locket didn't just get rid of the foliage and
throw down some tarmac. She claimed to be wealthy, and surely
it would make life easier?

It was a testing journey, but not a long one. Within ten minutes,
Beau had reached the end of the track, and another hacked
bush provided parking for around three vehicles - two if no one
wanted to reverse back up the hole infested track.

*Did the contract say no parties? I'm not sure who the hell is
walking down that track for a weekend bender, because they sure
as hell can't park their cars here!*

Beau grinned as she pulled up next to an old Land Rover and
peered across the expanse of land ahead which dipped gently

downhill. Before her was open meadow, lots of it, with a few scattered birch trees which were pushed eternally sidewards by the prevailing wind, as if reaching for something just out of sight. To the left, rising upward, was a pine forest as far as the eye could see. In the distance ahead, Beau thought she could see a glimpse of blue.

Is that the sea?

A small bubble of something climbed her chest. Terror, trying hard to disguise itself as excitement, and then the car door clicked open, and Beau swung round, slightly perturbed at the intrusion. Outside the car was the lower half of a man, his brown, muscled bare legs disappearing into brown laced boots.

Beau blinked, half wondering if she was about to be murdered, but surely no one else would be waiting at the end of the track except...

The man stepped back and leaned to look into the car, his bald head glinting in the light. His deep brown eyes, twinkled as he smiled, showing straight white teeth against dark skin.

'Good afternoon, Ms Winters. I'm Gerard. The caretaker.'

Beau felt herself pushed back almost to the passenger side at his presence, but his voice was deep and quiet, his accent soft. Beau felt her guard lower a little.

'Oh, yes. Hello Gerard, I'm sorry I'm so late. The traffic... I've come a long way, you know?'

'Aye, so it would seem.'

Gerard backed up and Beau got out of the car, straightening in the cooling air and taking his offered hand. She scanned the muscled giant in front of her, at least six and a half feet, she estimated, and then wondered how such a big man could have such a gentle handshake.

'Lovely to meet you,' he said, glancing across the meadow. 'I'm afraid we're losing the light, Ms Winters. You may have to leave some of your things here until tomorrow. We'll take what we can now, but we'll not be making two trips today, I'm afraid. Too far.'

Beau tipped a hand to shield her eyes as she looked across the field.

'Oh, I'm sure it won't take that long.'

Gerard smiled. Full teeth and gums on show. 'You're looking at an hour, maybe more with luggage. I'll explain what you need to know as we go.'

He rounded the car and popped the boot. Beau let out a small 'oh' as he pulled the case and two bags out and set them on the - thankfully dry - dirt.

'Anything else?'

He seemed amused and Beau opened the car the collect her handbag, which lay on the front seat. She hooked it over her shoulder and locked the car. He stared as though she should have more, and Beau shifted uncomfortably in the silence.

'That's the lot,' she confirmed.

Gerard ran a hand over his bald head. 'Suppose we won't need two trips after all then, and I'll be home for supper. You pack light, Ms Winters.'

Beau looked at the suitcase and flushed. It *did* look pitiful, and even more so when she knew it was the entirety of the clothes and shoes she now owned. She thought about all the things she had thrown away after the divorce. Clothes that Patrick had liked on her, clothes that she had brought because he had said he liked them, clothes that he had complimented her on, clothes that she had worn with him, clothes that he had touched...

I was actually pretty ruthless, she thought. Maybe too much.

She had been with the furniture too, what was hers after the split she couldn't stand to look at. He had touched them with his grimy cheating fingers, and she no longer wanted them in her sight. Almost everything had been sold.

'I'll take the suitcase and a bag. You take this one.' Gerard said, forcing her from her reverie as he handed her the lighter laptop bag. Beau took it.

'I can take the other one too, if you like.'

'No need,' Gerard said, slipping the strap over his head. The bag sat across his body, bumping at his waist. It looked insignificant against him as he pulled the suitcase up onto his shoulder as though it was nothing more than a nineteen eighties boombox.

'There's a long way to go, yet Mrs Winters, and I'm normally like a packhorse. I've never had so little to take to the cottage before. This is a six-month stint, you realise?'

'Call me Beau, please. And yes, I know. I guess I don't have much, but I have enough. That's what counts.'

Gerard scanned his eyes over her and pushed out his lips.

'What counts, Beau, is whether you have another pair of boots.'

———

Beau managed the three-mile hike in her heels. Not because she didn't have a brand new pair of hiking boots in her suitcase, but because three people had now scorned her dress sense since she had arrived not three hours ago, and she was blowed if she would be forced out of her favourite boots for the sake of three miles across a dry field.

What she hadn't thought about was how far three miles was to someone who didn't walk, and the fact that at least two of those three people had known what they were talking about. The land wasn't as luxuriously flat as it seemed. It was rutted and uneven, boggy in parts, and technically wasn't a field at all. It was open, untamed land, that Mrs Locket often allowed the farmer up the road to use to graze his sheep and cows according to Gerard's narrative.

There was no path to the house, just a worn line in the grass where people had walked over the years. It was truly unspoiled, and if not for the constant threat of a broken ankle, Beau would have enjoyed the scenery. As it was, she kept her gaze cast down and watched her step. Every so often, she looked up to find Gerard surveying her as he paused to let her catch up.

What felt like hours later, she heard him stop ahead and she glanced up for what seemed like the fiftieth time. Her thighs and calves screamed, and her ankles ached from trying to keep herself upright. She saw Gerard shaking his head and knew that she had slowed as time went on.

'I thought I'd be home for supper, but it seems it'll be a reheat job after all.'

'I'm going as fast as I can.'

'It'll be midnight before we get there.'

Beau felt her stomach drop. The sun was already low on the horizon and the thought of being out here in the dark was almost more horrifying than breaking an ankle. She moved faster, her heels wobbling precariously as she caught him up and he turned to carry on. Her shirt was wet at the armpits under her jacket, and she was panting hard, which seemed ridiculous when Gerard had carried the suitcase on his shoulder most of the way here and had barely broken a sweat.

'Is it really that much further?'

Gerard rumbled a low, deep laugh. 'I was joking, if you had decent boots and could look up from your feet you'd know it's not far now, see?' He swung his free arm forward and Beau looked up before stopping in her tracks with a gasp.

'Oh! Wow.'

She felt a grin spread across her face.

Ahead, the same green landscape dropped away, scattered birch to her right and pine forest to her left, but here, at the foot of the pines, was a small Victorian style cottage. The whitewashed walls, highlighted by the sun, glinted against the deep green of the pine, the lighter green of the scrub, and were framed by the dark blue of the ocean behind. There had once been a dry-stone wall that ran around the building, Gerard pointed out, but it had long since fallen. Only part of it remained, a short line that seemed to separate the cottage from the ocean across the landscape.

'Mrs Locket didn't see the need to rebuild it, so you may have visitors around the cottage. Just shoo them on.'

'Visitors?'

'Sheep, cows, deer. They'll not bother you, but if they come closer than you'd like, just wave your hands and holler, they'll soon go running.'

'Right.'

Just past the old wall, Beau saw, the grass, bog, and scrub give way to sand and ocean. Now that she was looking properly, she could hear the gentle lap of the waves against the shore and smell the salty seaweed scent that accompanied all the seaside holidays she had been on. A flicker of excitement joined the immediate punch of fear that the sea always brought. It was a strange contrast. She could appreciate how beautiful the ocean looked, and all the amazing times she had spent on the beach in close proximity, but the thought of being in or on it at anything more than calf deep sent her into a spiral of panic. She quickly turned her attention to the view across the ocean and the islands beyond, which was stunning. Was she really going to live here? This was postcard idyllic!

They continued to walk until they rounded the front of the building.

'Here we are, Bluebell cottage, so named because of the blue-bells that fill the wood behind each spring.'

Gerard fished in his pocket for a set of keys as Beau took in the quaint beauty of the small house. Faded red Victorian frill hung from the pitch of the roof, half hiding a small, circular, third-floor window, complete with red shutters that were open to the sides. There were just two windows on the second floor, cross paned, and complete with red shutters. The ground floor had just one shuttered window and the pale blue front door which sat to its left. A wooden porch wrapped around the cottage across the front and to the right, its roof and columns painted a peeling, faded red. The left-hand side of the house sank into the hill, which rose behind, and from the rise of the pines beyond, the back would tell the same story.

'The house is fairly sheltered down here.' Gerard said, admiring the cottage alongside Beau. 'Although winds from the ocean can blow a hooley. The porch looks delicate, but we've not lost it yet. It's perfectly sound. It runs around the side which faces west. You'll get some stunning sunsets over the ocean, especially this time of year. There's a swing seat round the corner that'll need removing from its chains in bad weather. I set it up already, and I'll show you how to take it down. It's pretty simple.'

'Okay.'

Beau followed Gerard up onto the wooden porch and waited as he slipped the key into the front door and went inside.

'Right, so here's the hall, living room directly on our right, ahead leads to the kitchen, and the dining room. Take a look.'

Gerard put down the suitcase and bag by the door and took Beau's from her shoulder to set down beside them.

'Thank you.'

Beau took stock of the hallway. The wallpaper was old, but not unkempt. Brown with a silver geometric pattern running through it. The floorboards were polished, and a brown patterned rug ran the length of the hallway. To her left, a flight of stairs ran up to the second floor and from here Beau could see the white spindles of the balustrade wrapped around to a galleried landing above.

Gerard gestured right and Beau stuck her head inside the small living area. An old rocking chair sat to her left, in the corner, and two small settees flanked another brown rug that sat in front of the fireplace. A small ornate glass topped coffee table sat between the chairs and the fire. The walls in here were half panelled; the top half wallpapered in a similar age to the hallway, this time pale blue with small white flowers. The room's two windows, one to the front of the house and one overlooking the ocean, made this small room light and airy despite the porch outside.

It looked cosy enough, but there was something wrong in here. At the moment, Beau couldn't put her finger on it.

'Not much to say about this room. It speaks for itself.' Gerard moved around her and pointed to a couple of single portraits that adorned the wall. 'These two beauties are Rector and Mrs Locket, circa 1954, before our Mrs Locket was even born. And the bigger picture over there is an old drawing of the cottage.'

Beau moved across the room to admire the bigger picture, which was a black and white shaded drawing of great detail, catching the house from about where she and Gerard had stopped to admire it earlier, and outlining a small wall which surrounded the property.

'It looks exactly the same! Except that I see what you mean about the wall. Why was it built? Was that to keep out the wildlife?'

'No,' Gerard moved next to her to stand before the picture. 'They were keen gardeners, and being so isolated, they obviously grew a lot of their own food. The salty ocean air and those fierce winds can ravage a lot of plants. That's mainly what it was for, I believe. Protection.'

'I see.'

Beau turned to look around the room and finally noticed what had felt odd when she first walked in.

'There's no tv?'

'No. The signal down here is pretty hit and miss. There used to be one, back when our Mrs Locket was young, but it was eventually done away with. No point, apparently.'

'Ah,' Beau said, wondering about her phone, but Gerard had her covered.

'The internet connection is pretty stable now though unless the weather is really bad. A tower was erected on the tor by the old church.'

Beau felt herself relax. 'Good news.'

Gerard showed his row of white teeth and gums. 'If all else fails, the record player in the corner works perfectly. There are plenty of vinyl records to choose from in the cabinet below. You'll need to switch the plug on first, though.'

Beau nodded and glanced at the socket he pointed to, before her eyes rested on the old player. Its smoked plastic top showed a record still sitting in position, and what looked like a long arm was hooked in the off position to the side.

She wasn't entirely sure how to set the player, or how to work it, but she didn't think she would need it, anyway. She had so many downloaded songs on Spotify that it seemed unnecessary. Gerard shifted.

'Shall we look at the rest of the place?'

They exited the room and moved down the hallway, past an ornate grandfather clock that Gerard said was over a hundred years old and no longer worked, to a door which led into a galley kitchen. The oven, hob, and sink were all integrated in the cupboards along the wall to her left, which also housed the only window. To her right sat another doorway into the dining room alongside a final cupboard and a fridge, which butted against the back wall next to an exterior door.

Gerard walked straight ahead to this back door, which sat snug between the microwave and the fridge, and unlocked the chunky old yale lock with the key that sat in the lock. He pulled the door inward, and Beau followed him out into an old extension. Windows ran the length of the house not two

paces in front of her, looking out into the darkness of the pine
forest outside. She followed Gerard to the right and frowned,
wondering why it had been built - the space was too narrow to
be useful. At the end of the passage was another locked door,
which Gerard said led onto the back end of the porch outside.

'I think this was used as a boot and coat room, but more im-
portantly, down this end is the old boiler and water heater. The
house has central heating, but it's old, and this beast can play
up. Both fireplaces in the living and dining room are functional
and plenty warm enough if the boiler throws a wobbler. There's
coal in a small bunker out back, and firelighters in the kitchen.'

Gerard showed Beau a few settings to try if the heating or hot
water went down, and then he led her back into the house and
the dining room.

'I'll have to write this down, or I'll forget by tomorrow.' Beau
tried to laugh, but the sound was high and forced and brought
goosebumps to her arms.

'No worries, Beau. That's what I'm here for. If you run into
trouble, or can't fathom what to do, call me, and I'll be here
within the hour.'

Beau smiled and touched his arm in silent gratitude as she
passed him into the dining room. This room was also bright
and had a window overlooking the ocean. It was half panelled,
just like the living room, and the pale-yellow wallpaper here
had scores of the same white flowers. A wooden table with four
chairs sat centrally, almost filling the space. Along the back wall,
a thin, waist high cabinet housed a row of pictures of the Locket
family, and on the wall next to her was a large painting of a
church sitting on a clifftop with a rough ocean behind.

'Rector Locket's church as it stood on Holly Tor. It's just above
the pine forest here.' Gerard gestured to the back of the house.
'There's a path, but the church is little more than a wreck now.'

Beau nodded. 'I heard it's well worth a walk up there, though?'

'It is beautiful up there, aye, certainly something to be seen.
Shall we go upstairs?'

Gerard led the way back into the hallway and up the stairs. She
had been right, she thought, as the second floor came into view.
The landing was galleried, and through the spindles, she made
out two doors.

Ahead, at the top of the stairs, was the tiny white bathroom. A shower bath with a white shower curtain, toilet and basin with a mirror were all that fit inside, but it did its job, and it was sparkling clean.

Beau pulled her head out of the space and looked back down the landing. The bedroom doors were now on her left, the balustrade running to her right. A large window at the end made this space bright and appear bigger than it would have done if there had been a wall alongside the stairs. A single armchair sat beneath the window, filling the space.

Gerard opened the door nearest the bedroom. A wooden plaque announced that this was the red room. Beau would have said it was more a sickly pink where the red wallpaper had faded over time. There was a single wardrobe and a double bed with a red spread and throw. The room had more old photographs on the wall, and two windows to the back and the side.

Which should make it light, but it just feels claustrophobic, urg.

'This used to be Mrs Locket's room, way back when she was a bairn. The red theme came later, when she got older, I believe. She continued to use this room when she lived here alone.'

'She liked red, huh?'

Gerard shrugged. 'Seems so.'

They left the room and moved down the landing toward the chair, which seemed to have no purpose other than to fill space and offer an opportunity take in the view. Maybe that would be a better pastime than it sounded. Beau thought she may have a little time to find out, at least.

A couple of steps down the small landing, Gerard pointed out a hatch in the ceiling which had a small pull ring in the door. Gerard was tall enough that he could reach up and pull the handle free of its clasp to tug on it.

'Stand aside.'

Beau moved back as a pair of ladders descended from the door and hit the floor with a gentle bump. Gerard pressed a light switch between the bedroom doors, which lit the area above with yellow light.

She blinked as he climbed the ladders and disappeared out of view. Then his head reappeared and motioned for Beau to follow him. She eyed the drop next to her as she climbed.

It's all the way down the stairs if you slip, Beau.

She focused on the rungs and thought that right now a wall would have been better than a gallery, after all. She was shaking when she rose into an attic space that held many boxes, pictures, and a few of pieces of furniture. The small round window she had seen from outside added some light to the space ahead.

'What on earth are we doing up here?'

'I need to show you something important.'

Gerard moved to the window and swung a latch in the middle to open the glass into two semi circular panes, which swung inward.

'This window is older and more delicate than the rest. It's important in windy weather that you close the shutters over the glass. All the shutters work the same, but they're not essential. This one matters.'

He reached his arms out and pulled the wood together, locking the boards together with a small central catch which snapped together with a firm click.

'See?' he said, leaning back for her to see. 'This works for all the shutters if you want to use them. The locks are identical.'

'Okay.'

Beau had no intention of using the shutters either way, so she wasn't paying much attention.

'After the shutter is locked, secure the window as normal.'

Gerard shut the small semi circles back together and swung the latch back down.

'Now it's secure, okay?'

'Yes. Leave it like that. I won't have a need to be up here, anyway.'

Gerard nodded in the dim light.

'As you wish. If you do come up here, you can open the window and shutters by reversing what I just did. Just remember to close the shutters over the glass if the wind rises.'

'I will.'

They descended back to the landing and Gerard pushed the ladder back up before shutting the hatch with a click. Beau let out a breath of relief and followed Gerard into the last room. Its plaque announced that this was the green room.

She rolled her eyes.

Great. Do I go for the claustrophobic room, or the sickly room?

Beau was thinking she may just take up residence in the red room, but the green room turned out to be pale, light, and fresh. It was almost identical to the red room, with a double wardrobe and a double bed with pale green spread and throw. Two windows. One to the front and one to the side, and an amalgamation of old pictures on the walls. This room seemed bigger though, and to Beau, it felt like it had more air.

'It's nice in here,' Beau said.

'I'll bring the bags up, then,' Gerard answered with a nod. 'And then I'd best be off, sun's a-lowering fast.'

Beau turned to watch him stride to the stairs with a jolt of reality.

He's leaving already?

Seconds later he was back with the bags over his shoulder, and her suitcase hoisted high. He crossed the landing and brought the luggage into the room.

My room.

A swirl of anxiety hit her gut.

My room, out here in the middle of nowhere.

'They okay there?'

Beau saw he had placed everything next to the bed.

'Great, thank you. Can I offer you a glass of something for your help?'

'I don't drink,' Gerard said as they walked back down the landing toward the stairs. 'But thank you.'

Beau struggled with the sudden panic.

It's going dark, and I'll be all alone here. There's no one for miles.

Is it safe out here all alone?

'How... how about a hot drink then? Tea, coffee?'

They reached the bottom of the stairs and Gerard handed her the keys and a card with a smile. 'No, thank you. I need to get home. Here's my card. Put the number into your phone, I'll always answer.'

'Right.' Beau looked at the card. 'Don't you want my number?'

'I don't need it, Beau, this is a work only phone. If I had to faff with everyone's numbers every year, I'd get in a muddle. I won't come down here unless you call or there's been especially bad weather. If you need me for anything at all, call, and I'll be here.'

'Oh. Okay.' Beau swallowed hard as Gerard opened the front door and disappeared down the steps of the porch with a wave.

'Goodbye, Beau. Nice to meet you.'

Words caught in Beau's throat and her heart thudded in her chest, so she held a hand up in a wave and watched as his long strides carried him away from her and the cottage.

She looked across the darkening porch to the ocean, which lapped and hissed at the shore. There was the call of a crow, a hurried flapping of wings, and then the gentle rustle of trees and bushes swaying in the breeze. The non-city silence filled her ears, and she swallowed hard.

Fuck, you are completely alone out here. Holy crap, Beau, you really didn't think this through.

Chapter 8

A S THE SUN LOWERED below the horizon of the ocean, stretching into reds, oranges, and even a splash of purple, Beau found herself sitting in the living room in silence.

It had been thirty minutes since she had cooked herself a banquet of beans on toast and the majority of the meal still sat on the coffee table.

Shame, she thought, as the bread had been a beautiful, fresh, crusty loaf she had found in the cupboard, but her stomach just wouldn't settle. Considering she had eaten nothing since her last stop at 3pm, when she had purchased a Dairy Milk with her coffee, she wasn't at all hungry. And despite the exhausting long drive, she was now wide awake, fuelled by adrenaline that wouldn't let her relax.

You could go and unpack, maybe set up the laptop in the dining area ready for work - heck, maybe that would inspire you to actually get to work and get a few words in before the first night!

She chewed on her lip as the sunset slowly deepened.

You could check what food you have and make a list of anything to add to your next shop. Or you could check out the swing on the porch, take some photos of the sunset and send them to Hannah...

She frowned.

...or maybe not just yet. Not until I've spoken to her and cleared the air a little first.

Beau's eyes drifted to her phone, charging on the coffee table, and then drifted further to her half full plate and cutlery.

You could take your dirty plate out and wash up.

It was the least appealing of the options, but the only one that stirred her into action.

I should probably do that.

With a little more resolve, she took the plate out, poured herself a glass of white wine, and made her way back to the front room, taking the cold bottle with her. As she sipped the cool liquid, she realised that she had killed all of five minutes.

The sky was beginning to darken outside.

The house was too quiet. Not even the ticking of a clock broke the eerie silence.

It was almost ominous.

Like every horror story you've ever written...

Beau felt her heart skip three beats and wobble back into rhythm.

Don't be ridiculous. It's just the quiet. You're a city girl. Born and bred. You've always had noise around you, always had **people** around you.

She thought about Hannah's last words. 'You won't cope alone, Beau. You've never been alone, ever.'

Beau took an uneasy sip of wine.

'I guess now we find out whether that's true, don't we?'

She smiled down at her glass. Her only friend in this unfamiliar place.

I don't feel too bad right now. I'm unsettled but–

Her thoughts cut off as the room darkened and she glanced up to see a large dark shadow pass the edge of the window.

'Oh, shit.'

She jumped up, spilling wine on the table and backed away from the settee, slowly heading to the doorway behind, her heart thudding frantically.

'What the hell was that?'

Her mind scrabbled for what she should do. Should she look, should she hide, should she approach whoever it was if she caught them?

The doors were locked. She had carefully locked all three, including the one from the porch at the back of the house, just after Gerard left. She was safe enough, she supposed, but whoever it was knew someone was here. The light from the hallway behind her would shine like a beacon across the darkening landscape.

What do I do?

Will they just pass on?

What if they knock? Do I answer?

Why didn't I ask Gerard whether it was safe to answer the door?

Shall I phone him? It's only 8.35pm.

Her mind was still in full flight, trying to work out the safest way to stay alive in this inhospitable place when the shadow came back, covering the window ahead of her and casting an eerie shadow across the room.

Beau's heart almost stopped, and a scream lodged in her throat, taking her breath.

She was fully aware that she was illuminated by the hallway light behind her. Whoever was out there had full advantage.

They see you!

She finally let out a strangled yell, and then she stalled as the shadow moved.

Whoever is out there has four legs, Beau.

She raised her eyebrows, and pressed a hand to her thudding chest.

Four legs?

She felt her momentum stall as she squinted into the dim light outside and the stag lifted its head, antler's high, its mouth chewing.

A deer? It's a deer!

Beau's vision wavered as the stag moved out of the lowering sunlight, the darkness leaving the room with it. She let out a breath and moved to the window, captivated by the animal, silhouetted against the deepening sunset beyond. He was only just beyond the porch - so close! - Beau had never seen a deer, and certainly never in the wild so close up. As she stood watching, more deer emerged from the forest on the left.

It's an entire herd!

They were obviously used to the house as they weren't bothered about how near they were, or that there was a strange, slightly panicked woman in the window. She watched them grazing for a while, snapped a few pictures on her phone, and then sat back down on the settee, appalled.

'Jesus Beau, you nearly had a heart attack over the wildlife. How will you ever cope here? It's the first goddamn night and already you're being murdered... by deer!'

She had to admit that the quiet was getting to her too, making her jumpy, especially after the scare, and there was the night to come yet.

'Oh, God, Hannah was right, you can't do this, you won't...'

Beau let the words trail off as Joe's voice filled her head. 'You'll hear things like 'you can't', or 'you won't', or 'you're useless'... When you hear those things, shut the bitch down. You have to tell her straight and prove her wrong.'

So, shut the bitch down, Beau.

In this moment, that felt harder than anything she had ever had to do, because what if this voice was right? What if psycho woman had a point? But then her mind produced another nugget of information that Joe had offered. 'If you kick her back enough times, one day she gets the message and doesn't come back out. After that? Living by yourself, and with yourself, becomes bliss. Everything gets easy. That's the secret.'

'That's the secret,' Beau whispered, putting the glass up to her lips and taking a sip. 'Thanks Joe.'

It should have made her feel better, and she did a little, but honestly, given the chance, she would have slipped out and driven all the way back to Hannah and Joe's with a big apology, because she wasn't at all sure she was cut out for any of this.

Not for living alone.

Not for living in dark silence, outside a city.

Not for living in the wilderness.

And not for living in isolation.

Hair rose at the nape of Beau's neck as she realised she may have just made the biggest mistake of her life.

Not only that, but you signed a contract. You're stuck with it. It doesn't matter whether you like it or not.

Chapter 9

T HE DOOR TO THE Antler Hotel swung open and a blonde woman walked in. She had made the reservation just hours before and had been apologetic, but the young man now watching her from the desk had been merely amused. It wasn't often this hotel was full; it was too far off the beaten track and had too many rooms. Mostly the hotel was used for weddings, and functions, or corporate away days where the point was to get outdoors and endure the elements. The guest to room ratio was always pitiful - even at this time of year.

The woman approached at a clip, dragging her suitcase behind her, and as she neared, he saw her cheeks were flushed and her blue eyes threaded with red veins.

'A room for-'

'Anna Lane.' The man finished for her with a smile, hoping that he was right, and she hadn't popped in off the street - although the hotel hadn't had someone 'pop in' for the entire term of his employment. To his relief, the woman relaxed and smiled.

'You remember,' she said, pulling a card from her purse with a smile that he was sure could light the whole of Manhattan if she hadn't looked so darn tired. 'Was it you I spoke to?'

The man shrugged and looked around at the empty foyer. 'Only me here, I'm afraid.'

'I see.'

'Just the one night?'

'Two, for now.'

He took payment and found a key card to connect to her room on the first floor as she watched him. He felt himself flush under her gaze.

'Just passing through?' he said stupidly as the connection failed. Stupid system, stupid question. No one ever passed through here. Everyone else was going up or down the country, and down here led to nowhere but back up the other side.

'Visiting someone. Is there somewhere to pass through here to... er...'

'Daniel,' he offered, 'and no, there isn't. I was just making small talk, I guess.'

Busted.

To his relief, Anna Lane laughed. A small titter that she hid behind a hand while looking up at him from under false lashes.

'Well, Daniel, it's a good job I have somewhere to be. I'm hoping to visit someone in Hollydale within the next few days, the next village along? but I'm not sure I'm staying there yet. I wonder if I may be able to come back and book another few nights here if needed?'

Daniel leaned on the counter and handed Anna the keycard.

'Plenty of room. It won't be a problem, Anna. Do you need me to help with your suitcase?'

Daniel saw the lady flinch a little at the use of her name and wondered if he'd overstepped the mark as she took the card from him.

'No, but thank you.' She paused, and then looked up at him. 'Interesting accent. Where are you from, Daniel?'

Daniel grinned. It was a question he got asked all the time down here - when there was anybody to ask it.

'Well, right now, my address is the Antler Hotel, but originally, I'm from Manhattan, in the Big Apple. You know, New York? I'm working my way around Scotland for the next six months, chasing dreams before going to university, if I ever go. I don't want to, but the old's have issues with me not being a lawyer.'

'Ah,' Anna said, her lips parting into a perfect red 'o'. 'So, you're out here avoiding your parents and a pre-planned future in law. Interesting way to do it.'

Daniel gave her a sideways grin. 'It's the only way I can delay the inevitable. My father travelled when he was younger, said it taught him all he knew. If I keep travelling, then he won't moan until I come home. So far I've been to Canada, Italy, Belgium, Poland, Ireland, and now Scotland.'

'And is it teaching you anything?'

'That avoiding responsibility is a fun and rewarding way to travel and meet new people.'

Anna dipped her gaze and then looked around the hotel.

'There don't seem to be many people here...'

She let the words hang, and he smiled as he met her blue gaze.

'You're here. What more could I want?'

'You're very charming, Daniel, and I'm very tired. Thank you so much for the room at short notice. Will I see you tomorrow?'

'That's a certainty. I have a room here in payment for the work. I'm always around.'

'Ah, well, goodnight then.'

'Goodnight.'

Daniel watched as Anna pulled the suitcase to the lift. She was old enough to be his mother, but his mother didn't move with the youthful grace that she did. She held up a hand daintily as the lift doors closed and he returned the gesture, marvelling that this little village could throw somebody like her onto his path.

Then again, it seemed to happen all the time. Travel was a constant surprise, people were a constant surprise, and that was what he loved about all of it.

Chapter 10

THE FOLLOWING MORNING, BEAU woke after the strangest dream that a bunch of deer with oversized antlers were surrounding the house. They stood, waiting. Watching. Crows sat on their backs and heads, stretching their wings, and cawing as though they wanted to tell her something. Beau had tried to shoo them away as Gerard had suggested, but in true nightmare style they had only watched, sending her scurrying back inside to lock the door and wonder whether she may end up stuck here forever. Then there had been a loud bang as the largest of the deer had stepped forward, bowed his head, and charged. His antlers thudded against the front of the cottage with a crash and a strange chime that had jolted her instantly awake with a scream on her lips.

It had taken her a good while to fall back to sleep as she lay in the darkness, and then, like magic, she was waking up in the early light of the morning.

As she lay in the warm bed, she remembered how hard her heart had thumped in the darkness, and how she had sneaked to the window to check for deer, only to find the landscape empty under the moonlight.

I haven't had a dream that realistic for ages. Probably the unfamiliar surroundings, and too much wine...

Her thoughts trailed off as she remembered something else in the darkness of the night. A metallic chime.

Had that been real, or part of the dream?

Beau shut her eyes and tried to remember. The deer had banged its antlers, and she had jolted awake. When her eyes opened, she had heard a chime for a few seconds... hadn't she?

From where, Beau? Nothing to chime in here.

Beau opened her eyes as she realised she was right. Letting it go, she turned her head to the window.

Dim light made its way through the curtains, and a look at her watch told her it was just after 6am. It was early, but knowing there was no more sleep to be had, she got out of bed and pulled her suitcase up onto it. She dressed and pulled the new hiking boots out, vowing to put them by the door when she went downstairs. Maybe she'd explore a little today, just the immediate surroundings. Her thighs and calves still ached from the walk yesterday, but maybe, the boots would help.

She pulled the laptop bag to one side too. She would leave that down in the dining room where she had decided to work while she was here, overlooking the ocean for inspiration while she was safe inside.

With a small nod of satisfaction, Beau moved to the curtains and swung them wide.

She blinked and felt her shoulders drop. The rain was almost horizontal across the landscape, its mist obscuring her view of the sea beyond.

Oh. Well, that puts paid to walking anywhere today.

She pouted and then felt herself relax with a small laugh.

You're here to write, Beau. Maybe this will be the perfect start, actually. You have six months to explore. Today we'll begin what we came here for.

Today we write!

She picked up her boots and the laptop bag and stepped out onto the cool landing, stopping at the bathroom to use the toilet and wash, before going downstairs and taking her time setting up her equipment on the dining table. The table was huge compared to the small desk at Hannah's and Beau found a satisfied smile creeping across her face as she spread out the things she would need without compromise. A minute later, she stepped back to admire her set up.

Laptop and mouse ready to go. A pen and a4 pad for thoughts and notes to the right. Her phone to the left, which was linked to the bluetooth speaker that sat just beyond. The speaker that had sat untouched for the last few months in favour of headphones.

No headphones today, Beau, you get to play the music as loud as you damn well like.

A swell of excitement filled her. A feeling in complete contrast to the evening before.

There was no one else here.

No one to worry about intruding on, no one to annoy her, no one to disturb her, no one at all. Heck, she could play the music at a hundred and ten decibels and dance on the table if she liked. There was no one around here to care.

Ha!

She felt that creative itch that pulled her toward the keyboard. The excitement of a new project and the fresh page that had thrilled her for the first two books now overtook any fear that she had of the blank page. It was a completely instinctive feeling. She felt a world away from the pressure of the publisher out here, a world away from anywhere and anything else to do.

First things first, this setup is missing just one thing.

Five minutes later Beau added a cup of coffee to a coaster by her notepad, and without further thought, sat down to write.

Beau was deep into one of the best flows she had experienced for a long time when the noise disturbed her. A small, slow, rhythmic creak that brought her back into the land of the dining room, blinking like she had risen from a doze.

She tilted her head and flicked the low music off.

The house was quiet. Only the tick of the rain on the window remained. She blinked, and then it came again, an eerie slow creak coming from the hallway. Beau strained to listen, the hair on her arms rising.

There's someone here.

Someone watching you.

She flinched and swung to the open dining room door. There was no-one there. The kitchen was still in the dull light.

The creaking stopped, and the cottage fell silent again. Beau sat listening for a few minutes before she felt her shoulders drop as relief settled her senses.

Probably the house settling under the rain.

Idiot.

One thing is fair to say, writing a ghost story alone out here? It's going to take an enormous amount of effort not to completely scare the shit out of myself.

She chuckled, raising goosebumps from her arms in the quiet. Rubbing them away, she checked her empty coffee cup and stretched, her stomach rumbling, and then she caught the view from the window.

The rain had all but stopped, and the sun was trying to edge its way through the heavy clouds, causing a shifting brightness that contrasted with the dull landscape. It was utterly mesmerising.

Beau had never been interested in the sky or its effect on a landscape before. The fact that she had never really had a view may have been something to do with it, but here everything was open and wide. The sky seemed to swallow her whole in its beauty.

And the beach, with its white sand and beautiful views. That beach needs exploring.

She swallowed a flutter of panic and chastised herself.

Look, if we're going to live with the ocean just ten feet away, we may as well make friends with it. No one says we have to swim, Beau.

She checked her watch and saw it was just after 1pm. She waited for the insults from the cursor, but it seemed happy with what she had achieved today. Even so, she was reluctant to leave her flow after doing so well.

Later. Grab something to eat and write while you're on a roll. At the moment, Bestseller Beau is back on track and has something to tell Lea at the publishers when she rings again. Write until 3pm, then you can explore the beach, deal?

Beau agreed it was a good plan. There would still be a good few hours of daylight left at that time. She looked down at her laptop and balked as she saw that she had written over five thousand words spanning two chapters.

What?

She squinted at the screen. She had never written that much in a day, let alone a morning. Even stranger was that she could hardly remember what she had written. She had felt this only once before as she had got into her first novel and the plot had seemed to carry her forward, and every read of the previous day's work had been a surprise, almost like she hadn't been there to write it at all.

It was a delight, and it got me a publishing contract with very little to re-write, and if that is anything to go by, then I'm in good shape already.

She shook her head, puzzled, and then laughed as she saved her work. Maybe bird man had been right that day in the park and she had simply needed her own space.

Thank God, and actually, I think I'll go out now. If I'm going to write that much every day, I'll have the book done within the month. Crazy!

She shut the lid of the laptop, picked up her coffee cup, and headed into the kitchen.

In good spirits, she hummed as she placed the cup by the sink, added coffee, and switched the kettle back on to boil. Rain was still spitting at the windows, but the sun was coming through stronger now, pushing the dark clouds aside.

Hopefully, lunch will give the day time to dry up before I go out.

She turned to the fridge to see what she could put on a sandwich and felt her stomach lurch.

The back door was open.

Not just open a little, but swung wide to cover the fridge door. A cool breeze circulated the small space.

But...

But that was locked. I locked it last night; I know I did.

More to the point, it's open, Beau. Not only is it unlocked, but it's open wide.

Beau moved to the door and peered out into the small extension with her heart thumping fast. Nothing was amiss, and the door onto the outside porch was shut. She moved down past the boiler to check it, and found it locked, just as she had left it.

She remembered how afraid she had been of the shadow passing the window just last night and gave a sigh of relief that she was still locked up tight. Still safe from the wilderness outside.

Just in case that shadow turns out to be something else at any point.

Back in the kitchen, she shut the door behind her and turned the key to lock it again. She shuddered as the lock clicked over and then she glanced back over her shoulder down the hall.

The front door remained tightly shut.

Thank God. I must have left this unlocked. I was tired, and it's an internal door, really. I didn't close it properly, that's all.

But as she sat eating her sandwich in the living room, her gaze was drawn to the hallway and fingers crawled over her scalp.

She hadn't touched the door this morning; she knew that. It was more than plausible that she hadn't latched it properly yesterday – although she was sure that she had, and even locked it - however, the thing that was putting her on edge was the timing.

The door had from 4pm yesterday to swing open during the evening or night if she hadn't latched it properly. It was closed when she came down this morning, so if it was prone to swinging open, why had it waited until now?

There had to be a reason, and yet, Beau couldn't think of one.

Maybe it was the floorboards as you moved around in the kitchen this morning?

But it would have opened then, or even last night, not later, surely?

So what is it, Beau, a ghost? You've been here one night. Get outside, call Gerard, and ask if there have been any problems with it. Solved. Christ, you're going to drive yourself nuts.

Chapter 11

GERARD HADN'T SOUNDED CONCERNED about the door. He admitted that it had opened a couple of times on the last tenant, and that he'd found it open on occasion when he'd popped in over the summer. He hadn't found the cause, but as it wasn't an outside door, he hadn't looked too hard either. He'd simply locked it back up. He offered to look at it again if she wished, but her inclination was to agree with him. The door wasn't integral to her safety, and if it wasn't an anomaly, then she felt better about the incident.

With the unease of the door off the agenda, Beau walked down to the beach. The sun had come out in force, and although the day wasn't hot, it was warm enough that Beau took off her new boots and socks, left them by the grass and buried her toes in the soft white sand. It was cool but felt like heaven. She closed her eyes and turned her face to the sun with a smile, feeling like she was on holiday.

Hell, I am on holiday, for six whole months, and this beach is all my own!

With a wide smile and a juxtaposing flutter of terror, she forced her way down to the shoreline, stepping over the brittle rows of seaweed that were littered with dead crabs, driftwood, smooth stones, and hundreds of shells. She bent to pick a couple up with sweaty palms and paused as a memory came to her.

Last time I was at a beach, I was collecting shells to make necklaces with Hannah. We laughed that there was only one shell every ten steps. It made it such a competition, and we never found enough to make even one bracelet. We should have come here instead.

Beau's smile slipped, and she let the shells fall back to the beach as she glanced at her phone to confirm that Hannah still hadn't messaged. Her stomach dropped. She hadn't.

She sighed and stood, eyeing the shoreline. The water looked cool and clear, and mildly terrifying, but in her admission to make friends with the ocean here she ignored her booming heart, rolled up her jeans and moved to the water to let the freezing waves lap around her feet. When her mind screamed at her to GET THE HELL OUT! she pushed the fear down and strolled across the inlet with as much fake nonchalance as she could muster. Instead of thinking about the freezing (*soothing*) water, she thought back to the many fantastic holidays she and Patrick had shared with Hannah and Joe over the years, and smiled.

When they had first met over ten years ago, Patrick and Joe had hit it off straight away. It had been perfect; the men had entertained themselves, allowing Hannah and Beau to do the same. It had been relaxed and easy, and the holidays together had come not long afterwards.

Turkey, Croatia, Egypt, Tenerife, Corfu, Portugal, amongst other places over the years. Sometimes four times a year, which often put a real strain on their budget, especially when Beau gave up work to write full time. Patrick had moaned, but it was time that neither of them would have missed.

She remembered the restaurant in Albufeira which had some of the biggest lobsters she had ever seen, the time they had been shopping as couples in Tenerife and Beau and Hannah had come back with the same new dress, and the laughing that she and Hannah had done as the men had checked Jet skiing off their bucket list with hilarious results. Then there was the time Hannah got duped into paying ninety English pounds by an Egyptian selling a slab of clay which had a few rudimentary figures painted on it. Hannah thought she had agreed and shook on nine pounds, not ninety.

Beau's smile faltered as she came to a halt. She watched the water lap around her feet with a frown as her fingers strayed unconsciously to the pendant around her neck. A best friend's necklace, brought in Blackpool. Half a heart. The other half belonged to Hannah.

Hannah.

Come to think of it, that afternoon in Egypt hadn't been so good. Joe had expressed his dismay at the loss of so much money, especially as he had tried to stop Hannah as she negotiated. She had waved a hand and ignored him. She was the negotiator, she'd said. Did he run a business? No, then maybe he should keep his damn mouth shut. It turned out that Joe was good at working out exchange rates and foreign currency – Hannah was not... she paid well over the odds, and it infuriated her. Not because of the money, but because she had got it wrong, and if there was one thing Hannah James hated, it was looking the fool.

The way she had treated Joe that afternoon was nothing short of bullying, and it had been hard to watch. Joe had taken it in good humour, and Patrick shrugged off the whole incident, but Beau was uneasy. She had seen a side to Hannah that she had never seen before and wasn't interested in seeing again.

You did see it again, though.

Beau bit her lip as a shudder ran down her back. She stepped out of the cold sea and stood in the safety of the warmer sand, looking over to the islands beyond.

It doesn't matter. Hannah was there for you when you needed her most, and if she wants to be in a mood because you left, well, you certainly know how that goes, and how bad it can get. Give her time and she'll come round. She always does.

Feeling a little off balance at how quickly her feelings had turned, Beau shook the thoughts away and began to walk across the inlet.

Ahead, sheltered by the rising cliff beyond, was a little wooden rowing boat. As she moved closer, Beau saw it was tied to the rock by a thick rope hooked through a metal hoop. She wasn't sure what it was tied up for. The tide line stopped a few feet beyond, and she now stood in soft white sand that must only ever see rainwater.

Maybe to stop people stealing it? Although I'm not sure I've heard of a thief who can't undo a knot.

Beau looked over at the water, and her stomach tumbled as she assessed the calm swell.

Maybe on a stormy day the water would reach up here?

Not really knowing the ocean, and not wanting to, Beau couldn't tell.

You'll find out when you have a storm, I guess... which you can watch from the safety of the cottage.

She shuddered and continued past the boat, following the curve of the bay to the very edge where it met the water once again. The view of the islands was different from here. Their edges dark as the white crest of the waves lapped against them, and beyond there was a glimmer of the vast ocean that stretched into nothingness until it met the horizon.

Beau felt her insides shrink as she wrapped her arms around herself. Beyond paddling on the shore – which she could push through – the sea worried her. The depth of the waves and the pull of the tides seemed too much of a match for one small person. There was so much out there that was unknown... or that *was* known and was terrifying. People who ventured into the ocean were taking their lives in their hands every second their feet had no contact with land. They were at the mercy of the deep blue. How people even slept on a cruise ship with all of that ocean underneath them for days was beyond her.

'Thalassophobia', Patrick had told her after she had refused a boat ride in Portugal. Hannah and Joe had gone on ahead, leaving Beau and Patrick to wander the beach. 'You have a phobia of deep, open water.'

Beau wanted to contest that phobia was a strong word, but looking out at the little boat Hannah and Joe had boarded that day, which had looked like a toy against the vast blue, her chest had constricted, and she hadn't been able to say anything.

Okay, she had a phobia, it was true, but it was one that would keep her safe on land, and she was more than happy about that. There was no controlling the sea.

Beau blew a steadying breath and looked back toward the other side of the inlet, where the land was much steeper, and the cliff much higher. The pine forest rose almost to the cliff top, where she saw...

Oh, wow, that must have been Mrs Locket's church! Or her dad's, anyway.

A huge stone arch spanned almost the width of the ruined stone building, reaching to the top of what was left, which was possibly still very near roof height, although there was no roof now. It must have been a phenomenal stained-glass window at one time, but now it was devoid of glass. Above the peak of the window, somehow a cross still appeared to be hoisting itself high, miraculously hanging on to the edges of the stone above the wreck.

Beau imagined rector Locket trekking up the side of that cliff each day to tend to his priestly duties and thought he must have been a very fit man, although the photographs had shown a man with a portly belly.

Maybe he puffed his way up there instead.

She smiled, and then paused.

Wait... didn't Mrs Locket say he had died up there?

Now Beau imagined his body sprawled lifelessly in the pulpit.

A heart attack, maybe? Or was it murder?

Maybe he had congregation trouble...

She shuddered as an icy breeze ran through her coat.

And you have imagination trouble, Beau. Let's go and get warm.

Shaking her head of the vision, she walked back to her boots and brushed the sand from her feet. She put on her socks and slipped into her boots for the trek across the grass. Animals roamed here, and she didn't want to step in anything she shouldn't. She was wondering whether to bother tying the laces when a handful of crows took off from the pine trees ahead, cawing loudly.

Beau looked up with a smile, watching as they took flight in a group, heading inland. As her gaze dropped to the little cottage, she shielded her eyes with a hand, admiring its quaint porch and red shuttered windows. Now that she was feeling relaxed enough to view it with appreciation, she realised how idyllic it looked.

Relaxed. Beau huffed a laugh - heck, she had even managed to work!

I think Hannah was wrong, after all. I'm fine alone. Patrick used to work long hours and sometimes nights and I was alone then... well, if he actually was working those nights.

Beau pushed the thought away as her eyes travelled to the thin extension that ran along the back of the house, almost at the tree line. She saw the door which led out onto the porch and wondered at the usefulness of the whole structure.

I'm not sure why you'd ever use the back door, it's not so far from the front, anyway. I mean, if you think about it, it's a pretty silly extension. Too small to put anything in it bar a chair, and what would you look at from all of those windows? It doesn't even catch the sun, must be north-

She paused as she caught sight of something red, just beyond the back door, not on the porch, but almost behind the extension.

Red. I'm not sure there was anything bright red there before and there's nothing red in the forest. What is that? Another shutter or something?

Beau squinted her eyes, only half convinced. The red remained half hidden by the structure. She frowned and walked forward and a little to the right so that she could see properly, but each time more of the extension came into view, the red seemed to move back.

Beau's heart fluttered, and she chastised herself.

It can't move. There's nothing out here, Beau, just you and the wildlife, and there's nothing bright red in the animal kingdom that lives here.

She continued forward, her mind in overdrive as the red seemed to shift again.

There's a rational explanation. Something blowing in the wind, that's all.

She moved faster, wanting to see what the thing was, and then maybe try to get some more work done before bed, and finally she was moving quicker than the object, but now she wasn't sure that was good.

It looked like a coat.

More to the point, it looked like there was someone inside the coat. An arm and a hand, then a body and a face.

'Oh!' Beau breathed. Her jaw dropped, and she and the person in the coat seemed to stare at each other. She wasn't close enough to distinguish features, but she thought from the size and form that it was male.

There was a beat of frozen shock where Beau wondered if she was seeing things in broad daylight - maybe she wasn't handling this isolation lark quite as well as she thought - and then the person turned and fled into the cover of the trees.

Beau gasped, tripping on laces as she lunged forward.

'Hey! What? Hey, wait!'

She lumbered toward the cottage, sand rubbing against her feet as the untied boots slipped up and down against her heels.

'Wait!'

She reached the edge of the porch where the person had stood and turned to face the forest. The trees swished and creaked in the breeze. Undergrowth rustled, but there was no hint of red. Nothing moved, and the only sound was Beau's rapid breaths.

'Hey!' she called again, cursing the birds who flew from the trees above her, making her jump and her heart race faster.

Nothing else moved. The figure - if it had been there in the first place - had gone, leaving Beau with battered nerves and a thumping chest.

Chapter 12

J OE THREW THE TEA towel over his shoulder and hooked the phone between his shoulder and the towel as he took the casserole from the oven, using oven gloves shaped like pink lollipops.

Leila was sitting on the tiled floor just in front of the oven, annoyingly close to the hot glass, and where he was trying to work. He put the steaming dish on the side, along with the tea towel and pink gloves, and tried the number for the third time as Leila scooted closer to the oven door.

'Leila, honey, just back up a little. You'll get burned.'

Leila moved back an inch and shuddered. 'But I'm freezing cold.'

'I know, I'm trying to sort it out. Did you put a jumper on?'

Leila held up two fingers and then shuffled closer to the oven glass again. Joe was about to move her away when Hannah finally answered, her voice clipped.

'Joe. I've been gone for a day. What is it? Is Leila all right?'

The cutting edge of her tone instantly raised his hackles. Yes, she had said to leave her alone while she attended to business, but Leila was her daughter too, and if she just allowed him to sort things out himself, he wouldn't have needed to call her at all.

Usually, at this point, he would have added a softener like, 'love you too, Han, yeah I'm fine thanks,' but today he couldn't be bothered.

'No. She's cold, Han. Did you call the plumber to look at the boiler?'

There was silence for a beat, and then:

'Why would I call the plumber?'

Joe turned away from Leila so that she wouldn't see his eye roll.

'Er...because that's what you do when the boiler is broken?'

He let the sarcasm drip through his tone. Honestly, had she not been listening to him for the past two days?

Probably not. There has been a heatwave.

Joe regretted his tone as Hannah's steely voice came back instantly.

'And I'm supposed to be psychic? You told me the boiler was playing up, and then you said it was okay. At what point did I say I was calling a plumber?'

Joe turned to smile at Leila, who was watching him intently, almost huddled against the warm oven door. He gestured a hand to move her back, but she only huddled closer.

'I said it was okay at that time, Han. I managed to get it going several times, as I said, but now it's off again and it won't start up. I thought you were calling someone out. That's why I didn't say anything more.'

'Well, I took that silence to mean the boiler was fixed.'

Joe heaved a breath and turned from Leila again.

'Great,' he muttered.

Hannah was quiet for a moment. Joe rubbed a hand over his face, braced for the outburst, but she was weirdly calm.

'I didn't know I had to arrange a plumber. I'm busy, Joe, just call the number in the black book. Henry Shipford, his name is, you'll find it under 'S' for Shipford. Call the number next to his name and arrange a date. Voila. It's simple.'

Joe clenched his jaw. She was mocking him, treating him like a child... again. The anger was rising into his chest, and he didn't want to argue in front of Leila. The child had been through enough. He tried to keep his voice calm.

'Well, it should be, but as you never fail to inform me, money is not my job. You're happy for me to wipe my arse, but the toilet paper purchase is your territory. If I'd known the job had been delegated, it would have been done two days ago.'

Small cold hands on his thigh pulled his attention to Leila, who began to whine.

'Daddy, I'm freeeeeezing. Is the man coming to fix the boiler today?'

Her small face looked pained and pale, and Joe stooped to pull her into his arms.

'No, darling, mummy didn't call the man, but it's okay, I'm going to call him now. Go and get the cashmere blanket from my room. We'll snuggle on the settee in that.'

'No, you bloody won't.'

Joe felt his temper snap.

'Well, we can't put the fire on; too much money to run, remember? I'm trying to abide by your rules here, Hannah, but the kid is cold.' He pushed Leila off his lap and rubbed her arm. 'Go get the blanket, honey.'

Leila ran from the room as the backlash he had expected from Hannah earlier finally came.

'For fuck's sake, Joe, it's not the bloody Arctic. Tell her to get another sodding jumper on, it can't be that cold. It's still officially summer!'

'It's all your tiled floors that are the problem. We've gone from a thirty-three-degree heatwave to nine degrees in the last two days. I can feel the cold from the floor right the way up my calves. What is so wrong with a carpet, anyway? It *feels* like the bloody Arctic in here.'

'Well, it'll feel like seven shades of hell if you let that child play in my new cashmere. I brought that blanket for show purposes.'

Joe blanched and a harsh laugh left his lips.

'What is the point of buying something for show when we can't afford to use the sodding fire? Sometimes, Han, I'm not sure what planet you're on. The other thing is-'

'Excuse me? I like nice things in my nice house, and I work damn hard to pay for them. Me, alone. What is the problem with that?'

But Joe wasn't listening. He'd had the 'I bring in all the money' talk more times than he could count.

'-*that child*,' he continued, 'just so happens to be our daughter, and she is cold. Surely that is more important than a dumb blanket that no-one will notice, anyway. Sometimes I wonder where your head is.'

'I often wonder where yours is, and sometimes I'm sure you ring just to piss me off-'

'No. I'm just ringing about the plumber, who I'm going to call now. I guess we'll see you soon?'

'Good, then you can put my cashmere away.' Hannah said, ignoring the question.

'I will when it's warm. Any idea when you'll be home?'

Hannah sighed. 'Not yet. This is an important deal, could be a few days at least. I'll let you know.'

'Great, and Han?'

'Yeah?'

He smiled as he heard the softness creep back into her voice. He knew what she was expecting. It was an age-old tradition after heated words, wasn't it? He should say that he loved her and couldn't wait for her to come home. They had some making up to do after this little tiff... wink, wink.

But he couldn't bring himself to say it. He wasn't even sure he felt it right now. Instead, he said what had been eating him for the last two days.

'Call Beau and make things right, will you? She's all alone out there and you're supposed to be her best friend. I'll speak to you soon.'

He pulled the phone away from his ear and cut the call before she could reply. Then, putting both women aside, he went to the drawer to find the little black book of telephone numbers.

Chapter 13

THERE WAS SOMETHING ABOUT working alone with her imagination on something as unsettling as the supernatural that put Beau on edge. She always had an ominous feeling when writing her stories; a cold draft, a menacing creak, being watched by something unseen in the corner. It was par for the course, and something that she could usually shake with just half an hour of normality. When the writing got too much, she would simply take a break and return when her nerves were back in order.

Here was different, though. There was no normality, nothing that was familiar enough to settle her jangling nerves after writing one of the spookiest scenes she thought she had ever written. The little ghost girl in this book had made an early appearance, not long after the main character had moved into the old house, and as Beau had written the scene, the hair on her arms had risen and her own sense of being watched had peaked. After writing another chapter and almost 7,000 words – a record day – Beau decided that enough was enough. The sky outside was darkening, and she was more than a little jumpy.

'I need to break there, or I won't sleep,' she murmured as she saved her work, and shut the laptop lid.

In the kitchen, with the back door shut and locked – and checked four times, no less – Beau took her speaker and played music from her phone app as she cooked herself a bacon and egg sandwich for tea. It wasn't the healthiest day she'd ever had with effectively two sandwiches making up her entire daily diet. Just a few months ago Patrick would have told her off for not eating enough and cooked her up something more.

But he's not here, and you're alone. You can do what you damn well like, Beau.

As she poached the egg, Beau wondered why that didn't feel as good as it sounded.

Because you feel alone, and between the story, someone in a red jacket, and being somewhere new, you're rattled. It would actually be nice to have someone else here. Even someone else badgering you to eat properly.

Beau stared at the two lonely slices of bread on the plate.

It would be nice to have someone else to share this meal with...

There was a noise from the hallway, movement, a *shifting*, and Beau snapped her head to the open doorway. The space beyond was empty and still and she let out a small breath of relief that didn't quite convince her heart to still behind her ribs.

...because you've scared yourself to death with your own story.

Unnerved, she tried to concentrate on the music as she added bacon to the bread, tried to shake the feeling of being watched as she laid the egg on top, and tried to shake the unease as she poured a glass of wine.

Chewing her lower lip, she glanced back into the hallway, which seemed to swell with an unseen presence. The lowering sun cast elongated shadows from the living room doorway and her hair prickled against her scalp.

Christ, what I wouldn't give for Hannah, or Joe, or even Patrick to be here now. All of them together would be even better.

They would be laughing and joking, filling the rooms with their noise, and forcing out the creepiness of an old and unfamiliar building. With others, you could push out a building's presence and occupy the space with your own, but out here alone, there was more of the cottage's presence than Beau's, and she almost felt the building watching her, testing her, reminding her that this was space that wasn't hers, that its energy was bigger and more powerful...

Enough, Beau!

Beau closed her eyes and blew out a shaky breath. Without vision the cheery music from the speaker blanketed her body in goosebumps and set every nerve on edge. In her mind she saw a scene play out, like every horror movie ever made – the one where the poor victim couldn't hear the noise of the danger over the music before it was too late.

With a shudder her eyes flew open and she turned the speaker off. The song continued to play from her phone at a much lower volume, but now she could hear the wind pushing against the building from outside. A little relief slid from her shoulders.

There. That'll be what you heard over the music, just the shifting of the cottage in the wind.

She should have felt better knowing this was true, but she didn't. She was still hyper aware, and still on edge.

Maybe I'll find a comedy on Netflix and watch on the laptop. Got to be better than sitting here thinking about how alone and creeped out I am.

Nodding to herself, she switched off the music app, put the phone in her pocket and picked up her plate and the wine. Then she paused.

The music was still playing.

Beau frowned and put down the glass and plate to check the phone. The music was off.

And yet, the music played on.

She leaned to check the speaker. Off.

But, the music continued.

That's impossible.

Beau shook her phone and then shook her head.

Where is that coming from? The music is off!

As she forced herself to listen she realised that the song wasn't coming from her phone, or the speaker, it was coming from the living room. The goosebumps, which had been receding, now stood to attention again as Beau's heart immediately began to hammer.

She looked into the hallway, and saw the living room concealed in semi darkness.

Her mind raced as she tried to push her trembling legs to the living room, only for them to stop by the grandfather clock, refusing to go any further. The music was louder here, and almost crackly, like the speaker or the connection was dodgy. She stood shaking as the song played on, not wanting to go forward, but knowing there was no one to do this for her. She had no choice.

Fuck, Beau, what have you done? Why are you here? It's night two and you're almost having a fit. Come on, there must be a rational explanation, just get it over with.

She swallowed hard and a small whine left her lips as she forced her rubbery legs forward to the doorway of the living room. As she reached a hand to find the light switch, she caught sight of a shadow at the far side of the room. Tall and black.

She screamed and thumped the switch, and the room illuminated before her. She stood, blinking in the light. There was nothing out of place. No shadow.

The only anomaly was the music, which came from the corner she thought she had seen the shadow - imagination, and God knew she had enough of that - but the music wasn't imagination, it was clear, and now the song sounded vaguely familiar.

It's like something from my childhood.

Beau moved across the room, hair rising at the back of her neck as she reached the record player and stared, her pulse pumping in her ears.

The arm was on a vinyl record, which spun underneath it. The name of the band, Simple Minds, and the song's name, 'Don't You (Forget About Me)' spun with it. The name meant little, but the tune was ringing bells.

Does it really bloody matter?

Beau felt a scream rising up the back of her throat as what she was seeing hit home.

How do I stop it? How does it work?

More to the point, why the fuck is it on? How is it on, Beau? Gerard didn't even turn the power on. He told me to turn the power on!

The power.

She stooped and flicked the power switch. The song cut off, leaving the record to spin as it slowed, the arm scratching rhythmically, sounding like a nightmare. Slower and slower until, finally, silence.

The air seemed to swell, and Beau felt a bead of sweat run down from her brow. The silence should have been better than the music, but it wasn't.

It was worse.

It took her a moment to gather enough nerve to turn and face the room. All was quiet. Too quiet. And now that the light was on in here, the hallway beyond seemed too dark and ominous.

The only sounds Beau heard were her own frantic breaths and the occasional gust of wind as she stared at the darkness beyond the doorway, her limbs frozen.

Well, this is fantastic, Beau. Why don't we just stand in the corner all evening like an idiot? Especially as your sandwich is now going cold in the kitchen. Of all of your great ideas, I think this one may be the best yet!

Beau struggled with her fear and then jumped out of her skin as a shadow passed the front window.

'Fuck,' she hissed, throwing her hands over her ears, and scrunching her eyes tight.

Her logical mind would have told her to check for deer after her experience last night. Unfortunately, her logical mind had slammed its door shut. A note on the front said that it would be away until further notice, leaving raw fear in charge.

Her fear said that the shadow belonged to someone who hung around isolated houses in a red coat. Someone who had scoped out the place earlier and had now come back to finish what he had started. Any minute now, he would knock on the door.

Slow, rhythmic, thumping bangs.

Because rushing a murder was nonsensical, especially out here, where no one would hear her scream.

In a near frenzy, Beau snapped from her frozen state and ran from the room. With every nerve screaming, and her eyes avoiding every window, she bolted for the stairs and into her room, shutting the door tight.

Up here, no one could see her. Up here she was the observer, and red coat was on the ground, and there was no way she would answer the door when he knocked.

She slid down the bedroom door, her heart thundering as she sat shaking, her hands still over her ears, willing the night to be done even as it had just begun, and wishing with all of her heart that she had never left the city.

She could have peered out of the window at that moment and she would have seen the deer grazing beyond the porch, it may have settled her flighty mind a little to know that deer were the shadow culprits, and this was possibly going to be a nightly thing that she shouldn't be too worried about.

What she may have been more worried about was the creak from the living room as the little rocking chair in the corner rocked slowly back and forth under the dim central light.

Creeeeak... creeeeak... creeeeak.

Chapter 14

A S BEAU WAS RETIRING early to her bedroom in Hollydale, Anna
Lane was getting frustrated in the Antler Hotel, a mere four
miles as the crow flies from Bluebell Cottage. She sighed as she
stared at herself in the large mirror that lined the wall in the
en-suite bathroom.

Start again.

'Hello, My Name is Anna Lane, do you...'

Anna shook her head, reset her jaw, and began again.

'My Name is Anna Lane. You may remember me from...'

Anna gritted her teeth.

'My name is Anna Lane, and I'm here because...'

Anna stared at her bloodshot eyes in the mirror. It was a minor
flaw in an otherwise perfectly put together face. The hint of
blush gave her skin a healthy glow, and her full red lips drew
the attention away from the red in her eyes. The blonde wig was
styled in a nineteen forties shoulder-length bob which flicked

back from the edges of her face appealingly. Anna shook her head, making the curls bounce as she pouted.

Then she rolled her eyes at herself.

'You are beautiful, Anna Lane, but that won't help you here. You need a story, and it has to be good.'

She bit a red lip as she stared at herself and narrowed her eyes at her reflection.

'Why the fuck *are* you here? Because the real reason will send everyone running for the hills, so what's the story?'

When the answer didn't reveal itself, she pushed away from the mirror and moved back into the bedroom. This hotel was exquisite, the rooms were big and grand. The bed was a genuine four-poster, and the large window was adorned with heavy swags and drapes.

Anna moved to the window, pretending she was in a film, her lips slightly parted as she sat on the sill and looked longingly over the dark huddle of mountains beyond. She dipped her chin and lifted her gaze, a trick to make her eyes seem larger and more innocent as she watched her reflection.

In this room, she could pretend she was the lady of the manor, an actress living in a mansion, having a break from the tyranny of stardom. She placed the back of her hand lightly on her forehead.

Oh, how I wish I could run to those hills and never come back... but I have four films lined up and everyone is depending on the great Anna Lane to make them as big a success as she is.

She swooned back against the corner of the window with a gasp, and then she began to laugh.

Oh, you would win Oscars in another life, Anna.

The truth was that she had worked hard at pretending, and now she had got it nailed to perfection. She could spin the most fanciful tale and make someone believe black was blue. She could change guises and accents at the drop of a hat. And while this sounded like a skill, it had simply been her lifeline. Pretending had got her out of the facility she had been placed in when she had... *hurt* somebody when she was young.

Anna cocked her head and brushed red nails through her hair as she pondered.

Yes. Hurt was a much better word.

Throughout her childhood, a worse word had followed her.

Stabbed.

Anna rolled her eyes and shook her head.

The teacher thought it was an accident at first as she rushed over to the screams that echoed from the young girl's mouth. It was one of the few times in her childhood that Anna had genuinely smiled, and it made her feel good. She saw and heard everything in a curious slow motion. The way the scissors disappeared first into the girl's clothes and then flesh, the way her face screwed up in pain, the inhuman noise that left her throat, the trickle of red that spread quickly into her white school shirt, the tears that squeezed from her eyes out of nowhere.

Anna had a single thought before the teacher arrived. She remembered it well. 'Serves her right.' Another followed quickly on its tail. 'This is fun.'

Genuine excitement flooded her veins, the intensity that only adrenaline can provide, and all seven-year-old Anna wanted to do was to feel it again, and again.

And so, she had stabbed. Again, and again.

Six times before the teachers had removed her from on top of the girl and her life had been changed forever.

The consequences were serious, but Anna never really understood why. The girl hadn't died after all. She hadn't *killed* anyone, and the scissors weren't even sharp. They were hardly a weapon. What was the harm?

And yet she found herself locked away from society for almost fifteen years.

It was ludicrous.

Luckily, she had managed to escape. Not *illegally*, that would have been silly, because now she wouldn't be here, free, and able to carry out her plan. She would have been hunted down and deemed even more unstable, especially after those first nine years of violence, kicking back, and weeks spent in isolation.

Nine years!

Anna shook her head at her reflection in the glass, appalled.

It had taken her *nine years* to realise that playing by the rules would get her further, and so she had played their game, bided her time, played by the rules, acted her butt off, until several members of staff had recommended her release at the grand old age of twenty-two. She had been rehabilitated, they said. She was remorseful. She knew what she did was wrong. She was BETTER.

Like she had been ill.

They bothered about whether she would be able to function in society and held her hand through getting her first job at a local shop, her first rental accommodation, her first bank account. She let them bother for a while, and finally they told her she had done so well that their care would amount to yearly assessments.

She had turned up to her appointments diligently and kept her house clean and organised for them to see. She was thorough and careful, always playing her role. She had flown through all of their checks over the years, not only that, but she had found a partner and now had a small child of her own. Sometimes she impressed herself with how well she was doing life like a normal human being, hell, a *successful* human being, and that eventually had meant the freedom she had today.

Freedom from the system.

Freedom from prying eyes.

Freedom to be here in this room. To be Anna Lane. Actress, debutante, submissive, elegant, but sharp.

Freedom to make a plan.

Anna let out a mirthless chuckle and stood up from the cold sill.

'If you can't get your story together, that plan won't work.'

Her hand drifted to twist her necklace between her fingers.

'There has to be another way, another opening, but you'll never find it in this room.'

Her stomach grumbled, and she had a flash of inspiration. It was 7.30pm. Early enough for dinner, but late enough that the young man on reception may be winding down for the evening. If the day had ever wound up.

'I need a different perspective. A different conversation. Let's see how far I drew this young man in yesterday. He looked pretty smitten. Let's see what he's learned from his avoidance of responsibility.'

It turned out that the youngster had company on the desk tonight in the form of the owner of the hotel, Lucas Carr. A portly man with a handlebar moustache and probably the owner of the motorcycle outside if his t-shirt graphic was anything to go by. Anna put on her most charming performance as she stood chatting to them in the empty foyer. She complimented the hotel's grand decor, complimented the room, complimented the staff, and gushed about how it was a shame it was placed poorly because it really should be accessible to more people. It *deserved* better.

Lucas agreed wholeheartedly. It was a special hotel, but in being off the beaten track, it meant that only special people found it, and that was fine with him. Lucas had a successful online business selling his wife's photographs. She was a busy wedding photographer but took stunning pictures on the side when she was travelling. He also made money selling meat from the red deer that had to be culled from the hotel's sixty acres each year. The hotel was simply a labour of love, an inherited extra that he and his wife had plenty of money to maintain. It didn't matter that it was mostly empty, he said - especially when people like Daniel turned up and worked wage free for a room and food.

'We've been lucky here. Good people seem to be thrown our way. Daniel is a great kid, very trustworthy, and then we get interesting guests like yourself. Never a dull moment. You look like you stepped out of a film from the forties, if I may say, very glamorous.'

Anna covered her mouth with a hand and laughed as the other hand waved him away.

'Oh, you're too kind. I love that era, it really resonates with me. Shame the clothes have to be quite so... modern. When I'm not out and about, I'm much more comfortable in a dress, you know? That won't do out here, though,' she gestured to her camel trousers that she had paired with a deep maroon blouse. She looked stunning, she knew, but wanted to play it down.

Guys loved modesty, she had found, and it seemed these two were lapping it up so far. She brushed off their raining compliments about her dress sense.

'Oh, please, you're too kind,' she said. 'But I didn't come here for compliments, what I was really after was somewhere to eat. I know it's late, is the-?'

'I'll have Betty cook you whatever you fancy, lass. Daniel has yet to eat too.' Lucas turned to Daniel who was smiling wistfully at Anna. 'Why don't you knock off now, lad, I can deal with the hoards in here.'

Anna painted a delighted look on her face. 'Oh, maybe you could join me, Daniel? It'll be awful lonely in that big dining room alone.'

Daniel quickly agreed and after a quick 'freshen up' as he called it, he joined Anna in the dining room, where she had already ordered a bottle of red wine and a steak. Daniel seemed impressed with her choice and opted for the same as he pulled out a chair and sat opposite her.

Lucas disappeared out into the foyer again and Daniel was immediately on her, leaning in, his arms resting on the table between them.

'So, what brings you out here, Anna? You said you had business in Hollydale?'

Anna smiled. He was a good-looking young man, full of confidence, no hint of nerves. It was refreshing.

'I do. Well, not necessarily business. I'm looking for someone.'

Anna cast her eyes down to the table and waited a beat. He didn't let her down.

'Who is it?'

Anna looked up at him from under her lashes.

'I don't even know if she's here. It was a long shot coming here at all, really. I'm looking for my sister.'

Lucas appeared with a bottle of Merlot, poured wine into each of their glasses, and left as they thanked him. Daniel picked up his glass, swirled the liquid, and then took a large mouthful.

'Sounds like big stuff. Did something happen?'

Anna felt herself start, a small plummet in her stomach, before she realised he was talking about her sister. She hoped her cheeks hadn't flushed too much.

'Oh, not really. We lost contact a long time ago. I don't even have a number for her. She used to live in Hollydale, but as I said, I'm not sure whether she's there anymore.'

'Big feud, huh?'

Anna smiled and sipped her wine. He was perceptive.

'Something like that.'

'So how long has it been?'

Anna swallowed.

'Oh, many, many years. I was a bit of a rebel when I was younger, got myself into some trouble. She, quite rightly, washed her hands of me. I want to make amends if it isn't too late.'

'Saw the error of your ways. What did you do that was so bad?'

Anna fingered the stem of her wine glass. The chat wasn't quite going the way she had planned and was lingering a little too far in the direction of a place she wasn't willing to go with anyone. Ever.

She looked at him with a smile. 'Nothing that needs repeating now. It's all in the past.'

Daniel cocked his head and narrowed his eyes.

'Right. Can I just confirm one thing?'

Anna felt her guard rise. If he was going to be annoying, then she would have to work this out alone after all.

'Sure,' she said, taking a sip of wine to avoid his eyes.

'I'm just checking... I'm not having dinner with a serial killer, am I?'

Anna almost spat her wine back into her glass, and Daniel laughed.

'Okay, okay, I'm sorry. I know, it just would have ruined the mood a little if you'd stabbed someone to death!'

Anna felt her chest constrict and fought to control her emotion. What did he know? Had he looked her up online? Was he toying with her?

Anna Lane has no connections with that girl. You just met, and there's no way he can know. It's just a coincidence. Relax.

'Anna?'

Daniel's face stalled mid laugh, and she pursed her lips, swirling her wine and watching the red that grasped the glass before losing its hold.

'Looks a little like blood, doesn't it?'

Daniel visibly paled as his eyes dropped to her wine. 'You're joking, right?'

Anna suddenly peeled into laughter and let her fingers fall onto his arm across the table.

'Of course I'm joking. This looks nothing like blood. You think I'm a murderer? All five-foot-three of me? Darling, come *on*. I haven't got the stomach, strength, or inclination to murder anyone.'

Daniel relaxed into a grin and put a warm hand over hers.

'I'm glad we got that out of the way.' He pointed a finger at her. 'You had me going there for a second.'

'Surely not. For heaven's sake.'

Anna put on her best innocent but slightly hurt smile.

Daniel grinned. 'Not really. I'm sorry I brought it up, I was joking. Look at you, you couldn't hurt a fly.'

Certainly not a fly, indeed.

'And I'm sorry I toyed with you. Let's start over.'

Anna took her hand away from his and used a small mirror from her pocket to straighten her hair. Not that it was out of place, she was just giving him a moment to admire her. She checked her lipstick and snapped the hinged mirror shut.

Daniel *was* staring, although when her eyes met his, he had the grace to shift his gaze and fluently change the subject.

'So, there's no-one at all you could have contacted to find your sister before coming out here?'

'No. My parents passed away years ago, and I've no other family. She's all I have left. I'm realising as I get older just how important family is. My sister has no one either. It's an awful situation, to have living relatives and to struggle alone thinking they hate you. I just... I need to make that right, and I just hope she's here. I really do.'

Anna sighed and used the napkin to dab her eyes, hoping he hadn't noticed they were dry. Her fears were put to bed as Daniel nodded ahead of her, his face solemn.

'Well, if she lives in Hollydale, that's not too far. I know a little of the area, maybe I can help you find her?'

'Oh, you don't have to do that... although...'

'Although?' Daniel tilted his head again and Anna found it rather endearing.

'Well, maybe if she doesn't know that it's me who is looking for her at first, I may have a chance of finding her. I'm worried that the village will shut me down and hide her - small villages do that, you know? If I know where she is, especially if she is still at the house, I can just turn up. At least then I have a fair shot at explaining things before she turns me away.'

Daniel seemed to consider it. Maybe he was questioning how morally right that was, but then he was nodding.

'Well, okay, I suppose I can see why you'd want that. I guess I could stake things out for you first, do a little asking around here, try to get a feel for where she may be without being too obvious.'

Anna put a hand to her chest and tried on her best grateful look.

'Oh, Daniel, would you do that for me? It's not as bad as it sounds. The village will know of her, of course, but if she's still at the cottage, that's all I'd need to know. You don't need to knock on doors or ask around.'

'So there's a house you need me to check?'

'A cottage. It's isolated, by the sea, a few miles out. It'll be a walk. Just see if there is anyone living there, that's all I need.'

'I'm sure I could find it and check it out for you. I've been walking over that way a lot.'

Anna let her face fall into a relieved smile.

'That would be amazing. You don't need to speak to her, I don't need her getting suspicious. Just keep an eye out and let me know if there's a woman living there. I would be so grateful. You're happy to do this for me?'

Anna looked at him from under her lashes. Daniel tucked his bottom lip between his teeth in thought, and then he smiled.

'Sure, I'd be honoured, Anna. I can call you Anna, right?'

Anna almost rolled her eyes, but with practiced will, suppressed her instinctive reaction and smiled back at him.

'Of course you can.'

'Great. And where am I looking for again?'

'A place called Bluebell Cottage, it's down in a bay just outside the village. I can't give you directions, but I can find it on a map if you have one.'

'In Hollydale? I'll find it, don't worry. Hang on a sec.'

Daniel grabbed a pen from the foyer and wrote the name down on a napkin before folding it and placing it into his jeans pocket. A few hours and a couple of bottles of wine later, the napkin would flutter out of that pocket to land on the floor of Anna's bedroom in their haste to get undressed. She would press it to his chest as he left her room with a small kiss and a promise to find her sister. Anna knew that he would keep his word, especially if she kept up the interest in him. It may take a few more nights, but he was good looking and great in bed. That would be no hardship.

But that was in the future, a plan she had already mapped out. For now, Lucas arrived at the table with the steak, which looked delicious and perfectly rare. Blood pooled into the boiled potatoes and tender stem broccoli. Deliciously red.

Perfect, Anna thought, simply perfect.

Chapter 15

C HIMES WOKE BEAU FROM her sleep. She blinked into the darkness, wondering where she was for a moment. A scan of herself didn't make things any easier when pulled straight out of a dream. She was fully dressed, even to the shoes, and was lying on top of a bed...

...in the bedroom in Bluebell Cottage... yes, that's right.

The chime came again, and she sat upright, her head swimming with a dream where she was out on a boat called the Antler, complete with deer skull on the front and the stag watching her from the shore. Her heart was thudding in the darkness from both the dream and the noise. She lifted her arm to illuminate the time and squinted at the bright numbers.

12.02am.

Far too early.

The noise drifted away, if it had ever been there at all, maybe it had been part of her dream. Kicking off her shoes and clothes, Beau got into the warmth of the covers and allowed her eyes to drift closed with a yawn.

There was light on Beau's face, warm and bright, and birds were singing somewhere close by. She snuggled down further into the warmth of the covers, keeping her eyes closed.

Just ten more minutes. It has to be early yet.

She didn't want to get up, but the longer she lay there, the more she wondered why the room was so light, and the more her bladder called. After a few minutes of trying to ignore the urge, she finally got out of bed with a sigh and found out why it was light. The curtains were open.

Wow, weird. I must have been tired last night.

She shuffled to the bathroom, where she got the second surprise of the morning. It was just 6.15am.

She yawned.

Curse of the open curtains, I'll just close them and grab another couple of hours.

As she entered the bedroom, though, she was caught by the beauty of the view, and instead of closing the curtains, she crossed to the window and opened it wide. A gentle breeze ruffled warm fingers through her hair and Beau leaned on the sill as she checked out the landscape. The ocean was almost turquoise as it lapped quietly onto the white sand, (a small jolt crossed her chest and receded). No white heads today, the sea was almost as calm as a loch, (A slight pattering of the heart, but not too hard). Beau grinned. The sun was warm too, even this early. It seemed it was going to be a hot August day, quite different from yesterday.

What to do today then, Beau? Another seven thousand words?

The grin widened.

Maybe not so many. I have my own beach, and it looks like it's going to be warm. I'll take my book out onto the sand this afternoon. Who would have thought that being in Scotland would be like being in the tropics, or that I would be relatively calm looking at the sea from my bedroom window?

She dressed quickly and picked up the thriller she had brought over a year ago and hadn't yet read as she poured all of her time into writing words that never came.

The first feeling of unease came as she descended the stairs and caught sight of the living room. Freezing air pressed itself around her and she stopped in her tracks, not quite up, not quite down.

That room. The record player, and the shadow... had that been there? Did it happen? Was it just my imagination? I fell asleep easily enough. Maybe the whole thing was a dream.

Beau blinked as she remembered the terror of the frenzied run from the living room up to the bedroom. How she had huddled at the back of the bedroom door, waiting for... something.

She frowned, her hand resting on the bannister.

That seems far too dramatic. It must have been a nightmare. In fact, didn't I wake hearing strange chimes at some point too?

Yes, and I woke fully dressed... Except that I didn't wake fully dressed. I woke in my underwear, as usual. It was a dream, Beau, all of it. Just a dream.

The feeling of unease gently subsided, and with a small laugh, she began to descend the stairs.

I hope the seven thousand words weren't a dream too.

As she turned down the hallway toward the kitchen, the last bit of tension left her body at the sight of the shut back door.

Good. Everything is in order, see? Now, let's get the coffee on and get to work.

The living room looked bright and cosy as she passed and she was feeling almost normal until her eyes found the uneaten bacon and egg sandwich, and the glass of wine that sat next to it untouched on the kitchen side.

A buzzing started up in her head, a million flies swarming in her brain.

I didn't eat the sandwich. Or drink the wine.

She stared and then poked the stale bread with a finger. It was rock solid. The hair at the back of her neck prickled.

I didn't eat the sandwich because...

The record player *had* been playing.

Beau turned her head toward the hallway, goosebumps blanketing her body. It didn't look ominous, right now it looked warm and inviting. And yet the record player...

I have to know. I have to know, because if the song is Simple Minds then...

Beau swallowed hard.

'Then it wasn't a dream,' she whispered. 'The record player, the shadow, and running upstairs from a possible intruder. It wasn't a dream.'

It was a surreal feeling as she moved back to the living room, tentatively, her heart in her mouth. The room was warm, the front window letting in a strip of morning sun. All looked normal, and yet looks could be deceptive.

With her heart banging, she walked to the record player and looked down through the perspex lid.

Simple Minds. Don't You (Forget About Me) adorned the paper at the centre of the vinyl.

Beau gasped and stepped back, the air leaving her lungs, her mind whirling. If she had the song right, then chances were high that the shadow had also passed the window, and that she had bolted for the stairs and huddled in the bedroom, too.

Because an intruder had been circling the house. An intruder in a red coat?

Beau felt frozen to the spot.

Oh shit. Oh shit. I can't do this! I need to get out. I need to get out. There was someone here, someone staking me out! I need to go!

Beau ran into the hallway and had a hand firmly on the front door handle, ready to bolt the three miles to her car in just her socks, when a voice stepped forward in her mind.

No! You need to stop this silliness, and you need to work, Beau. You are here for a reason, and you signed a contract. It's just six months. Get over it and get on with the damn book before you lose it all and get sued in the process. Ghosts and bad people are your forte. They're what you know best, what you write about, and they're the first thing that ever enters your mind if something can't be explained, but they should be the last. Lots of things could have caused the record player to run, and the shadow was probably deer, just like the night before. You're getting spooked by the very nature of the thing you're here to do - write a horror novel. That's all.

Beau hesitated, knowing that she had a point, but not quite ready to stay. Then Joe's advice about the voice in her head came to the fore.

The psycho bitch, who is trying to ruin my life. Am I going to let her, or am I going to kick her back into her box?

She chewed on her lip and gave a resolute nod, and then before she could argue, she forced herself into the dining room, opened the laptop, and sat down to type, losing herself in over four thousand words before coming up for air and deciding to stop for the day.

An hour later, Beau was laying out a towel on the beach. She had no swimsuit, but the breeze was chillier now that she was out in the open and she found her jeans and t-shirt were just warm enough. The feeling of getting out of the house and just being in the open air had already lifted her spirits, but now her excitement at reading on the beach in the quiet waned and her heart gave an unexpected pang.

The last time she had been somewhere hot with a beach, she had been with Patrick. It was difficult to think that today she would be here alone. In fact, everywhere she went now, she would be alone, in more ways than one. There was no other half, no one to lean on, to laugh with, cook with, drink with. No one but herself.

At least with Hannah and Joe, there had been company; people, noise, laughter, tears, sex - even if she hadn't been a direct part of it. It had been all around her, there if she had wanted it.

Infuriating me and putting me on edge... until it wasn't there anymore.

'No one to make any noise around here, Beau,' she said, smoothing an edge of towel that flicked up in the breeze with her toes. 'No one but the elements and the animals. Is that enough, or are you going to go mad in the silence?'

The hair on her arms rose at the sound of her own voice, and she brushed them down with her hands. 'Oh, for crying out loud, it's been two days. I need a strategy to get through this or I *will* end up going mad. Inside or out here.'

A writer will go mad if he's constantly alone with his own mind.

Beau hesitated as she felt the words tiptoe their way through her mind and leave again with almost a whisper. She stilled and looked out across the sea with a frown.

Who said that?

When she couldn't come up with a name, she wondered if she had made it up.

I'm going crazy already.

She shook her head and sat up on the towel, placing the book beside her, and pulling out her phone. She would message Joe. The silence from Hannah was becoming all-encompassing, like a ghost standing behind her that she couldn't communicate with. Had they ever not spoken for this long? Beau didn't think so, and the pang of nostalgia filled her chest. She wanted to hear her friend's voice more than anything. In fact, she would even chat with Patrick or Lara right now. It was that notion that made her realise she would do anything for human company at this moment.

'I'll ask Joe how she is before I message her, just in case she's still mad,' she muttered.

Then? What's the plan Beau, because the last couple of days have been insane and I'm not sure you can do a whole six months swinging from a state of terror to joy and back again without a soul to talk to.

Beau bit her lip as she scrolled.

I need to just throw myself into work and learn to relax into the quirks of the place. I'm out here alone, and that's the issue, just as Joe said. I see danger everywhere, and yet the only real danger is in my very overactive imagination.

She found Joe's name and began to type.

Hey Joe, Hope you're all well down there. How is Hannah? I haven't heard from her and I'm not sure if she wants to talk? I could do with a chat. It's lonely up here.

Beau sent the message before she could think further and then chastised herself.

Why did you put that?

Because it is lonely out here. Very lonely.

She sighed, and a single tear hit the screen of her phone as it began to vibrate and ring in her hand.

Chapter 16

'**B**EAU, HOW ARE YOU doing?'

Joe cleared Leila's lunch plate and shooed her off to play while he put the dishes in the sink.

'I'm good, I think. Thank you for calling, Joe. You didn't need to. I was just feeling the pinch.'

'Of only the wildlife to talk to? That's why you messaged after Han, huh? When every other source is exhausted-'

'No! That's not it-'

Joe cut her off with a laugh as he ran the tap, trying to find the hot water that was hit and miss with the broken boiler.

'Chill. I know, Beau, I was only joking. Truth is, I have no idea how Hannah is. Not dead, I know that much, so that's all good, eh?'

Joe heard Beau's hesitation and immediately regretted the pointed remark. None of this was her fault, and he shouldn't be taking his frustration out on her.

'I'm sorry, that was too much.'

Beau sighed as Joe heard the boiler fire, felt the water warm, and plugged the sink to catch it before it gave out again.

'Are you okay, Joe?'

Joe laughed again, hoping it didn't sound as flat as he felt. He had called to cheer Beau up and give her a small lie about Hannah being on a trip and how she had said she would contact in a few days, not to drag her down with him.

'I'd be just great if this weather would piss off. We were freezing yesterday after the heat wave disappeared and the boiler broke. Now someone is coming to fix the damn thing, we're back in the twenties and dressed in shorts again. Fucking weather. How is it up there?'

'Warm. I'm on the beach.'

Joe switched off the tap and shook his head.

'The beach? I thought you were up there to work? What the hell are you doing on the beach?'

'Sunbathing. Reading a book. Listening to the sound of silence.'

'There's a beach up there with no one on it?'

'It's mine. For the next six months, anyway.'

Joe laughed and turned to sit his backside against the counter-top.

'Whew, came with the house, huh? Get dinner ready, we'll be up in a few hours!'

Beau joined his laughter, and Joe felt his earlier apprehension slide. He wondered how long it had been since he had spoken to another adult in a casual conversation and thought the last time had been Saturday, the day Beau left. It kind of put them in the same lonely boat, and it was a bit of adult conversation he would miss now that she wasn't around.

'You're on. I'll pick up some things for the barbeque,' she said.

'A barbie on the beach? Hell yeah, that sounds like a plan. Want me to bring burgers?'

'Nah, there's a shop three miles away. It wasn't open last time I looked, but it can't be shut forever, eh?'

'Sounds like a kicking village.'

'It wasn't kicking anything but old men in a dark pub when I arrived.'

'Literally?'

Beau laughed, and Joe grinned with her.

'It was like a ghost town, seriously.'

'Shit. And that's on a Saturday!'

'Well, it's not like I'm near enough to find out whether it's different on any other day. It's a three-mile hike just to the car from here.'

'Shame. It may have cured the lack of people to talk to. Maybe you should get up there, Beau, get out and see. It can't be good for you sitting alone twenty-four-seven.'

'I might. For now, I'm relaxing on the beach.'

Joe swung behind him to flick the kettle on and grabbed a cup from the cupboard.

'Good call. So how is the writing going, or shouldn't I ask?'

'Great actually, yeah. I mean, I've got the first five chapters down already.'

Joe paused, his hand halfway to the coffee jar. 'Really? I thought you said you were blocked?'

'I was. I guess I'm cleared.'

'That's all it took? I mean, it's been two fucking days!'

'I know. I suppose that's the beauty of a new place. I couldn't write a thing down there, Joe. Up here... I don't know, it's kind of like the flow turned back on. I have the story mapped out, and the chapters are coming easily. And yeah, it's been two days. The great thing about a new space, I suppose. I may go insane from lack of human contact, but I won't be poor as I descend.'

'Such a catch. Patrick was a jerk.'

Beau laughed. 'I know, right?'

'It's great to hear you're finally working, though. Not only that, but getting out and relaxing in the sun too? Sounds like it was a good move.'

'It was, if only someone was here with me, but I knew the score before I came. I can hardly complain now, can I?'

Joe poured his coffee and moved to sit at the dining table.

'Well, me and Leila would love to come up to visit, but someone took the car.'

'Hannah?'

'Who else?'

'Joe, what happened?'

'You don't need to hear my problems, Beau.'

'I really have nothing else to do out here. Spill. Has she left you again?'

Joe smiled and narrowed his eyes at the garden beyond the bi-fold doors.

The bi-folds that she wanted, paid for, and got, and the perfectly maintained garden that she designed and brought someone in to maintain. Even after I said that I wanted to do it.

Joe remembered the flippant way she had laughed at him. 'Let's just get the professionals in, Joe. At least they won't ruin it. Do you know how much that magnolia tree cost? If you kill it, I'll end up killing you. Besides, you have far too much to do educating your daughter... if that's what you call what you do together, anyway.'

'Joe?'

Joe sipped his coffee and swallowed the hot liquid.

'I'm still here. It's a valid question, but no, not this time. A business trip came up, an emergency, she said.'

'What? Since when does she ever have *emergency* trips? Is the business doing okay?'

Joe sighed and chewed his lip. How would he know? He got an allowance paid into his account every week, besides that he saw none of the money that Hannah made. She made it and she deserved the bulk of it, she said, but what that bulk amounted to he had never known.

'I have no idea. She gets grumpy when money is short, and she didn't seem grumpy. She was flippant, like it was no big deal. Just another trip away for business.'

'But it's not though, is it? She has business trips and meetings planned months in advance. I didn't know about this one just three days ago.'

Joe pursed his lips as he stared at the perfectly trimmed hedge that bordered the lawn.

'That makes two of us.'

'So where has she gone, and how long for? Maybe you can all come and visit when she gets home?'

'Three questions, and I can't answer any of them, I'm afraid.'

Joe felt his cheeks redden and was glad there was no one in the kitchen to witness just how little control he had over his own life. He was stuck here with no vehicle and very little money, for God knew how long, and until God knew when. He'd had to cancel Leila's party invite to the kids play centre because he couldn't afford the present, and while he normally just asked Hannah - and she would always begrudgingly give him extra as it was for Leila - after their last talk had been loath to call again. Apprehensive even.

She hadn't really sounded herself, and he'd asked her to contact Beau, but clearly, she hadn't. He wasn't sure what was going on, or that he wanted to know, but he knew she wasn't being totally honest. Especially about not knowing how long she would be. Hannah was a time person. To the second. The first questions she always asked were 'What time?' 'How long?' and 'how much?'

In that order.

It simply wasn't feasible that she didn't know what was happening.

It's her bloody company, for God's sake. Of course she knows.

Then why is she keeping it from me?

'Joe?'

'Here,' he said, raising the cup to his lips.

'Did you go into dreamland? I said, what do you mean you can't answer them?'

'Just that. I don't know the answers. She hasn't told me where she has gone, she says she doesn't know how long she'll be, and obviously I don't know whether she'll be up for a visit. She was still pretty damn mad when she left.'

'But I did nothing wrong.'

Joe shook his head and stared at his coffee.

'No, you didn't, but you know what she's like. You know better than anyone, Beau.'

Beau gave a sigh, and Joe felt a flicker of unease. He'd told himself that Hannah was simply at a meeting, but he also knew that he had glossed over what he knew to be true. She didn't work like this, not at her very core. Of course she knew what was going on.

'I know, and now I'm worried, Joe. She's gone off in anger some-where, hasn't she?'

Joe shrugged.

'I honestly don't know. She was pissed off with pretty much everything on Saturday; you, me, and the non-existent dog. She said it was the lateness that the meeting had been thrust upon her.'

'Do you believe her? About any of it?'

Joe smiled at the empty kitchen, but there was no trace of warmth behind it.

'Do you?'

'No.'

'Me neither. And as the two people that know her best, I suppose that's not good.'

'Not good at all. Where the fuck has she gone, Joe? And what for?'

Feeling his stomach roll, Joe rose and tipped the last of the coffee down the sink.

'I only wish I knew.'

Chapter 17

C HIMES. THERE WERE DEFINITELY chimes which pulled Beau out of a dream and into darkness for the third consecutive night.

12.02am.

Again?

Her heart was banging at the intrusion into her sleep, and she swallowed hard as she remembered being woken at the same time yesterday and the day before.

At the same time?

She propped herself up on her elbows and frowned.

Chimes.

She searched the house in her mind and came up with one option that would be so precise: the grandfather clock. It was the only thing that fit.

Beau swung her legs from the bed and put on the bedside lamp. As light lit the room another chime bellowed and she yelled, throwing the covers aside and finding herself on her feet by the door.

Fuck, fuck, fuck.

Her heart was thudding with renewed vigour as she stood listening to the tingle of the chime peeling off. The house felt heavy in the resulting silence and Beau heard her ragged breaths matching the rapid rise and fall of her chest as she gasped for air.

Right Beau, this is crazy, go check the clock. If the chimes are coming from there, you need to call Gerard and get it sorted out. You can't keep being woken at 12am.

She nodded in agreement but made no move. It was warm and light in here, and something about going downstairs in the middle of the night in this house had her trembling.

If you can't live with normal life, you should stop your imagination running so wild with the ghosts and stop writing, Beau. This is ridiculous.

She chewed her lip as the house fell back into silence.

Maybe I should just get back into bed and...

...have the same happen tomorrow? Go check it out now. If it's the clock, Gerard can fix it. It's simple...

She stared at the bedroom door.

And yet, so hard...

Just go! The damn thing won't be moving at all by the time you get down there, and you'll be doing this tomorrow instead. Get over yourself, this isn't a ghost, it's a damn clock!

As Beau reached a shaking hand for the door, a series of heavy bumps came from above. She stopped to listen to the thick silence that followed, her knuckles white on the door handle, before shaking her head.

Just imagination. It's nothing.

She pulled the handle, opening the door just a crack. Light spilled out into the hallway, which looked normal.

As opposed to what?

She opened the door wider and sent light spilling out over the landing and the top of the stairs. A shadow slipped quickly toward the chair under the window and Beau gasped and placed a hand on her thudding chest.

Imagination. Just imagination.

She peered around the door and found the chair empty, moonlight coming through the window above.

See? No shadow. In fact, it's quite light!

Beau let out a shaky breath.

Because your eyes have got used to the dark while you've been standing here scaring yourself again. The shadow came from the light that was cast around from the bedroom as the door opened. Nothing more.

Beau felt a slither of relief lower her shoulders, it sounded right, especially as the landing looked and felt serene in the moon's half glow. It was really a beautiful old cottage when you took the scary writer's imagination out of the mix.

Taking a few calming breaths, Beau moved from the room onto the landing and stilled, feeling the quiet in the air. She was about to move on when the noise came from above again. A series of muffled bumps, like something - or someone - was in the attic.

What is that?

She listened, and the noise abruptly stopped.

Rats. Mice. Nothing to be scared of. Let's just check the clock. That's of far more consequence. Gerard can do pest control, I'm sure.

Swallowing hard, and now wearing a blanket of goosebumps, Beau moved to the balustrade ahead and peered over. Moonlight streamed through the window by the front door giving her a clear view of the stairs and empty hallway below. Feeling better she descended quickly to the grandfather clock. A light not lit was one that she wouldn't have to turn off and make it dark again afterward – although now she was standing before the clock, she wondered whether she needed to see more. The clock appeared silent and motionless, and Beau realised didn't know the first thing about these clocks and wouldn't know where to look for any action if the chimes *had* come from the old timepiece.

She peered closer through the glass, and in the gloom, saw something that may be relevant. The long-weighted chains that hung under the clock face were moving. Not a lot, in fact barely, but they *were* swinging.

Did that mean it had chimed? Or was this just wind, or the floorboards that had moved under her feet, subtly moving the clock, and causing them to swing?

She shuddered.

Well, you can ask Gerard tomorrow, but it has to be making the noise. Let's get back to bed. It's cold.

With a yawn, Beau turned to walk back to the stairs.

There was a click behind her, which stopped her in her tracks and raised the hair at the back of her neck. She turned back to the kitchen to see the back door swinging slowly inward with a long, drawn-out creak.

She almost let out a scream but couldn't draw the breath as she gasped for air. The door moaned to a stop, causing every nerve in her body to thrum as she stared.

Why now? Now I have to go and shut it.

She blinked as her heart almost faltered and gave out.

Do I? It's not an outside door after all. I could go to bed and do it in the morning.

Beau almost turned away, and then she chastised herself.

You are the custodian of this cottage, Beau, and you know the door is faulty. Just turn on the light and go shut it.

She lurched forward for the light switch that sat by the front door, thinking that may make the situation better, but now the kitchen seemed darker and more ominous.

Then put the kitchen light on too.

She brought a shaky hand to her mouth as she stared down the hallway into the dark mouth of the kitchen. She had to get there first.

So move.

Beau took a shaky breath, steeled herself, and then made herself walk to the kitchen. It took all of her effort not to run to the light switch, but simultaneously took all of her effort to move toward a door that had just opened itself.

At the doorway, she reached round and pressed the switch. Light illuminated the kitchen. The door was the only anomaly, but the air felt stirred, wrong somehow, and the open doors to the dining room and living room behind seemed to mock her.

Before her mind could run, Beau licked her dry lips and headed to the door, grabbing the handle before peering round the corner into the small extension. It was dark and empty.

Gerard said the door opens, no big deal. There's nothing here, Beau. Nothing.

With a sigh that dropped around seven kilos from her shoulders, Beau stepped back and swung the door shut, but just before the door connected with the jamb, something passed the windows outside. A flash of something that Beau just caught in the light of the kitchen. Something red.

She blinked and swung the door wide again with a gasp, moving into the extension to stare out of the windows into the darkness.

Red.

Whoever that was the other day, they had a red jacket.

Is this the same person?

At the word person, Beau's heart went into overdrive, and her legs nearly gave out.

It's freaking midnight, Beau. Why the hell would a person be out there? Why?

She couldn't think of a good reason, but suddenly the locking of the door between the extension and the inside of the house seemed imperative for her safety.

She slammed the door shut, turned the key that sat in the lock, and ran for the stairs.

At the top, she ran into the back bedroom, the red room, and to the back window. The one that overlooked the back of the house.

She could see the roof of the extension, and see the dark forest behind, but nothing moved, and there was nothing red.

Beau felt a shiver run down her spine.

Had she seen it or not?

Christ, Beau, you write horror. How easy would it be to imagine someone hunting you down in the woods out here alone?

Oh, easy. So easy, it's almost natural.

And wasn't that all the answer she needed?

There's no-one out there, Beau. You flipped under the intensity of the situation and saw what wasn't there.

With goosebumps and a pattering heart, Beau took a last look around before stepping away from the window.

Yes, that must be it. There's no one out there now.

As she headed out onto the landing, she realised the lights were still on downstairs, but going to turn them off was no longer within the remit of what she was capable of handling tonight. Instead, she headed back to bed, shutting the bedroom door against the peculiarities of the cottage, and tried to get some sleep.

Chapter 18

'NO, I'M ABSOLUTELY SURE. The dangly things below the clock face were moving.'

Beau hooked the phone between her ear and shoulder and turned the sausages in the pan.

'Well, they're the weights, but the clock doesn't work, Beau. The pendulum is stuck. It can't chime. Are you sure you didn't dream the noise?'

'Three nights in a row? At exactly the same time?'

Gerard sighed. 'Well now, I suppose that's odd. Could it be something else? Did you set an alarm on your phone or something?'

'It was the clock. I'd swear it. Gerard, I'd let it go, seriously, but there were noises in the attic, and the back door swung open again in front of me too. Scared the bloody shit out of me, and now I'm freaked out. Is there any way-'

'I'll come up and check it out for you, aye. Just after lunch, okay?'

'I'll be here, like there's anywhere else to be.'

Gerard gave his deep, gentle laugh. 'You'll be glad of it soon. It's always disconcerting at first, the quiet can get to you, play tricks, you know?'

'You think I'm overreacting?'

'Not specifically, it's just an insight. There have been a few house sitters before you, remember. I've seen all this before, and it always happens in the first few weeks. That's all I'm saying.'

'I'm overreacting.'

Beau turned to take the butter from the fridge and set it next to the loaf of bread with a sigh.

'I'll be up after lunch. Don't worry, this is all normal.'

Beau thought he sounded like a shrink. She rolled her eyes.

I'm overreacting. So be it.

She thanked Gerard and said goodbye before taking her breakfast and a coffee to the dining room and opening her laptop where she could forget about the weirdness of this world for a while and enter the spookiness of another.

'How are you finding it here, Beau?'

Gerard opened the glass front door of the clock and checked the weights and pendulum, running his fingers over the hanging brass.

The clock chimed quietly.

'That's it, that's the noise!' Beau said. She stood watching him from the living room doorway, her arms crossed over her chest, her shoulder against the doorjamb. Gerard raised an eyebrow.

'I mean, yes, I'm good. I like the place, apart from the back door and the chimes, anyway. I heard some noises from the loft earlier too, maybe mice or rats?'

'No. We had a mouse problem last year. It was all dealt with, no sign of them since.'

'Well, there were noises from the attic. What else could it be? Has anyone else said anything about that before?'

Gerard huffed as he rose to check behind the face of the clock.

'Aye. Last year. When there was a mouse problem. Now there's not.'

'How can you be sure? Could you check again?'

'The holes we found were blocked up, all five of them. I last checked just before you moved in.'

'Maybe there's one no-one noticed? Or maybe they found a new one? There was someone hanging around the outside of the cottage a couple of days ago, too. Do you think that's worth worrying about?'

Gerard stared at her, and Beau felt her cheeks redden as he assessed her.

'No. I think it's probably someone out hiking. Did you say something about a coffee?'

Beau pushed off the wall.

'Oh! Yes! Coming right up!'

She felt his eyes on her as she edged past him into the kitchen.

Too high pitched, Beau, too falsely bright and breezy.

Too late now.

The kettle had boiled a few minutes ago, and she flicked the switch back down as she turned to the hallway to find him staring at her, his lips tucked under his teeth.

He was quiet as she made the drinks and handed the cup to him. He moved into the dining room and she followed, shutting the lid on this morning's four thousand words as they sat, Beau uneasy.

'Nice day outside,' he finally said after a sip of coffee.

Beau nodded as she noticed the sun streaming across the landscape and glinting off the sea. 'I suppose it is. I've been working, I hadn't noticed.'

'What sort of stories do you write, Beau?'

'Ghost stories. Formless shadows, creaks on the stairs, unseen things in the room with you, you know.'

She chuckled, expecting the normal reaction of 'you don't look like someone who could write horror!', but Gerard just smiled.

'Opening doors, noises in the attic, chimes from a clock that doesn't work? That sort of thing?' he added.

Beau rolled her eyes and let out a long sigh.

'I know how it seems, and I know my imagination can run away with me, but you said the back door has opened on other people before-'

'The lock is a little loose, aye. I'll get it changed when the parts arrive, but it's not supernatural.'

'I know that. And the noises in the loft could be mice or rats. That's not supernatural either.'

'And the clock?'

'Maybe it works after all? Maybe the last sitter fixed it.'

Gerard shook his head. 'The mechanism is stuck, the gears are worn, and a hammer is missing. None of them have been replaced or repaired. The clock can't be wound, Beau, and therefore can't chime.'

Beau frowned. 'But it does chime. You made the noise just.'

'That was just the weights knocking against each other.'

'But that was the noise! How does it do that?'

'It's impossible. It can't, not by itself.'

Beau opened her mouth, sensed the pointless argument, and nodded.

'Okay, well, maybe I did dream it then. I'm not suggesting this place is haunted at all. That's not it.'

As the words left her mouth, she remembered something else. The record player that had played Simple Minds - all by itself.

Not right now, Beau. He already thinks you're mad.

Gerard took a sip of coffee and dropped his gaze to the laptop.

'How have you been getting on with the book?'

Beau stumbled at the sudden change of topic.

'Er, well, great actually. The plot is really taking shape and I'm finding it easy going. I wrote over nine thousand words yesterday, which means I'll have the book finished in a couple of weeks if this inertia keeps up. The cottage has been a phenomenal writing environment. I think the peace and quiet was just what I needed.'

Gerard nodded.

'You've been writing a lot then.'

It was a statement, not a question, and Beau felt the dig.

'It's my job,' she said defensively as Gerard reached into his back pocket and produced a folded piece of paper.

'This place, the peace and quiet? It can seep into the mind. It can make you see and hear things. Get me? Too much of your work will amplify that for certain. When was the last time you left the cottage?'

Beau blinked. 'I went to the beach yesterday. I spent the entire afternoon outside.'

'Two steps outside. I mean when was the last time you went out? Walked to the church, or took a drive, or went into the village?'

'Well, not yet, but I've only been here five days. I'll be running out of food soon, so I'll have to go out to the shop either way tomorrow or Saturday.'

Gerard frowned.

'It's not enough. We need people, or we go mad. Why do you think isolation is used as a form of punishment?'

Beau glanced at the sun-drenched land outside.

'Okay. I hear you. I'll get up to the church this afternoon. Mrs Locket says the views are worth the climb and I'm intrigued to see the ruin.'

Gerard nodded and spread the paper open in between them.

'That's a great start. I also need to give you this.'

He pushed the paper toward her, and she read the neat, inked handwriting.

My dear Beau,

I'd like to invite you to the next ladies evening at the Quill and Feathers, Thursday 15th August at 7pm. Fun, laughter, good company, wine and nibbles all complementary. Please come. It will be nice to put a face to the name and hear about your extraordinary life as an author!

Let me know if you can make it by messaging or calling the number below.

With much hope and crossed fingers,

Your neighbour, Ophelia.

'This sounds lovely!' Beau smiled, and then she started and checked her watch. 'Oh, but that's tonight?'

'Aye. I would have brought this over to you this morning whether you had called me or not. Ophelia asked me to drop it to you yesterday, but I ran out of time.'

Beau felt a flutter of apprehension. She would be walking into a group of ladies that knew each other, and pretty well by the sounds of it. What if they didn't like her? What if she felt uncomfortable? She had been alone for almost a week. What if she didn't know what to say?

'Well, it's a little short notice. Maybe I can join them next time. I'll message-'

'Beau.' Gerard looked at her pointedly. 'Ophelia is a lovely lady, very welcoming, and very keen to include you and help you integrate into village life. She does it with all of the sitters and they all seem to have a great time. Maybe just let your guard down and go.'

'Oh, my guard isn't up, don't worry, it's just that it's only a few hours away, I mean-'

'What else are you doing tonight?'

Beau chewed her lip as she stared at him.

Listening to record players that play themselves, watching locked doors open, listening for thuds from the attic, watching shadows pass the house, listening for intruders in red coats...

That sounded about the length and breadth of evenings here.

'Beau? You said you'd already written a lot, and you can get to the church and back in just a couple of hours. You have plenty of time.'

Beau swallowed and nodded. 'Yes, okay. I do. I'll message and say I'll go.'

Gerard nodded and seemed to be waiting, so beau nodded back at him.

'Go on then,' he said, gesturing to her phone.

Beau flushed. 'I can do it later.'

'She'll be waiting to see how much food to buy, and I'm already a day late with the note. Do it now.'

'Now?'

'No time like the present.'

Beau found herself picking up her phone.

I suppose not, and this will do you good either way. Company. Female company, and if you don't like it, you can just leave.

She fired off a message, thanking Ophelia and saying that she would love to attend. Only when she placed the phone back on the table did the thought hit her.

If it doesn't start until seven, and it'll be almost dark by then, what time am I coming back? And over three miles of wilderness?

Oh, crap!

Beau's face must have told a picture because Gerard began to laugh.

'You'll be fine, and don't worry about getting back. They're all-nighters normally. The Quill and Feathers has a spare room, Ophelia lets people from the cottage stay. She knows about the walk back. This place will survive without you for one night.'

Beau wasn't sure how she felt about that, especially with the someone who was lurking outside, but now a message was pinging back.

Oh, Beau, that's wonderful. We're dying to meet you. I'll get extra food in, Bread, cheese, and tapas! It's going to be so much fun!

Forgot to say that we have a spare room, you won't need to get back tonight, so don't worry about a thing. Let us pamper you and give you a proper Hollydale welcome!

Beau looked up at Gerard with a shrug that denied the nervous swirl of anxiety. 'I guess I'm out for the night then.'

Gerard rubbed his massive hands together. 'Great news, Beau. See how things will change when you start getting out. The fun will soon begin, and all of this weirdness will stop. You won't even notice it.' He rose from his chair before the offense crept under her skin. 'Well, I'll be away. Thanks for the coffee. If you don't need me beforehand, I'll be down with the new lock in a few days. Do you know where the Quill and Feathers is?'

Beau nodded. 'I saw it on my way through.'

'Ophelia will open the shop door at the front tonight at seven, be sure to start out good and early, five thirty at the latest. Keep your back to the sea and follow the trail in the grass where you can. You can't miss the car after a while, it's always harder to find the house in the dip than it is to find the car on the hill, but you'll be fine tomorrow in the light. If you really think you can't manage, just call me. Have a good time, and have a good walk to the church, too. The sun is lovely today, but it'll not last.'

Beau felt the warmth of the sun as she saw Gerard out and watched him walk away across the grass. She felt a mad urge to call him back, to ask him to wait until five thirty to escort her to her car, or at least draw her a map, but she knew it was silly. He told her to keep her back to the sea and watch for the trail. All she had to do was trust him. He knew what he was talking about.

Hopefully, he knew what he was talking about with this ladies evening too, and she wasn't about to be fed to the Hollydale lions, because let's face it... how many ladies evenings had he ever been to, anyway?

Trust, Beau. He obviously knows Ophelia. Just chill out and trust people.

Too late for anything else now, anyway.

Her stomach churned with a swirl of social anxiety that she hadn't felt for a long time. She knew that she'd never manage lunch on these nerves, so she decided to put her shoes on and get walking.

Maybe that would calm the nerves. Maybe not.

She would find out either way.

Chapter 19

A NNA HAD PROMISED HERSELF that she would stay away from the village, at least until Daniel had information for her, but he was slow going and the lag was driving her nuts.

It wasn't his fault; he didn't understand the severity or the immediacy that she needed to get hold of her... her...

She almost stumbled over her words and felt the heat of anger in her cheeks.

Sister. I know she's a bitch, but she's your sister, it's not hard. Fuck, if you can't get it right in your own head, how are you not going to stumble outside of it? And your name is Anna. Anna Lane. Don't undo what's been done. You've come so far. Keep your composure, it's not long now. Don't fuck this up.

She let her thoughts drift to Daniel as she navigated the lane. He was a good kid, easy on the eye and good in bed, but he was both a blessing and a curse.

He was eager to help, like a little puppy, and he helped to pass the time in the shitty hotel, but God, he was slow! It was like extracting teeth from a whale. She had only expected a couple of nights with him, but at the rate he moved, they would be celebrating their fifty-year bed-iversary before he had information.

His last three days amounted to hiking to the cottage on two evenings and on one lunch break - which was pretty impressive in an hour and a half as he'd said the hike was around five miles. Each time he'd arrived back, she'd devoured any information he could give her, but over the last two days, that had amounted to little more than the first.

Yes, he'd found the cottage, yes, he'd peered inside. 'It looks really old-fashioned, like something out of a time warp! Wooden doors and windows, nice shutters, porch could do with a lick of paint. Quaint place.'

Anna had smiled at this. It was one piece of news she welcomed. Wooden doors and windows, and old locks, meant easy entry was almost guaranteed when the time came.

And then:

No, he hadn't seen who lived there, although it *did* look lived in. There was a laptop set up on the table in one room.

So she was probably there then. This was good news, but not quite enough. Christ knew she wasn't walking all those miles to find the house empty. She needed more, needed a plan and a bit more routine. She needed solid evidence.

And soon.

This was her fourth night at the hotel and while she had always known this would take an amount of time, she hadn't expected the restlessness and growing agitation that would come with waiting longer than she had predicted.

It made her think about how many hobbies she didn't have. If she read, or knitted, or wrote, she could fill her time with those pursuits. Unfortunately, the only things in her head were revenge, and anger, and blame. And these were all-consuming, day and night. This episode of her life had to be nipped in the bud, so that she could continue with whatever life held for her in the future, not that she could see what that was. She couldn't see further than the elimination of her... *sister*.

Such a hard word to say. Why was it so difficult?

Because she's a bitch?

That brought a smile to Anna's face as she drove into Hollydale, lowering her speed so that she could get a good look at the tiny village. Her last slow drive through on her way to the hotel had revealed nothing but a closed, dusty, shabby village with a handful of mournful grey houses and shops that looked like they never opened. It hadn't changed this evening except for a splash of golden orange sunset to highlight the tired buildings.

It was pitiful and lifeless. How anyone survived here was a mystery.

She crawled past The Stone Bull and saw lights behind the small windows. Something is open then. She wondered if she should stop for a drink and humour the old men that probably never left the bar.

She felt the cool wine on her lips and subconsciously pushed out her tongue to taste the liquid.

A *good idea*?

No-one would know who she was, but she would stick out like a sore thumb here and that meant that she would be talked about.

Is it worth it really?

There was the beep of a horn from behind and Anna glanced in the rear-view mirror with surprise. A small car waited behind, its driver a silhouette in the lowering sun, and Anna realised she had come to a halt outside the pub. She eyed up the front door.

Not tonight, Anna. Go back to the hotel and find Daniel.

Raising a hand to the waiting driver behind like a good citizen, she pulled into the small layby outside the pub. When the car had passed, she turned her own car around and prepared to drive back to her abysmal room at the hotel.

She had known that nothing would come of the drive here; it was merely a chance to get out of her room for an hour or so and quell the agitation. Now that she felt calmer, she felt she could deal with a few more days' wait. At least she had a handsome young man to share the time with, and really, what was the rush? What was there to go home to, anyway?

Words her useless therapist had once said suddenly filled her mind in an unexpected stampede.

Enjoy the present, for it's a gift. Stop looking back and stop rushing forward. What's here that you can enjoy right now? Find it You'll find all the worry and agitation will fall away, and more gifts will follow.

Anna grimaced and rammed the car into gear with a crunch.

Fuck off, Barbara.

She pulled out of the layby and her headlights fell on a woman standing outside a shop ahead. The light was dimming, and the shop looked shut, but there she stood, and Anna's heart staggered and thumped as the car slowed.

The hair, the posture, the clothes, the stance. She knew it all and knew it well. God knows she had studied every inch of this woman over the years.

It was her!

Crap.

Anna pushed her foot onto the accelerator and slid down into the seat. Not that she would be recognised with the blonde wig, but just to be sure, after a last sneaky confirming look, she turned her head away as she drove past with a small whoop of exhilaration.

Fuck me, Barbara, is that a gift I see?

Anna allowed herself a grin and then put the lid on her excitement. Confirmation put her a step nearer, but it wasn't time for action yet, she had to be sure of the location. That time would come, and when it did, she wanted it to be perfect.

Nothing would jeopardise this plan, she would see it through whatever it took, but right now she would go back to the hotel, toast the win with wine, and start preparations, because *she* was here.

She was *fucking* here!

Chapter 20

B EAU FROWNED AS THE car started away at speed. She didn't recognise the car or the driver, and there was nothing odd about getting lost and turning a car around in the village, the lanes didn't allow for many three point turns before or beyond, but the way the car had slowed, and then accelerated off had been a little weird.

Or you're just a paranoid writer, she thought as she crossed to the door of the Quill and Feathers. It opened immediately, and a woman floated out to meet her. There was no other word for it.

The material hanging from her long-layered skirt, the hooded arms on her top and a shawl with tassels around her shoulders, combined with a mane of light pink hair that, even pinned back, curled thickly from her face and down her back. All of it floated ethereally around her like she was some kind of angel as the wind caught it, and the way each layer lifted made her look like she was literally walking on air.

The next thing Beau noticed was the smile. Wide and warm and welcoming, it squashed all of Beau's unease in one fell swoop.

'Welcome! Welcome! I'm Ophelia, Gill is upstairs, and Edamine has literally just arrived, it'll just be the four of us tonight. Usually Fern joins us too, but she's recently had an op, poor thing. She'll be joining us in spirit instead.'

Beau's heart skipped and her face must have shown the horror she felt at the statement.

'Oh! What? Well, er... you mean she-'

Ophelia laughed and placed a warm hand on Beau's arm.

'Oh, no! I don't mean she *died*.' She pulled her mouth back in a grimace. 'Heaven's no, it's not that serious, she's just resting up, god bless her.'

Beau blew a breath and raised her eyes skyward.

'Well, that's a relief! Hi Ophelia, I'm Beau.'

Beau smiled and offered her hand, and Ophelia took it warmly in both of hers while looking straight into her eyes.

'I know. You're also spiritual.'

Beau opened her mouth and then shut it again, unsure what to say.

I am?

Ophelia waved her free hand in front of Beau's face. 'Your energy. You're in tune with the other side. How wonderful.'

There was a moment where Beau faltered and wondered what on earth this woman was talking about, and then she got it. The other side.

'Oh yes, I write ghost stories. I'm fascinated by the paranormal - in fictional context, anyway, and outside of my home, of course.'

She laughed politely, noting that Ophelia was still holding on to her hand. Ophelia narrowed her eyes.

'Hmmm, indeed. Maybe we should consult the ball, or the tarot, whichever you like. There are hidden things here, that maybe you don't know?'

Beau tried to find something to say but couldn't follow the question with anything that fit.

Ball, Tarot, hidden things?

Am I dreaming?

Then Ophelia laughed again, a soft, fluttery sound that made Beau think of butterflies.

'Oh, I am sorry, Beau. I just presumed you knew what I did. Listen, let's start over and go inside out of the cool, there's plenty of evening left, and the others are dying to see you. A fancy-pants author, your kind doesn't pass by our village often. This should be interesting. Come, come!'

Beau followed Ophelia through a shop floor that was crammed with much more than quills and feathers. She saw crystals and wands, oracle cards and dream catchers, chakra charts and crystal balls, a large Ouija board and incense sticks, bottled potions and Buddhas, and books on everything from tarot and astrology to mediumship and ghosts. The walls were draped with material of all colours, creating a cosy tent-like effect that seemed to hug you from inside, and although Beau had never stepped inside a shop like this, she felt her interest pique as she passed by the shelves.

She wondered if she should say what was on the tip of her tongue, especially as she didn't know this woman, but in the end, it tripped out anyway.

'I don't see any quills or feathers,' she said as Ophelia pulled open a door that led to a set of stairs.

'Over on the left, third shelf down. Quills with feathers.'

Beau was glad Ophelia couldn't see the heat in her cheeks. 'Of course, that's what a quill is. I'm such an idiot.'

Ophelia chuckled as she moved up the enclosed stairs.

'Well, it's not as if we use them daily anymore, is it? Although we all should. A quill is a magnificent writing experience, its energy differs completely from that of a ballpoint pen. It really makes you stop and think about what you're writing, you know. When you have to dip and conserve ink, you're not lax with your words.'

'I'll take your word for it,' Beau said as they emerged into a small room filled with a couple of cosy looking sofas and a platter of food and drink on a small table between them.

Two women were sitting talking. The one facing her had shoulder length brown curls with streaks of grey and thick blue glasses that turned up at the corners like cat's eyes. Her lips were bright red and her shirt an explosion of flowery colour above her jeans.

'Hi,' she said, catching Beau's eye with a small wave and a big smile, 'you must be Beau. I'm Gill. Lovely to meet you.'

The woman with her back to the stairs turned and Beau saw a familiar face, one that had torn a strip off her a little less than a week ago.

'Hi Gill, you too, and... Mrs Locket. Nice to see you again.'

Mrs Locket's gaze was aloof and serious.

'Nice to see you can turn up somewhere on time, Ms Winters. It's seven o'clock on the dot. Well done. Must be the sensible shoes you're wearing, although they don't quite do the same for your outfit, I must admit.'

The other women fell silent, and Beau felt her jaw drop as the back of her neck bristled. She had intended to put her heels in the car to change into when she got here, but she had forgotten them. Now she kicked herself.

She was about to retort when Mrs Locket broke into a smile and the others laughed as she used her cane to stand and took Beau's hand.

'I'm joking, Beau. You look lovely, and please, call me Edamine. How are you getting on at the old place?'

'Er, good, great, thank you. It's beautiful out there.'

Beau wanted to say more, but she felt off kilter at the sudden change in manner. Part of her still wanted to retort angrily, the other was still processing the smile and the confession of the joke.

Gill handed her a glass of red wine, which softened the ruffled feathers a fraction more.

'Edamine is a bugger for this. Never know whether she's joking or not. When we first met, I thought she hated me for above a week because of the poker face and cutting words. Then I realised that's just a hard shell, crack it and a wicked sense of humour flows out, just like a Cadbury Caramel, right Edamine?'

Gill knocked gently on the top of Edamine's head. It was a funny sight; Edamine being so tall that Gill had to stretch to her tiptoes to get there.

Edamine raised an eyebrow in disdain and Beau felt her insides shrink, and then the smile was back, lighting a twinkle in her blue eyes.

'I can be any version you like. It depends on what I see. You took some working out, Gill, but now I know you are just the silly woman I thought you were. No games played. Beau?' She turned to Beau with her eyes narrowed. 'Beau, I still have to work out.'

Ophelia patted Beau's shoulder and laughed as she moved to a small kitchen area and placed a bowl on the floor. A black cat appeared from nowhere and began to eat.

'You're her landlord, Edamine, and you're scaring the poor girl to death.'

'I'm deciding whether she needs it.'

'She doesn't. Her energy is wonderful.'

Edamine winked at Beau. 'I work with what's in front of me, Ophelia. None of your energy bullshit.'

Beau grinned at the word that left this regal lady's mouth as Ophelia smiled unfazed.

'We're all energy, Edamine, whether yours is bullshit or not. In fact...' Ophelia wrinkled her nose and sniffed. 'Can you smell something?'

'All I can smell is the pondweed spewing from your mouth,' Edamine countered, folding her arms across her chest.

'No, it's more like...' Ophelia lifted her nose and sniffed a little more. 'Shit.'

She said the word so softly and eloquently that Beau actually giggled. She hadn't meant to. It just slipped out.

Edamine turned to her with a straight face. 'Do you smell something, too?'

Beau pulled her mouth straight as her eyes widened. Her head unconsciously followed the shake of Edamine's, which was slowly moving from side to side.

'No. Nothing to smell here.' Beau said carefully.

Edamine raised an eyebrow, and then Gill broke the tension.

'For heaven's sake, let's stop toying with the girl.' She looked at Beau. 'It's just our humour. You'll get used to it, but it's certainly been an indoctrination. If you wish to leave, there'll be no hard feelings. I know we're a bunch of weird old women, but give us a chance, we won't bite, I can promise you that.'

'I can't, but I'll try my best,' Edamine said with a smile. 'And I refuse to be old, thank you, Gill.'

Gill shrugged and rolled her eyes, and Beau looked at each of the three women. Gill, who seemed down to earth, warm, and comforting, like an apple pie. Ophelia, who was soft and ethereal, almost like an angel, and Edamine, who was tough and crass, and clearly said what she thought.

These three could be great characters in a novel, she thought, as the three women looked quietly back at her with an air of expectation. Beau smiled and sipped her wine.

'The wine is good. I'll stay.'

She laughed as three lots of arms raised in the air with whoops of joy, and then Ophelia wrapped her in a warm hug.

'I'm sorry, my love, usually we start much more gently. I'm afraid Edamine was so excited to meet you again that she's been quite wound up.'

'I can't believe that,' Beau said as she was escorted to a sofa and told to sit. Edamine raised her wine glass.

'It's true, dear. All true. I'm dying to know how you got on walking three miles in those heels, and how your ankles are faring up.'

Beau looked at Edamine, trying to gauge whether she was picking at her again, but all she saw was a soft smile and a mischievous twinkle of those blue eyes.

Joking, she's joking.

Beau shook her head with a grin. 'They're doing much better now, but it wasn't pleasant. Hence the walking boots tonight!'

The other women laughed and Edamine pulled her walking stick from the side of the chair to tap Beau's boots.

'Much better. Don't say I didn't warn you.'

'What can I say? I'm a little stubborn.'

'Oh, I know. I see it that fire, and I like it, Beau. I like it a lot.'

Ophelia gasped and pointed to Edamine, Gill, Beau, and finally herself in succession.

'Earth, air, fire, and water! We're complete tonight. Do you realise how powerful this is?'

Gill grinned, but Edamine grumbled and put her hand to her head.

'It's going to be a long night, Beau. Hold tight, it'll all be over soon.'

Chapter 21

T HE DAY WAS DROPPING dark when Joe called Leila away from the play park.

'Come on honey, time to go.'

'Just five more minutes!' Leila shouted from the climbing frame.

Joe sighed. 'It's past bedtime Leila, you know what your mum would say if she was here.'

'She's not here.' Leila called back, continuing her climb to the top. 'She won't know unless you tell her. I'm not going to.'

Joe grinned.

The kid had gumption, and as much as it grieved him, that side of her certainly didn't come from him. She was right though, he thought, and what harm could it do? It was only eight thirty. Still early really.

The last few evenings he had let Leila stay up to watch movies with him. He was lonely rattling round the large house alone for hours until he went to bed, and Leila never slept until after nine either way. They may as well be awake together, than be awake in separate rooms, right?

'Five minutes,' he shouted, and smiled at Leila's whoop of joy.

As he sat back on the bench, his phone began to ring. He pulled it from his pocket and saw Hannah's name light up the screen for the first time since their argument three days ago.

Shit. And we're at the park after bedtime. This won't go down well.

He wondered whether she would notice that he was outside. It wasn't a video call – she only did those with Leila – and the park was empty aside from a pair of twin boys that looked a year or two older. He saw their mum on her phone on the other side of the park, possibly taking comfort in the fact that someone else was still out here at this time too.

The phone rang off and Joe felt the tension loosen in his chest. He stared at the device in his hand and realised he was trembling.

Okay, it was okay. He would just call her back later and say that he had fallen asleep.

He stood to call Leila so that they could get back and save his bacon, but then the phone rang again.

Joe clenched his jaw, and a headache brewed over his right eye. He swiped a hand over his mouth and swallowed hard.

Last time it had taken him a couple of calls to get him to answer, she had given him hell for not being available. There was no way he could let her ring off again. He just had to hope she didn't notice.

He swiped to answer and sat back on the bench, trying to control his rapid heart rate, and breathing so that he sounded like he was sitting chilling in their living room and not like he had run a marathon... or that he was petrified to answer.

She's going to pick up on this.

When did you get so scared of her, Joe? Why are you letting her control you? Just tell her you're at the damn park and if she doesn't like it, she can come home and sort it out herself.

The thought sideswiped his air, and he found he couldn't speak. As usual, Hannah stepped in for him.

'For fuck's sake, Joe, are you there or not? Why can't you answer the phone like a normal person? In fact, why can't you just answer the fucking phone? This is the second time I've had to call! Joe?'

Joe sat holding the phone to his ear, the new revelations circling his head, and he suddenly had the urge to end the call. Just cut off her jibes and her anger. He had to think. What did this mean?

His body told him he was scared now that he was listening to it, and that wasn't so new. He spent so much time trying to brush off her anger and placate and calm her, he always felt tense. It made his adrenaline spike, but that was Hannah. She went off like a bomb and was just as passionate about making up. That bit he certainly wasn't scared of. But control?

Control, Joe?

Joe felt a flush of anger. Even when he had worked, he had been the boss; he had never been controlled. Where was this coming from?

Hannah cut into his thoughts.

'Joe, if you don't answer me right now–'

'You'll do what? From wherever you are.'

Hannah stalled.

'Pardon me?'

Joe blinked.

What are you doing, Joe? Rocking the boat, and for what reason? Is it worth it?

He ignored the voice in his head, the anger pulsing through him.

'I asked what you were going to do about it, from wherever the hell you are.'

He heard Hannah sigh and wondered whether his jaw would come unclenched when he next had to speak. His teeth seemed welded together, sending pain through his jaw and his head. His whole body was shaking, and for some stupid reason, he couldn't stop it.

'Joe, Joe, Joe. You *know* where the hell I am. I'm working. Hard. I've only just got out of a meeting, and it's eight thirty-six. I'm tired, and I called to apologise for my behaviour the other day. I wasn't in the best-'

'It took you three days?'

Hannah paused and Joe ploughed on.

'Three days for you to call and apologise? You haven't spoken to your daughter in three days because you've been angry at me. How does that compute in your mind, Hannah?'

'I've thought about Leila every single day.'

'And you could have called every single day. There's nothing stopping you.'

'You fucking stop me, you moron. Listen to yourself. I called to apologise, and this is the response I get? Fuck you, Joe.'

Fuck me.

Joe huffed a laugh.

'You won't be doing that when you get back either... if you get back at all.'

He heard the confusion in Hannah's voice.

'What the hell are you talking about?'

'The make-up sex. I know it's your way of controlling the situation, of controlling me. Of ending a fight in your favour, of letting you get away with the things you say and do.'

'No, Joe, that's not it. I enjoy sex with my husband. I love you. Is that so wrong? Why are you being such a fucking idiot? You think I control you?'

'Don't you?'

'I have enough problems controlling my business without my personal life getting involved.'

'So what was that with the cashmere throw? We were freezing, Han, and we couldn't use the best blanket to warm up?'

Hannah stalled again, and Joe gave her time to catch up, his heart thudding furiously.

'Right, so this control thing is about a throw? All I was saying-'

'No, it's not just about a throw, it's about all the other little things over the years too, and not just me, it's everyone. Look at the fuss you've caused about Beau leaving. She is doing this for herself because it's what she needs, and you've called her all the names under the sun and ditched her. How is that being a friend?'

'I have not ditched her, she-'

'Have you called her yet?'

'I haven't had time. I'm busy working, you asshole. Why is Beau getting involved now? This is not about fucking Beau. She has my number too, you know. Has *she* called *me* yet?'

Joe sneered. 'Why the hell would she call you?'

'To apologise for leaving me in the fucking shit? I have no fucking friends down there Joe, I'm stuck with you and Leila.'

'Stuck with us? I thought you loved us a minute ago, loved me, and thought about Leila every single day. They were the words from your mouth.'

Hannah let out a high-pitched screech that Joe could only think was frustration. Good. He was getting to her.

'Of course I love you both, but it's not the same. You don't understand. I work so hard, I need playtime, not family time. Beau knew my position, she understood, and still she fucking left!'

'She left because she had no other choice. She couldn't write here, did you not hear that?'

'Well, she could have got another job. She doesn't have to write. She could have lived here, I'd have even waived the rent-'

Joe laughed, and Hannah paused. He could almost feel her anger climbing out of the receiver, but he noticed something else. His heart was still racing, but he was no longer shaking. He felt in control.

'Maybe she wants to be the author she's supposed to be, and when that gets hard, she doesn't want to quit. How would you feel if this was your business we were talking about?'

'That's the whole fucking point, isn't it? I'm running a business, not sitting on my arse creating fairy stories. How long did she think it would last before she landed in reality? Patrick was supporting her all the way, and when he left, I supported her. She can't sustain a hobby and expect to fucking live off it.'

As Hannah got angrier, Joe felt himself get calm. It was eerie, but it felt good.

'We supported her. And I'm pretty sure she was a best-selling author last time I checked. That's not a hobby. She has contracts to fulfil, just like you do. She works as hard as you do. It'll be interesting to hear what she thinks of your little summary of her life.'

Hannah gave a low laugh.

'Beau got lucky because she's beautiful. Nothing more. How interested are you in her, Joe?'

'I'm interested in whether she's doing okay up there alone, unlike some of us.'

'She's not *your* friend.'

'We were friends as couples before she came to stay with us Hannah, did you expect me to ignore her? Not to care? I've known her as long as you have. Don't you wonder how she is?'

'Well, you obviously do, so why don't you fucking call her and then you can stop relying on me for information you're obviously too fucking star struck to get yourself? Here, I'll give you her fucking number if you like.'

'I have her number, and I've already called her.'

Hannah went quiet, and Joe smiled. He was enjoying how this was going; he had the upper hand, and he was surprising her at every turn. It was fun keeping her on her toes.

Is that why she likes it, too? Is this the way she feels with you?

'You called her?' Hannah's voice was low and dark, and Joe knew he had hit a nerve.

'Yes. She messaged me first and seemed down, so I called. It's what friends do.'

'But you're not her fucking friend. I am!'

'I'm more of a friend than you at the moment, Han. Do you know how she's getting on, or whether she's broken the writing block, or whether she's lonely?'

'Why don't you tell me, if you know so much?'

'No. Why don't you call her?'

Hannah made a sound that Joe couldn't quite distinguish. Maybe a gargle? He wasn't sure. He frowned and pressed the phone closer to his ear. What was she doing? Then her voice screeched as hell let loose, and Joe yanked the phone from his ear.

'Why don't I call her? Why? Maybe this is fucking why. I gave her a roof over her head when she had nothing, I gave her a shoulder to cry on for months over her blithering idiot of a husband, I listened to all of her miserable whining over the useless prick, and she left me when I needed her. *She* left *me*! And now to top it off, when things get tough, she messages my fucking *husband*?

'You think you've got this all worked out, but you're so wrong, Han.'

'You just said - from your own mouth,' she said, mocking his earlier words with a version of his voice. 'That she messaged you. What was she after, Joe? Was she lonely? Did she want you to go up there and make her feel better?'

'She asked how *you* were and how *you* were feeling. Then she asked if I thought it would be a good move for her to message you, bearing in mind your mood.'

'My fucking mood? What the hell is that supposed to mean?'

'Well, listen to yourself. What are people supposed to think? Beau knows you well, she knows what you're like and she knows everything you've done. Why wouldn't she be cautious?'

'Um... because she was my best friend?'

'Well, maybe you should treat your friends better.'

'Maybe they shouldn't be calling my fucking husband when they're lonely.'

Joe sighed and rubbed a hand through his hair.

'I called *her*, and it wasn't like that. Just message her, Han.'

'Maybe if she wasn't such a fucking bitch, I would, but she just crossed the line. Nobody calls my husband. She's a selfish prick and there's no room in my life for whores. Who the hell does she think she is? Does she think she's getting her hands on *my* family now she fucked hers up? I don't shitting think so.'

Joe frowned, his heart beginning to beat hard for a different reason.

'Hannah, there's no need for that. Beau called asking about you. She cares. Please, just call her and sort this out.'

'Absolutely fucking not.'

'You just said you needed a friend.'

'Oh fuck you, Joe, and fuck Beau, too. She won't come crawling back to me, I'll make sure of it. She's a selfish whore that I don't need in my life, just someone else to let me down. And you? You're a fucking arsehole, Joe. I hate you both. Do you know that? I fucking hate you!'

Joe was so used to the screaming in his ear that the silence as she cut the connection almost caught him off guard.

'Hannah? You there?'

He looked at the screen and saw that she had gone.

Shit.

Joe looked across the park at his daughter, now at the top of the climbing frame, and realised he was still scared, but however scared he was of Hannah and the way she was losing control again; he was ten times more scared for Beau.

When Hannah had fallen out with the last friend ten years ago, it hadn't ended too well. In fact, Hannah didn't do friends well at all.

When Joe had taken her back after the last attack, she said that she had learned her lesson, had promised that she would never do anything like that again. She knew that it was wrong, and that she had to change.

She promised to change.

And yet, she was losing control again. She got too close, and when she got too close, bad things happened.

Joe knew her, he knew how it went, and so did Beau, to an extent.

But Beau didn't know what had happened to the other girl - the last 'best friend' that Hannah had latched on to.

Right now, Joe wondered if she needed to, because then she may have a chance at protecting herself, and although Hannah had said nothing about hurting Beau, Joe couldn't be certain that she wouldn't, and the way Hannah worked, neither of them would see her coming.

Chapter 22

'Y OU'RE HAVING SOME TROUBLE.'

Ophelia stared into the crystal ball with a frown.

'Of what kind?' Edamine said as she glanced at Beau. 'I don't need trouble at my cottage.'

Beau shrugged. 'There's no trouble at the cottage.'

'I see you walking around with unease.'

Beau felt her insides shrivel under Edamine's gaze. 'I'm not uneasy. The cottage is fine, I promise you.'

Ophelia frowned. 'Maybe it's subconscious, dear. My visions are never wrong and it's early days at the house. Settling in unease, possibly?'

'Possibly,' Beau muttered, the hair at the back of her neck beginning to rise.

'Your visions are sometimes suspect, Ophelia.' Edamine added, giving Beau's hand a quick squeeze. Ophelia smiled.

'But not wrong. Sometimes you just have to think around what's been shown, and sometimes these things will come to light later.'

Beau said nothing. She hadn't intended on relaying her fears to any of these ladies tonight, and especially not Edamine, but now it seemed the information was flowing from a ball without her consent.

The crystal ball had started out as a fun game. It was after 11pm, and the night had gone quickly. The atmosphere had been relaxed, and the food was all gone save for a tin of chocolate orange shortbread and a box of luxury desert chocolates. The third bottle of red had all but gone, and Beau had been feeling open and relaxed in a way that only wine could induce. Ophelia was the only one not drinking. She was on the elderflower cordial, which she said made her feel giggly enough. When the ball had been suggested, Beau was imagining party games, but no one was suggesting what to play. Edamine had merely rolled her eyes with a smile, and Gill had eagerly agreed. Only Beau had been a little flummoxed, the wine making her head feel so slow that she couldn't grasp understanding.

'The ball?' She asked, thinking she must have misheard, until Ophelia had retrieved a large glass sphere which sat on a decorative base of wood. Meanwhile, Gill had lit two purple candles that had appeared on the table, and placed a smooth, almost translucent crystal tower between them before turning the lights low.

'Selenite.' Gill had whispered with a wink, as though Beau should know what the hell that was.

Beau watched in amusement as Ophelia had taken five minutes in silence to 'ground herself and call in her guides', and then she had stared at the ball and immediately given some advice to Edamine about her cat, who was not too happy about the new food that she had been given. 'It's giving her a bellyache,' Ophelia said. Edamine huffed but admitted that the cat hadn't eaten much over the last few days. Gill had only grinned, and Beau had been intrigued.

'How are you doing that?'

Ophelia only stared at the ball on the table, two candles flickering either side of her in the low light. It was Gill who answered.

'It's called scrying. Ophelia looks into the glass and sees moving pictures where we see nothing. It's why we don't have a tv up here. She's all set with her own movies while I have to suffer the silence.'

Edamine laughed, and Ophelia grinned. 'Not true,' she said, keeping her eyes on the glass. 'Someone broke the tv with her backside and we haven't purchased a new one yet.'

'What?' Beau asked, wondering if her mind was fully with her in the room.

Was it the wine? Was she in a parallel universe? What the heck was going on here? How did this go from relaxed chats with food, to... crying, was it called?

She felt a little like crying right herself now. The whole scene was a little too far out of her comfort zone. She thought crystal ball gazers were phonies who resided in booths at the seaside, waiting for those gullible enough to be lured inside.

'I admit, I sat on it.'

Beau's mouth dropped open as she looked at Gill. She didn't quite know how to answer, but Ophelia saved her the trouble.

'From a great height. She fell through the roof while putting something in the attic. It's a tiny space. You can't even stand upright. I don't even know how she managed to fit between the floor joists.'

'Are you saying I'm fat?'

'I'm saying you sat on the tv and broke it. I'm not saying anything about your weight, honey.'

Ophelia leaned over the table to stroke Gill's cheek and blow her a kiss.

'I sprained my wrist, had to have stitches in my leg, and destroyed my favourite pair of dungarees too. They stayed upstairs while I came down.'

'Luckily, she landed butt first, lots of padding.'

'Even more if you'd have fallen.' Gill turned her face away from Ophelia in mock annoyance and pushed away her hand. Ophelia chuckled.

'I wouldn't have fallen, honey. I'm far too fat to fit through the joists. The tv would have been safe if I'd gone up there, so would your dungarees.'

They had all laughed, and the atmosphere loosened for Beau, who was beginning to feel more normal again, and then Ophelia had been 'called' back to the ball, and now she sat chewing at the inside of her mouth as she waved a hand at her face, which seemed to be burning up.

'I suppose it has taken a while to settle in. The house and surroundings are very new to me. I've lived in the city all my life and never on my own. I'm doing okay though-'

'Wait.' Ophelia held up a hand and staring at the glass with a frown. There was a moment of silence. 'I hear something.'

All Beau could hear was the hum of the refrigerator and the thudding of her own heart. No one said a word until Ophelia spoke.

'I'm not clairaudient as a rule. I don't hear psychic information, and so this is very rare and might be nothing, but I'm hearing a song. It's familiar, well known, I feel. A few years old now.'

The group waited, and then Ophelia smiled and looked up.

'No. It's gone. Let's put the ball away and find some more wine.'

Later, when Beau had retired to her tiny room to get ready for bed, there had been a knock on the door.

'Yes? You can come in, I'm decent.'

Gill poked her head around the door. 'We're doing hot chocolate if you fancy before bed, just a wind down in the lounge. If you're tired, no worries, we just wanted to invite you out with us.' Gill gestured at her. 'We're both in our PJ's too, don't worry.'

Gill stepped into the doorway to reveal full pink unicorn pyjamas. Beau looked down at her own brand-new highland cow pyjamas. She usually slept in her underwear but living alone in the countryside and in an unfamiliar place she had felt pyjamas would be safer – not that she had used them yet. She hadn't known there would be sleepovers at friend's houses, but she was glad she'd bought them right now.

'I'd like that, actually,' she said. 'Although I'll have more water first. My head is spinning a little.'

'Sounds like a plan. We'll see you in the living area.'

The door clicked shut and Beau continued to fold her clothes ready for the morning, placing them on a small chest of drawers opposite the bed. She lay her phone on top and left the room to see Ophelia and Gill snuggled on one sofa. Beau opted for the other as Ophelia rose to pour her some water from a jug. She had a long floral nightgown that made her look like something from the eighteen hundreds while simultaneously being perfectly her style.

'Here you go,' she said, handing Beau the water before sitting back down. 'We always have a little time-out after a big evening. It helps the energy settle so that we can sleep better.'

Gill curled her fingers and pointed a thumb at Ophelia. 'What she said. I have no fricking clue whether it makes a difference or not. I'm not sensitive at all and not interested in being.'

'Sensitive?'

'Psychic.'

Ophelia nudged Gill with an elbow. 'Intuitive. I don't like psychic, it has too many connotations. As much as you have seen me acting like the local fortune teller tonight, that's not a side that I bring out in public. I am intuitive, and I do get downloads of information, but I don't ask people for money. In fact, I don't even tell them usually. Unless it's Gill, Fern, or Edamine, of course. Close friends. I save these sessions for our ladies' evenings, a bit of fun, something different, and it's nice to surprise people when I get it right. Of course, usually we don't have new people to join us. The village is a bit stagnant, that's why I love to invite the ladies who stay at the Cottage.'

Beau nodded with a grin. 'I can understand that. I've been in this village twice and both times everything but the pub has been shut down. I need some groceries in the morning. Any idea when the store is open?'

'That's Fern's domain. She's been holed up in bed after her op, but I'll see if I can deal with it in the morning for you.'

'So the shop is shut because Fern has had an op? Won't the produce go off?'

'Stan, her husband, is supposed to open it. He prefers the pub. I told Fern I'll sort it while she's off her feet, it'll only be a couple more weeks. Hopefully, she won't lose too much - in takings and produce.'

Beau nodded. 'I may have seen him in the pub when I first met Edamine. Older man with a cap. He seemed a bit sullen.'

Ophelia and gill laughed and exchanged glances.

'Putting it mildly,' Gill said. 'He's even worse now he has to look after the shop, too. Grumpy old bugger. Do you want a hot chocolate now, Beau? I'm making.'

Gill got up as Beau downed the rest of the water. Both her head and her stomach were feeling more settled already, but now she was a little cold. She shivered. Hot chocolate sounded perfect.

'I'd love one, thank you.'

Gill moved to the kitchen area and Ophelia threw Beau a wool blanket.

'Here. It gets chilly in the evening. Don't be afraid to tuck your feet up too. We're not proud. Our home is yours too.'

'Thank you,' Beau said, wrapping her feet underneath her and pulling the blanket on top. 'So how long have you and Gill been living together? How did you meet?'

Ophelia smiled and tucked up her own feet.

'Funny story, really. We met at a Mind, Body, and Spirit convention in Edinburgh twenty-five years ago and we've been together ever since. Gill was manning a stall full of crystals, and all I saw was a halo of gorgeous energy. I was mesmerised. It was only later I learned that the energy was nothing to do with Gill and everything to do with crystals, but by then I was already taken with her. What could I do but give her a crystal shop to front? Hence Quills and Feathers. Now she's constantly radiant energy - or I can pretend she is, anyway.'

Ophelia winked as a cry came from the kitchen.

'What a load of crap.' Gill came back to the table with three hot chocolates. 'I'll tell you the real story, shall I? I was indeed manning a crystal stall at the convention. It was absolute torture. I had been dragged there by a friend to help out. Just taking money, that's all I was supposed to do, but it was busier than either of us thought. I was surrounded by all of these new age types taking aura photographs and having energy healing, and so many people asking what crystal healed what, or protected against what, or was good for negative energy, or good for increasing intuition or wealth. I was at my wit's end, and then Ophelia appeared, and she not only knew what she was talking about, but she offered to help out. This angel spent all afternoon helping people choose the right crystals for their needs, and by the end of the show, I was smitten. Unfortunately, she thought I was happy manning a crystal stall, and five years later we end up here manning our own bloody new age shop.'

'You love it,' Ophelia said, as Gill sat back down and pulled the blanket over her, too.

Gill grinned and Kissed Ophelia's cheek. 'I do. At least I now know what crystals do what, and I know psychics aren't all fake either. I've seen firsthand what happens with Ophelia, and I have no idea where she gets the info from, but she's usually bob on.'

Ophelia smiled and held out her hands.

'That's because the information doesn't come from me. I was right with what I saw tonight too, wasn't I Beau? You're uneasy.'

Beau blinked.

'Oh, I'm fine, really. Settling in nerves, like you said. Life has been a bit of an unpredictable rollercoaster since I left Patrick. I can't say I haven't been uneasy since then really, what with losing everything, living with my friends and not being able to write. Now I'm alone up here in the wilderness when I've always been surrounded by people. My foundation is a little unstable, I suppose.'

She smiled, but Ophelia was shaking her head, her face scrunched into a frown.

'That's not it. The vision was very specific. It was the cottage you were uneasy with. What's happening at the cottage?'

Beau felt her stomach clench. 'Nothing. Really.'

Ophelia pursed her lips and looked down at the blanket over their legs. She paused a moment and then looked up.

'I heard music. Old. Like a record player.'

Beau swallowed hard.

'Uh-huh.'

'As I said, I don't hear things often, but when I do, it's usually because the message is stronger.'

'Right.'

Ophelia sighed, and Gill placed a hand on her shoulder.

'Okay, I'm going to tell you what I saw, and what impression I got. I had hoped to tell you gently but you're stubborn, Beau. You're not giving anything up.'

Beau's heart was hammering against her ribs as she blinked at Ophelia. She half wondered if this was a joke.

'Fine,' she croaked and reached for her hot chocolate with shaking hands.

'I'm not trying to scare you, but I felt an energy in the cottage. There was a large clock, and a door at first. The door had an abnormally large lock, which suggested to me that there is a problem with it. I saw you moving around as though looking for things that weren't there. When I heard the music, I saw you standing over an old record player, looking at it. The song that played was a band I can't recall, but I knew the song. It was 'Don't You Forget About Me'. Does that mean anything to you?'

Beau felt her lower lip tremble as Ophelia hummed the tune and Beau saw the spinning disc complete with Simple Minds. It was the same song, and she would never forget that label. Fear edged up her spine as Ophelia continued.

'Okay, well, I saw some other things, too. A round window with shutters. There was a small face behind it, but it wasn't you. The image was fuzzy, but the hair seemed dark, long and dark, and the face pale, the mouth was huge and black, usually my sign for someone who likes to shout or argue. There was something else too, just briefly, but this had a slightly different energy, almost like it wasn't connected, but this felt male and connected with a rocking chair. I also saw a red coat. Bright red in-'

Beau let out an anguished sob as she put a hand over her mouth. She had meant to keep everything in and assess what she was hearing when she was alone, but everything matched perfectly, and the list was just too much.

'How can you know all of this?'

Ophelia's face fell, and she moved to Beau's sofa to clutch her hand. 'Oh, I'm sorry. I said too much. I shouldn't have pushed. I never usually tell people what I see if they don't agree to hearing it, but Beau, I feel strongly that I need to tell you.'

'Are you trying to scare me?'

'Not at all, no, I would never do that. I want to help.'

Beau felt an uneasy mixture of fear and dread and mistrust. Had Edamine put Ophelia up to this? Why had they invited her here, anyway? Neither of these ladies knew her, but Edamine certainly did. Did they always try to frighten the cottage sitters? Was it a game?

And then Beau's thoughts stalled.

How can it be a game? There is only you at the cottage that has heard the record player or seen the back door open, or heard the clock, or caught sight of the man in the red coat...

'Beau? Please say something.'

Beau felt a flicker of anger and she knew she had figured it out. She was right. There was no other explanation, but this one fit perfectly. Who owned the house, who had keys, who knew people around here, who knew that Beau wasn't used to isolation, and who had access to Gerard? To top it off, she had been late on that first Saturday here. There was motive.

She felt her cheeks flush.

'Edamine. This is her, isn't it? We got off to a bad start when I got here late, but I'd had an eight-hour drive. Eight hours! The traffic isn't something I can control.'

'Sorry?' Ophelia sat back with a frown.

'She's organised someone to scare me. It's not hard out there, is it? Someone in a red coat to hang around the house, someone who has a key and can let himself in and mess with the doors and the clock and the record player? Is Gerard in on it, too?

Maybe he's helping out? You're all having such a good laugh about it, but it's not funny!'

'No one is laughing, honey, I don't understand what you think Edamine has done, or why, but I can guarantee you that she knows nothing about this.'

Ophelia tried to reach for Beau's hand, but Beau snatched it away as she thought about the noises that she had heard in the loft, too. Footsteps? She had forgotten about that, but Ophelia had obviously been primed because she had mentioned a face behind a round window. The attic window. So maybe red coat is living in the attic, that way he can move around and make noises all night.

Beau rolled her eyes and huffed a laugh.

'Of course she does. This is her cottage after all, she holds all the cards. She knows I come from the city and that I'd be easily scared. It's payback, right?'

'No, Beau, you've got it wrong. If I'm reading the energy around the situation right, you need to be careful out there, that's why I felt I needed to tell you. Something feels wrong, but I can't put my finger on what it is, and it worries me that you're alone out there. It's an energy I'm not familiar with and it feels dark, but the reason I said nothing in front of Edamine is that I felt similar around her too, but I'm not sure what that means. I didn't want to alarm her with what you're going through, and I didn't want to have to bring up everything I saw and felt.'

Beau knew that her face was stony as Ophelia sat wringing her hands next to her.

'Oh God, I've done something wrong, haven't I? I shouldn't have said. I'm so sorry, I shouldn't have said anything more. I know not to get involved and I go and do it every time, but it's only because I care!'

Beau thought the theatrics were pretty good. This woman should have her own stage show. What with the seeing things in the glass and then crying that she's said the wrong thing. The drama was entertainment, that was for sure.

'I'm sorry Beau, please, can you forget that I said anything? Just forget it all. I'm sorry, it probably means nothing.'

'Oh, you know it means something. You all do, that's the issue.' She looked at Gill. 'Thank you for the hot chocolate, it was lovely, but I think I'll go to bed now.'

All Beau actually wanted was to leave, and her body was trembling with as much restrained anger and confusion as fear, but where would she go? She couldn't get back to the cottage tonight, and there was no way she wanted to sleep in the car out in the middle of nowhere.

There was no choice but to stay, but she didn't have to sit here and listen to this.

She rose, thanked them both for letting her stay, went to her little room and shut the door. After a moment, she pulled the little chair from the corner and wedged it under the door handle. She didn't know if that would stop them from entering, or whether they would even try, but at least the chair falling would cause her to wake.

She grabbed her phone from on top of her clothes, intending to sleep with it under her pillow, and then she paused and shook her head.

What are you doing, Beau? These women may be playing a game, but they're not bloody murderers!

She tilted her head in thought.

How would you know? And it would be two against one.

She took her phone to the bed, but as she pushed it under the pillow, she noticed a missed call amongst the notifications. Her heart skipped.

Hannah?

She pulled the phone back out to read Joe's name.

Joe? At 11pm? Why on earth would he phone so late?

There was no voicemail, and no message.

Strange, but obviously not urgent. I'll call him in the morning.

She got into bed and yawned. She was tired and regretted accepting the hot chocolate after all that wine. It was sitting on her stomach wrong, lying heavy. Each time Beau closed her eyes, she felt the room sway, and the chocolate swayed with it. She also felt the niggle of her bladder.

You didn't even ask where the toilet was, and probably you should have gone before bed.

She lay with her eyes open in the dark.

No way I'm going back out there now, I'll just have to suck it up.

She blew a few steadying breaths as her eyes adjusted to the dark and her thoughts turned to the evening and the revelations.

She hadn't come across anyone like Ophelia before, and she hadn't delved into the world of psychics very much, but she hadn't believed it was real. She thought they all had generic lines that they spewed to everyone.

You're happily married... you're going to have a long life... you'll have two children... you'll holiday in Costa Brava.

All things that could never prove anything - except the marriage and the wedding ring, of course.

But Ophelia hadn't said any of those things and hadn't specifically been looking into the ball for her, but what had come out was uncanny.

'And Edamine was here before you. It was all pre planned Beau. Every bit of this was planned to make you scared,' she whispered.

But she didn't sense that was the truth.

If it was, why didn't Ophelia say all of this stuff with Edamine here? Why wouldn't they all want to see how you reacted?

Beau rolled onto her side, felt the movement in her stomach, and carefully rolled back with a sigh.

The other thing that was playing on Beau's mind was the fact that Ophelia had said that the same energy was around Edamine and that she didn't want to alarm her, that's why she'd stopped the reading as though she had lost the visuals.

If Edamine was in on this, why would Ophelia bother waiting until she had gone to speak to Beau?

But if Edamine wasn't in on this, then how the heck would Ophelia get such specific information?

And if Ophelia was indeed a psychic crystal ball reader - which seemed ludicrous - but if she was, and she was warning Beau to be careful, then what did that mean? Be careful of the person in red who was messing with her? Were they actually dangerous, after all? Were they getting in and moving things? Were they getting into the attic?

Beau felt her stomach flip over. She clenched her teeth and sat up, breathing carefully, as she waited for her stomach to settle.

Sick with fear, or sick with wine?

Beau couldn't tell. She wished she knew for certain that these women were playing with her, at least then she could put it aside and move on. Not knowing left an opening that she didn't like too much. An opening where she may not be alone out at the cottage... and that was terrifying.

This is so stupid; you're going to drive yourself nuts.

Beau reached behind her pillow for her phone, thanking the lord her plan had unlimited data, because this could be a long night and she hadn't hooked up to the Wi-Fi, but she had to know more.

Unlocking the screen, she loaded Google and began to type.

How does reading a crystal ball work?

Good place to start, she thought, sitting back to read.

Chapter 23

NEXT MORNING BEAU ROSE to the smell of pancakes and bacon. Her stomach grumbled, last night's wine forgotten and leaving a massive hole in her empty stomach, but she refused breakfast saying that she needed to get back to work. Her words had resulted in both Gill and Ophelia looking so crestfallen that Beau almost physically felt the stab of pain.

Ophelia apologised again profusely and insisted that Beau keep her number, or at least Gill's. She professed that she had meant no harm and hoped that she and Beau could put this aside and be friends. Both she and Gill had enjoyed her company immensely, and they had both hoped to repeat the experience again soon.

Beau agreed to nothing. She didn't know how she felt, but this morning, she did know that both women seemed genuinely upset.

Ophelia was also as good as her word about opening the grocery shop and helping Beau pick up a few items from next door. Fern was nowhere to be seen, and Beau was glad. She didn't know how normal she could act meeting anyone new after the night she'd had.

She was driving back to the cottage when she received a phone call from Edamine. Still in a dark mood, and with the Bluetooth still acting up, she contemplated leaving it, but as the woman was her landlady, she felt obliged to answer. She balanced the phone on her knee and turned it on to speaker.

'Hi,' she said, not sure whether to call her Edamine or Mrs Locket now they were back on business terms.

'Good morning, Beau. I hope you slept well, and that Gill and Ophelia were good hostesses?'

'Yes, thank you.'

Beau glanced at her dark rimmed puffy eyes and pale face in the rear-view mirror and was glad she wasn't on a video call.

'Good, that's good. I had a lovely evening. It was nice to get to know you a little better, especially after my rude interlude when you first arrived. You must have thought me to be very harsh. I was in a lot of pain with my legs, and I wasn't looking forward to the nurse. You just came on top of a pile of gripes that I'd been sitting on all day. I know I said all this last night, but I just feel the need to apologise again for my rudeness.'

'Oh, it's no trouble, really. The only thing you caused that day were my aching ankles when my stubbornness took me across the land in heels.'

Edamine laughed, and Beau couldn't help the smile that travelled across her own face. Whatever had transpired last night, when she wasn't placing them under suspicion, Beau realised she had enjoyed the company of all the women last night.

'I really like that fire about you. I was going to tell you I've never had a woman like you at the cottage. Usually, they're hardy loners used to the isolation and the harsh winters; ruddy cheeks and calloused hands giving away their predisposition. You were quite unexpected, I have to admit. Calling from the city, never having being away from the crowds, and yet wanting to place yourself here. I couldn't decide whether you were mad or admirable.'

Beau smiled. 'Yet to be determined, I supposed.'

'You were certainly *determined*, I'll give you that.'

Beau laughed as she pulled the car into the tiny parking area and turned off the engine.

'I was desperate. That's what I was.'

She looked out over the landscape ahead, which was thick with morning mist.

Just three miles to cover with shopping. This should be fun. Hope I don't get lost.

'Well, whatever it was, I know I made the right choice. I don't want anything to jeopardise your position at the cottage or make you feel uncomfortable, and I don't want to make an issue of what was said last night, but I do want to say that if you're having any trouble at the cottage – anything at all – please tell me. I don't want you to suffer in silence. I'm sure whatever the issue, we can work something out.'

Beau felt her heart skip. Now they were finally getting to the real issue, weren't they?

'I'm not having any trouble, I promise.'

Edamine was quiet for a beat, and Beau wondered what she was thinking. She waited, not wanting to add anything to the bonfire just yet.

'Are you certain, Beau? I... I mean, even if it's just a small thing that you're worried about, you can tell me.'

Beau frowned across the landscape. As she stared, a stag appeared, cutting through the mist, its antlers large and majestic. It looked like something from a fairy tale and Beau's breath caught.

'No problems. It's really beautiful here, Edamine, and I'm writing lots. I'm incredibly grateful for this opportunity.'

'Hmm.'

Beau didn't dare move as she and the stag seemed to lock eyes, or at least the stag watched the car, but Beau could swear she almost felt the animal look into her soul.

'Don't you believe me?'

'It's not really that, it's more that I've known Ophelia for so many years.'

'And?'

'Well, she's not normally wrong with her predictions, that's all.'

The stag finally moved on, and Beau let her attention move back to the call.

Is Edamine pushing because she knows? Or because she's concerned?

Beau didn't know what angle this conversation was coming from. She scrunched her eyes shut and leaned her head on the steering wheel.

'I don't know what to say, Edamine. There's nothing.'

Edamine finally seemed to let it go. And was that a sigh of relief? Or frustration?

'All right, maybe she got this one wrong, or maybe there's something to come. Either way, I want you to know that you can tell me if anything comes up, and between us and Gerard, we'll sort it out. And Beau? I know that the contract states that I will sue if you leave before term, but I also want you to know that I would never go that far. I would never stop you from leaving if you wanted to, especially given your city background. I just wanted you to give things a real shot, I didn't want you running at the first hurdle and leaving me in the lurch, that's all, but if you're worried about anything and you don't want to stay, I won't stop you from leaving.'

Beau blinked.

This conversation is getting weirder the more it goes on. Does she want me to go? Is that why she's scaring me? Or is she being kind?

Beau couldn't fathom what the intention was, and her fuddled mind didn't make it easy for her usually sharp brain to figure it out. The little nuances that she usually picked up on were fogged with last night's wine and a lack of sleep.

What do I say?

'Um, thank you? I assure you, though, I'm having no trouble, and I don't want to leave. Not at all.'

Where the fuck would I go? Back to writers hell? Not now Hannah is in a funk.

Beau's lip curled as Edamine gave in.

'Fine, that's good to hear. I used to love it out there. I'm glad you're doing well.'

'I am. Do you get down to the cottage yourself much these days?'

Edamine gave a soft laugh.

'Not anymore. I can make it when it's been dry, and the ground is harder, but my legs give me hell. I try to see the place every once in a while, though. I'm very fond of the cottage.'

Beau had no idea what was going on in her mind until she said it.

'Well, we've had no rain for three days now, and it's likely to be dry today. Why don't you come over later and I'll make us some dinner? I've picked up a couple of steaks from Fern's store. We could have new potatoes and salad?'

'Do you have egg and chips?'

Beau found herself grinning. 'Egg and jumbo mushrooms. No chips, but I can make them. I used to back at home.'

'Then you have yourself a deal, on one condition.'

'What's that?'

'We eat early, before 3pm? That way I have enough time to get back. It takes such a long time for Gerard to help me get to the cottage now.'

'No problem at all. Do you want me to meet you where the car is?'

Edamine huffed.

'Goodness no, Gerard and I have a routine when I visit. He'll see me to the door and take me back again, don't worry.'

Beau shook her head.

Of course.

'Shall I plate up extra–'

'Oh no, no. He won't expect that. I pay him handsomely, and he's used to leaving me down here alone for a few hours. I used to stay overnight at times. He will bring me down and pick me up when I ask him to. He doesn't expect anything, he's a good man.'

He must have a lot of patience, Beau thought. That would drive me nuts, especially as it's an hour or so each way for him.

'Okay, well, shall we say around two then? Give me time to spruce the place up and get cooking?'

'I have the nurse at half-past twelve, so I may be a little late after the journey, but I'll be as close to two as I can. I'll keep you updated.'

Beau nodded.

'Okay, I'll see you later, then.'

'Thank you, Beau. I'm very much looking forward to it. You've brightened my dull day, no end.'

'It's a pleasure.'

They ended the call, and Beau sat back in the car seat with a frown.

What the hell was that all about, Beau? Like you're not tired enough, now you have to clean and cook for your landlady?

The very landlady who may be playing games with you and trying to scare you?

Beau sat with that thought.

For what reason, though? Why would she pay for a sitter only to scare them out after a week and tell them they could go, too? Why bother?

It simply didn't make any sense. Edamine appeared to be amiable, and she didn't seem sadistic, so Beau was sure she wouldn't just be doing this for fun...

Or maybe that's just it. Maybe this is her thing, and she does this for kicks? Who knows what actually goes on in people's heads? Look at Hannah. She seems all sweet and hardworking. A loving mother and wife with drive and ambition, but if you peel away the layers and poke at the sore spot for too long, she turns nasty. Very nasty. You know that firsthand.

At the thought of Hannah, Beau felt a small flutter of unease, although why she would feel that up here, she didn't know. Hannah was miles away discussing business - or maybe she would be home by now. She certainly wasn't up here in the middle of nowhere.

When the unease didn't shift, Beau shook her head and climbed out of the car. She picked up the two shopping bags and her overnight bag and stared ahead.

Well, whether you have a penchant for attracting psycho women or not, the only major obstacle at the moment simply is getting the shopping home.

Beau tittered.

How many people can say that?

The cottage appeared both normal and yet ominous as Beau came closer, her legs tired, her arms and hands screaming, and her body craving coffee. She wanted to get inside and take the load off, but simultaneously wanted turn and run as far away as she could.

It was disconcerting, and her senses were on overload.

She came to a halt a few meters from the house, frozen, as though she had hit an invisible wall. She eyed the cottage, feeling like she couldn't breathe as it stared back. Cool air passed through her jacket and onto clothes that were wet from the long walk in the mist. She shuddered.

Placing the bags down at her feet, she pushed away the strings of wet hair that had stuck to her cheek and fingered the front door key in her pocket. It would be ridiculous to walk three miles back to the car and...

Go where, Beau? Where are you going? This is home for the next six months. Here is where you belong, and there's nothing wrong.

Still, her body hesitated, and her mind whirled.

What if someone got in while I was away? What if the man in red had got in and messed with my stuff? What if he touched the laptop and ruined or deleted my story? Worse, what if he has taken the laptop?

A little 'oh' left Beau's mouth, and she picked up the bags to stumble the last few meters to the front door, the critic in her mind stamping and shouting.

You idiot! Why didn't you take it with you? Why did you think it was safe? And let's face facts, Beau, you're not the only one who knows about the man in red, are you? Which means he's not in your imagination. There's really someone out here and you left everything valuable unattended at a cottage in the middle of bloody nowhere!

The critic finally fell silent at the front door as she slipped the key into the lock, her heart pounding behind her ribs.

Please be there, please be there, please let everything be okay.

Beau swallowed the lump in her throat as she turned the key and entered the hallway, dropped the bags to the floor, and paused.

The cottage was warm and silent. Nothing seemed to be out of place...

You're in the fucking hallway, Beau. What would be out of place, the grandfather clock?

She let out a breath, shut the door to keep the heat in the house, and stooped to untie her boots. They were soaked and Beau thought she may have two small blisters on the back of her heels, but as she kicked them off, she saw her socks were dry. Her feet sighed, and she congratulated herself on what she thought had been a highly expensive purchase. As the only dry part of her attire, right now, it turned out they had been worth it.

She stripped off her jacket, hung it to drip from the coat stand beside the door and began to move.

Right. Downstairs first, and then up and changed.

Her initial reaction appeared to be correct. Nothing seemed out of place, and nothing seemed moved or disturbed. The back door was shut and locked, as was the extension's door behind it. Her laptop sat shut on the middle of the dining table as she had left it, with the speaker behind, and her notebook neatly closed with her pen on top.

Just to be sure, she pulled open the lid, loaded the screen, and entered the password. The document was as she left it.

A weight dropped from her shoulders and a relieved sighed left her lips.

It's okay Beau, everything is okay, see? But next time you go out, take the bloody laptop, will you? That was the quickest way to have a heart attack!

She chuckled as she filled the kettle and pressed the switch before scanning the living room and ascending the stairs.

Bathroom. Check.

Red room. Check.

Green room. Check. Even her clothes were strewn over the bed as she had left them yesterday.

No-one has been here. It's all fine.

She moved to the window and scanned the landscape. Outside was quiet and motionless, and the sun was finally beginning to burn off the mist. Another nice day to come.

Beau smiled and finally felt at ease enough to strip out of her wet clothes and step into a hot shower. The water was bliss, and as thoughts about Edamine's visit later ran through her head, she was grateful that she wouldn't have to do much at all. The Cottage was almost spotless.

I'll catch up with some writing and then maybe get some air before cooking.

Yes, she had just walked three miles, but Gerard's words from yesterday were still hitting home and as she showered, she realised he was right. She wasn't getting out enough, and maybe she *was* seeing things that weren't there or attributing reasons to occurrences which simply weren't true. Maybe she *was* too hemmed in, too close, and with no one to take away her thoughts or the silence, wasn't it obvious that she would feel like this?

When Joe had told her living alone would be hard, she had imagined silencing a voice in her head and had been prepared to try to catch it out, but what she was getting wasn't voices, it was images and thoughts that were driving her insane.

Same coin, different sides?

As she dressed, her mind wandered to Joe and the memory of his late-night call. It was an odd time to phone, but it couldn't have been urgent. She'd call him later.

After running a brush through her hair, Beau opened the bathroom window a crack and stepped out onto the landing.

A square of white paper caught her eye by the bannister. She frowned and stepped toward it. There was something else, too. Tiny bits of scattered yellow fluff.

She stooped and fingered the yellow substance, which looked a little like candy floss, and then she turned her attention to the white paper, which felt like aged card between her fingers.

She turned it over and saw it was an old photograph. The colour was muted, a little overexposed, and there was a crease through one side. The photo showed two small girls, both in dresses, holding hands in front of the cottage. Something was written in small cursive hand on the bottom white edge of the picture. Beau squinted closer.

Best friends, 1981.

Beau wondered if one of the girls was Edamine, and then the picture was momentarily forgotten as she remembered where she'd seen the yellow fluff before.

Insulation. It's loft insulation... from the attic.

Beau felt her stomach clench as she looked at the loft hatch just above her. Her mouth was dry, and her scalp prickled.

She and Gerard had been in the attic on that first day, but surely, she would have noticed this over the last six days.

The photo caught your eye as you came from the bathroom. How many times have you been in and out of that room since you've been here? The picture wasn't here. It wasn't here yesterday either, I'm almost certain.

Beau looked back down at the photo in her hand, and then back to the hatch.

Someone had been in here while she had been away. And what about the footsteps she had heard from above in the middle of the night? Were they up there that night while she was asleep just underneath? Had they been up there all along?

Beau recalled Ophelia's warning from last light. *It worries me that you're not alone out there.* Her heart lurched as she let out a gasp, all of the air leaving her body in one breath.

The idea was terrifying, but the insulation suggested that they'd left, didn't it? Or at least they'd come down at some point while she'd been out.

But did they leave, or are they still up there? Are they up there now?

Goosebumps littered her flesh as Beau looked at the hatch. It was shut tight. There was no way of knowing unless she went up there.

Absolutely not.

You should check. How will you sleep otherwise?

Are you fucking crazy? I'm not going up there while I'm here alone. What if there's some psycho up there?

Well, who the hell else is going to go up there and check for you? You live alone now in case you hadn't noticed.

Noted. And as long as the psycho stays in the attic...

Beau paused mid thought and almost swooned with relief. Gerard. Gerard would bring Edamine this afternoon, she could ask him to go up and check.

You'll have to think of a good excuse, or he will be calling the local asylum and booking your place.

I think I can manage that, she thought, as she looked at the innocent white square in the ceiling and shivered. She listened. Were there any sounds from above? Any footsteps, shuffling, or movement?

There was only silence as Beau's eyes bored into the hatch, and then a click and a hiss downstairs made her jump out of her skin. She swung to the stairs, her heart almost coming out of her chest, and then she blew out a breath and placed a hand on her thumping heart.

'It's the bloody kettle, Beau. The kettle you put on for a coffee just five minutes ago. Maybe you should stop looking for anomalies and drink one, and then you can get the hell out of here and clear your head. Christ on a beanpole, if you stay here much longer, I think you may actually go insane!'

Chapter 24

D ANIEL MATHERSON ZIPPED HIS coat as he crossed the single-track road and sauntered down the path toward the cliff. It was a couple of miles to get to the ruin, but there was no rush. Lucas had sent him on break until 2pm when they had another customer checking in. That was to be the highlight of the day at the Antler Hotel.

Still, he couldn't complain, he was getting free rent, room, and meals, for doing nothing much, and while that may have been boring to some, he was a perpetual learner, and he supposed that made him different. There was always something that he wanted to explore, most of the time several things, and there was never enough time for him to get fully absorbed at home like there was here at the Antler.

Perpetual learner.

Daniel smiled as he followed the faded track in the grass to the crest of the hill that revealed the twinkling ocean beyond. It was perfect here. Not only the scenery, but the ability for motion. It had been the motion that had pulled things together. From his time here, Daniel understood that he was a self titled 'instinctive motion learner'. The motion and meditation of walking allowed him to mull over and process what he had learned, allowed him to cement the learning and twist it into different forms and analogies that allowed perfect recall when he needed it. The walking during his travels, and especially here, had taught him as much as the research. That was the part that never connected at home, where he hadn't been allowed to go out with friends, and girls were nowhere in the mix. He hadn't minded. There was too much information to dig into at home after all, but now that he had left and had the freedom to travel, it was like the final pieces of the puzzle were slipping into place.

He'd earned the perpetual learner title from his father at eight years old when he'd stepped into Daniel's room early one Sunday morning and found him watching a video that took him through the detailed design and engineering of his favourite plane: Concord. That the plane flew at supersonic speeds had him enthralled, and Daniel gorged information, only to spit it back out to anyone who would listen. He wanted to know everything. From the engineering and aerodynamics to the seat layouts and the uniforms of the captain and crew. Everything from wingspan to the cockpit buttons, and from the warning alarms to the speed and altitude, and that fatal Air France crash on his birthday – the twenty-fifth of July.

He had been so enthralled with the plane that his mom had once laughed that he had been aboard that fatal Air France flight before later being reincarnated as a Matherson. That had been during a large Thanksgiving dinner with the family where even Daniel could admit, looking back, that he'd been more than a little annoying as he regurgitated every bit of information he could on his new audience. It had started a love affair with knowledge, and he just couldn't get enough.

A nerd. I'm a nerd, and proud of it. I just love information.

His dad had initially been amused and impressed with his son's dedication, but then, as Daniel got older and his whims had taken time away from studying what he should have been, he had got angry. A fond pat on the head and 'come my little perpetual learner' had turned into a spat 'Son, you're a perpetual annoyance', and Daniel felt his father's intense psychological wrath daily, because as much as Daniel loved science and engineering, he was supposed to follow in his father's footsteps and become a lawyer. He would continue partnering at the firm his father co-owned and live the life that had been put in place for him. Daniel, who had little interest in law, found every way he could to scrape by so that he could study what he really wanted to. Space, ecology, warfare, nuclear fission, global warming, and everything in between. He adored deep diving into things which tested his brain and taught him new ways of looking at the world, and hated the old essays, archaic rules, and strictness of law.

As the ruined church came nearer, and the brisk warm wind caressed his cheeks, he wondered if he would ever go home and thought probably not. The thought made him a little sad, but mostly excited for his future. He couldn't sit indoors, behind a desk, with a planned out future, 2.5 kids, and a 401K. He'd die. Just wither and die. Life was so much more exciting out here on his own terms. He could go where the wind blew him, and that was just fine.

Well, right now it's doing its best to blow you back to the hotel. Maybe that's a sign Anna Lane is waiting for you.

Daniel grinned as he hunkered down and pressed on. The church ruins were in sight, and once he got behind the church walls, he'd be fine. He'd take a rest and then head on down to the little cottage, because Anna was almost certainly waiting for him. She was pushing for an answer about her sister, but as of yet Daniel had only seen one person down at the base of the cliff, and they hadn't been at the house at all, but on the beach. The woman could have been a hiker for all he knew, and until he was certain, he wouldn't be saying anything.

At the moment, he was getting exactly what he wanted from Anna. It was sweet, and the longer he held information back, the more she would give. It was perfect, and she was a perfect enigma, but he wasn't under any illusion that it would last. She was trying to keep him on side, trying to extract information, and he wasn't stupid. She would move on when her sister turned up, and Daniel would put her down to an exciting part of his adventure.

For now, though, he would enjoy every moment of being here with her and helping her solve her mystery.

He strode on to the church, pulled by the view of the ocean and the islands beyond that he knew he would see on a day as clear as this. And it wasn't only the view out to sea, the edge of the cliffs shaping the land was just as alluring. Edges were the highlights of his trips to both Ireland and Scotland, where he had been by the coast. He loved the edges of land, the years of strata in the rock, the fossils he had found on the beaches below, all those billions of years of history. He found he was loving the outdoors more than he thought he would too, after years stuck inside on a computer in his spare time, he was loving the wind against his skin, and the warmth of the sun, and even the occasional pelting with hail. Natural science and history really came to life when you were surrounded by it.

When Daniel finally rounded the corner and came upon the church, still holding its own right on the edge of the cliff, he stalled. There was someone else blocking the best view from the top, and he was so startled that he almost yelled. In all the times he had been up here, he had never crossed paths with another living soul.

He blinked and shook his head, but she was still there, silhouetted in the vast arch that was once a huge, stained glass church window. Granted, the window would have been impressive, but not as impressive as the view from the open gap now, he bet. The woman under the arch had the best view right now.

Daniel assessed her. She didn't seem to be dressed for hiking, and her red hair wasn't fixed like someone who had walked miles, it cascaded down her back, blowing back from her concealed face. But if she wasn't hiking why the hell else would she be out here? To get out to the church was at least three miles across any terrain.

As he moved closer, his eyes dropped from her brown waist cut leather jacket, to her jeans and...

Hiking boots. I guess I read her wrong after all.

Daniel curled one side of his mouth as he huffed a laugh. Should have known. Increasingly on his travels, he was learning not to judge a book by its cover.

And now how to approach a lone woman on a cliff edge in the middle of nowhere?

Daniel was a big guy, he knew that, so he decided to introduce himself. He understood what it was like to want to be alone to appreciate the view with your own thoughts, but if she turned and saw him, she might panic at his presence, and he didn't want that. Instead, he strode forward, lifting a hand.

'Hi! Lovely morning.'

The woman turned as he approached, and he relaxed. She was less afraid than he thought, a smile fixed to her face in greeting, a pretty face, too. One he had seen before.

'Hi.'

She pushed her hair from her face and the smile faltered, as if she suddenly realised her predicament up here with a stranger. She took a step back, and Daniel's heart skipped over.

'No, don't.'

He lunged forward, catching her arm as her foot caught the low wall where part of the underneath of the window had collapsed. Beyond was a sixty-foot drop which led to the ocean. She yelped as he pulled her upright, his heart in his mouth.

'That was close.'

The woman gasped as he held onto her, and she swivelled her head to the see the small ledge of grass that was all that would have saved her from falling to certain death.

'Thank you. I... I...'

Daniel moved back from the ledge, pulling the lady with him. She was older, he surmised, perhaps in her forties, but looked good for her age. A little like Anna, but with more of a modern vibe. Strange how these women were suddenly turning up out here. Where were they coming from? And where did he know this one from? He was sure he'd seen her before.

'No problem. I startled you, I'm sorry. I'm Daniel.'

He held his hand toward her, and she stared at it for a while before looking back up at him. Not as unafraid as he'd thought. He took his hand away.

'It's okay. I hike around here a lot. I have to say I haven't seen anyone else up here though yet, you're the first. Where have you hiked from?'

The woman crossed her arms over her chest.

'I've seen you before.'

Daniel faltered. Of all her responses, he hadn't expected that one, but then, he'd had that nagging feeling of familiarity too when she'd turned.

'Yeah, I get that too. You seem familiar somehow. Where did we meet? Was it here? Or do you travel around? Maybe I've seen you on my-'

'Down at the cottage. I know it was you, I recognise the coat... well, the colour. It doesn't blend in with the scenery when you're trying to hide.'

Daniel felt himself physically reel back.

'Hide? Why would I...'

And then it came back to him in a flash. This was the woman on the beach. The woman he had run from rather than have to explain why he was watching her from the corner of the cottage.

'Oh! Right, you were the lady on the beach last week.'

'I certainly was, and you were watching me.'

Daniel swallowed, trying to think of a good explanation. He *had* been watching, as he watched any beautiful woman, although she was a little older than he first thought now that he was up close, and he had been staking out the cottage. Neither of which would go down well here, but Daniel was a firm believer that truth was always the best option. Lies just twisted you into knots, which only pulled tighter.

He dropped his gaze and pursed his lips, trying to look innocuous.

'I was. I'm sorry.'

The woman, whose face had become both defiant and steadfast, opened her mouth. If she was going to speak, then no words were coming out, and Daniel thought he'd better explain further.

'Look, I'm a young guy, and you looked beautiful out there. Your hair was blazing in the sunset. It was quite a sight.'

The lady rolled her eyes and looked away.

'If you were that intrigued, why didn't you introduce yourself? You've had no trouble today.'

Daniel wanted to show her he was genuine, to make her feel more comfortable. He hadn't meant to frighten her that day, or any day, and yet he had. He'd done the wrong thing.

'Well, this place is a little more open, and I didn't want to startle you if you turned and saw me waiting to admire the view.' He gestured at the large arch of the window. 'It's pretty spectacular, right?'

The lady shrugged.

'What's the difference between up here and down there?'

Daniel blew out a breath.

'Like I said, it's more open. The cove is enclosed with the sea behind it, I could have been perceived as threatening, and you may have felt trapped. I hate that men get the rep of being up to no good if they come across a woman alone in an isolated place, but I understand that I'm a big guy. I didn't want you to panic.'

'So you ran? Like that would make me feel better?'

Daniel held up his hands. 'It was the wrong thing to do. I know that now.'

The lady still had her arms crossed over her chest; she wasn't giving him an inch. Whatever was eating this woman wasn't his fault. She clearly had issues, and she was ruining his morning stakeout on this rare, cloudless day.

'Well, I'm sorry. Be a little more careful around the edge. I'll let you get back to your day. Nice to meet you.'

I think.

He turned toward the slope at the side of the hill and stepped over the low wall.

'Wait! Where are you going?'

Daniel paused and looked back over his shoulder, unsure what she wanted. 'To continue my walk.'

'That way?'

'Why not?'

The woman seemed to be churning something over, and so he waited.

It was silly, really; he owed her nothing, but it was the way he had been brought up. Be kind, smile, people are generally good, even when they seem like they're not. People have issues, his mom had once said, and we have no idea what they are or how they're dealing with them, Daniel. Sometimes a smile will go a long way in their day.

His mom was the kindest woman he'd ever met, the only reason he'd been reluctant to leave home, and the only reason he'd cried on the plane to Poland. It had broken his heart... which was also silly when he still spoke to her at least twice a week. Not too much info, just enough that she knew he was okay, and vice versa.

'There's nothing down there. Only the cottage,' the lady finally said.

'And a beach.'

They stared at each other, and Daniel really couldn't understand the problem. He sighed heavily and fell back on his theory that honesty was best.

'Look, if I'm being honest, not that it has anything to do with you, I'm trying to locate the person who lives in the cottage.'

There was silence, and then.

'Why? What do you want with them?'

Daniel headed back towards the lady. Obviously, this conversation wasn't over, and there was a small chance that she knew something.

'Do you know who it is?'

'I might. Why do you need to know?'

Daniel felt a grin spread across his face and a weight lift from his shoulders.

'You know her? That's amazing. You certainly meet people for a reason, don't you think?'

The lady's mouth was a straight line, and Daniel wished she would lighten up.

'Why do you need to know who lives there? If you're fishing for whether it's abandoned so that you can squat-'

Daniel felt like he was in the twilight zone. So much of this conversation felt unreal.

'Actually no. I'm not. I need to find the woman who lives there. I have some... information for her. I don't want to scare anybody and I'm not trying to hurt anybody.'

'Well, *Daniel*.' He flinched at her use of his name. 'There are alarms all around the house and CCTV inside and out. The place is isolated, but it has security and deadbolts. There are security guards who are on alert and can be at the house within ten minutes should anything happen. Big men. Tough men. Men who make *you* look like a weed.'

Daniel felt his jaw drop. He knew the terrain, and if he knew one thing for sure, there was no way anyone could walk there in ten minutes. Maybe there was an access road? Not that he'd seen one. And why the hell would a cottage where no one came need that kind of security, anyway?

'Okay. How would you know that? It looks old, and I haven't seen any cameras.'

He had looked too, just in case he was had up for trespassing, because let's face it, it would look suspicious when he had been there a lot over the last couple of days but had never seen a living soul.

The lady seemed to be working up to something, and then she blurted out words that were music to his ears.

'I know because I live there, and I may look old to you, young man, but I'm a black belt in karate, too. Just for reference.'

Daniel almost laughed with relief. This lady was on edge for certain, and she was trying to keep him away from the cottage, but if she really lived there, then he didn't have to go down again anyway - unless he fancied a dip in the sea on that side. He assessed the lady in front of him. She looked around Anna's age, and Anna had said that there were only a couple of years between them, so that would be right. She was pretty like Anna too, in a slightly different, more spiky, way. The family obviously had good genes. But a karate black belt? Nah.

'So what information do you have for me that has you staking out my cottage every day?'

Daniel blinked, and his smile slipped.

Oh shit, Anna said not to speak to her, and she'll be mad if I go into the reason.

Well, it's not my fault I bumped into her up here. Anna said that her sister wouldn't want to know her, but maybe there is a chance that she does. They haven't spoken for many years. How would Anna know what her sister wants?

Not that she looked very accommodating at the moment, he supposed.

Just tell the truth. What harm can it do?

'Look, I'm sorry. I've been in contact with your sister. She's searching for you, wants to make amends or something.'

The lady raised her eyebrows. 'My sister? I don't have a sister.'

Daniel shrugged. 'Yeah, she said you might say that. Apparently, there's some big feud you guys are having?'

The lady wrinkled her nose and shook her head. 'I have no idea what you're talking about, or what you're trying to achieve here. I do not have a sister, I promise you.'

'But you do live in the cottage, right?' The lady stared at him and Daniel let it drop. 'Okay, wrong person, clearly. I didn't mean to offend you... again.'

'What does she look like?' the lady suddenly asked.

Daniel laughed. He couldn't help it. That was a clear insinuation that she *did* have a sister and coupled with the fact that she lived at the cottage and had the same petite features, this was definitely the woman he was searching for. No more needed saying, really, but he'd humour her.

'A little like you, but blonde. Slim, petite, big blue eyes. Your eyes are prettier though, I'd say, that's quite a colour.'

'It's green.'

'A striking green.'

'You have a real way with adjectives, don't you, Daniel?'

Daniel grinned. Maybe this was the opening to make this woman a little less spiky. He didn't envy Anna the task of trying to apologise and make amends with this lady, though. Tough call. Either way, for now he would back off, try to keep her unsuspecting, and throw her off the scent until he could speak to Anna.

'Maybe. I just say what I see. Listen, I'm sorry, I must have you confused with someone else. I'm sorry to have bothered you. I obviously have the wrong cottage. You won't see me around there again.'

The lady nodded and then finally uncrossed her arms with a sigh. 'Thank you. I suppose it's good to know that you weren't staking me out for other reasons.'

'Not at all.' Daniel looked at the clear blue sky and rolled his shoulders. 'Well, I'll be off now. Enjoy the rest of your day.'

'You too.'

He turned back the way he'd come and then took another path to the right, which led to the coastal path, and down to another beach further along. He didn't intend to go there now, but he couldn't go back yet either. His adrenaline was on fire. He'd obviously found Anna's sister, and Anna had been right to say she wouldn't be welcoming, but now that left Daniel without a mission and a cause. This was the only thing Anna had asked him to do. Now she would continue alone, and he would be back to the internet and a quiet hotel.

Oh, well, it was fun while it lasted, Matherson. Now you just have to hope you've done the right thing.

Right, because Anna is obviously a murderer! The worst that will come out of this is an even more prolonged feud and a bit of bitch slapping... probably from the redhead.

As he walked along the coast, Daniel found himself wondering what it would be like to have the both of them. Maybe his next mission would be to charm his way in with the redhead. She had a fire and a steeliness that he liked. Anna had been easy to bed, but her sister would be a challenge.

First, though, he had to find out if she lived alone. If there was a husband or lover involved, he wouldn't stoop that low. Then things became not fun, fast.

Mission 1a in succession, and maybe I won't tell Anna about this one.

Chapter 25

B EAU SLIPPED ON LOOSE earth, just about caught her balance, and stumbled on, hurrying back down the hill to the cottage. The one person she hadn't expected to see on her church excursion was the man in the red coat - or maybe that should be the boy – and she hadn't expected him to admit that he had been hanging around the cottage, either. Her heart was still hammering at their altercation, and she still felt that she'd had a lucky escape somehow, although he hadn't made any move to harm her.

She didn't believe his story any more than she believed Edamine was guilt free in what was happening at the cottage, but at least now she knew what she was up against if she caught him hanging around the cottage again.

Is he a stalker?

It wasn't an unknown; she had one in the past which had turned out fairly innocent in the end but had been pretty scary while it had been going on. Patrick had done all of the heavy lifting back then though, and he had protected her at every turn.

Now you have no one.

It's ridiculous anyway. How would a stalker know that I'm out here? I've not posted anything since the split with Patrick. No-one knows I'm here except Hannah and Joe.

Maybe it's from when he saw you on the beach?

How would he recognise me from that far away? That's ludicrous, I'm hardly Julia Roberts.

Halfway back down the cliff, Beau's phone rang, and her heart plummeted. If that was Edamine calling to cancel, then she wouldn't be able to gauge whether she knew anything. She also wouldn't have Gerard to check the attic before tonight.

Shit, no, no, please.

She stopped, fumbled in her pocket for her phone, and pulled it out to see Joe's name lighting the screen. She blinked and stared and then her brain clicked into gear as the call rang off.

Joe. Joe called last night. I didn't ring him back.

Her hands shaking with relief, Beau called him back, he answered almost immediately.

'Hi, Joe, are you okay? I forgot to call you back. I'm sorry.'

'No, I'm sorry it was so late. I was in such a hurry, I didn't look at the time.'

'A hurry? What's going on? You should have left me a voicemail or messaged if it was urgent. I saw the call last night, I just didn't want to call you back that late.'

'Don't worry about it. It was my mistake, and it's not so urgent that I couldn't speak to you today, anyway.'

Beau saw a large smooth boulder sunken into the ground at the edge of the path. It was a perfect place to sit, sheltered from the wind, and fully sunbaked. She on the warm stone and stared out across the cliff edge to the ocean, trying not to think about the dark forest behind her.

'So what's happened? Is it Hannah?'

'How did you guess?'

Beau grinned and Joe told her about the call with Hannah, and he and Leila being out past her bedtime. As she wondered why this was such urgent information, the deep blue swell ahead lulled her. She couldn't see the cliff edge or the shore from here, but she could hear the hiss of the waves from the beach by the cottage further down. Birds chirped and called all around her and somewhere a cuckoo called incessantly. Aside from the wind rustling through the trees, there were no other sounds up here. It really was peaceful.

Peaceful. Cut off. Isolated. Lonely.

Nice one, Beau. Shut the hell up, idiot.

She focused her attention back on Joe's voice.

'...I don't think she noticed in the end because she was that pissed off with you.'

Beau felt herself wince as she smiled. 'What? I'm nowhere near her, haven't spoken to her for days, and she can still get pissed off with me?'

'Yes.'

There was a beat of silence, and Beau rolled her eyes. Honestly, this was a friendship she would definitely keep at arm's length when things got back to normal. Funny how people showed their true colours when you did something they didn't like or agree with.

Funny how Hannah takes everything to catastrophic proportions!

'Okay, I guess I won't bother texting her any time soon then. Thanks for the info, Joe, and I'm glad she didn't catch on to you being out. God, life wouldn't have been worth living!'

She was half joking and expected Joe to laugh with her, but he didn't. Weirdly, when he spoke, he sounded almost nervous.

'I know. I almost crapped myself when I saw her name on the screen. Luckily, there weren't really any other kids on the park to make a noise. It was fairly quiet. I'm thanking my lucky stars.'

Beau laughed. 'Come on, Joe, you almost sound serious. I know she can be opinionated and feisty sometimes, but was it really that bad?'

There was another silence, and Beau heard the wind rustle the trees above her. The sun briefly hid behind a cloud, and then came back out again.

'It was bad. The whole call was bad. I know that you've seen how she can be, right?'

Beau frowned. 'I remember her paying too much for the Egyptian clay, and taking it out on you for days, although you had tried to stop her.'

'Exactly. And there's worse. More that you haven't seen.'

'But you didn't seem bothered at the time. I was uncomfortable, but it seemed to roll off your shoulders. I remember thinking you were the most laid-back man on earth.' Beau pursed her lips and swallowed hard. 'I may have used another word in my head, to be honest.'

'Gullible?'

'Along those lines. I didn't know why you put up with it, but then you're obviously both very much in love. Twelve years and still going strong. That's to be celebrated, Joe.'

Joe coughed.

'Maybe. I don't know. A lot of our life is her way or the highway. I get little say in anything.'

Beau frowned and felt an urge to defend her friend.

'Come on, Joe, she works hard so that you don't have to. You get to be at home with Leila all day, you get to have that fun relationship with your daughter, and you get to do what you want. It would look pretty perfect to someone slogging a nine to five to pay bills they can barely afford. They'd love your freedom!'

'You don't see it. It's not freedom, Beau. It's a prison.'

Beau stumbled and found she couldn't respond. This demeanour was so out of character for happy-go-lucky Joe that she wondered if she was talking to an imposter.

'It looks idyllic to the outside world, I know that,' he continued. 'I have everything I want, and all the time in the world to appreciate it. And I *do*; some of it. Leila is an angel, and that's why I don't complain. She's the reason I put up with so much, but I... Christ, what's wrong with me?'

Beau caught the sob and felt her heart stagger. Hannah would be devastated if she knew he was talking like this, but her heart also went out to Joe, who did put up with a lot. Beau knew that. She had seen it.

'Joe? Are you thinking of leaving?'

There was another sob and Beau let him have his moment.

'No. I... I can't.'

Despite her unease, Beau felt a trickle of relief slide down her spine. Hannah would not be happy at all if he'd said yes, because despite how she treated him, Beau knew that she loved him dearly. Beau had also heard about the other side of the boyfriend before him, who called it off after he found someone else more interesting. That revenge had looked like breaking into his house and smashing all she could get her hands on, ending with the man himself. Lucky for him she'd had no weapon, but she had spent six months in jail, and if you asked her now, it was still the most satisfying thing she had ever done.

Beau's mind flashed back to the moment Hannah had told Beau the story. They were drinking cocktails in a downtown bar, and it had seemed hilariously funny. They even laughed about how she had slashed every item of clothing.

'I may have been in jail, but he was using student loans and debt to pay for new underwear. I never spoke to him afterward. There was a restraining order against me, but I was staking him out for quite some time, making sure he suffered like I had. It was great fun.'

They both laughed and sipped more cocktails and, as happened in new friendships, Beau put the story down to exaggeration and showing off. Hannah liked to seem a little 'out there' while keeping a perfectly normal outside façade. She liked to think she was clever, and Beau knew that she was, but she didn't believe she would have gone that far for a romance that had lasted just four months. It was just too farfetched.

Now that the memory of that evening was coming back, there was a small thread of fear winding through her stomach. Had Hannah really done it? Had Beau been wrong to dismiss it? Did Joe know about it?

Her hand was shaking, and she pushed the phone into her cheek to stop it knocking against her face. Joe was sobbing openly, and Beau fought against her own emotions. Was it really as bad as she thought? Maybe the story had just been that... a story.

Or maybe not. What then?

Joe began to sniffle and apologise, and the swirl in Beau's stomach wanted her to say - *please, Joe, don't do it - or if you do, make sure you do a moonlight flit somewhere far, far away, where she'll never find you.*

What she found herself saying was: 'It's okay, Joe, let it out. Things are going to be fine. You can work this out. If you still feel that you love her, that's good, and things can be changed. All you need to do is sit down with Hannah and talk-'

Joe heaved a sound that sounded like a strange mix between a sob and laughter.

'Have you ever tried to talk to Hannah? Especially about your feelings? It'll end up in an argument and she'll just let me know where I stand again. That's how things work in our house.'

Beau nodded, and the fear in her chest made it hard to breathe. 'I know. She loves the fights because she loves the making up. To be fair, you both seem to enjoy the making up...' The attempt at lightening the mood fell flat, and she trailed off, her cheeks red.

'No. You don't understand Beau. I hate it. I hate the arguments, and I hate the making up, because it's false, and it's controlling, and it's... it's... it makes me feel sick. She doesn't know, but if we've been fighting and I know the next bit is coming? I have to slip a blue pill. And if I forget to take it and it doesn't get...hard... she's vile. She tells me I've got problems, and I need to book an appointment to get myself sorted. She threatened to cut it off in my sleep once. Needless to say, I moved to the settee and didn't sleep a wink.'

Beau blinked and was glad she was already sitting down, because at that statement she felt that she may have fallen.

'Er...what? I don't get it, Joe. Surely you know she was joking, she would never do something like that!'

There was a sniff. 'I don't know if she would or not. That's reality. This is life for me, Beau, and I want to reiterate how bad it is. I feel like I suddenly see, and I want to hold nothing back. It's important for two reasons. One because I'm sick to death of playing happy families, and two, you need to know what she's really like.'

If Beau thought the world was off kilter before, it was definitely hanging by one thread and swinging sideways now. Bile rose into her throat.

Had Hannah been telling the truth about that poor guy? *Did* Joe know?

And you were laughing and egging her on?

'Joe, I-'

'Beau. I need you to listen, for both of us. Can you do that?'

Beau closed her eyes and tried to swallow her vomit, before spitting on the ground beside her. She half wondered if she'd wake in bed.

Please tell me this is a bad dream.

'Beau? Please, I need to say this.'

She opened her eyes and stared at the deep blue ahead, some-how knowing this was a pivot point. After this? Things would change, and there would be no going back. She felt it, deep in her bones.

'Okay, I'm listening.'

Chapter 26

F OR THE SECOND TIME that morning Beau was stumbling down the hill toward the cottage, but this time there was a pit in her stomach so large she didn't think she'd be able to eat, let alone focus on cooking and entertaining Edamine. She had vomited once as Joe told his story, and then twice more on the way back. She was shaking and depleted of energy by the time the cottage drew near.

Joe hadn't known about the previous boyfriend, and hadn't known about the jail time, but he took everything Beau said on board, because, well, he had lived with Hannah for twelve years and unlike Beau when she had been a new friend, Joe knew she was perfectly capable.

It had reinforced what he had always secretly feared. He could never leave.

He told Beau that lately he had been a little more authoritative and stood his ground more - now he regretted that stance. What if he wound her up further?

Beau had agreed that if he wanted to get out - and she didn't blame him at all after the things he told her - he needed to be very careful and plan every single detail. This was a woman who was profiling serial killers for fun, remember?

Beau had attempted to project the statement as humour, but it had felt wildly true and had hit a nerve with both of them, especially when Joe got down to the real reason he was calling.

Hannah was a leech (Beau didn't change his wording). She loved to latch onto one person and become their world, and of course she was to become theirs too. She was a one friend girl and gave all to the relationship, doting on that friend like there was nobody else, and there really wasn't for Hannah. She was all in.

Beau had nodded her agreement. She and Patrick had other friends they saw initially, but eventually Hannah commandeered all of Beau's time and they began to go out separately. Patrick would meet their friends, and Beau would meet Hannah. At the time, Beau had thought it healthy. She had always relied on Patrick, and Hannah was giving her confidence and allowing her opportunities to do things she would never have done otherwise. In the end, Patrick had seen it as being pushed away and had walked into the arms of one of those friends. Hannah had jumped on this as evidence that Beau couldn't trust anyone but her and had moved her into the house almost immediately.

Looking back over that with hindsight made Beau feel sick. What Joe said next forced that vomit out.

What Beau didn't know was that Hannah had been searching for another friend for about nine months before Beau came on the scene. Before that, there had been someone else. Cassie.

Hannah and Cassie had been friends since college. They were tight, close, and did everything together. Hannah had even moved Cassie into her one bed flat so that they had more time together - flat mates. When Hannah met Joe and they fell in love, Joe moved into the bedroom with Hannah, and Cassie slept on a pull-out in the tiny lounge.

Sound familiar?

Joe said that things were tense as the space was so small, but every time Cassie suggested moving out, Hannah shut her down. After a tense couple of years - yes, *years* - Cassie finally moved out. Joe said that she literally moved down the street, but Hannah swung between distraught and furious.

She had given her a place to stay? Didn't she appreciate that? How could she be so selfish?

'Attachment issues,' Beau had muttered.

'She has attachment issues, for sure, but that's just scratching the surface.'

It had been the first Joe had seen of her 'other side', but he wasn't too concerned, he knew Hannah loved hard, and she had been friends with Cassie for many years at that point.

The crux came when Cassie drowned in a lake three months later.

Beau's heart had almost stopped when he said that Hannah was never found guilty, and never admitted guilt, but he had found all sorts of information on her laptop that said otherwise. The main thing was that Cassie couldn't swim and Hannah knew that when she suggested a weekend in the Lake District and planned a day boating on the lake. She said it was a tragic accident. Cassie had tried to stand and had fallen overboard. Hannah had tried to pull her in - and there were witnesses to that - but how hard? She said that without paddling, the current from the wind was sweeping the boat away from Cassie, but while she was paddling, she couldn't get her friend out of the water. It was a no-win situation.

In the end, Hannah jumped in and tried to rescue Cassie by towing her back to the boat, lifesaving style, but the boat drifted, and Hannah ended up almost drowning herself as people came to the rescue. By the time rescuers reached them, Hannah was in trouble and Cassie... well, Cassie had already gone.

Joe had paused here as nausea swirled in Beau's stomach.

What's wrong with that story? He had asked.

Beau knew immediately. Hannah was a strong swimmer and had swum competitively when she was younger, she also had a lifesaving certification and had been a lifeguard at the local pool for many years before starting her business three years ago.

'Right. There were a few articles about the incident, not many, because it was said to be a tragic accident, and Cassie's family obviously knew that Hannah loved her like a sister. They grieved for Hannah's loss almost as much as they did for their daughter. There was no way Hannah had contributed to Cassie's death, was there? But if you look at the picture printed in the Times on the date of the accident? - look online so that you can zoom in on the picture, Beau - It almost looks to me that Hannah is holding her underwater. Not only that, but look at her face. It's pixelated, obviously, but as someone who knows every inch of Hannah as much as I do, just have a look and see if you come to the same conclusion. Look hard because it's not obvious.'

Beau stumbled as she went over the conversation in her head, and finally came to a stop. She leaned on a tree at the edge of the forest and heaved breaths so large she didn't know whether she was trying to breathe or trying to throw up again. She closed her eyes against the spin of the land and tried to calm herself.

It's okay. Just because you and Joe exchanged stories doesn't mean anything. She's better, now. Whatever happened to each of those people, it's in the past. Hannah is a different person.

When Beau met Hannah, she had been going through coun-selling for an issue that Beau now understood was Cassie's death. Joe said that she had abandonment and trust issues, she said, which stemmed from her mother leaving the family home in a sea of wrath every few months, only to return days later and pretend that it never happened. She told Joe the correct terminology and what she had been told to do, mainly to respond instead of reacting to people. If she felt the anger come up, she would take herself away from the situation for a while and reflect on the response she wanted to give, not the impulse reaction. Joe said that he had been proud of her as she worked through her issues with a therapist, but he said that she had ditched all form of therapy just after she met Beau, and that her anger and control now seemed worse than ever.

'Doesn't mean history will repeat itself.' Beau whispered. 'Han-nah loves you and Joe. She's just angry. If she had control and abandonment issues, then it makes perfect sense why, doesn't it?'

Then another thought hit Beau as her breathing slowed.

'That's why she's gone away! She told Joe it was a business meeting, but that doesn't make any sense. She's never done that before so suddenly. So, she's taken herself out of the situation, as she learned to do, and will be back when she has processed it. It's obvious she's still angry, that's why she snaps at poor Joe, but the point here is... she's done the right thing. She's not coming for any of us. She's done what she was supposed to do.'

Beau felt a swell of pride, and tears came to her eyes as she thought of the way they had just discussed her, like she was some sort of monster.

I need to message Joe and tell him. He obviously hasn't thought of it like that because of the pressure he's under.

Beau stepped away from the tree and walked the final few meters to the cottage. The land flattened out and the thunder of the waves came to her ears. The wind was up, and clouds were scudding across the sky with more dark heaviness than earlier.

Pulled toward the inlet of sand, she stopped to stare at the waves. Their sound rhythmic and almost calming she realised as she pushed down her fear before it rose.

Did you ever think you could be calmed by a wave last week?

Beau raised an eyebrow.

Never. Not by water and especially not by the ocean. That's a first.

She closed her eyes against the cool breeze and stood, breathing in and then out, until each crash seemed to soothe her soul.

See? Everything is fine. There's nothing to worry about here, nothing at all.

Pretty amazing how you're changing already, writing, and now being soothed by the sea? You'll be out in that boat next!

Beau opened her eyes and stared at the small boat still tied to the cliff face. Her heart lurched and she swallowed hard as the suppressed fear raised it's head.

Maybe not just yet... if ever.

She looked back at the sea and noticed the sky over the islands beyond. Black and thunderous. Wind pushed her hair away from her face, and she knew it was headed this way.

A storm? I should have checked the weather. Maybe I'll message Edamine and see if she wants to rearrange. It's already getting cold.

She crossed her arms against the cool air as a shiver ran through her, and then she turned back to the house with a smile. It'd be pretty cool to watch a storm over the ocean from her bedroom window, especially now she was becoming more acquainted with it.

Her eyes travelled up the cottage with the first ripple of fondness she'd felt.

It's not so bad here, is it? I can do this after all.

She almost stuck a finger up at Hannah, wherever she was in the world, and then she felt a wedge of guilt. Hannah had been angry when she said those things. She was trying, she just needed...

Beau's heart stalled as her eyes fell on the small round attic window and she recalled Ophelia's words.

There's a girl, long dark hair, and a huge mouth. She likes to argue.

Beau searched the darkness behind the glass, and then let out a small breath. There was nothing up there, no movement, and if Daniel Red Coat was done hanging around here, then she could bet that there wouldn't be movement at all.

He had dark hair, although it wasn't long... but he wasn't female...

Beau shook her head.

Get over it Beau, it's time to leave the run of your imagination in your stories where it belongs. This is doing you no good.

It took her almost reaching the wraparound porch to realise what had been wrong with that whole scenario and come to a halt. She stared back up at the window with her heart banging.

The window. She could see the glass, and yet last week when Gerard had showed her how to open the window, he had closed the shutters over the glass. Not only had she asked him to; she had watched him do it.

You saw him! He hasn't been up there since, and you sure as hell haven't, so who opened the shutters, Beau? Who opened the damn shutters?

She tried to calm her racing mind.

Gerard will be here in a couple of hours. He'll shut them over before the storm.

But who the hell opened them?

Gerard will check the attic. If there's someone there, or that has been there, he will find them.

Why are they fucking open, though? Why?

Chill Beau, they could even have blown open, they're old! Let Gerard check it out later.

I'm not happy. Not at all.

Not happy, but certainly getting cold standing in the shadow of the house, Beau decided she was right. It was all she could do. Gerard would be here soon, and until then, she had dinner to prep.

Unless you're going up there to check (and you're NOT), then forget it until later. Put it to the back of your mind.

Beau tried.

And then she entered the cottage.

Chapter 27

S ITTING ON THE BED in her room, Anna paused, her hands
poised over the keyboard of her laptop. A cigarette burned
in a small saucer on the bedspread. She picked it up, flicking
back her long dark hair and feeling the brush of silk against her
upper arms. The dressing gown sat low off her shoulders, barely
covering her silk camisole and shorts bed set. She adored the
sensual feel against her skin. Blowing smoke and replacing the
cigarette, she looked back at the laptop screen and bit her lip
as she read. Her cheeks were flushed with adrenaline, and her
heart was pumping with desire as she looked over the titles she
had written.

**Walk and attract no attention? Take the car and have it pos-
sibly witnessed after the event?**

Sneak attack or full-frontal entry?

Hands or weapon?

Chat first or move on with the plan?

If she's alone, or if she has company?

Use the wig, or let her see my identity?

This was the title that had made her pause. If she was seen and identified as Anna Lane crossing the countryside, or leaving Bluebell Cottage, there would be almost no trace back to her aside from the booking at the Antler. However, her ego really, *really*, wanted to spring not just a surprise attack, but one where the fear and the recognition went hand in hand. Where the pleading and the energy were that of being able to stop the events that were in full flow because they *knew* each other.

Not that there will be any chance of stopping anything. It's much too late for that.

Anna leaned back on the bed, rubbed a hand through her hair and gave herself a mental high five. This idea, born of the boredom and frustration of waiting for news and the need to be actioning something, had been a great one. It may even send the plan off even more flawlessly and stop her flailing if anything went wrong. Cover every eventuality.

She narrowed her eyes as she added to her work, listing the pros and cons under each title, what she could do in each situation, what she could do if something went wrong, and any other notions that came to mind while writing. So far, it spanned three pages. She was good at brainstorming ideas.

In fact, come off it honey, that's what made you your money. You're fucking great at brainstorming ideas!

She smiled and began to write under the last title.

Probably should wear the disguise to get there, but inside the cottage? I want to see every line of recognition on that bitch's face, every trace of confusion, and every little breath of the fear that will follow. I want to hear her beg, listen to her plead, and watch her scream. I want to build it up, drag it out. That the Cottage is isolated is so perfect. No one will hear the noise, and there will be no one around to identify me. If I can do it well, I should be able to walk back out of there without leaving a trace, and this will be just another unsolved murder in paradise.

Anna was deep in planning mode when the knock came at the door. She knew the rap well.

Bam, ba-ba-bam, bam.

Fuck. Not now Daniel, evenings only.

She looked over at the door, and considered ignoring him, pretending she had been napping when she saw him later. Then his voice filtered through the door, offering the words she had been dreaming about for days.

'Anna, are you there? I have news.'

Anna felt adrenaline that was readily available burn in her chest.

Shit. Fuck. Daniel, bad timing!

'I'll be right there, darling. Give me a minute.'

She pushed the open laptop under the four-poster, and then she climbed off the bed, placed the lit cigarette and saucer on the side and turned the duvet over as though she had not long woken. She grabbed the blonde wig that lay on a side table, looked in the mirror, and began stuffing her hair up into it quickly. When her real hair was concealed, she ran her fingers through the full shoulder length locks.

Fuck.

The wig was a mess, certainly not her best look, but it would have to do. There was no time to straighten it out, and anyway, she had been napping, right?

She quickly checked the wig sat right in the mirror, added a fresh coat of red lipstick, and sprayed fresh perfume on her neck. As she trotted to the door, she shrugged her shoulders into her gown and tied it at the waist. With time for a small breath of composure, she unlocked the door and opened it a crack, leaning against the frame.

'Hey. Were you taking a nap?' Daniel broke into a wide grin as he scanned her from head to toe. Anna kept her eyes on his face and tried not to roll them. Men were so predictable; he probably didn't even know that he had given away all of his feeling and intention right there in that look. 'I have to be quick. I only have twenty minutes of my break left.'

'Have you found her?'

'Yeah.'

Daniel nodded, and she smiled as he passed her. She checked the corridor both ways, shut the door, and placed her back to it. He had moved to the bedside table and was picking up her cigarette, which was still smouldering. He flicked the long stream of ash into the saucer and held it aloft.

'Bad girl. There's a strict no smoking policy at the Antler.'

Anna fell into character, looked at him from under the lashes she luckily hadn't removed, and shrugged demurely.

'Are you going to tell me off?'

He grinned and kept his eyes on hers as he lifted the cigarette to his lips and took a drag.

'How can I tell you off looking and smelling like that?'

He blew smoke as she moved toward him. Slowly, hips swinging. She knew what game he was playing, and she had built up enough desire figuring out her plan that she would play it. He understood she would quickly move on when he had revealed the information she was looking for. He wanted her before he gave her the news.

So *obvious*.

What he didn't realise was that she may be back for more yet. He was damn good in bed, and she was enjoying the young energy he offered. Maybe she could give it a few days and fulfil her work from here, depending on what he said next.

She kept a restraint on her feelings, which wanted to know everything RIGHT NOW, and finally reached him. She took the cigarette from his fingers and took her own drag before squashing it out on the saucer.

'All gone,' she murmured, her lips inches from his.

He gave in first and she pulled back.

'News first.'

'But-'

'News.'

Anna sat on the edge of the bed, her legs crossed, making sure her gown fell away from her hip, revealing the small shorts.

Daniel's eyes fell to her hip.

'Anna, I–'

'I know what you want, and you'll get it, but the longer you dither with the information, Daniel, the less time we'll have.'

That seemed to spur him into action.

'Okay, so I took a walk along the hill to the ruined church this morning. I usually go that way to the cottage to check it out for you. I saw a woman down on the beach last week, but she saw me spying and shooed me off. I didn't know whether she lived there, or she was just a walker, so I didn't say anything. I had been hoping to get a glimpse of someone, maybe her, inside the place, but never did. Anyway, I get to the church this morning and there she is. Same woman. Looking out through the arched window over the sea.'

'Did you push her?'

Daniel raised his eyebrows, and she gave a small, husky laugh.

'Just joking. So, what makes you sure she's the one?'

Daniel counted on his long fingers.

'One. She told me outright that she lives there. Two. She told me to stop snooping around or she'd kung fu my ass. Three. She also told me she didn't have a sister. Four. She was super spiky, didn't want to know at all, just like you said.'

Anna felt the worry slide from her shoulders. She didn't need to hear any more. She was still there, and that made all of her planning and her work from this morning very real, and very close. It took all of her will not to power punch the air. Instead, she leaned to Daniel and kissed him.

'Thank you. Now shall I repay you?'

She began to unbutton his shirt, and he made no move to stop her.

'Don't you want the details?'

'They can wait,' she murmured as her lips found the skin on his chest and he slipped off her dressing gown.

A mere fifteen minutes later, flushed, and sweaty, Anna rolled off him and excused herself to the bathroom as she always did, taking her dressing gown with her. She had no idea what he thought of this little ritual, but she had to make sure she was still in place. She couldn't relax after a session until she knew that everything still looked like Anna Lane.

She locked the bathroom door and inspected herself in the mirror. Her lipstick was smudged. She sighed - now she'd look like she'd been punched in the mouth until the pigment wore off. The bane of bright red, and so annoying.

Annoying?

Anna smiled at her reflection.

Nothing could possibly be annoying right now, Anna. Not one thing.

Everything was falling into place and soon she would execute the only goal that she had come out here to achieve. It was almost literal bliss, the sweet reward after the days waiting to hear. Daniel had come good. Okay, she had been frustrated, and thought him slow, but he had done an excellent job - a *thorough* job - of finding out, and he had waited until he was certain before giving her the news.

He was an absolute darling and would be a great accomplice to have around. Shame she would be moving on soon.

I think he's too good of a boy, anyway, Anna. Much too good for you. And you have a family to go back to, mores the pity.

She checked the placement of her wig, please to see that no dark patches were showing at the hairline, and briefly brushed her fingers through it to tidy it up. Although it was real hair, it felt synthetic when it was a mess. Probably because she felt like a nineteen-forties femme fatale barbie.

She scrubbed at her mouth, washing away as much of the red as she could, and then applied a fresh coat from the matching lipstick she kept in here after that first night together. Anna Lane was a particular and well put together woman. She didn't like to give the impression that she didn't wake up looking as glamorous as she went to bed each evening.

Anna checked her eyelashes were in place, smacked her lips, used the toilet, and then wrapped the dressing gown back around her.

With one last mirror check that confirmed she looked like a Hollywood Icon, she unlocked the bathroom and slowly opened the door.

She had intended to discuss more of what Daniel had found out, maybe smoke another cigarette together before the end of his break, but when her eyes fell on the bed, she realised he had gone, and so had his clothes.

Anna blinked and felt a flood of anger.

Who the fuck does he think he is? He knows it's over, so he fucks off without a word?

The hurt stabbed at her chest until she saw the white sheet of paper on the bed. It was a folded napkin, the one that he had written on when they met six days ago.

He had kept it. Not only that, but he had written her an endearing message on the other side, embellished with hearts.

My dear Anna, I had to go. My break is over and I'll be in trouble. I'll see you around the hotel for as long as you're here. Our journey may be over, but it will forever stay in my heart. Take care, my 1940s sex kitten. Stay one of a kind. Daniel.

Anna pressed the note to her chest with a rush of affection that she hadn't felt in some time.

It was a shame she was married, a shame he was a good boy, and a shame she didn't have the time to see if she could change him, because right now she wanted very much to keep him alongside her.

It can't happen, Anna.

She turned to the bed and threw herself onto the place they had just consummated their deal. She moaned into the bedclothes and then pushed up onto her elbows with a sigh.

There was no point wishing for what couldn't be. She had a plan to get on with, and she had to focus now. The big day was almost here.

She edged across the bed on her elbows and peered over the edge at her laptop, which still sat where she had pushed it when Daniel had knocked.

She pulled it toward her by its open screen, and then cursed, her heart turning over in her chest. The screen was still lit; her plan still open for all to see.

Shit! That was a close call. What if he had noticed?

He didn't notice anything but you. Calm down.

But what if he had? You need to be more careful, Anna, you could have blown it all. Stupid woman, you know better. Don't get lax for the sake of a man.

She pulled up the laptop, sitting before it, and found the setting to apply the screensaver at five minutes before adding a pin. Both of which she had removed when she first had the machine because she had thought them too much trouble.

Silly. Little. Mistakes.

She shook her head and moved to scratch a tickle on her arm.

She looked down, and when she saw what was there, she almost screamed.

If Daniel hadn't seen the screen, then surely he had seen this, and that would put everything in even more jeopardy. He would know that she wasn't who she made out to be, and although that wasn't the end of the world, it would place her under suspicion earlier when the news came out, for sure.

She hopped off the bed to the mirror, her heart thumping wildly, as she turned to assess the damage.

Hanging down her back was a thick strand of long dark hair, which fell from the bottom of the blonde wig like a disjointed ponytail.

Like a secret that wouldn't be concealed.

Had he seen it? Had he taken notice in the throes of their lust?

His note didn't seem to say so, and that was all she could go on right now, wasn't it?

Maybe, but now you have to get out of here as soon as possible, no more relations with Daniel, it can't happen again. Even if he didn't see it, today was just too close. Too close.

Her heart lurched, and she turned to throw herself onto the bed, beating the covers repeatedly with an angry screech.

Fuck, Anna! Fuck, fuck, fuck!

Chapter 28

BEAU HEARD THE FAMILIAR music before she put the key in the lock, it's low thump vibrating around what should have been an empty cottage. Her fingers trembled as she pushed open the door, and peered inside. Frigid air met her on the threshold, sending a chill down her spine, and raising the hair on her scalp as something dark passed into the living area. She flinched.

'What the hell-?'

Her brain tried to catch up with the startling activity, and her heart drummed as she tried to process the influx of information.

Someone just passed the doorway. There's someone in the living room!

That little fucker, it has to be!

Beau found movement and strode into the living area. The room was cold but looked untouched. There was no one inside, and yet Simple Minds played emphatically from the corner. If these things were considered alone, she could have been forgiven for thinking she was going out of her mind, but there was more. The smell of cigar smoke was pungent and beside her there was a slow creaking that made the hair stand up at the back of her neck.

She held her breath as she turned toward the sound, and her heart almost gave out at the sight of the rocking chair, moving almost too slowly in the corner, as though whoever had been in here had knocked it on the way out.

Beau's senses were on fire as she remembered the sudden blast of freezing air as she had opened the front door.

They went out the back. This is real. This is someone real. This is not a ghost like in one of your stories. You're not being haunted; this is an actual person. Someone is messing with you out here. Someone with a key. Someone who literally just left!

Beau stood frozen, gasping for air, as the rocker slowly came to a halt and the cigar smell dissipated. The only remaining anomaly was the music.

Unplug it, just unplug the damn thing.

Beau turned back to the record player and made herself move toward it. Underneath the plastic lid, the record spun, its movement and circling label making her feel nauseous.

She swallowed hard and looked down at the plug socket. On. Although she had flicked the switch off last time the player had come on, she knew that for certain.

A shiver ran down her spine with such ferocity that her whole body shook.

Someone is messing with me!

Lunging down, she ripped the plug from the wall and dropped it, stepping back as the music slowed and distorted to a stop. Silence roared in her ears. The last bit of sun outside the window cast warmth over her, and then a cloud swallowed it, and the landscape darkened. Her mood darkened with it, leaving anger to replace the jolt of fear.

She strode back toward the doorway, looking out into the hall. Nothing moved.

'Who's there?' she yelled. 'I know you're in here. If you come out now and leave, I won't call the police. This is your only chance.'

Her voice brought goosebumps to her arms in the quiet that followed.

No movement. No noise. The house was perfectly still.

Impossible! There was someone here. I saw them!

She strode from the living area and down into the kitchen. The unruly back door was shut and locked, she found as she marched to it and pulled the handle. Only pausing for a beat, she crossed the threshold into the dining room, her breath coming in gasps.

They have to be in here. There's nowhere else for them to go.

Again, there was no one. Nothing was out of place, and her laptop sat closed as she had left it.

Beau blinked sweat from her eyes as the wind left her sails, and a creeping unease returned.

This is bullshit! I saw them down here, by the living room. They didn't pass me; they passed into the room.

And yet, there's no one here. There's nowhere to hide. You've seen every corner down here.

Fuck.

What is going on?

Beau moved back into the kitchen and to the living room, which was as empty as it had been seconds ago, and almost nause-atingly bright and cheery now that the sun had made a brief reappearance.

She stared, her chest heaving, and then shook her head and rubbed her eyes.

Did that even happen, or am I insane? Was the music actually playing? Did I see the chair move? Did I smell the cigar smoke? Or is something wrong with my brain?

The house sat passive in the quiet as tension crawled up Beau's spine. *Maybe I'm living too much in my books here, maybe all that imagination is filtering into the real world. Maybe I'm seeing things that aren't there.*

222REBECCA GUY

She moved into the living area and saw the plug to the record player lying on the floor where she had dropped it.

Or maybe you're being messed with.

She shuddered and checked the windows, which were still locked. There was simply no escape, not within the time that she had unlocked the door and stepped into the living room. The chair had still been rocking, and the smell of smoke had still lingered. She had *seen* them, and yet, there was no one here.

Am I mad? Is this my version of living alone and going insane? Is this what Joe meant when he said I'd have to fight my inner demons?

Beau chewed her lip.

Are these inner demons or outer demons?

She heaved a sigh.

Well, whatever is going on, it seems to be over for-

A shrill noise emanated from the hallway. She threw her hands instinctively over her ears as she whirled toward the hall. Her heart banged and her skin was crawling.

The sound cut to leave shrill silence, and then immediately began again.

Phone. Beau, it's your phone.

Beau closed her eyes and took a breath, her last nerve hanging on a precipice. The phone cut off and began again, and she finally moved into the hall on legs of jelly to take it from her jacket pocket. Seeing Mrs locket's name, she forced a full smile onto her face, and answered the call with a false lightness.

'Hi, Edamine!'

'Hello Beau. I hope I'm not interrupting you.'

Beau felt the smile slip and her eyes narrow. 'Not at all. I've just noticed the storm clouds out over the ocean. Is that why you're calling?'

'No, no. The storm isn't due to arrive until later tonight, so that's not a great concern, but I was wondering if it would be a big deal if I made my way over to you now? Gerard has some things to do, and bearing in mind how long the journey will take, he would like to get it over with now, if he can. I said I'd run it by you.'

Beau grimaced. 'Get it over with?'

Edamine laughed softly. 'I know I'm a pain. Let's get that out of the way. He's a good man, and I'd like to go along with his plan to bring me earlier, if that's okay with you, of course. It makes no difference to my day now, the nurse just cancelled and booked me in for tomorrow instead.'

Beau shrugged. It made no difference to hers either, and the lady was hardly coming from next door. She was at least an hour away yet.

'Sounds fine to me.'

'Wonderful. I'll let Gerard know and be on my way. See you soon.'

Edamine's call couldn't have landed at a better time. The fear that had been sitting in the pit of Beau's stomach subsided to sheer relief. Before long Gerard would be here to check things over, and after that, she would have Edamine for company for a few hours. All she had to worry about right now was preparing dinner. She shot a triumphant look at the living room as she had passed to the kitchen.

'Let's see you do your shit when the owner's here.'

In the kitchen, she put on some of her own music, poured herself a small glass of wine – just to settle her nerves - and lost herself in the forward plot of her own book as she prepped and seasoned the chips, peppered the steak, and chopped the salad.

Cooking had always come easy to Beau, and she slipped into a lull as she chopped and seasoned and tossed, allowing her left brain to busy itself with mundane tasks, which in turn seemed to light up her creative right brain. 'Ah-ha' moment's about the plot of her book came thick and fast, and she often found herself staring into space as she collected her thoughts, and the major points of the storyline fell into place.

Have you ever written like this, Beau? Like you have here?

She chopped cucumber as she thought.

No. Certainly not this fast, and maybe that was why she was getting super creative and having flashes of insight as she chopped salad. The speed and intensity at which the story was coming together was something she had never experienced before.

You never pushed this hard before. You never tried to write a novel in six months, and therefore you never did. Maybe, though, this is something to take forward. Keeping myself fully in the story for so many words a day, it's almost like my mind never stops creating. It never fully steps out of the fictional world.

Beau stopped chopping.

Maybe that's why you're so on edge about what's going on here. Maybe there's a perfectly legitimate explanation for everything. Maybe you're looking for the unusual, the paranormal, because you have one foot in the present and one in the fictional world.

She pushed out her lips and began to chop again.

And maybe Edamine - or someone - is trying to scare you and get you to leave?

What Beau couldn't figure out was why that would be. Edamine had given her a job to do and was paying her for the privilege. Why change her mind six days in?

I'm not going anywhere anyway, the writing is going too well. If that little squirt is living in my attic, I'll just have to show him my karate skills... well, after I've researched them on YouTube, anyway.

She tittered and felt herself relax, even singing along to the songs that played from her speaker as she worked.

She waited in the least inviting room in the cottage - the living room - as it was the only place to watch the front of the house. It was either that or sit in the hall, which she thought may look a little strange when Edamine and Gerard turned up, so she stood by the window, wine glass in hand, contemplating. She pretended to be one of her characters, living in a haunted house, and trying to find a way through the experience.

What felt wrong in this room, exactly? Cold, uninviting, sinister?

None of the above.

She turned to place her backside on the low windowsill and looked around the space.

It's pleasant, actually. A nice room, feel wise. It's only because I've seen things happen in here that I know there's anything wrong with it.

Not at all like my books...

Beau huffed a laugh and finished the wine in her glass, then she took the glass into the kitchen and rinsed it before going back to her viewing post.

It was a little early, but there was movement just over the rise, going down into the dip. Beau squinted through the window, and then the funniest sight appeared.

A quad bike. Edamine was driving, laughter on her face, as Gerard - twice her size - sat behind, holding onto her waist, looking like a kid at a birthday party. They looked like the strangest couple on an adrenaline filled date, rather than the caretaker bringing his disabled employer to her cottage.

Beau grinned and ran to the door, waving as they came to a stop just shy of the porch.

'Hello!' Edamine yelled as the roar of the engine cut out.

'That looked really cool! I wish I'd been offered the VIP transport when I arrived.'

'It's a one off,' Gerard said, swinging his leg over the vehicle. Then he pointed at Edamine, 'and that's the last time you drive!'

'It's a two-off. Best fun I've had in a long time, and I'm driving back.'

'Not on my watch.' Gerard threw an arm around Edamine's waist and helped her from the bulky machine, handing her the walking stick as her feet touched down.

Beau laughed, her voice carrying across the landscape. 'Gerard loved it. You should have seen his face, Edamine, looked like a kid in a sweet shop.'

'I did not,' Gerard disputed with a wide grin. 'It was like the world's worst theme park ride.'

Edamine tapped Gerard's leg with her stick and shot him a scathing look as she reached Beau and gave her a warm hug. Beau immediately let down her guard. There was no way this lady had anything to do with what was going on. She just couldn't. She was too nice, too kind, and too full of fun.

Gerard faked pain and then broke into another full grin before placing a hand on Edamine's back. 'Well, I'll leave you ladies to your fun, and- '

'No!' Beau shouted. Too loud and too quick. Both Edamine and Gerard looked a little startled at her outburst. 'No, I mean, wait. There's something I need you to help me with in the attic first.'

Beau expected the questions and was half ready for them, but Gerard looked up at the third-story window and smiled.

'Got them open and now can't shut them, eh? Well remembered though, Beau, if the storm had rolled in with those open, we could have been seeing damage.' He nudged Edamine with a smile. 'See, I told you she was a good one. She'll look after the place.'

Beau's smile slipped.

'You've been discussing me, I see?'

Edamine only smiled. 'Of course. I'm the owner of an old cottage, and he's the caretaker. I can't get over to see what's going on, and he can. He has more dealings with you sitters than I do, and he can give me the information I need. That's why the relationship works.'

Beau nodded. She supposed that made sense.

'Okay, well, let's lock the attic shutters so I can get back.'

Gerard ushered them into the cottage ahead of him and then motioned Beau upstairs. Her heart staggered.

'What? You need me, too?'

'If you can't do it, then you didn't see properly last time. Do you want to have to call me down here every time you need them shut?'

Yes, please, I think there's someone up there.

'No, I suppose not.'

'Let's go then.'

'I'll wait in the living room,' Edamine said as she peered around the doorway and disappeared inside.

Beau went ahead of Gerard up the stairs and then stood back, staring at the small pieces of yellow insulation that were still scattered around the balustrade as he pulled the ladders down and began to climb.

'Wait, um, be careful. Anyone could be up there.'

She felt herself flush even as she pretended to make a joke. A joke that her face said was an obvious truth.

Gerard paused, his head almost through the gap, and looked down at her, a crease in his brow, and a smile playing around his lips.

'You really *are* a horror writer, aren't you?'

Beau forced a grin and shrugged. 'Every eventuality. Play along with me and be careful.'

'Okay,' Gerard nodded, looking back into the space above and then he gave a sudden harsh whisper. 'Beau, I think there may be someone in the attic!'

Beau felt her stomach roll over as he rose higher, and she heard his low laughter.

'Not funny,' she grumbled.

He was almost fully inside when he suddenly gave a shout and fell backward against the loft hatch.

Beau screamed, and then Gerard disappeared inside and peered down at her from the dark hole. 'Guess what? There's no one here!'

'What's going on up there?' Edamine called from downstairs.

Beau stared at Gerard, not sure whether to laugh or cry. 'Gerard is messing about, that's all.'

Gerard grinned. 'She thinks the attic dweller is going to attack me.'

'You should always be careful of the attic dweller,' Edamine shouted, and Beau nodded at Gerard. 'See?'

Gerard shook his head and motioned her up the ladder. 'There's no one up here. Let me show you while it's light.'

Beau climbed, and just inside the hatch, she quickly scanned the area and the boxes. There were so many places for people to hide up here for sure.

'Could be, over there.' She pointed, her hand shaking. She hoped he wouldn't notice, but he covered her hand with his warm one and pushed it down. He was shaking his head when she looked at him.

'No. Do you know how I know?'

'Do you know for certain?'

'One hundred percent.'

Beau doubted that, but she was ready to listen to the voice of logic up here in the scary attic... which didn't seem so scary now that she was up here again. With the shutters open, it was light enough to see most of the items up here, and now Gerard turned on the light, dispelling the darkness that remained.

'What's the theory?'

'Look at the floor.'

Beau dropped her eyes but couldn't see what he wanted her to look at.

'I don't understand.'

Gerard crouched and ran in a finger across the floor next to one of the boxes. It came up with a thick layer of dust and Beau suddenly understood.

'Here, where we've walked and I've taken the other sitters every year before you, there is only a trace of dust, and this print here?' he pointed to a large footprint that pointed toward the small window. 'This is mine, but you can see further out nothing has been disturbed. It's thick.'

He rose and placed his foot where his finger had been, leaving loose dust and a huge footprint behind.

Beau nodded as her eyes scanned down the attic between the boxes. There were no prints of any kind. The dust hadn't been disturbed, and she began to lose the unease that had followed her around for days.

There can't be anyone up here because there would be evidence!

'Can I go down there?' Beau pointed to the other side of the room, where the boxes were packed high.

Gerard gave her a puzzled look. 'Aye, if you remember next time that those prints are yours, and don't scare yourself to death thinking they're the attic dwellers.'

Beau rolled her eyes as she moved among the boxes. The attic wasn't large and after a quick scan of any hiding places, Beau realised Gerard was right. One hundred percent right. One look at the mess she had made walking over here suggested that no-one had trodden this way for many, many, years. No one had been up here.

'Convinced now?' Gerard said from by the window. 'The last time anyone came up here and wandered about would have been before Edamine took over the place after her mother died in 1992.'

Beau baulked. 'That's over thirty years ago!'

'Hence the dust.'

'Why doesn't she want to look at all this stuff? It must be like a treasure trove of history and memories for her up here.'

'Aye, I'm sure it is, and that may be the problem. There are some memories that she'd rather forget. It's public knowledge that her father hung himself from the church rafters in the eighties. I won't go into the reason. That's not my place.'

Beau felt her mouth drop open, but Gerard continued.

'Edamine's diagnosis came a year or two after her mother died, and after that she couldn't get in and out of here safely, so all these memories are left to dust. As I say, maybe that's where she wants them.'

'Diagnosis? Is this about her legs?'

'She has Limb Girdle Muscular Dystrophy. It's a degenerative disease. When I first met Edamine twenty years ago, she was only thirty years old and struggling to live here. She hired me to help her out and collect what she needed. The deal only lasted five years before she had to leave. She just couldn't manage the stairs. The bed was moved downstairs, into the dining room, but the toilet is still up here, see?'

She purchased a property in the village, but it broke her heart to leave this cottage, and she fell into a deep depression. I kept the cottage for her without payment for the best part of a year before she was ready to look at her options. She didn't want the place rented - too much like their own and they could change the decor. She wasn't happy about that, and besides, she had been left enough money; the rent wasn't needed. But she didn't want the place sitting empty, where it would eventually become derelict and gratified like the church. I suggested the idea of a house sitter, and she suggested just over the winter. That way she still had control of the cottage, and she could come over here in peace in the drier months if she wished, and she did, a lot over the first few summers, but for the last ten or so it's just sat empty. The travel here takes a lot out of her and the toilet is almost out of bounds.'

Beau didn't know what to say. All Edamine had ever said was that she had trouble with her legs, nothing more. It shocked her that this went so deep, but she hadn't said a word.

Why would she? She doesn't know you.

'That's awful, but why not just install a toilet down in the back extension, or have a stair lift fitted?'

Gerard shook his head. 'The toilet could have been do-able. The three stair lift companies weren't happy about trekking themselves and their equipment three miles over the land. They advised having some way they could get their vans through first. Edamine refused. I think the other big reason that pushed her to leave was company. As much as she loved it here, she couldn't get into the village, and that made her very isolated and very lonely. I saw that slip from a vibrant young woman into a recluse who would stare at the ocean for most of the day. She was miserable.'

'And she was getting worse?'

'Aye, she's a lot worse now than when we met, and the speed of the disease is increasing. She won't say anything, but I know she's getting worse by the day. I know her so well now, I can hear it in her voice.'

'Oh, that's so sad.' Beau hesitated, and then decided to say what was on her mind, anyway. 'You sound like she's at death's door, but she can't be that bad. She managed the stairs at Ophelia's ladies evening, and she drove the quad bike over here just now.'

'One ladies' evening a month. That she can manage if some helps her up the stairs, and Ophelia always meets her at the bottom. Same with the bike, although she'll suffer for that later. It's the constant everyday up and down that she can't manage at all now. The disease progressed slowly at first, but of late she has gotten frail very quickly. Don't let her hear that I've said that though. She'd cut me from her life and break that stick over my back!'

Beau laughed, wanting to hear more, but Gerard changed the subject.

'Well, times passing, let me show you these shutters again, then I'll take the swing down outside, and then I've really got to be off.'

Beau was glad that Gerard turned away and couldn't see the flush of her cheeks. Despite the impending storm, she hadn't given a jot of thought to the swing or the shutters... just the attic dweller.

The attic dweller who clearly doesn't dwell in the attic, she thought, rolling her eyes.

Five minutes later, as they descended the ladder, with the shutters closed safely back over the window, Beau was almost certain she saw movement.

Get over it Beau, there's no one there, that dust hasn't been disturbed in thirty years!

Then the yellow insulation caught her eye as she touched down on the landing, and her heart gave a small skip.

So where the heck did that come from? And the photograph? What is going on? Who is up there that doesn't disperse dust as they move around?

Pushing down her unease, annoyed that it was back so soon after she had checked the space herself, she picked up the yellow insulation from the floor and slipped it into her pocket as Gerard replaced the ladders.

Out of sight, out of mind.

As they said goodbye to Gerard, she knew that would be easier said than done.

Chapter 29

'T HIS IS ABSOLUTELY WONDERFUL, you're a great cook, Beau.'

Edamine sank her knife easily into the steak, and Beau smiled and took a sip of wine. Earlier, she had moved her laptop onto the sideboard and set up two places at the dining table after realising she hadn't eaten a single meal here since she had moved in. She would eat here more though, she thought, it was more relaxing than the living area with its spooky nuances, and the view over the ocean while she ate was both commanding and soothing.

'I'm glad you're enjoying it.' Beau said, placing her glass back on the coaster. 'It was a little thrown together in the end. I panicked a little.'

'That was all my fault. It's perfect. Could be that the company and the atmosphere are great too, that always helps with food, don't you think?'

Beau shrugged. 'It does, but I think maybe it's just that you're home.'

Edamine lowered her fork to her plate and smiled. 'I *am* home. Thank you so much for this, Beau, you don't know how much it means to me to be here again. It's been almost two years now, and I wasn't sure I'd make it. Gerard suggested the quad bike – which was a whole heap of fun, I have to tell you – but I'm paying for it now.'

Beau swallowed a mouthful of salad.

'It looked absolutely brilliant. I wish I'd recorded you coming over the rise, I was so shocked!'

'I wish you'd recorded it, too. It was brilliant fun. I'd love to have shown the girls in the village.' Edamine chuckled and looked toward the pictures in the cabinet. 'My father would have hated it. He loved nature, that's why we never had a driveway. He always said that the walk would do us good and that the wildlife and ecosystems would thank us for it. Any type of motorised vehicle coming over that land would have made his hair curl.'

Beau took another sip of wine.

'Catch twenty-two, I suppose. It's really unspoiled like it is, and very beautiful, but a driveway would certainly make the place much more accessible.' Beau thought about the stair lift companies that Gerard had mentioned. 'Maybe you could still have been living here, if you had direct access.'

Edamine raised an eyebrow as she sank her knife into more steak. 'That may be so, but I wouldn't have been living here in peace. My father would have turned in his grave. He already used to make his presence known from time to time after his death.'

Beau blinked, wondering whether she'd heard right. 'What, here?'

Edamine laughed. 'Where else? Through Ophelia's crystal ball at the Quill and Feathers? He didn't believe in any of that stuff!'

'Do you?'

'I do now. When Ophelia moved here with Gill and opened that metaphysical shop it raised more than a few eyebrows, including mine, but when odd things began to happen around here, I thought she may know a thing or two. I spoke to her, and luckily, she did. To cut a long story short, my father was troubled, and she helped me to cross his spirit over. I never had any problems after that. No one has complained of anything since.'

Beau looked at Edamine, trying not to let her mouth gape open. Was this about last night and the crystal ball? Is that why she was bringing this up, or was this a fact?

'You had problems with a *ghost* here? Is that what you're saying?'

'I did until he crossed, but no one should know more about this type of thing than a writer of ghost stories, eh, Beau? Are you a believer?'

Edamine had spoken to Gerard or looked her up at some point then. She knew what she wrote, even if she hadn't read either of her books.

Beau shrugged. 'I'm on the fence, I suppose. It's just a subject that has always fascinated me, but I've never had any personal paranormal experiences.'

Edamine sipped her wine and narrowed her eyes. 'Interesting.'

Beau almost felt as though Edamine could read her mind... or maybe it was that she had set this whole thing up after all. She decided to tread carefully. There had to be a way to know for sure without upsetting Edamine and causing an atmosphere that she couldn't walk away from. Outside the sky was darkening, and as she chewed her steak she noticed the first few droplets of water land on the window and slide down the glass.

'I think that's rain,' she said. 'Maybe the storm is heading in a little earlier than expected, after all.'

Edamine turned to look back at the window with a nod. 'I think you may be right.'

There was a beat of quiet where the only sounds were cutlery on plates, and Beau wondered why Edamine didn't seem too bothered.

Maybe she knew all along and that's why-

Beau shook the thought from her head, and took another sip of wine, feeling the slight tremor in her hand.

Stop it Beau, just relax. Change the subject for God's sake.

'So, what was life like living here as a rector's daughter? The cottage and the pictures are beautiful, like a time capsule. I suppose I can understand why your father wouldn't want to leave this place.'

'Ah, no. You understand nothing, Beau. I wish it were some chick-lit, light hearted, fun adventure that my childhood skipped through, but unfortunately, it wasn't. It was pretty horrific and left me scarred for quite some time afterward. The eighties were particularly bad, I wish I could scrub that entire decade from my mind.'

Beau remembered Gerard's admission in the attic and suddenly felt her cheeks flush. She had said the wrong thing.

May as well admit you know.

'Was that when your father...'

Edamine sipped from her glass as Beau left the sentence hanging.

'You've done your research, I see. I suppose it's not hard to find when you Google the area.'

'It was Gerard, actually, when we were in the attic. I asked why you'd leave all the stuff up there untouched for so long. He suggested that it may have been the reason.'

'Some of it. Most of it is my legs and this blasted disease. Did Gerard mention that too?'

Beau grimaced and shrugged. 'Only a little.'

Edamine sank more wine.

'He's a loose-lipped bugger,' she sighed. 'He's not wrong, though. It's been a strange life, looking back. I often wonder why so much was thrown at me so young, and why so many opportunities were taken from me, and mostly why I couldn't even just live a quiet life in my own damn cottage.' She placed her glass down. 'Would you like to hear a horror story, Beau?'

Beau took a gulp of her own wine, feeling she may need it. 'I'm partial to horror, but only if you want to tell it.'

Edamine smiled and gestured to the cabinet along the back wall where there were still a few pictures of the family. 'The pictures in this cottage are the ones that my mother used to keep hanging around before she died. She loved having pictures of family around her, and this room, the cabinet here, used to be crammed full of them.'

Beau turned to look. She hadn't looked at the photographs closely, but she knew they were of three people - mother, father, daughter, and a couple of a black and white border collie. All were taken around the house and grounds, up at the church, or down on the beach. In one the rector sat on the porch with a newspaper, in another a child swam in the sea while the dog ran on the sand, in another a woman stood with her arms around the child's shoulders outside the front of the house, and another the child curled up with the dog on a chair in the living room. They looked like your average happy family photographs to Beau.

'I don't remember a lot from that time, but I do remember knocking into that cabinet once and mother scolding me and telling me to pick up every one of the pictures and place them back correctly. The task took me over an hour.'

Beau's mouth dropped open. 'Why? Because you got the positions wrong?'

'Oh no, mother wasn't that strict, it was simply the volume of pictures in there. When people visited, she would get them out and line them up on this very table, boring the guests with the story behind every one as though she were afraid she would forget if she didn't. She loved family life, and she loved living here. Before what happened, life was almost idyllic, I suppose, but after, mother cleared through all the photographs in the house, leaving only these out. The rest she put away for good.'

'In the attic?'

Edamine finished the last bite of steak and placed her knife and fork on the plate with a nod.

'Yes, they're all still up there. I'm surprised the weight hasn't brought the ceiling down. She never touched any of them again. Too much pain, I suppose.'

Beau finished her own steak and waited, not wanting to push for a story that was going to be hard to tell, whether Edamine had offered it or not. She watched as Edamine finished her wine, poured herself some more from the bottle on the table and topped Beau's half full glass back up. Then she rubbed a thin hand over her face with a long sigh.

REBECCA GUY

'Edamine? You don't have to say what happened. It's none of my business, and I know it must be tough to talk about.'

'Tougher than I thought after so many years, but I think you may find it relevant.'

Beau frowned at her. 'Relevant?'

Edamine swigged more wine and began to talk.

'My father was a good Catholic man, and very strict. He was the serious one in our lives, and Sundays were particularly stressful for mother. Everything had to be in order, his gown and cassock cleaned, ironed, and starched to perfection, and we all had to be at church, dressed in our best to meet the parishioners and greet them into the service as a family. Father practiced his sermons in front of mother countless times on Saturday night after we were in bed. I think he thought we couldn't hear, but I did. I knew them by heart. I heard them so often, I can still recite them even now, and the way he delivered them, the way he used his voice; it was powerful. *He* was powerful, and that power was something I aspired to have. I loved the way people fell before him just from wearing that robe and shouting a few lines from a book. Even at an early age, I was very aware of how powerful the bible was. If things had worked out differently, I might have been rector in that church even today. I was hell bent on taking over from him until the accident, but after that, things went tits up, really. Spectacularly tits up.'

'The accident? Your father took his own life by accident?'

'No, no, he was very much in a place where he thought he had no other option by the time he went. He left mother a note saying how sorry he was and how he wished things had worked out differently. He hoped that by removing himself, he would give us the peace we deserved.' Edamine shook her head. 'No, he meant to do it and do it well. It was both the best and the worst bit of the whole thing looking back. Horrific, and yet... it worked.'

Edamine heaved a long sigh, and her eyes flicked to the photographs in the cabinet. She was quiet for a while, and Beau reached a hand to place it on her arm, which felt cold and bony under her cream jumper.

'That's very sad.'

Edamine gave a wry smile. 'Yes. The whole situation was and still is, but he had to pay one way or another, I suppose. I do wonder if he ever went to hell, and I hope not.'

'I'm sure he didn't go to hell, Edamine, you said yourself that he was a good man. Why would you think that?'

'Because good men do bad things, and he did a terrible thing in Nineteen-eighty-three. Something that would change our lives forever, and something that would start a terrible spiral of many awful things here.'

Beau saw Edamine's hand shake as she picked up her glass to sip her drink.

'What did he do?' she said after Edamine's gaze was pulled back to the cabinet of black and white memories. Edamine pursed her lips, and then she turned to Beau. Beau thought she looked a little pale. 'You don't have to–'

Edamine waved a hand.

'He killed my sister, Constance. His daughter.'

Beau physically reeled in her chair. Of all the things she had been expecting, this certainly wasn't one of them.

'He what?'

'It was a terrible accident, they said, and he never fully recovered, especially with what followed. That's why I always thought he'd go to hell, see?'

Beau blinked and found her own gaze travelling to the cabinet. Her eyes strained to see anything of the man who held this terrible secret that she hadn't known, and then Beau noticed something strange.

'Your sister? But there are no photos of a sister, only of the three of you. I thought you were an only child.'

'I am. I wasn't. As I said, mother put all the other memories away. I don't know how she managed it so quickly, but she was a tidy up and carry on kind of woman and I suppose she wanted to protect me and my father. It was better to brush it away and keep moving. Chin up, shoulders back. No point in being upset after the milk is spilled. We clean the mess, and we carry on.

It hurt me immensely, and I hated and loved them both with an intensity that I hadn't known I could feel. It was literally like they swept Constance under the rug. I still don't understand much of their reaction, although I tried to later, but mother was ill by then, both in body and mind. We were a sick family, Beau, so sick when you peeled back the perfect layers.'

Beau felt her mouth drop, and she searched for something to say, but the revelation was so far from what she had been expecting that she couldn't find any words that seemed right.

'How... what do you mean?'

Edamine looked up with a tight smile. 'Sick? Just that. There was a lot of tension, a lot of covering up behind those carefree photos. Father had a rage that pushed him over the edge more than once, but his need to be a perfect, calm, and patient rector to his disciples - that's what he called the people who came to his church - was just as strong.' Edamine gave a low laugh. 'In fact, I remember when a villager came to the cottage to ask him for prayers for his wife, who was dying. I had been caught sneaking the last of the bread, and he was midway through spanking me with his belt when Mr Patton knocked. Mother made sure that my tears were dry and then she straightened my dress while father greeted him with such charm and warmth that I could barely believe he was the same man who had been whipping me seconds earlier. We all had to gather in the living area to listen to father read from the bible and we all had to join in the prayer for Mrs Patton. My backside was throbbing so much that I couldn't sit down. I stood behind the couch, hoping to get away with it, but mother noticed and told me it was impolite. It hurt so bad when I sat that I couldn't help but cry, but I knew better than to say anything. Mother hugged me and rocked me on those sore cheeks until I could have screamed, telling Mr Patton that I was upset about his wife as she brushed my tears away.'

Beau felt her stomach shrink as Edamine shook her head.

'I *was* upset when Mrs Patton died, she was a lovely woman, but not that day. That was the day I swore I'd never steal bread again, and I haven't, not to this day. Are you building a picture of what our family looked like, Beau?'

Beau said nothing. She looked at Edamine and wondered how there was no emotion. She looked as steely and as strong as she usually did. Her manner was still forthright and nothing she said carried any frills. She said it as it was. Either way, having a happy childhood where she really was carefree, this story was not only shocking to Beau, but heart breaking. What a strain to have to live with that constant tension, especially as a child.

Edamine patted Beau's hand.

'Good, so you see, mother was just as sick. She never raised a hand to us, and life could be pretty carefree when father wasn't around, it wasn't all bad, but she was on her guard as much as we were when he was home, and she helped to cover up more than one of his crimes without question. She married him and she would stand by him to the last. It was simple.'

Edamine stopped to take a sip of wine, taking her time, rolling the liquid around her mouth before continuing.

'Later, just after Constance died, mother developed throat cancer, and I always felt it was because of what she kept inside, squashed, and hidden. All of those lies built into physical lumps in her throat and eventually they killed her.'

'Oh, Edamine, I'm sure that's not-'

'I'm sure it is.' Edamine smiled at Beau. 'It's also the reason I've never married. I won't be tied to a man like she was, and I won't help anyone cover their crimes and injustices. I have no interest in love and marriage if that's what it entails.'

Beau nodded and thought of her own marriage. It had been good... until it wasn't. She had certainly never had to lie for Patrick, although she did understand the camaraderie of the sealed unit. The projection of the family to the outside world. Beau had felt that, even with just the two of them and with no children involved. They were married, and they stuck together, through thick and thin, for better, for worse.

He lied to you, though. For quite some time.

Beau felt a lump of ice sit heavy in her abdomen. Would she ever trust another man? Or would she end up like Edamine from here on in, going it alone?

How can you trust someone when they can abuse it and lie straight to your face, and you never know?

Beau felt Edamine's cold hand touch her own and for the first time she took in how frail it was, which left her wondering how far advanced the disease was.

'Beau?'

Beau tried to smile up at Edamine. 'I was just thinking about my marriage and thinking you may have it right. I never had to lie for Patrick, but he certainly lied to me. It works either way round, doesn't it? You just never know who's being as faithful, and loving, and truthful as you are.'

'You never know what another is thinking, and that's what had my whole family tied with sickness. Father raged his rage, and mother covered it up. I thought nothing of it really, until Constance. Then I wondered. Does covering things up go as far as murder? Or was it really an accident like they always said?'

Beau felt her heart almost stop as she swung to face Edamine.

'You questioned it?'

Edamine shrugged and finished her second glass of wine. Beau reached over to pour the last of the bottle into her glass.

'Thank you, and yes, of course I questioned it. Later, after father died, I questioned mother too. I told her it didn't matter how things happened, but she stuck to her story. Whether she was protecting him, or whether it was the truth, I suppose I'll never know. All I really know is that his spirit couldn't rest. What does that tell you?'

Beau fingered the stem of her glass and thought.

'It tells me that he felt guilty and responsible, but he would have felt that whether it was an accident or not. In fact, possibly more so if it was an accident, wouldn't he?'

'Ah,' Edamine said, her head tilting as she looked out of the window and toward the sea through a now persistent patter of rain. 'I suppose I thought guilt was guilt, but maybe you're right. We all grieved after it happened, of course, but it just seemed to me that the both of them could move on much faster than I did. Within weeks, life was moving on without her, and that killed me. That worries me too. If he did it on purpose, then he wouldn't have been so bothered now, would he?'

Beau shrugged and shook her head. 'I'm not sure, Edamine. People deal with things differently, don't they? Like you say, he had a job to do, he was holding up a parish, and he had a front to put on. He was so serious about that role that he could spank his daughter one minute and be full of smiles and charm the next. It says a lot about his character, and his ability to either process quickly and move on, or that he also suppressed things like your mother.'

Edamine smiled. 'You're much less suspicious and more forgiving than I am, Beau, but you make a good point.'

'What happened that day, Edamine? Why do you question it?'

Beau didn't fear asking like she had done a few minutes before. Edamine was treating this like a story that wasn't her own. She was detached and analytical, like she had been over this a thousand times, and it no longer hurt, although Beau didn't know how that could be true.

Edamine answered quickly, almost as though she had been waiting for the permission to offload.

'Constance was sick too, in more ways than one that day. She was just seven years old when she died, but I could already see the same rage that father carried. She was fiercely loyal and protective of me, possibly because she was father's favourite. Not that she didn't feel his wrath - she did - I just got it worse. A lot worse. She noticed it, and she hated it. She played on father for what she wanted, of course, and she was often at the church helping out in the week after school, always she would come back with a pack of sweets for herself, but she also often cried with me after a spanking and tried to help me tend my wounds. She was an extremely sweet child, but also very headstrong. I remember once when father was yelling at me, I ran to our room - the red bedroom. Constance was in there playing and she whipped into a such a fury, so quickly. She slammed the door in his face and told him to keep the hell out, and to keep away from me. Her little face was as red as beetroot, and I was filled with both admiration and horror.'

Edamine shrugged.

'We both got it that day, and we cried together, tending to each other's wounds. We were best buddies. The only problem Constance had with me, and the only fights we ever got into, was when she got a spanking and I didn't do the same. I would help her after, of course, but I would never outwardly protect her against father. I used to stay quiet. I didn't want a spanking too, that's how it was. She was braver than me, I suppose, but that belt hurt.'

'How old were you?' Beau asked.

'I was eleven years old the day it happened. We had gone to school as normal. The school is seven miles from here in a bigger village up north, and as mother didn't drive, father used to take us and pick us up. We were always at school, never late, and never in trouble. That's who we had to be. We were Rector Locket's daughters.

That day, apparently the school had called mother and said that Constance was sick and needed collecting. Father was leading a group that met on Tuesday mornings, and was apparently none too pleased that he would have to finish halfway through to collect her. He ranted, apparently, as he always did when things got in the way of his plans, but he picked her up just the same.

However, when Constance got home, mother said she admitted there wasn't a thing wrong with her. She had made it up so that she could 'have a day to herself' because she was tired. According to mother, father hit the roof, especially as he had cut his session short. There was a lot of shouting and screaming, I would imagine, and finally Constance announced that she hated him and hated her life, and ran out into the forest. We had a pathway that only we knew, in and out of the trees, skipping around corners and through the vegetation. Mother said that father followed her through the forest but couldn't keep up. He was growling, she said, red in the face. She thought he was going to have a heart attack! I only wish that he had. It would have stopped the altercation altogether.'

Edamine paused and Beau paused with her, barely breathing at what she knew would come next.

'So they reached the top of the hill, all three of them. Mother said that Constance ran for the large front door of the church, but father had locked it after he left, so she ran around the back instead. Have you ever been to the church, Beau?'

Beau nodded. 'Yes. I walked there this morning. It is isolated, and wild. An incredibly beautiful setting.'

'Did you go around the back of the church, where the large stained-glass window used to be? It provides a convenient arched frame for artistic pictures of the sea and the islands now, but it used to be beautiful in its day.'

'Yes, I saw it.'

'Well then, you may have seen just how little cliff top stands between the church and the drop into the sea. The weather was particularly wild that day, and mother said that both of them shouted at Constance to come back as she made her way down the ledge. Their mistake, I think, was to corner her. Mother stood at one end, and father the other. There was no way out except into one or the other's arms. I'm pretty sure Constance wouldn't have wanted to have been in either. Mother said that she was too scared to step foot at the back of the church, but father and his bullish ways,' Edamine rolled her eyes and shook her head with a sigh. 'Well, of course he went, sliding himself down the back wall to get to Constance. She screamed and apparently as father reached for her, she jolted away from him and slipped, falling sixty feet down into the sea. The rest is history. I came back from school and Constance was gone. Over the next few days there was a search of the water and police came, but it was put down to a tragic accident. After all, father was the rector, and mother a witness. Constance's body was never found.'

Beau could feel her heart pounding in her throat. 'That's awful. I'm so sorry.'

Edamine smiled. 'It is. You know the worst thing? Worse than not getting her body back? It was arriving home from school to find mother in tears collecting up all of the photographs and putting them into a box.'

Beau frowned. 'That soon?'

'Oh, yes. She picked up every scrap of Constance's life over the next two days, packed her into a box, and put her in the attic. Out of sight, out of mind. She always said that it was better for our grieving if all traces of her were gone.'

Beau felt her chest ache. She reached for Edamine's cold hand and squeezed. 'I'm so sorry, maybe it was shock?'

'Quite possibly. Either way, that wasn't the end of the story. From that day forward, we were terrorised. Someone started the rumour that father pushed Constance, making him a murderer. Where they got the information from, I don't know, but it came quick and hard, and only around five days after the accident. People would walk to the cottage and throw eggs at the windows and shout the most awful things at us. The once I was sitting in the living area and a large rock was thrown through the window. We had the police here constantly, and it was terrifying, especially living out here, but it was father who took the worst. Not only did he get several beatings on his way to and from church, but his 'disciples' were leaving in droves. A month or two after Constance died, he had only two parishioners left. We simply couldn't keep the church going, and when father tried to sell, no one was interested, especially as the church was in a little disrepair, and by now graffiti was appearing inside and out as people broke in and trashed it. It was heart breaking.'

Beau looked at Edamine and realised that the only tear she had cried through all of this story was finally letting loose. She got up to fetch tissues from the kitchen side and handed them to her, watching as the lady dabbed her tears.

'Thank you. My life was turned upside down after that day. News of the rector who got away with murder travelled far and wide, but we never knew the reason. There was nothing to fan the flames. Father was never arrested or even questioned again. The police saw it as a shut case. There was no evidence to suggest there was any foul play. On the contrary, they looked after us well. We had a stationed officer with us for quite some time. They thought the rumours would fizzle out, but two years later, although the abuse was declining, so were we. We had no friends, no visitors, no dignity, and father was half of the man he used to be.

I think what really pushed him over the edge was the window. He went up to the church one Sunday to meet his remaining parishioners, only to find the doors broken and the inside demolished. The large stained-glass window had been almost completely destroyed, as had many of the other windows. His sanctuary had been demolished, and so had his life. It was later that night, when mother and I were asleep, that he went up to the church and hung himself from the arch. Mother found him almost six hours later. She saw him first, from the small bay where she was out with the dog. She said that she felt someone walk over her grave and looked up to see him swinging in the wind, his body almost over the cliff edge, before swinging back again. She said that she knew it was him before it had even been confirmed.'

Edamine dabbed her eyes and Beau shook her head.

'That's so awful, and you being such a young girl.'

Edamine blew her nose and nodded. 'As I said, father left a note saying that he wanted a better life for us, and his life insurance policy made sure that we were more than comfortable. It was like the ultimate sacrifice. After that, things really did begin to get better for a while, but then I began to question everything. Why would Constance want to come home to have time to herself? Why would she run to the church? Why would father chase her down the back of the church knowing that one slip would cause her to fall? She was seven years old. It just doesn't ring true to me. Why did father really kill himself? Was it a sacrifice? Or was it cowardice? Was he guilty? Is that why the rumours wouldn't settle while he was alive? But then how would anyone know except mother? And to that end, was mother telling the truth? Or was she covering his tracks again? I wanted answers. I wanted to know what really happened to my sister, but all I got was the same story, over and over, until mother died almost ten years later.'

Beau touched Edamine's arm lightly.

'Maybe she was telling the truth.'

'She may have been, but I just... well, let's get it out of the way, I didn't believe her. There's something. Something in the way she could just pack Constance up.'

'What makes you think she was doing wrong?'

'I don't know. I could never put my finger on it, and I may never find out now. Some things are probably best left in the past, I suppose.'

'You're probably right.'

Edamine smiled as she dried the last of her tears. 'So, what do you think of the story? It's a clincher, isn't it? Worthy of one of your novels?'

'I don't know about that, it's a little gut wrenching and gruesome for my books, I write spooky ghost stories, not crime!'

'Well, it has a ghostly element in the middle, after all of the bad stuff.'

'That bit I'd be interested in.'

Beau realised she had played into Edamine's hands if the lady was trying to scare her out here, but Edamine simply laughed.

'I'm sure you would, and I'm sure you'd write it well.'

Beau felt warmth circle her stomach. She was grateful for the sudden lightness of the mood almost as much as the compliment. 'So, what is the character arc here? How does it end, this story?'

'You have the end. I don't know what the hell went on with my childhood.'

'No, no. Think much later than that. Things usually come full circle in a story. What happened? Did you pursue your dream and become a rector in the village church, helping the people of Hollydale? That would be fitting.'

Edamine raised an eyebrow.

'No, I found I had a blasted disease that was eating my limbs. It sent my dreams off kilter somewhat. For as long as I could work, I was at the Stone Bull, helping the old men of Hollydale prop their beer on the bar. I was always taught that alcohol was the devil's sin, although father drank every day, of course. I found his secret stash. He would have been ultra proud of both my job and of my detective skills don't you think?' She raised the glass with the last of her wine to the ceiling. 'Cheers Rector.'

Beau smothered a surprised laugh, and Edamine patted Beau's hand.

'Life is a real shit show, right? Come on, raise your glass!'

Beau raised her glass to meet Edamine's, and as their glasses chinked, there was a loud crash from the kitchen.

Beau jumped up from her seat as Edamine yelled and spilled wine onto the table.

'Let me get that,' Beau said, her heart thumping as she rushed into the kitchen to see the back door swinging shut after crashing into the fridge, which now had a small dent in its own door.

She almost expected a flash of red outside, and to see the man, Daniel, rushing away, but there was nothing. As the door clicked shut, Edamine's voice next to her ear made Beau jump.

'I guess he's not happy with our toast.'

'Who?'

'Father.' Beau turned, hoping to see Edamine laughing - it's a joke, see? - but she was serious. 'I feared this would be the trouble. We can chat about it later. For now, let's lighten up. Bring another bottle in Beau. Let's have more wine.'

Chapter 30

'W HAT'S THE MATTER, DADDY? Just sit and watch the film, you'll walk a hole in the floor!'

Joe forced a smile at Leila, who looked up at him with big blue eyes that looked so much like Hannah's he wanted to cry.

Where had this all gone so wrong? How had he let it get so far, and why couldn't he go back to knowing nothing about what was going on - or what he thought was going on? He couldn't be sure, and that was the clincher. If he could just find out where Hannah was, hear some sort of noise that would give her position away, or even just trust her, he would feel so much better.

He rubbed a hand over his mouth, aware that Leila was still watching him.

'My legs are all achy from the zoo, honey. I feel like they need stretching out.'

Leila wrinkled her nose. 'When my legs ache, you always tell me they need a rest.'

'This is a different ache. Listen, I'm just going to make us a snack and a drink. What do you fancy?'

'Popcorn and Crunchie bites with chocolate on toast and strawberry milkshake.'

Joe tried to paste a look of horror onto his face but had trouble twisting it into anything but worry.

'What? Your mother would have a cow, especially before your dinner.'

Leila laughed. 'She's not here.'

Joe shook his head and placed his hands over his eyes, and Leila giggled.

'You're right,' he sighed. 'She's not here.'

Where the fuck is she?

'So I can have it? Everything?'

'Everything,' Joe said, forcing a smile.

'You're so much *fun*, daddy.'

Translates into you're such a pushover, Joe, remember that when she's walking all over you like Hannah does.

'I bet. Popcorn, Crunchie bites, and chocolate toast with strawberry milkshake coming right up.'

He grabbed his phone from the coffee table, leaving Leila snuggled in the cashmere blanket, watching The Jungle Book - one of her favourites. It was warm now that the heating was fixed, but Joe had been feeling rebellious at the time and they had snuggled in the 'best show cashmere' until late most nights. Since it was only 3.40pm, today had started even earlier. A kind of middle finger up at Hannah.

At the moment, I think Hannah may break it off in her attempt to murder you.

Maybe put the cashmere back, Joe.

Joe thought he may consider it. In the kitchen he brought the popcorn and Crunchie packet out of the cupboard and popped four slices of toast in the toaster - he was partial to Nutella on toast himself and Leila would expect him to join in - it was a glorious life when Hannah was away.

It used to be anyway.

He left the bread in the toaster for the moment. Leila would give him a good fifteen minutes before she came looking, he estimated, and that was enough.

He picked up the phone and dialled Hannah. She answered almost immediately.

'Joe! I'm so sorry. I've been thinking about you all day. I know I've been a bitch. I'm just miserable here, and it's driving me insane. I want to come home, and I take it out on you, that's all. I'm so sorry, I really am.'

Joe let his mouth drop open, his pre-planned speech dropping away at the difference he had expected in her tone. He felt warmth flood his chest. This was Hannah, his wife, and she wasn't perfect, but over the last few days, he had made her into a monster.

Didn't you think just that she would murder you for having a blanket out? Jesus, Joe!

'Joe? Please, I don't expect you to forgive me. I know I was hard on you, but none of what I said was true. I love you. I love Leila. Our family is all that's important to me right now. I'm sorry, I really am, do you believe me? At least say you believe me.'

Hannah's voice caught, and Joe's heart stumbled in his chest.

'I'm sorry, too, Han. I shouted as much as you, and I didn't mean any of it either. I'm just frustrated at the situation.'

'Me too, like you wouldn't believe. This is never happening again. I'm done!'

Joe felt his smile slip.

'With the company?'

Hannah sighed. 'No, of course not with the company. I've poured my heart and soul into it. I'm done with being called out to places I don't need to be. These decisions could have been made so easily, they're not integral to the company's operation.

It's annoying. These people just can't seem to function without me.'

That's because you don't let them, just like you don't let me run the household. You won't let go of the control, not for a second.

Knowing that insight wasn't going to go down well, Joe changed the subject.

'We miss you, Han. When are you coming home?'

He expected more excuses – lies? – and was shocked at her answer.

'Tomorrow, possibly the day after, but that's at most. I can't stay away any longer, I want to be home with my family. Joe, I've had a lot of time to think up here about what the therapist used to say to me about Cass.'

Joe felt blindsided. He swallowed hard. 'What about her?'

'Not about her, exactly, but of that time when she moved out, and I felt like I was being squeezed out of her life, and I hated it. I pushed her away by holding too tightly. The therapist gave me the analogy of a bird he befriended when he was small.'

'You never told me.'

'I didn't? Well, long story short, he made friends with a robin in his garden when he was a child. He spent almost a year putting seed out every day until it was tame enough to eat from his hand. Each morning he was late, the bird used to sit on his bedroom windowsill and tap at the glass. He said that he loved that bird like nothing else. As time went on, he'd sit with it in the garden and the bird would land on his hand or his knee, but one day he got it into his head that the bird was free, and that it could leave at any time. Again, long story short, he tried to put the bird in a cage he brought from the local pet shop using his pocket money. The bird wasn't happy, his parents weren't happy, and a fight ensued, he grabbed the bird and held it close trying to stop it from being frightened while his parents screamed at him to let it go free, but he squeezed too hard and...'

'It died,' Joe finished.

'Yeah.'

'That's how friendship feels for you?'

Hannah paused, and then she laughed. A light, fluttery sound.

'Well, not quite to that extreme, but kind of. I understand that I get too attached, and that it's not healthy.'

Joe shook his head with a smile that melted all the tension in his shoulders away. It was going to be okay, of course it was, and he could cope here. He'd had a meltdown to Beau, and that made him feel better, stronger. He had thought he could decide what to do about his situation when she was back, but there was a difference here. Maybe Hannah had changed, maybe she was learning. Maybe Beau had been right, maybe they could sit down and talk it out after all. He was busy making a monster of her, and she wasn't a monster. She was a human. A human with issues, and wasn't that applicable to most humans?

'I am sorry, Joe. I've been awful to you, my amazing husband, to Beau, who I think of as a sister, to everyone around me. I'm toxic.'

'You're not toxic. There are things in your past that have caused these reflexes, that's all. We can work through them.'

Hannah sniffed, and Joe almost held his breath. Was she *crying*? Actually crying?

'I just have one thing left to do here and I'll be home. I'm going to make this better Joe, I'm going to make it up to you. To everyone. I promise, everything will be okay. It will all be okay.'

Joe scrunched his eyes against his own tears as he heard her struggle with emotion. It was a side to Hannah he had never seen. Ever.

This is some breakthrough.

'I'm thinking we could move when I get back. Live somewhere different. You always said you wanted to be by the sea, didn't you? We'll move wherever you want, right when I get back. Just pack up and go. Let's just go, Joe, far, far away from all this crap.'

There was wet on his cheeks and Joe realised he was crying with her.

'I don't want to uproot you, Han. You said Chester is the best place for your business. We're okay here-'

'We're not okay, and you haven't been okay for a long time. I know it, I've just been turning a blind eye. This trip has made me reassess a lot, and I know how I've been – how I am – and I'm going to make it all right. I'm going to do what's best for us, best for everyone.'

Joe hadn't known just how much tension he had been holding over the years until that moment when a barrage of pent-up emotion left him in a flood.

Leila appeared in the doorway, cashmere blanket dragging on the floor behind her. He sat down, his back against the cupboard, and held out an arm, unable to say anything. She climbed onto his lap and snuggled close, squeezing her little arms tight around his back.

'I hate her,' she whispered, and Joe shook his head, another sob leaving him.

Leila was perceptive. They were too close for her not to feel how he hurt, but she didn't understand.

'Joe? Please don't hate me,' Hannah was saying down the phone. 'Please, give me a chance to put this right.'

There was a commotion, and then laughter. Voices. Joe sniffed.

'Where are you, Han? It's noisy.'

'The restaurant stops serving lunch soon. I've had to come down to eat.'

Joe felt a current of something strong run through him.

Lunch? At 4pm?

Maybe she's in a different time zone. You don't even know where she is.

Still, the actual time didn't matter. She was going to eat right now? They hadn't even finished their conversation. Did the woman who didn't do crying really walk into a restaurant with tears rolling down her face?

She could have wiped them. Her voice sounded pretty normal now.

She's going to lunch while I'm busy breaking my heart?

A mixture of anger and disappointment ran through him. It didn't matter what she said, she still didn't get it.

'I'll let you eat, Han. We'll see you soon.'

'Okay. Ow, watch it, I could have been carrying a drink!' A heavily accented man apologised and explained that his wife had fallen ill. Hannah huffed. 'I wish people would look where they're going. It's not even like it's busy! I have to go, Joe, but I'll speak to you soon. Love you.'

'Love you,' Joe whispered as she cut the call, and he realised his tears had dried at the strange ending. She had been trying to make amends, and yet all he was left with was emptiness, disillusion, and a shit ton of questions.

How could she be crying one minute, and then at a restaurant the next? And when he was sobbing on the other end of the phone, too?

He thought about what she had said.

Could she change that much in just over a week? Had she really reflected, or was it lip service? Would she change her mind about moving from this prison when she returned?

I won't fucking let her. I'm done here. I'm holding her to it.

Joe put the phone down on the floor and wound his arms around Leila.

'It's going to be okay, Leila. We're moving to the sea, and things are going to be better. I promise.'

The words trailed off as he hugged his daughter close, and a ter- rifying realisation swept over him. The accent. He recognised the accent of the man she had cursed in the restaurant.

Hannah was in Scotland.

Had she been there this whole time?

Joe felt his body begin to shake.

She said she has one thing left to do. Is it a coincidence that she's in Scotland?

As much as he wanted to believe that she was genuinely on a business trip, he couldn't shake the terror that now clutched his heart

I have to warn Beau.

Chapter 31

B EAU COULDN'T DECIDE WHETHER it was the wine or the story that was making her head thump. They had chatted easily after lunch, and a couple of hours had passed by with wine and laughter as the weather had worsened outside, but now the conversation had turned to Edamine's father and his return from the grave.

Beau hadn't invited Edamine over to learn about the horrific things that had happened here, although she hadn't minded Edamine offloading, and it had shown her fierce and commanding character in a completely new light; and she hadn't invited her over to discuss the odd things that were now happening around the cottage and stamping them with a paranormal label.

She loved to write about her characters being terrorised by ghosts, for sure, but she did not need to be terrorised by them herself while she was writing - especially when she had never really believed they existed. They were a great platform for terror and invoking terror in others through story - that had been true for centuries, maybe even since time began, but that's all they were. Stories and illusion.

She bit at her lower lip.

So, if you're sure about that, what's been happening here? You thought someone was living here and messing around with you... maybe that person is still here and trying to mess with you?

Beau looked up at Edamine. She was sitting on the settee at a right angle to Beau's in the living room, holding a mug of coffee in her frail hands.

'I thought little of it at first,' she was saying. 'It began small, just tiny things to let me know he was there. I'd smell cigar smoke when I walked into this room. I thought I was making it up for a long time, but then I'd see the chair over there.' Edamine pointed to the rocking chair in the corner. 'It would rock and rock with this awful creaking. I tried to put the chair on a mat to get it off the floorboards, anything so that I could block out the sound, but I heard it all the same. Creeeeaaaakkkk. Creeeeeaaaaakk. Oh, the god-awful noise used to drive itself into my brain and I...'

Beau felt the hair at the back of her neck prickle and pressed her fingers to her temple as she took a sip of coffee and let Edamine's voice trail off.

Did I smell cigar smoke when I came in here earlier? Did I?

Does she know? Is she playing with me?

Oh crap, we shouldn't have sunk two bottles of wine with dinner. How am I supposed to assess what the hell is going on here? I'm not sure if I'm drunk, if Edamine is drunk, or whether I'll even remember any of this tomorrow.

Beau jumped as rain splattered against the window, sounding like someone had thrown a handful of small pebbles at the glass under the pressure of the wind. The storm had snuck up with a sudden ferocity that unnerved her, and she placed a hand on her chest with a small laugh.

'I'm not sure that's called for when we're talking about the supernatural.'

Then the whole cottage seemed to shift as a moaning whine whistled around its edges, and Edamine looked to the window.

'You get used to it. The angles on the cottage, and the depth of the porch, trap the wind until the moaning and creaking has you thinking the thing is going to fall down around your ears. Never has up to yet, though.'

The cottage creaked as another gust pushed the rain at the window.

'Let's hope tonight isn't the night. At least we know *that* isn't supernatural.'

Edamine chuckled. 'No, no. That's definable. I could never define why the rocking chair rocked, or why the smell of cigars I never smoked hung around in the living area well after my father had smoked his last.'

Again, Beau felt the prickle at the base of her neck.

I smelled cigar smoke earlier. I did.

Oh shit.

What does that mean?

'Was... was there anything else that ever happened here?'

'Just the back door, but that was very occasional and not as forceful as today. I often wondered if the lock was just broken, but Gerard could never find anything wrong, and it didn't happen often enough to worry me.'

Beau chewed at the side of her mouth.

The door has opened a number of times on me in just the last week.

Is it better or worse that it's the same activity that Edamine experienced, only it seems to have intensified for me?

Is it really Rector Locket, or someone else? Someone real?

Beau decided to play along with Edamine for now.

'When did you find out it was your father that was here? You seem pretty certain.'

'I am. One-hundred-and-ten percent. I was at ninety-seven when I sought help from Ophelia. I didn't know her well back then, but I knew she was friendly because I'd spoken to her in the pub when I was on shift, and I knew she owned the shop, but thinking the place was to...' she paused, looking for the right words and finally put her coffee on the table to hold her fingers in inverted comma's. 'Woo woo' I'd never been inside.'

Beau grinned. 'I thought exactly the same, and then I asked her why she had quills but no feathers…'

Edamine's eyebrows shot up and her eyes crinkled with humour as she got the mistake straight away. 'Oh, well, I'm sure she won't talk about you too much.'

They laughed, and Beau pursed her lips and shook her head. 'I still feel like an idiot. Anyway, carry on.'

Edamine took a sip of coffee as another whine rolled around the house and rain lashed at the windows.

'Well, I sleep light, so after being woken for at least three weeks in a row by the blasted rocking chair, I asked her what she did, on a hunch, really. She told me that she and Gill worked with crystal therapy, pendulum dowsing, scrying, and tarot, and other wonderful things which I had no idea about. I still didn't know if she could help, but when she offered to show me around the shop, I agreed.' Edamine grinned at Beau. 'By the end of the evening, she was drawing my cards and using the crystal ball, all in much the same manner as we did last night. It's still as fun now as it was then, but what drew my attention to the fact that she was no fake was that she told me about the problems here before I could tell her. She 'saw' the rocking chair and 'smelled' the smoke. She told me an older gentleman liked to sit in the cottage and watch over me. He was anxious and wanted to get a message to me.'

Beau sat forward, hanging onto Edamine's words with a little worry. If Ophelia had got Edamine's father before she even knew her well, then it was perfectly acceptable that she got Beau's trouble out here, too.

But why would the rector want to watch over me?

Maybe he just wants you out of his cottage.

She pushed the thoughts away.

'So, what happened?'

'Ophelia and Gill came down here, and that's when I learned Ophelia is also a medium. She can talk to the dead. Apparently, he approached her as soon as we entered, and she described him perfectly, although I had never told her the history of our house or that he was a rector. She said that he was a 'man of the cloth', which is what he often called himself, and described his cassock, gown, and silk scarf.

I confirmed he was my father, and she asked him if wanted to cross over. He said that he had a message for me, and that I was to see the doctor about my arms as soon as possible.'

Edamine sipped her coffee.

'It was strange, you know, because I'd been suffering in silence. I hadn't told a soul. I was almost twenty-five back then and I couldn't understand why my arms no longer wanted to reach the top cupboards. They just wouldn't rise enough. They hurt and ached, and although it was annoying, I wasn't really bothered, more intrigued. I was young. What could possibly be so wrong?

Ophelia told me he wouldn't cross unless I saw the doctor, and so I did. Like I said, I wasn't expecting anything mind blowing, certainly not life altering, and it didn't seem like a huge ask to have the chair still and the air clear again. He told me he loved me; I kept my promise to see the doctor the next day, and from that moment I never heard from him again.'

Beau shook her head at the strangeness. Was this actually real?

Did she look a fool for believing this? Or was Edamine being truthful?

Her face was serious, and she didn't seem to be joking. Earlier, she had said that the story of her father was relevant to Beau, too? What did that mean?

'That's strange, especially with your diagnosis, too.'

'That's how I know. One-hundred-and-ten percent. My father had come back over that period to make sure that I got the care I needed. The disease could have progressed much faster without the right care, physio, and medication. I may not be here now. He was looking out for me, and after what happened to Constance, I was grateful. It made him a little less of a monster if you get me?'

'And I suppose if you said nothing to Ophelia, and she got it spot on, then you had no reason to doubt her.'

'Not one. I told her nothing, and she stepped in here and knew everything. It was both surreal and weirdly comforting to know that she could cross those spaces for us to communicate. As I said, I've not heard anything from him since. I think he was making sure I got the best care I could as early as I could.'

Beau smiled and reached to squeeze Edamine's hand.

'That's a really nice story, especially after the one about your sister. I suppose it would kind of redeem him a little for you.'

'Exactly right. It was a strange but enlightening few days after meeting Ophelia and Gill, and I've been good friends with both ever since. I feel a little indebted even all these years later.'

Beau nodded. 'I can imagine. Edamine, you said that the story of your sister was relevant earlier. What did you mean by that?'

Edamine finished her coffee and placed her cup down with a small smile. More rain attacked the window and Beau flinched. If this carried on she thought her heart may actually give out, but Edamine didn't show any sign of noticing.

'Back when Ophelia told me what she saw, she began by asking if I was having trouble at the house. I said I could be, and she elaborated. Last night she said that you were having trouble here-'

Beau felt her cheeks redden as she cut Edamine short with a laugh. 'Oh, no. I understand what you mean, but no, there's nothing like that.'

Edamine stared.

'Ophelia is rarely wrong in my experience, and the terms she used were the same. It triggered a sense of déjà vu, almost.'

'Well, she's wrong this time. I'm-'

'Having trouble with the back door?' Edamine said, stopping Beau in her tracks.

There was a moment of silence as Beau scrambled for a suitable story, as though both Edamine and the storm were waiting for her answer, but Beau couldn't think of anything to say.

'I... I mean...'

'You didn't seem surprised that it had banged open. In fact, all you said was 'I'll get that,' as though you knew it would be the door.'

Beau opened her mouth, shut it, and then tried again.

'I did know it was the door, yes.'

It was incriminating, but it was all she could think to say.

'So you've had this happen before.'

It was a statement, not a question, and Beau tried not to roll her eyes.

There was no way that she was sitting with Edamine talking about the ghost of her father haunting the Cottage she was renting for the next six months - especially as only a week had passed by.

'Yes, but I'm sure the lock is just broken, that's all.'

'I thought the same until the night my father crossed over and it never came open again. To my knowledge, it's not opened since... until now. And Beau? The door never blasted open like that for me. It sometimes did it so quietly that I wouldn't know until I walked into the kitchen.'

Beau felt herself flush.

'What are you trying to say, Edamine? That your father is back to watch over me - a complete stranger? Or that he wants me out?'

Edamine let out a soft chuckle. 'He doesn't want you out. He's never been a problem for the sitters here since I first began employing them over twenty years ago. No, that's not it.'

'Well, he doesn't know me, and it's just a door. I think you're getting carried away here.'

'Just a door?' Edamine raised her eyebrows.

Beau nodded and held her stare. 'Just a door.'

Edamine pursed her lips. 'Okay, but you're not the only one Gerard spills secrets to around here. Let me tell you that.'

'Gerard?'

'He told me you've been experiencing more than the door.'

Beau sighed, and then she huffed a laugh. 'Bloody Gerard.'

'Loose-lipped bugger, I told you.'

Beau nodded, and a certain weight slipped from her shoulders. She didn't need to hold back anymore. If Gerard had spoken, then Edamine probably knew most of it anyway, except for the attic. Had she told Gerard about the attic before today? Or the record player? She couldn't remember.

Bugger.

'What's been troubling you here, Beau? Maybe if it is father, we can get Ophelia down here again. No point in you being scared to death too, and maybe he has another message. Maybe that's why he's back.'

'I'm not scared.'

Much, anyway.

'So, tell me.'

Beau sighed as another gust of wind and rain battered the old cottage.

This storm was certainly settling in. There was no way Edamine was going anywhere just yet, and it was early in the afternoon.

So just tell her everything. Let's get it out of the way and we can move on.

'Okay, well, there are only a few things, nothing major, and I certainly wouldn't call them trouble-'

'I'm listening, and we have all the time in the world by the looks of this storm. I want to know everything.'

Chapter 32

D ANIEL SHUT THE DOOR to his small room and flicked on the light. It was only 4.30pm but felt much later. The sky outside was black, the rain thunderous, and only the odd streak of lightning lit the outside world. It was typical that Lucas had let him off early in this moment, right when he could have done with a walk to dissect the knowledge in his head.

He blew out a long breath, grabbed his laptop and sat on the bed, hearing the first rumble of thunder as he switched it on.

He swallowed hard. Normally he would go and see Anna – make a nuisance of himself, she always said, but she never turned him away. He knew she was grateful for all that he was doing for her, and today she had been extra grateful.

Because you found her sister.

His heart thumped as he loaded Google and punched 'Cottage, Hollydale, Scotland' into the search bar. His hands were shaking, and he couldn't seem to keep his focus on the screen. He had known that it probably wouldn't return much, and he was right. After sifting through three pages of holiday cottages that eventually weren't even in Scotland, he shut the search down and heaved a breath.

Come on, Matherson, you're better than this. What was the name of the place?

He glanced out of the window as more lightning lit the sky and he saw the rain driving down in sheets. He tried to calm his mind and gather his scattered thoughts, wishing that of all the idiotic things he had done over the last week, he hadn't left Anna with the napkin that he had written on the evening they first met.

The evening you fucked a possibly deranged woman, or one that certainly isn't who she says she is. The evening you got carried away, didn't even see the weirdness of Anna wanting to find a sister that she couldn't find herself in a village with a handful of houses and three shops. Couldn't see the problem with her sister possibly not wanting to be found.

Daniel clenched his jaw and scrubbed his hands through his hair.

He should have snuck up on her earlier, more than once, and then maybe whatever was going to happen next could have been averted, because he never would have told Anna that he had found her sister at all.

A bead of sweat rolled down his back as he thought about the story Anna had told him. The story he had taken at face value. It was only now that it was too late that he questioned it.

Why didn't she want to see you, Anna? Why would she cut you off if she knew you were hunting her down? Is it because you're a psycho?

Hunting. Had Anna used that word? Or was that just in his mind after what he'd seen?

Daniel huffed a grunt of frustration and got up, breathing heavily.

Okay. Calm down. Just calm the fuck down. What you saw doesn't mean she's a psycho. So, she wears a blonde wig over her dark hair. Is that a crime?

His jaw worked as he began to pace.

That may not be a crime, but the laptop under the bed said a lot of things that could lead to criminal behaviour. Covering identity while hatching a plan to break into a cottage and hurt someone? That's suss as hell.

Daniel swallowed bile as he remembered his note to her.

Forever in my heart. 1940s sex kitten. Stay one of a kind.

All of it he had written to throw her off the scent, because he couldn't stay after what he had read, but now the thought that she had read and believed it made him feel like an idiot; played, and terrified.

He couldn't stop thinking about what he had seen on the laptop and how close he had come to simply asking her - they were in this together, right? But then he had come to his senses. She wouldn't tell him anything, and if she was planning a crime, even if it wasn't murder, she would wipe the evidence.

Should have taken a photo. Should have taken a god damned photo.

Daniel banged his palm into his forehead repeatedly, and finally leaned his head against the wall, panting hard.

What do I do with this information that may or may not be incriminating? What do you do when you're not sure?

He closed his eyes, and it was his father's voice that came into his head.

You're going to be a lawyer, Daniel, so act like one. Sit down and do the goddamn research you were going to do before you wound yourself up again. Sit the fuck down and see if there's any truth to this story. Get the facts, the evidence, and then decide what to do with the knowledge. Guilty or not guilty? Find out, and fast.

Daniel's breathing slowed, and he nodded as the words hit home. He had been around this type of talk all of his life, he understood, he had seen his father at work, had spent long hours at the offices with him as a child. He had hated it, but he got it, and suddenly he knew what to do.

He pushed off the wall and sat down before the laptop with renewed purpose, and a renewed perspective and focus that left him feeling in control.

It was funny what perspective did, and after years of cursing his father for trying to push him into a profession he had no interest in, Daniel was finally thanking him. A mere five minutes after changing tactics and researching the history of Hollydale, he had his answers – and was kicking himself for not remembering the name of the cottage; Bluebell. So simple.

Idiot.

The Cottage had once been a rectory, housing the family of the priests who oversaw the old, ruined church that Daniel loved to visit at the top of the hill. Apparently, the church had fallen into disrepair, and the rectory received a new name following the suicide of its last priest in 1985.

Daniel pulled a notebook from his desk and wrote the details down, ready to expand on them. Now he had something to search, a way forward.

1985. Near enough to be the family that Anna was part of? Or was she part of a new family that had brought the cottage afterward?

How many years did she say it had been since they had spoken?

Daniel felt his mind focus in on that first conversation. He didn't think she had said exactly, but he remembered her saying it was many, many years ago.

Chewing his lip, he wrote her approximate age, mid-forties, at a guess, and then tapped the pen on the paper.

Let's say she's forty-five, and they haven't spoken for twenty years. That would make it around 2004. Even thirty years would make it 1994, and then she would only be fifteen, hmmm.

It's not looking likely that she's the rector's daughter if they had a fight and didn't speak again. It doesn't fit. So who owns the house now?

On a roll, he searched sales details of the cottage and came up with nothing. Nada.

He scratched his head and tried a few more sites, but nothing was forthcoming. Apparently, the house hadn't been sold since the times of the internet, and yet 1985 was pretty close, that sort of information would have been added for sure.

Daniel turned back to history. Maybe a historical document would give him more of a clue. He searched for the last rector's suicide and had too much luck - pages and pages of luck. There was a lot to sift through, and it wasn't light reading. He scanned a few articles, taking notes as he came across things which piqued his interest, getting into the tragic story, even if it didn't match Anna's.

The church had been smashed and vandalised just the day before the rector had hung himself from the large church window.

That figures. The church was his life... and death, literally. Yet he left behind a wife and a small child? That doesn't figure.

But then he read further and found more. The rector's seven-year-old daughter, his second child, had tragically fallen from the cliffs at the back of the church just two years earlier, killing her instantly. Reports of vandalism at the church began at around the same time and had continued until the rector's death.

Oh, wow, that's bad luck, Daniel thought, rubbing a hand across his mouth. He thought about how much he enjoyed his walks to the church, sitting in the quiet of the ruins, and photographing the sea through the arched window. The arched window the rector hung himself from?

Well, that will make a pretty picture when I go there now.

Daniel wrinkled his nose and felt his time at the Antler Hotel coming to an end. The events of the last week, and the things he was digging into now, were tainting the area a little for him.

Well, mostly Anna, and what she'll do from here, and whether I should do anything about it. That's the real issue.

He blew air from his lips and looked back to the article, skimming his eyes down the page, past pictures of the ruined church and the cottage that he was so familiar with now. He hadn't expected to find anything more, it was pretty obvious what had happened, but to Daniel's surprise, he found a link to another article, this time a blog post, written much later in 2005.

Accidental Murder at Holly Tor church?

Twenty years after a tragic accident saw a seven-year-old girl killed falling from the cliffs behind the church atop Holly Tor, speculation continues as to whether it was, in fact, murder.

The enigmatic story of Constance Locket and that of her father has followed residents of Hollydale since the mid-1980s. With the benefit of hindsight, is it possible to determine the truth of what happened that day? And what fuelled the rumours of murder, which resulted in the vandalism of a sacred church and the subsequent suicide of its rector?

Constance Locket was one of two children born to the rector and his wife. The eldest, Edamine, was born in 1972, and her sister Constance followed in 1976. It was said that Rector Locket was a fair but stern man. He and his wife were older parents and several of the church's regular patrons report him having little patience with the sisters, who were seven and eleven years old respectively, when the accident happened in 1983.

'They were always there at the church doors on Sunday morning, freshly starched and ramrod straight…[sic]… It's no life for a couple of bairns now, is it?' one patron is reported saying at the time. Does this allow us a glimpse of the children's lives at home, or was it a show for the patrons of the church? There is no way of knowing.

It is said that the younger child, Constance, had not been to school that fateful day. She was feeling unwell and had been allowed to stay at home with her parents at Hollydale Rectory.

The rectory, a pretty two-story, whitewashed cottage, surrounded with a cosy porch, lies in a secluded position in the valley between coastal cliffs. Photographs give the place an idyllic feel but looks can deceive and who knows what went on behind closed doors, or what poor Constance was subjected to that morning while her sister went on to school without her.

From the father's testimony, it is understood that an argument broke out just after lunch, and as the argument intensified, Constance, whom he deemed to be hotheaded, fled from the cottage. Fearing for her safety, both he and his wife followed her as she ran up the hillside to the church.

Why she ran to the church is a mystery, but being a rector's daughter, she would have possibly believed that the church was a safe haven, and that God would protect her. That day it wasn't to be. Constance found no sanctuary at the church, just locked doors. No safety for a small, scared child.

With no access, Constance ran to the back of the church, possibly to hide, but as corroborated by both the mother and the father's testimonies, they cornered her at the top, in a move to stop the chase and take Constance home. It is obvious that the small girl would now only feel trapped and terrified, on little more than two feet of cliff edge that is uneven and treacherous. Her mother tried to coax Constance out, but admits that Rector Locket barged his way toward her, no doubt red faced and angry, having lost all control at the insolence of his small daughter. When he reached her, she panicked and slipped, tumbling from the edge, and plunging sixty feet into the ocean below.

A tragic accident.

Or was it?

Speculation, and witnesses to the rector's temper, suggest that she didn't fall, but that her father's fury led to him pushing her over the edge, putting an end to her insolence for good, and showing her sister what would happen if she didn't play by the rules. Rules that had been seen enforced by a few regular patrons who often saw the younger girl at the church with her father after school. When questioned by one as to why the girl was cleaning pews at eight-thirty on a school night, the rector simply laughed and said that she was after extra sweets, but another patron said that he had told her on a separate occasion she was being punished for 'not playing by the rules'. A strange statement not only from a father, but from a man of God.

After the accident, the rumours came thick and fast, but the rector, if he was guilty, was never brought to justice. He was found hanging from his church window just two years later, after the establishment had been heavily vandalized, leaving the stunning, stained-glass window broken.

Was Constance's death an accident or murder? It is a question that has hung over the small village of Hollydale for over twenty years, where the ruin of the church, and a question with no solid answer, both stand to this day.

Did the innocent rector hang himself over the rumours and the vandalism of his church? Or because he was guilty of the murder of his own daughter?

What really happened on top of Holly Tor that day will be lost to history forever, a secret of only the sea, a rector, and his small daughter.

Alison Murdoch, 7th April 2005

Daniel jotted some notes and sat back, shaking his head. Who knew that such a story could hang around a village with only a handful of people resided? What a scandal. It was no wonder the rumours spread, and gossip would have kept it alive.

He wondered who had started it, and whether there was any truth to it, or whether it had been fabricated into a much more thrilling story to tell. Especially when a child was involved.

Lightning flashed outside, and a long rumble of thunder followed, but Daniel barely noticed.

People loved a tragedy, but if there was murder involved, especially involving such a prominent member of society, it would make it especially juicy.

Daniel huffed a laugh and then shook his head. People just couldn't stop their judgment of others could they?

Anyway, on to Anna...

...oh, wait a minute!

'I guess that solves that,' Daniel murmured. 'How can she be the rector's daughter wanting to make with her sister if her only sister died?'

No, that doesn't make sense. There's more to this story, more to Bluebell Cottage after the rector. I just have to find out the next chapter.

Either that or Anna really wasn't who she said she was at all, and she was here on a totally different mission, and that meant that he would have no chance of finding out anything.

A flash, and a loud crack of thunder made him flinch, and the ominous air of the storm sent a shiver running down his spine.

Chapter 33

'I'M NOT SURE HOW I'm getting back across the land in this,' Edamine said as she used her stick to stand and look out of the window.

The sky was inky black across the ocean and rain hurled itself at the windows as the wind whipped it into a frenzy. There was a moan and a long creak from the cottage that Beau tried to ignore even as it raised the hair on her arms.

'Don't be daft, you're not going anywhere tonight. You can't go out in that, I won't let you. You can stay in your old room.'

Edamine chuckled and turned to Beau. 'That sounds wonderful Beau, but my legs are shot, I won't even make the stairs.'

'I'll help you up them, we'll manage. Gerard can't come back out here in this, and you certainly can't go out there.'

Edamine raised her eyebrows. 'I suppose we agree on that. It would be suicide for me, and it appears to be getting worse. I think the storm came over early after all. I can't get up the stairs though, so as much as I'd love to sleep in my old bed, I'll just have to sleep on the couch down here.'

Beau joined Edamine at the window and placed a hand on her arm with a smile. 'Wherever you sleep, I can't say I'll be upset to have company after the conversation we just had about ghosts.'

Edamine laughed. 'I don't have to imagine. I've been there.'

'You really think it's your father?'

'Things match up, don't they? The door and the cigar smoke?'

'But what about the clock and the record player? Oh, and the noises in the attic?'

'Maybe he got more inventive over the years.'

Beau blinked, and then Edamine began to laugh. 'I'm not sure Beau. Like you said, what would he bother to come back for? I'm no longer here, and he doesn't know you. No other sitters have had any problems. Maybe it's coincidence.'

'Gerard said that the door played up last year, but he didn't mention anything else.'

'And certainly not to me. Are you sure you aren't hearing things? Especially with your line of work, you know?'

Beau rolled her eyes. 'You sound like Gerard.'

Edamine grinned back out of the window as the first streak of lightning lit the room. 'It's an obvious thing to say, isn't it? You're an imaginative soul, and you're writing ghost stories in an isolated cottage, all alone.'

'Right, so what was your excuse?'

'Oh, I didn't need one. He was my father, and he was here to warn me about my condition.'

'Fabulous. That makes you sane then.'

Edamine chuckled and Beau shook her head with a half-smile as her phone began to ring. She turned her head to the kitchen. 'I'll just see who that is. It may be important.'

'No problem, I'll just wait here. The storm is fabulous!'

Beau thought she may have used a different word as she made her way to the kitchen with the cottage creaking under the wind. She picked up her phone, and her stomach dropped.

Joe again? Something's happened.

She called to Edamine that she would just be a moment and swiped to answer. On the other end, Joe was already speaking.

'Beau? Beau, Beau! Are you there?'

Beau glanced at the phone in shock and then put it to her ear, her heart drumming as her adrenaline spiked.

'Joe? I'm here. I'm here. What is it? What's happened? Are you okay?'

'Beau, thank God, are you okay?'

Beau blinked, feeling like she was in an alternate universe. 'Um, I'm fine. Are you okay? You sound... strange.'

'I feel it. Beau, have you heard from Hannah at all?'

'No. Not a thing. I've given up thinking I will, or that I want to after our last conversation.'

Beau began to laugh, but Joe cut her off.

'Did you check out the newspaper article? The picture I told you to look at? It's worse. So much worse than our last conversation. Please believe me. You have to be careful.'

Beau felt her stomach roll over. 'I haven't looked yet. I have company. Joe, what's the matter? What's gone on?'

'I had a phone call from Hannah, and now I'm worried we're both in trouble, or at the very least, you are. It was weird.'

Beau's heart thumped hard under her jumper.

'What happened?'

Beau listened as Joe explained that Hannah had called full of apologies and saying that she was homesick. He also told her that Hannah had been keen to move and make things better between them when she came home in a couple of days. Beau struggled to see what was so wrong.

'Surely that's a good thing?'

'I thought so. She never cries, and she seemed to understand what was wrong with the way she processed friendship and the way she wouldn't let go of the control. She seemed to understand that there was a problem with us and said that she was going to make it okay, she was going to put everything right. Like you say, it should have been a good thing, but there are a couple of reasons I've just got a massive hunch something is wrong.'

Beau swallowed hard. 'What are they?'

'First she was crying, and she doesn't cry.'

Beau thought back. 'No, I must admit I've seen her tear up, but never actually cry.'

'Me neither, in almost twelve years, and yet yesterday she sobbed on the phone, really sobbed. So much so that I was crying with her. It was like a literal breakthrough, like we had a moment, and I thought she may actually be aware of her actions.'

'That's great, so what was wrong?'

'In the middle of this, the very middle – as in I was still sobbing, and she had literally been sobbing two seconds before - she went to lunch... in a restaurant.'

Beau felt confusion ripple through her.

'She went to lunch?'

'Lunch. She just stopped crying and said, oh, I have to eat before the restaurant closes. Just like that. I was still crying. *Crying*, beau, and she's like 'I have to eat'!'

'That sounds...'

'Like Hannah. Unfortunately.'

Beau pursed her lips. Where Joe was concerned, she had to admit that it did.

'Yeah. I get it.'

'I was still wiping my tears when she ended the call.'

'I'm so sorry, Joe.'

'You don't need to be, I'm used to it. What was strange was that someone who never cries suddenly wipes her tears and steps into a restaurant?'

'Red eyed and all, I know, and no, it doesn't sound right.'

'It sounds like she was faking the whole thing, like it was a fuck-ing performance. She just kept saying she would make things right, and the last time she was so adamant about that, Cassie died.'

Beau felt her stomach lurch as goosebumps littered her arms.

'But she said she was coming home, right?'

'Tomorrow, or the day after. The point is, she said she had something to take care of first, and when she entered the restaurant, I heard a couple of people speak to her. Beau, their accents were Scottish. She's in Scotland.'

'Scotland? She's up here?'

'Yes, she has to be. Do you see what I mean now? She puts on a performance, tells me everything will be okay, and says she will be back after she has sorted something out. The only thing that I feel needs sorting is the way she left things with you, and then she's in Scotland? It's almost too coincidental.'

Beau felt a chill travel down her spine.

'Right. I'm following you and thank you for making me aware. I did show her where I was before I left, so she may just be coming to apologise or-'

'No, Beau, did you hear what I said before? The last time she acted anything like this was a week before Cassie's accident, and if she is up there, then I'm not sure she's coming to put things right as we would. This is putting things right as Hannah would, and I don't like it. I just get a feeling. Please be careful. She could be on her way to you at any point and I have no idea what she is planning.'

The icy chill enclosed itself around Beau and she shivered.

'I'm really sorry, Beau. I wanted to warn you, just in case.'

'Okay, thanks Joe, I'll keep a lookout.'

'Be on your guard. If she gets to you, message me so that I know you're okay. If I haven't spoken to you by the time she gets home, I'll message you, and hopefully that's that and I have it all wrong. She says you're like a sister to her. Let's hope that means that's she not planning anything bad. I know this sounds farfetched but look at the photo I told you about. You'll see what I mean, then you can judge for yourself.'

'I will. You take care too, Joe.'

'Stay safe.'

Beau put the phone down on the side feeling sideswiped. An inkling of something stirred in her brain as Edamine called from the living area.

'Everything okay, Beau?'

Beau remembered something up by the church, something with a man... Daniel! Daniel said that he was watching the cottage for a woman who was tracking her sister. A sister who lived in this cottage.

'Beau? I've just had a call from Ophelia.'

Feeling off kilter, and with her train of thought interrupted, Beau made her way back through to the living room with Daniel still on her mind.

'Ophelia?'

Edamine nodded, her face serious. 'She's uneasy that we're together down here, she says the girl with the angry mouth is close. Any idea what that means? Because if Ophelia's manner was anything to go by, something is about to go down.'

Beau stopped in her tracks as though she had hit an invisible wall.

'The girl with the angry mouth?'

'She said you'd know. I will say, what she didn't know was that I was down here with you. I haven't said a word, but it's not unlike Ophelia to hit things on the nose.'

Beau felt the room tilt and reached to the fireplace for support.

'Shit.'

Edamine tilted her head. 'Beau? Do you know?'

Beau saw Daniel in her head, watched him say that he had been staking out the house, watching her, looking for the sister of this woman that she didn't even ask the name of... wait! He said that the woman was blonde!

Beau looked at Edamine, at her head of white hair that had possibly been blonde at some point. Of course, Edamine was the owner, after all.

'Do you-?' she began, and then cut herself short.

Stupid, Beau. Of course she had a sister, but she really doesn't now. What the hell have you been talking about all afternoon?

The uneasy feeling crept back over her.

'Do I what?'

'I was going to say do you have a sister, but that's a stupid and insensitive question.'

'It's a moot question.'

'It is, and one that I think may provide us an answer to the girl with the angry mouth. I've just had a rather weird phone call, along with an unusual conversation with a man up at the church this morning. Those, coupled with Ophelia's message? I have to say I'm a little on edge now.'

Edamine patted the settee next to her, and Beau moved to sit down.

'Come and tell me. You've gone white as a sheet.'

'I don't know where to start.'

'The beginning,' she said.

And in the corner, the rocking chair began to rock.

Chapter 34

A NNA WORKED HER JAW as she watched the rain streak down the windows of the dining area, the steak sitting on her plate almost untouched. Not that it hadn't been cooked to perfection - it had - but right now, knowing that she had to act fast, and without a proper plan in place, her stomach wanted to reject everything she gave it.

And now this.

She glowered as lightning streaked the sky, and a gust of wind sent rain belting across the windows.

Couldn't be more fucking perfect.

'Is the steak okay, Ms Lane?'

Anna looked up to see Lucas standing ahead of her, and she tried to paste a smile on her lips.

'Perfect. I just don't feel too well, to be perfectly honest. I may go and lie down. I have a big day travelling tomorrow.'

'You're leaving us, are you? Ready to move on? Did you find your sister?'

Anna almost choked and picked up the napkin to pretend to cough into it.

'Yes, I found her, thank you.'

'The old rector's cottage, wasn't it? Quite the scandal there forty-odd years ago, but I don't suppose it was your family caught up in that.'

Anna blinked. 'No.'

'I didn't hear it had been sold on, but there we go. Who were the family back when the rector lived there?' He clicked his fingers and pursed his lips. 'Ah, almost had it... Lockley? No-'

Anna felt fury rise from her stomach. Could he not just shut the hell up? Did she say she wanted small talk?

Calm down, don't blow it just yet. You're quiet. Demure. If you explode now, there will be consequences for sure.

'Locket! That was it,' Lucas said with a triumphant grin.

Anna coughed into her napkin and pushed the chair back to stand. 'I need to lie down. I feel quite unwell.'

Lucas reddened and stammered. 'Oh, of course, Ms Lane. Settle up before you leave tomorrow, don't worry about it now, I'll stick the meal on your room tab.'

'Thank you.'

Anna pushed around the table and almost had a clear run to the exit when Lucas spoke again.

'Was everything all right between you and your sister, Ms Lane? Only you seem to be in a hurry to leave now you've found her. I hope everything went well.'

Anna clenched her teeth hard, pasted another smile on her lips, and turned to him.

'No, Lucas. It didn't go well, that's why I'm leaving first thing tomorrow. Thank you for asking though. It's a sad situation, but not everyone wants to let the past go.'

'Sorry to hear that, pet. Do you want me to tell young Daniel you're free? I'm not sure he knows you're out of here and I know you've built up a friendship. I think he has a little crush to be perfectly honest-'

Anna felt the anger turn in her stomach, and she fought to keep it contained. 'No, thank you. It's fine.'

Not wanting to engage further, Anna strode from the room, leaving the door to slam shut behind her and echo around the roomy reception.

On the way to her room, the rage seethed and swirled just below the surface. She understood she had told Daniel he could say she was after her sister, and agreed he could ask around if needed, but to tell *everyone* the *entire* fucking story?

Even where she was looking?

That wasn't on. In so many ways.

Anna swung through the stair door and stormed up the stairs.

Stupid. Stupid. Boy.

Now when things went down at Bluebell Cottage, all fingers would be pointed at the blonde stranger who was asking about the place at the Antler Hotel. They would suspect she had something to do with it, and they would be right.

Anna reached her room, let herself in and threw herself face first onto the bedclothes with a long screech.

Fuck. Fuck. Fuck. How is this all turning out so wrong?

She flipped over onto her back and stared at the cracked plastered ceiling.

I never should have asked Daniel to help!

But then you may not know anything. It was Daniel who found her.

He wasn't supposed to blab to everyone.

He may have only blabbed to Lucas.

Shit! This isn't good. Now I have no choice but to go tonight. I've been pushed into a corner.

I fucking hate being pushed into goddamn corners. I needed time to prepare properly. I only learned she was there today, for fuck's sake. Give me a goddamn break!

Seven days ago, no-one knew who I was and what I was here for. Now the whole of the Antler Hotel knows, and probably Hollydale too, and what for? What fucking for? Where are your brains, Anna?

Lightning lit the room and Anna stared for a full five seconds before the thunder hit.

The clock on the nightstand flashed 5.06pm.

I'll go later under the cover of total darkness, get out of here without being seen. That leaves a couple of hours to go over a good plan, and for this blasted storm to run itself out.

With a half plan that allowed her time to go over her primary plan, Anna felt her anger dissipate as she pulled her laptop from under the bed and tried to focus on what she had written.

Chapter 35

T HE ROCKING CHAIR ROCKED so slowly that it defied logic, but it continued anyway, like someone had a hand at its back, or someone was sitting in it... someone invisible.

And that noise. That rolling creak of the rockers on the floor.

Beau felt every hair on her body rise as she let out a whimper. 'I... I can't do this Edamine, I'm already on edge and that is freaking me out. I can't deal with this.'

Edamine smiled and leaned forward on the settee. 'It's okay, he won't hurt you, he's just listening to the story. Maybe he is here to help you out too, maybe he likes you. Do you like her father?'

The chair simply creaked on, and Beau shuddered. To hear Edamine address an empty chair like that, so tenderly, was horrifying.

'H... he doesn't know me, and he's scaring me to death. Edamine, I n... need to get out of here. Can we get out of here? We c... can talk in the dining room.'

Beau's legs felt like cooked spaghetti as she tried to stand, but Edamine only sat back into the settee, and Beau dropped back onto the very edge of the chair, ready to run at a moment's notice.

All the way to her car if she needed to.

Heck, all the way back to Chester.

Then her heart slammed harder as she remembered Hannah. This wasn't only a supernatural situation, Hannah was coming too, and she had business to take care of, according to Joe.

Beau felt a frantic wave of panic swell through her. 'Edamine!'

Edamine stared at the chair. 'Ophelia said that if I asked him to stop, then he would. He didn't want to scare me, he only wanted to get my attention. I never needed to ask because he crossed over, and I went to the doctor to be served my life sentence. For the remaining time I had left here, all was quiet.'

Beau was struggling for breath as she kept her eyes fixed on Edamine, the creak from the corner gouging itself into her brain.

'Well, can we do that?' Beau finally whimpered.

Edamine opened her mouth and shut it again with a small sigh. She closed her eyes and shook her head. A small shake, almost as imperceptible as the speed of the rocking chair.

'Edamine?'

'I don't want to,' she snapped, looking back at Beau with a glint of something hard in her eyes.

Beau floundered, surprised at the sudden sharpness. Then she swallowed hard.

'You... you don't want to ask it to stop? Or you don't want to move rooms?'

'Both. Either.'

The air was incredibly tense, and Beau felt a small circle of horror climb up to her chest at the sudden change in the scene.

'Edamine?'

Edamine stared at the chair so hard that Beau wondered if she had been hypnotised, or even worse, possessed by whatever rocked there. She wondered if she should break the spell... and then her thoughts staggered to a halt.

Shit. The book, Beau, the book.

Beau felt a shuddering breath leave her body cold at the coincidence.

In the book she was writing so well here, a malevolent spirit had taken control of the daughter of a priest and was causing mayhem and devastation for the people around her who weren't yet aware. The irony wasn't lost on Beau that Edamine was a priest's daughter, even if she wasn't a child.

That's great, Beau, but the end hasn't yet been written, so what am I supposed to do? What do I do?

Covered in a panicked cold sweat, Beau was certain that her book was coming to life in the very walls it had been written... and then she saw a tear roll down Edamine's cheek and drop to land on her jumper. Beau instinctively reached a hand out to the lady's arm.

'Edamine?' She said softly.

Edamine finally moved a hand to wipe her tears, and Beau reeled with relief.

'You don't understand, Beau. I haven't had the chance to be around him since the night Ophelia came over. I was very frightened back then and I wanted nothing to do with it. It is frightening, I know that, but after... when I knew it had really been him looking out for me, all I wanted was to see something, or hear something again. I wanted to speak to him and know that he was okay. I wanted to thank him, but I didn't get the chance. Ophelia always says that he knows, even if I just say it in my head, but I've never felt that's enough. Not for me. I've been away so long, and I promise you I never thought I'd enter this house again. I didn't think I could, but finally I come home, and my father is here too? It's like he knew...' Edamine paused and raised a hand to her head briefly. 'It's like he was waiting for me to come back, and he's here, but now I don't know what to do. I can't ask him to stop, Beau, because I've wanted this very moment for so long.'

Edamine sniffed and shook her head.

'The other thing that scares me is that it doesn't stop. Does that mean it's not my father at all? I couldn't take that thought, not after so long, I'd rather not know. At the moment I feel a... a connection. Even if it's coincidence. Even if it's not him. I just feel comforted by the rock of the chair. It was where he always sat, and how he always rocked, very slowly, because mother would get irritated by the noise.' Edamine sniffed again and patted more tears with her fingers before turning to Beau. 'Do you see my dilemma?'

Beau pulled her bottom lip under her teeth with a small nod. 'Yes, I understand. I'm just... I've never experienced anything like this before. I'm bloody shitting myself, Edamine.'

Edamine chuckled softly. 'Says the writer of ghost stories.'

'Well, the operative word there is story... *story*. I don't need to experience anything like this in real life. I'm quite happy doing it in the imagination.'

Edamine's chuckles faded, and she stared at the chair.

'Please help me, Beau. You must research for your work. You must know something about these things, and I'd really like to... to connect. You can help me, can't you?'

Beau felt more horror slide into her gut.

'You want to connect with him?'

'I'd like to say thank you, and I'd like to say goodbye, if nothing else.'

The rocking chair creaked to a halt, and the silence was so loud in the dip of the storm, that both women turned to the space it occupied, Beau relieved, Edamine distressed. She threw an arm out, clutching Beau's with a strength she wouldn't have thought the lady possessed.

'No! He's gone! Father? Oh, Beau, he's gone, and I had a chance. I won't be here again, I missed my chance! I missed it.'

Beau flinched as goosebumps littered her arms. 'I'm sure that's not true, Edamine, he's been hanging around since I arrived. I'm certain he'll-'

There was a small click and a crackle from behind that Beau couldn't quite place, and then music suddenly blasted from the corner, making them both yell.

'...forget about me. Don't. Don't. Don't- '

'What in the...?' Edamine got to her feet looking startled, one hand heavy on the arm of the chair to assist, the other at her chest. Beau, also on her feet, swung to the record player with her heart thumping.

The record player.

She stared, trying to make sense of the situation as Edamine was reaching for her stick.

I unplugged it at the wall this morning. This isn't possible.

Breath clogged Beau's throat, and it took her a minute to speak as the song played on. Edamine looked at Beau, her face a mix of fear and awe, and Beau reached a hand into the space between them.

'It's okay, it's the record player. This was what I told you about, it was playing when I got back earlier, too. This is what it does.'

Even when it's unplugged from the wall, ironically.

She swallowed hard, and then, feeling sick, she approached the machine, and almost turned and fled at the sight of the plug, which was back in the wall.

I didn't do that! I didn't plug the thing back in! Was it Gerard? Edamine? Is it on a timer?

Beau floundered, the music played on, and she felt the panic rising in her chest.

Move Beau, shut the thing off before it drives you mad.

She reached down and yanked the plug from the wall, cutting the power and stepping back. Ice slid down her spine as the music slowed to a stop, distorted and edgy.

'Oh, please,' Edamine said, throwing a hand to her ear. 'Raise the needle first, that's awful and you'll break the machine.'

Beau felt the heat in her cheeks as her heart continued to pound in the new quiet, her ears ringing from the change.

'Sorry, I didn't know how it worked.'

She expected Edamine to chastise her while showing her sternly how to take off the 'needle', but when Beau turned, Edamine was smiling.

Well, beaming would be more appropriate.

It sent an uneasy shudder through Beau.

'It doesn't matter. That was him, Beau, for certain. He loved to play that song. You're right, he's here, whether he's in the chair or not. How can we speak to him? How can I say what I need to?'

Beau stared at her, breathing hard. I could leave, she thought irrationally. I could hand Edamine the key and leave her to it. There's no need to be here just to write, I could write in a hotel.

'Beau? Please, I need help.'

And Beau cracked, despite her fear. There was such genuine pain and loss and desperation on Edamine's face, that alongside her terror, Beau felt her heart go out to her. Edamine really believed this was the rector. She really wanted to talk to him, really needed some kind of closure that she never got the chance to have. Beau understood the desperation, and whether she was spooked or not, she could try to put her fear aside, for tonight anyway.

She swallowed, her throat dry as sandpaper. 'Um... didn't Ophelia say that he would hear you if you asked him to stop if he scared you? Surely that means he can hear you when you speak either way. Maybe you should just talk to him.'

'But that's ridiculous. How will I know if he's even getting the message, how do I know if he wants to chat?'

To chat?

A faint waft of cigar smoke found Beau's nostrils, and she tried to keep her voice neutral despite her fear, for Edamine's sake. 'Well, I don't know whether there's much else to do where he is. I suppose he may be busy, but then why has he been hanging around here for a week?'

Edamine frowned and then her face changed to surprise as she sniffed dramatically.

'Cigar smoke! Do you smell it?'

Beau nodded and everything seemed to spin. She had to get out of this room. 'Yes. Are there any more signs that you need? The chair, the record player, the smoke? This is the most activity I've had here in one go, and I'm about to have a breakdown. I think he's happy to talk, so talk. I'll make us a fresh coffee.'

'Coffee.' Edamine nodded. 'Yes, I'd like to settle myself, and then we'll talk to him.'

Beau balked. 'We'll talk to him?'

'I can't do this alone, Beau. I'm frightened.'

'Of what? You said that you wanted to say thank you and good-bye.'

Edamine fingered the cross at her neck and looked toward the chair as the smell intensified.

Maybe because she doesn't know if he's a murderer.

The thought came from nowhere, and Beau felt the room tip. She grasped the arm of the settee as Edamine spoke, proving her wrong.

'Last time he came back, there was a reason. He was trying to tell me that I was ill. I'm afraid there will be more bad news, especially with what Ophelia just said.'

Beau swallowed hard.

'That may be so, but you don't live here anymore, Edamine, and unless his spirit is tied to this place, and not you, then he could find you wherever you are. He'd find you if you moved to Norway.'

'How do we know whether his spirit is tied here?'

'It's not. He wanted to get your attention last time, and then he was happy to leave. As far as my research has led me to believe a spirit who is tied to a place has a reason to walk there and unless that reason is resolved, or they are happy to cross over, they will continue to walk. Many people will experience phenomena in that case, so the other sitters before me would have experienced this. It's about the building, not a connection to anyone living there.'

'So, what are you saying?'

The smell of cigar smoke was finally subsiding, and Beau felt her thumping heart slowing as the room settled slowly back into normality.

'I think - and I'm no expert - that he came back for you. He told you what he wanted and then he left. There was nothing more to keep him here, and as you said, no one has heard from him here since - including you.'

Edamine fiddled with a silver cross at her neck, running a thumb rhythmically over the centre crystal.

'So, you're saying if this was about me, he would have found me in the village?'

Feeling more stable now the phenomena was gone, Beau thought back over her research.

'Apparently, loved ones who have crossed are more than able to find us wherever we are. I don't think this is about you, unless he knew that you were coming here tonight, of course.'

Edamine shook her head. 'I didn't even know that I was coming. How would he?'

Beau shrugged. She didn't know enough to know whether that made a difference to the spirit world or not, but she thought she had read that they were aware of everything - past present and future - or maybe she had made that up.

'Which leaves you, dear,' Edamine said, looking less pale now that the emphasis seemed to be off her officially, and back to Beau.

Beau felt her slowing heart gaining speed again.

'I still don't see why he'd be bothered about me.'

'You're in his place, and it is as it was when he was alive, Beau. Maybe he's protecting the space.'

Beau nodded and blew out a long breath. 'I suppose we'll find out if we can get him to talk. We need to check whether it is your father first though, this could be any spirit playing with us.'

'There's nothing else here. I already know. I feel it.'

'You *want* it. We need to double check. Think of something to ask, something only you and he know, and I'll make the drinks.'

The room darkened as thunder rumbled overhead and Beau turned the light on as she left. It was dim, but dim light was better than half dark, especially for what was to come.

Chapter 36

'F ATHER, IS THAT YOU? Give me a sign if you're here.'

A coincidental streak of lightning flashed through the room and Beau closed her eyes, waiting for the heavy thunder that would follow close on its heels.

She sat next to Edamine on the settee with two cups of coffee steaming on the table ahead. Their eyes were fixed on the chair, but Beau was more worried about a sudden outburst of Simple Minds from behind. She wondered if they should face the record player instead; the creak of the chair didn't have the effect of making her soul leave her body like the record player did.

While she made coffee, Edamine had contacted Ophelia to ask how to speak to spirits. Ophelia, not batting an eyelid, had given Edamine a rundown of things to ask and things to watch for. 'They're just people, but people that can't answer without expending energy. You need to give him a way to answer quickly and easily. Try tapping, and call me if you need more help, I'd love to be there with you!'

Beau had almost asked if they could trade places, and she could sit with Gill drinking coffee, while Edamine and Ophelia sorted the spooks out. It was a real shame that the place was so far off the beaten track, and that they were in the middle of one of the worst storms Beau had witnessed, or she would have been out like a shot.

She had been feeling sorry for herself when Ophelia said something that changed her perspective.

'I bet Beau is loving this. Just think of the new experience she can bring to her writing now. It's like on-the-job research, I bet each experience brings an extra dimension to her work...'

Ophelia had blathered other things over the speaker, but these were the words that stuck. Beau was a writer of ghost stories, but she had never lived through her own experience. Maybe she *could* think of this whole strange and spooky scenario as research. She could put on her writer hat, maybe even take notes if her hands would stop shaking so much. She heaved a sigh as Ophelia said goodbye and an eerie silence wound round the cottage, even the wind seemed to have dropped still in anticipation.

Had it ever been this silent here? She thought not. It was almost eerie.

'Ophelia said to try tapping?'

The wind chose that moment to come back with a vengeance, howling round the side of the house with a moan. Goosebumps littered Beau's arms as a featherlight breeze wrapped itself around her. She hoped it wasn't supernatural, surely it was just the wind finding its way through the cracks of the building. Before she could mention it, Edamine called out again.

'Father? It's me-'

Edamine cut off, and Beau gasped, as the rocking chair creaked into motion.

'Oh,' Edamine stammered, 'is that you? Can you give me a sign?'

Beau swallowed hard. 'I think... I think that is your sign,' she whispered.

'Oh, sorry,' Edamine said as cigar smoke penetrated the air. She sniffed. 'Well, *that's* got to be a sign.'

Beau nodded and took a sip of coffee, almost slopping the contents over the table at the shake of her hand. 'I think you've got your sign. Just ask the question, you know, the one that shows it's really him?'

'It's him-'

'Edamine! Even Ophelia said to check.'

Edamine shrugged. 'Okay, if you insist.'

Beau gave her an incredulous look. 'I do. I have to live here. If you upset a demon, I'm leaving, whether you sue me or not.'

Edamine seemed to think Beau was joking and let out a soft chuckle. 'I told you I wouldn't sue if you wanted to leave.'

'And I'm telling you I'm not joking.'

'Neither am I.'

Thunder cracked and rumbled over the blustery thrash of the rain, and to Beau it felt like the Cottage shook on its foundations.

Edamine, who paid no mind to the possibility of the cottage falling down around them, looked at the creaking chair. 'I need to know if you'll chat with me. If you're really my father, Rector Harold Locket, will you answer a question?'

Despite her fear of both the storm and the spirit, Beau almost rolled her eyes as she interjected. 'Tap once for yes, twice for no. Like this.' She curled her fingers into her palm and rapped on the coffee table. The sound of her own knuckles almost sent her skittering into the dining room.

The chair stopped rocking and there was a strange silence inside the Cottage, juxtaposed with the roar of the wind and the rattle of things loosened outside. Wood from the porch banged, windows rattled, and rain battered the glass, and Beau had the strange notion that this was the second coming and that they would need Noah's Ark to ever leave again - if the cottage didn't get lifted to Kansas like Dorothy's had.

The thought of deep water made her chest constrict... and then...

'Was that a tap?' Edamine said, turning to Beau.

Beau's heart was thundering a hundred miles per hour, and the resident cigar smoke was beginning to actually taste acrid in the back of her throat.

'I'm not sure,' she said truthfully, taking a sip of coffee.

'Could you do that again?' Edamine asked.

Beau heard it this time. A small rap over by the doorway, almost too quickly to be a coincidence. Her heart jumped into her throat. She had read about this time and again, but never in a million years did she think she would ever be chatting to a real ghost.

...If there was such a thing, because although she was here, and petrified, Beau still wasn't sure this wasn't just a bad dream, the effect of too much wine and a killer of a story.

I'm going to wake any minute now.

'Oh, thank you. I knew it was you, father.'

Beau blinked. 'Edamine the damn question.'

'Ah, yes. I wonder if you could tell me the year that you died, just to... to prove it's you, of course.'

Beau felt herself sway. This was some strange dream. 'Edamine, how the hell is he–'

She cut off as there was a low tap, and then a period of silence.

Lightning flashed, and then the taps began again.

'One...' Edamine said, and then she began to count the next set until the taps stopped. 'Nine.'

There was a moment again before the taps started up again, almost like morse code.

'Eight,' Beau murmured with Edamine.

The taps began again.

'Five.'

They waited, but the tapping had ceased. His answer was in. Edamine's grin was almost Cheshire Cat as she looked to Beau and thunder crashed overhead.

'1985.'

Beau shrugged.

'It's right.' Edamine said, and then she huffed. 'Okay father, I'm going to list the months of the year. Can you tap once on the month that you died?'

They waited and Beau thought their run of luck was over, but then there was a single tap and Beau's jaw dropped as she looked at Edamine.

'You're a bloody natural.'

But Edamine was already saying the names of the months, giving a brief period in which he could answer when she got to the right one, which he did.

November.

Edamine nodded, and then she went further. 'Could you tap out the date in November the day you died, just the number?'

Five distinctive raps, and Edamine clasped her hands at her chest.

'Thank you. Thank you so much.'

'Was it right?'

'5th November 1985. That's right, all of it. It's him Beau, there's no doubt.'

Beau felt that she would have liked a little more proof, just to make sure, but Edamine was already in a flood of tears beside her.

'I didn't think I'd get this opportunity again, Beau. I didn't. This is wonderful, and you made it happen. Thank you, thank you so much. I didn't think I'd ever speak to him again.'

Beau grabbed her hand, swallowing her own emotion at the woman's sudden outburst.

'Well, then, speak to him. You have the floor.'

⎯⎯⎯ ⎯⎯⎯

The pleasantries had been nice, or as nice as chatting to a ghost could be. Beau had looked on, unable to decide if she was full of pure terror or pure wonder, but as Edamine had asked each question, even when they had to wait, or she'd had to repeat the question, she had been answered with far too much precision to be coincidence. She was still in tears as her father said that he was at peace, and with her mother, but that's when things began to get strange.

'Father, I have some questions about Constance, some things that I'd like to clear up. Is that okay?'

There was a tap, and Edamine nodded, wiping her eyes, and blowing her nose before adding the tissue to the growing pile on the table. She heaved a sigh and Beau dropped her gaze. This was like voyeurism at the worst level.

She had a front-row seat to the movie of Edamine's life and what had happened all those years ago. The air felt weirdly palpable, and even the weather seemed to cease its fury outside, hushed at what was to come.

Edamine took a breath.

'I'd like to ask about what happened... at the church that day?'

There was no response and Beau saw Edamine swallow, her Adam's apple bobbing.

Beau knew how important this question was to Edamine. She wanted to understand what happened, but the answer would either settle her fear or pull apart her world all over again. She would have no idea which until he answered, and Beau felt the fear and anticipation as though it was her own.

Rain battered the windows as Edamine continued. 'I just... I just want to know if you pushed her. That's it, and I won't judge you either way, there's no point now. But the allegations of murder, and the harassment, it was... it was almost unbearable. I want to know if there was any truth to the rumours. Was there...?'

Her voice faded off, and she pulled another tissue from the box. Beau reached to squeeze her arm in comfort. There was nothing else that she felt she could do but be present with her.

There were two taps, and Edamine slumped forward with relief and a fresh barrage of sobs. Beau rubbed a hand at her back.

'Do you want me to ask some more for you?'

Edamine nodded. 'I don't think I...'

'I know.'

Beau looked at the wall next to the chair, where the taps seemed to come from, for lack of anywhere else to look. She took a breath and saw herself as part of a movie, a movie where she was speaking to an invisible dead rector in her own cottage - well, her own for the next six months, anyway.

This is ridiculous.

And yet, he's here, just speak Beau, Edamine is in bits.

Beau cleared her throat.

'Um, hello Rector. It's me, Beau... the one you've been scaring the hell out of for the last week. Um, could I ask some questions on Edamine's behalf?'

Stupid. Ridiculous.

And yet the thump was clear above the noise of the storm. One. Yes.

'Rector, can you just confirm it is true that you didn't push Constance? That you did *not* murder your daughter?'

Edamine gave a small whine, and Beau regretted her choice of words, but the answer came swiftly. One knock.

Yes.

Beau licked her dry lips. 'Right, the rumours were false Edamine, your father isn't a murderer. He didn't push her.'

A long moan left Edamine's mouth, and she relapsed into more sobs.

'He's not a murderer. He didn't kill her, Edamine. In fact, you loved her, didn't you, rector?'

One knock.

'And you just wanted the best for her, is that right?'

Again, a clear knock.

Beau blinked and felt a circle of cool air chilling the sweat at her armpits. Was she doing this? Was she really? Or was she dreaming?

Pull it back Beau, this is for Edamine, get a grip.

'I'm so sorry rector, I bet it was awful watching her fall and knowing there was nothing you could do.'

Two taps.

Beau nodded, and then her smile faltered.

'No? Were two taps for no?'

There was a tap as Edamine nodded and sniffed. Her eyes were puffy and red rimmed, and her breathing had an accompanying small wheeze.

'One is yes, two is no,' she said, her voice thick.

She gazed at Beau, questions in her eyes, and Beau felt lead in her stomach. Something was wrong here. She almost didn't want to ask what.

'You didn't feel awful watching Constance fall from the cliffs?'

Two taps. Quick and close.

'No,' Beau frowned at Edamine, whose tears had dried in the confusion. Edamine shook her head.

'Father, did you see Constance fall?'

Two taps.

Edamine frowned. 'I don't understand. The story they both told me was that they were there at the cliff edge and father tried to save her as she fell. If he didn't see her fall, then how could that be true?'

Edamine hadn't asked a direct question, but there were two taps all the same.

'Is it true what Edamine was told?' Beau asked. 'Were you at the cliff edge with Constance?'

Again, two taps.

Beau shook her head. 'Did Constance fall at all?'

Two taps.

Beau felt bile rise up into her throat. It was looking like Edamine had been spun a lie. A big lie. 'What in the hell happened that day?' she whispered.

Edamine shook her head, looking completely lost. 'I have no idea what is going on. Maybe this isn't him after all. I think I've made a terrible mistake Beau, I think I got my hopes up and I'm wrong.'

There were two taps, and Edamine shrugged. 'If I'm not wrong, then where do I go from here? What do I do?'

There was an enormous crash from above which sent Beau skittering from the settee, her heart thumping. Edamine stood behind her, looking startled.

'What was that?'

Beau shook her head. She peered out into the hallway, but the front door was closed, and a look at the back saw that closed too.

Thank God for small mercies.

She checked herself in the presence of the rector.

Sorry.

'The doors are closed, maybe the wind blew a tile from the roof or something.'

'Or blew a window in. You'll have to check Beau, I struggle with stairs.'

'I will.'

There was nothing Beau wanted to do less, but as the custodian of the cottage, she knew Edamine was right. She stepped out into the hallway and heard the eerie whistle of the wind as she turned toward the stairs. Her heart was drumming and her already sweaty palms felt slick on the bannister. She felt watched, like something was holding its breath, looking back at her, as she peered up into the darkness.

When had it got fully dark?

'If that's you, rector, I'd appreciate you not pulling anything just now. I may have a heart attack. Seriously.'

A flash of lightning lit the stairs and landing ahead of her as she yelped.

'Are you okay?' Edamine called.

'Fine, just found out that lightning is not good when your nerves are shot.'

Beau flicked on the landing light, blew out a breath and began to climb.

She saw what was wrong before she even reached the top. Through the spindles of the bannister, she saw legs. Thick and still.

Shit!

Looking up to the ceiling confirmed her fears.

The attic door had come open, and the ladder had fallen down like an invitation. She climbed the rest of the stairs and huffed uneasily at the open door. She wasn't as tall as Gerard, she would need something to stand on to push the ladder up and click the door back into place.

'Everything okay?' Edamine called.

'The attic door came open. It was the ladder that made the crash. Everything is fine. I'll just find something to stand on to shut it and I'll be down.'

'There's a coincidence. Has that happened before?'

Beau frowned as she leaned over the bannister so that she didn't have to shout.

'Noises from the attic? You know they have.'

'No, has the door come open before?'

'No.'

Beau frowned as Edamine went quiet and a rumble of thunder crashed over the house. She wished the storm would blow over, but this one seemed to want to stick around.

'Could be the weather, but you have to go up,' Edamine finally called.

Beau let out a laugh as her insides shrivelled. 'Oh, I don't think so. It's blowing a gale up here, and I don't want to be anywhere near the roof.'

'It's father. He wants you to go up.'

Beau looked at the dark hole above her, and her skin crawled. Nothing seemed less appealing.

Of course he wants me to go up. What else?

She shuddered, and Edamine appeared at the foot of the stairs, stick in her hand. She looked up at Beau.

'He wants you to go up, Beau, please, it's important.'

Beau glanced at the attic and shook her head.

'You'll have to give me more than that, Edamine. I'm not just going up there with no further instruction. Not for anybody.'

Edamine raised her voice against the crescendo of wind and rain.

'Father. Is there something specific in the attic we need to find?'

Beau heard nothing, but Edamine smiled.

'There's something up there.'

Beau rolled her eyes. 'There's a lot up there, Edamine, hundreds of boxes. It would be like finding a needle in a haystack.'

'That's it! Is it a box, father? Do we need to find a box?'

The answer must have been yes, for Edamine continued. Beau wished she'd hurry. The longer she stood here under that gaping hole, the more she felt something was waiting up there for her, grinning out of the darkness. She shuddered as Edamine continued to question.

'Can you tell me if it's by the window?'

'By the West side?'

'At the back?'

And then the best news that Beau had heard all afternoon.

'It's by the hatch. Is there a box right next to the hatch that stands out?'

Beau looked at the black hole above her. She didn't want to go up at all, but Edamine would surely kick up a stink if she refused and might attempt it herself. Beau didn't want her to fall, and this could solve the childhood dilemma, so she stepped onto the first rung of the ladder and began to climb.

There *was* a box right next to the hatch, which sat at an angle to the rest of the boxes. Beau wasn't coming up here again, so she shouted down to Edamine.

'Ask him if it's the one I have my hand on. I presume he can see me?'

'Yes,' Edamine stated.

'Yes, what?'

'Yes, that's the one.'

Beau blinked. She hadn't assumed it would be that easy.

'I'm coming down,' she said, testing the weight of the box and coming down the ladder a little too fast. At the bottom, she quickly retracted the ladder and pushed the door hard. It swung up but didn't catch.

Typical.

She found a stool in the bedroom to stand on and give the door a push. As it clicked, she could have sworn she heard laughter.

'I'm glad you find this funny, Rector Locket.' Beau whispered as ice slid down her spine.

Then she picked up the box and bolted for the stairs.

Chapter 37

ANNA CHECKED HER WIG, turning fully and using her phone camera and the mirror to check her back. There were no dark strands hanging this time, nothing to give away that she wasn't blonde. Not that it would matter once she reached the cottage, at that point she had decided she wanted to be recognised. She wanted to see the confusion, and then the joy. She wanted that big reunion before she slammed her intent on the table. Then the joy would be gone, and she could get on with what she really loved to see. Fear. Terror. Shock. Panic.

Delicious.

She teased at the front of the wig and brushed the style forward until all traces of her own hair were gone, because until she reached the cottage, it was important that her identity was completely concealed. She paused, a small frown crossing her features.

Where was the point, the exact point on the map, when she went from conceal to reveal?

A paradox.

She let out a giggle, which upset moths in her stomach, and she frowned, assessing her reflection as she put the brush on the table and blew out a breath.

So close now, let's not fuck it up.

Easily said from the end that she could control. She only hoped that Daniel hadn't told anyone that she wore a blonde wig, and was really dark haired. She also hoped that Lucas hadn't told anyone she had come to see her sister at the cottage in the dip by the sea 'yes, that little place where something bad went down for the second time in forty years', and that she'd had a weird blowout in the restaurant 'which was totally out of character'. Most of all, she hoped that they didn't get together and conclude that what happens from here on in is any more than coincidence... at least before she has a chance to be miles from here by morning.

Anna closed her eyes as her heart began to thump under her silk shirt - stupid clothes for going out in the rain, but what choice did she have? She pressed a hand to her chest and willed the beating to stop. Pounding hearts made silly mistakes and there could be no time for mistakes now. It was show time.

She took a few calming breaths and opened her eyes to see her reflection looking back at her. Steadfast, cold, in control.

That's all I need.

It doesn't matter if they do talk. By the time they hear of the cottage and try to link anything to me, or even realise that I've given them a false name and address, I'll be long gone.

She nodded, and then her heart flipped and began to thump harder.

It's all in order, Anna. What's the matter with you?

She knew what it was.

The car.

The hire car was the only anomaly that she couldn't think her way out of. The road was single track, leaving it at the side of the road would attract attention. Driving it into Hollydale and leaving it there would attract attention, and driving it down the track that seemed to lead a little way to the cottage could attract attention. The only place the car wouldn't attract attention was right here, in the car park, because that was exactly where it was supposed to be.

If all went to plan, she wouldn't be seen leaving, and no one would bat an eyelid at the car of a patron who was in their room on a stormy night. By the time she got back to the car, all being well, it would still be dark. She could just drive away into the night before anyone got up and noticed she was gone.

She pushed all thoughts of CCTV away. Quite probably, the owners didn't have any out here, but you never knew. All she could hope was that they checked it days after she'd gone, giving her time to get back out of the country.

The only other sticking point was getting to the house at all. Five miles across open countryside she had never trekked was not going to be much fun, especially in the dark and stormy weather.

When she had realised how far it was, she had contemplated taking the car to the nearest point anyway, the end of that little track, and walking from there, but the app she had downloaded showing her hiking routes and rights of way in the area hadn't shown a direct route from there, she would be on her own walking aimlessly toward a house with no directions and no idea of the land underneath her feet.

From the hotel, if she crossed the road, there was a long path that led right up to the church ruins. From the ruins, another path led right down past the cottage to the inlet and up the other side of the cliff.

It left Anna with one logical choice.

Walk three miles with no guide to follow? Or walk five on marked paths that hopefully would be easy to follow in torch-light and less liable to contain trip hazards?

How far can five miles be, anyway? Daniel walks it most days in his lunch. Ninety minutes, did he say?

If she planned for a couple of hours, she thought she'd be good.

Thunder rumbled and groaned outside, fighting with the howl of the wind and the thrash of the rain. Anna sighed and moved back to the bed, where her small suitcase and a large rucksack lay. She knew it looked strange to bring a small suitcase and a large bag when she could just use a single large suitcase. But the rucksack had a secure pocket for her laptop and accessories, which were fundamental. It had to come with her, no questions. And the large pocket at the back had been useful for shoes and cosmetics so that she could lie her second wig - identical, just in case - in the suitcase on her clothes without it getting ruined.

Now she swapped everything around, taking the laptop - she didn't need anyone finding that in the car if anything happened - and anything else that may lead to unwanted conclusions. She also packed the spare wig, a long pair of pointed scissors, a steak knife that she had stolen from the restaurant two days ago, and pepper spray. Even armed, you could never be too careful out there in the wilderness after dark.

Not that she knew, of course, she just presumed.

Silly really, the only scary thing in the wilderness tonight would be her, and if she came across anyone wanting to fool around, she would show them why they should be scared.

'I have a knife... and I'm not afraid to use it.' She said aloud. 'Although, I'd rather not. I don't want too many bodies on my hands tonight, so if you like to step aside...'

She tittered. If that didn't send most people running, she didn't know what would, especially after she showed the knife glinting in the moonlight, rain running down its silver sides, teeth ready to bite into soft flesh–

On track, Anna. Get on track.

Shaking the image away, she packed the pair of brand new hiking shoes she had brought on the way up here, and a spare pair of socks, lastly she packed the brown envelope with the items that Anna was sure would pack the best punch she had ever witnessed - not that she had witnessed many since being on the road of the good girl.

As she stuffed the rest of her things into the small suitcase, and sat on the top to do the zip, lightning flashed outside, lighting up Anna's grin and a darkness on her face that was ready to spill over into her soul.

She was going to enjoy tonight, storm or no storm. She felt herself unwinding, loosening the control of the good girl, pushing her back into the corner with each move she made toward her outcome.

Tonight, she would tempt out the bad girl, the darkness that had been pushed down for so long, and she would let her run wild.

With the suitcase heaving and the backpack a little lighter than it had been, Anna scoured the room one last time, and then, with blood raging hot and black in her veins, she left the room.

Chapter 38

I T WAS ALMOST NINE-THIRTY when Daniel saw Anna from his small window, which thankfully looked over the front of the hotel car park. She was moving quickly, her bag at her back, suitcase dragging behind her, blonde head bent forward against the gusting wind.

Orange lights flashed on her little car as she opened the boot to place the suitcase inside, and then moved to the driver's side of the car.

Where is she going in a storm? And why? Is this it?

The thought sent shoots of worry up his spine and before he knew what he was doing, he had grabbed his waterproof from the back of the door and stuffed his feet into walking boots.

If nothing else, he had to get to the cottage and make sure that the red-haired lady wasn't in trouble. He knew the cottage couldn't be reached by road from any angle, so wherever she was going to park she had to walk, but from the bulging suitcase it was all too obvious that she wasn't intending to return.

If he left now, he had more than a hope of getting across the land before she did. He had walked to the church many times in the daylight. How much harder could it be in the dark?

Daniel left his room and ran up the corridor to the owner's quarters, his bootlaces flying. At the door where Lucas and his wife lived, he hammered his fist against the wood.

Lucas opened it briskly, looking confused, and then even more confused to see Daniel in a dry raincoat, stooping to lace up his boots.

'I have to go out,' Daniel said, looking up from his boot. 'I need you to be available for the desk.'

He realised how it sounded as Lucas took a step back and raised his eyebrows. 'Excuse me?'

Daniel switched to lace the other boot with a shake of his head.

'Sorry. I meant I won't be available for the desk. I'm not sure how long I'll be out, but I'll be back to work in the morning. I'll do a double shift. I have to go now, though. It's an emergency.'

'What sort of an emergency?'

Daniel swallowed hard and licked his lips as he glanced to the corridor which led to the main doorway.

Has she left already? Probably.

'Please, Lucas. Trust me. I wouldn't do this if it wasn't vitally important.'

'And I wouldn't ask if it wasn't important. What's going on, lad?'

Daniel closed his eyes and saw her speeding up the road in his mind, brake lights glinting in the rain.

He was losing time.

'Anna. I've just seen her go out in the storm. I don't think she's coming back because I have reason to believe she may be up to no good. She isn't who she says she is. She wears a wig and has probably given us a false name and address. I saw some very incriminating things on her laptop yesterday that seemed to be plans to attack somebody. I need to stop her. The lady she is after is alone, and she isn't safe.'

The words came out fast and jumbled. The entire story in perhaps thirty seconds and, God, if Lucas wasn't standing there like he was processing the paragraph at a word a minute.

'Please, I have to go. I can fill you in later, everything, I promise.'

'Anna? Sounds like trouble, son. Where are you intending to go?'

Daniel tapped at the architrave, a quick and fast beat. 'Lucas, I have to go now. Trust me. Please. I'll fill you in later. Just trust me.'

Lucas looked at Daniel and gave a slow nod.

'I do, which is why I'm letting this slip. I hope it comes to nothing, but the temper I saw on the woman at dinner tonight was barely concealed. It was a look I've never seen before, like actions, words and reality didn't mix. I asked her a question about her sister, and she almost jumped down my throat and made excuses to leave. Thought she was having a bad day.'

'I think she is, but I think it's her sister who will get the brunt of it. I have to get to the cottage before her.'

'You'd do well to keep your nose out of people's business, lad, but you're not going to listen to me, are you?'

'I can't. If anything happens after what I saw on her computer, I'll never forgive myself. I can't be here right now, I have to-'

'Go, aye,' Lucas said, pointing to the corridor. 'Go, but don't be getting yourself into trouble lad, I can't be watching your back now. I have a business to run.'

Daniel turned and sprinted down the corridor, pulling the hood over his head as he shouted back. 'Thank you, I won't. I'll speak to you when I get back.'

'I'll be up and waiting. Oh, wait! Hang on!'

Daniel clenched his jaw as he skidded to a stop and turned back to see Lucas in the corridor.

'Be careful. I almost forgot. She took a steak knife from the restaurant two days ago. If we had been full, I probably wouldn't have noticed, but when there's only one person eating, and a knife goes missing? Well, it sure as hell wasn't me, that's all I'm saying.'

Daniel felt his stomach roll and his heart pound against his ribs.

A knife? That's a weapon.

He nodded, and then he was out of the door, sprinting into the rain and howling wind, running headlong for the small track that led to the church.

Then his eye caught something that shouldn't be there, and he stumbled.

The car. She hasn't left yet!

He skidded and tried to backtrack behind the cover of the side of the building, but a handy streak of lightning showed him all he needed to know. The car was empty.

He slowed to a jog and rounded the car to peer inside.

No bag. No Anna.

He glanced back to the hotel.

Had he got this all wrong? Had she gone back to her room?

Maybe she was just getting her things together for an early start tomorrow?

His heart was pounding as he looked from the hotel to the car and back again. His adrenaline was firing on all cylinders, and the last thing he wanted to do was find she had gone back to bed... and yet, that would be the most amazing thing to find right now, too.

Daniel swung his gaze to the road and the little track to the church. Icy rain pelted his face as the thunder rumbled above. It wasn't as fierce as it had been earlier, but it was still a good storm, and still not pleasant to be out in.

He wrinkled his nose and pulled the drawstring of his hood close around his face, the small peak just about allowing him vision that caught something across the road.

Something was moving.

Across the road, just inside the bushes.

He squinted and began to jog as stealthily as he could across the lane and onto the track. He paused and dipped his peak to squint into the rain again.

There!

Now he not only saw the person and the small light flickering ahead, which wasn't nearly bright enough for this terrain, but it highlighted the large backpack they carried. He knew the shape of her well, but the glint of blonde in the light gave her away.

Anna.

Was she really walking to the Cottage, in the dark, and in a storm?

That couldn't be good news. Not at all. Especially not with a possible weapon.

She moved at a decent pace and Daniel crept behind her, staying a good distance back, thankful that the noise of the weather would disguise and footfalls or crackle of foliage that may alert her that he was following.

He wondered what she had in her backpack and thought of all the things that she may have stowed to use as a weapon alongside the knife. Then he chastised himself.

Christ, Daniel, you could give her the benefit of the doubt. She may just be going to visit her sister. There is no way to get there other than to walk either way.

At 9.30pm?

And wouldn't they have called it off in this storm?

His guts squirmed and writhed. Something was very wrong here, and with all the evidence mounting, it all just felt... wrong. Off. Hokey.

Those were the only words he could come up with, not that they would stand in a court of law, but maybe it would all be okay, maybe she was just visiting, and that was fine. He would follow her to the cottage, and if she was, he could just turn around and walk away with no harm done but a good soaking.

Lost in his tumbling thoughts, Daniel failed to see that she had stopped. He came to a halt much closer than he wanted to be and froze as she kicked something on the ground with a curse that he couldn't quite make out. Holding his breath, he crouched low, hoping to look like foliage if she turned, although if she turned her light toward him, he was screwed. He didn't think that she would have seen many red bushes in her life, especially man shaped ones.

He watched as she opened the bag and took something out. Rain ran from him in rivulets and his leg cramped, but he didn't dare move as she took her time changing into another pair of shoes.

He would have thought it a good call if he hadn't been so terrified.

She pushed the old boots into her backpack and stood to put the straps over her shoulders, turning so far toward him he thought there was no way she wouldn't see.

Why did you get so close?

And then it was over, and she was walking again, tramping over the dark ground, her light barely picking up the ground in front of her.

Daniel checked his pounding heart and dropped back to a safe distance, following the tree line where his steps were more uncertain, but she was much less likely to see him if she turned.

He hoped she wouldn't turn, because he didn't dare to think what she could do to him out here with what may be in her bag if she really was intent on harm.

A spooked woman could give him an injury or two, and that would be fine.

A spooked psychopath with a bag of goodies... well, that was a whole different ballgame, and one he desperately wanted to avoid.

Chapter 39

T HERE WAS AN OMINOUS flash of lightning as Edamine opened the box on the coffee table. It was a special kind of creepy, as it seemed Rector Locket had decided to join them in his favourite rocking chair.

The creak was fortunately only really heard when the wind and rain let up for a few moments, or thunder wasn't rolling around the cottage. It was the movement that kept catching Beau's eye which was disconcerting.

He's in here, on the chair? Is that what the rocking is supposed to mean? Is he watching us from there?

She shuddered, and turned to Edamine as she gasped and pulled out a stack of photographs.

The chair stopped, and Beau felt relief fall from her shoulders as she looked at Edamine.

Thank you, Rector, let's keep it like that for now.

'It's the things my mother hid from the day Constance died.'

Beau remembered the photograph that she had found on the
landing and moved to the mantlepiece where she had left the
old picture.

'There's this too. I found it under the loft hatch this morning. I
presumed it was you and a friend?'

*This morning? So much had happened in the last few hours, it
almost seemed days ago.*

She shook the thought away and handed the picture to
Edamine.

Edamine smiled sadly at the picture. 'It's me and Constance. I
never had any friends over, neither of us did. I'm not sure why.
Maybe people thought it was too far, or maybe it was because
we were the rector's daughters? I don't know, I just know we
asked, but no one could ever come. Constance is here on the
left, see? We *were* best friends for the most part.'

Edamine thumbed the writing at the bottom. '1981. She would
have been just five here. Five, two years before she died. So
young.'

There was a creak out in the hallway and Beau felt her stomach
clench.

'I'll just check that.'

She moved to the door and saw that nothing was out of place.
The front door was shut. She moved to it and double checked
it was locked before looking out of the small pane of glass next
to it.

The landscape moved, tugged and pulled by the ferociousness
of the weather outside.

*You'd never know if someone was out there or not. Probably won't
see her coming.*

Beau's heart jumped, and she pushed away the voice.

She's not coming in this weather, I assure you. No way.

But the words sat with a sharp edge against her heart.

Joe said that she was back tomorrow, which means she must intend on coming today - but now it's evening and she's still not here.

Maybe she won't bother after all. Maybe Joe has her wrong, and she's not a psychopath. In fact, come on Beau, you know her. She has her quirks and her problems, sure, but murder?

Beau chewed a lip as she continued to peer out, memorizing the shapes the trees made, the movement of the bushes, the grass.

A large thud thumped and thrummed just outside the door and Beau jumped back with a scream, her heart racing a million miles an hour.

'What on earth are you doing out there, Beau?'

'Just checking. What was that bang? Did you hear it?'

'I thought we agreed earlier it could be a board from the porch. It's been banging on and off most of the evening?'

'Was it the same sound?'

'From in here it was.'

'Should I check it?'

'Not unless you want to get very wet and possibly hit by flying debris. Repairs can be made afterward. Inside is safer at the heart of a storm.'

Beau swallowed hard, her face back at the window as the wind whined. When she turned back, Edamine was standing in the doorway of the living room watching her.

Beau tried to smile but thought it may have come out more of a grimace.

'I'm sorry Edamine, I'm just on edge after the phone call.'

She headed back to the living area as Edamine put a hand to her mouth.

'Oh, Beau. I'm so sorry. I got carried away with my own problems and I completely forgot about your call and this lady you were talking about.'

Beau took Edamine's arm and turned her back into the living room, trying to ignore the darkness now pressing against the windows from outside.

'It doesn't matter. I don't think she'll be coming in this weather, anyway. Let's see what's in the box.'

'Oh no, it's just the old photographs and memories, and probably some papers from the church. To be honest, they're tearing at my heart a little, especially looking at them in the Cottage. I'll have Gerard take them back to mine and I can sort them out there.'

Beau was a little downhearted. She wouldn't have minded seeing the girls and their lives out here.

'I do have something funny to show you, though. Look at this.'

Edamine handed Beau a picture which showed her and Constance with a large stick on the beach. The collie ran off to the left, toward the water, and something was written in the sand that Beau couldn't make out. It was the girls that caught her eye, though. Edamine holding the stick, her head up, smile wide and bright. Constance, her arms folded tightly across her chest, scowling up at her sister.

'This was us,' Edamine said with a chuckle. 'Best friends one minute and best enemies the next. I remember this day well. Mother wanted to take a photograph that she could send to Gran of us wishing her a happy birthday. Constance thought it would be a good idea to write a message in the sand, and mother agreed.'

'So, what was all this about?' Beau said, pointing to Constance's face.

'Mother wouldn't let her write the message. Being four years older, I had neater writing, and so she said I should do it. Constance was so mad that she looked at me just like that for four days afterward and hit and poked at me every chance she got. She was furious.'

Edamine chuckled and shook her head. 'Needless to say, she refused to smile for the picture, and so the picture was never sent. She was a darling, Constance, but goodness, she had a foul temper.'

There was a tap from the doorway, and Edamine laughed.

'Father agrees!'

Beau grinned and put the picture back in the box. 'Have you said all you wanted to now?'

'Yes. I'm not sure why he's still hanging around, but it's nice to have him here. Maybe it was for you after all.' She shut the box and pushed it to the side of the table and turned to face Beau, 'So tell me everything, what's been going on that has you shaken up? And who is this girl with the angry mouth?'

The rocking chair began to creak, and Beau shook her head.

'Oh, no. I'm sorry, I can't have that. You need to stop the rocking, Rector, it freaks me right out.'

Chapter 40

T HE CHAIR DID STOP rocking. If Rector Locket was still in it, then he was doing what she had asked and Beau couldn't be more grateful because telling her story was testing her nerves, and making it seem more possible.

She made fresh coffee to replace their cold cups and then she told Edamine everything. About Hannah's behaviour, Joe's call and concerns about the friend who had died and the picture in the article, running into the man at the church and what he had said about a sister, and finally Ophelia's vision of a woman with dark hair and an angry mouth in the attic window.

Beau's heart skipped as she thought of the laughter she had heard up there just an hour ago - or thought she'd heard, anyway.

She sighed and shifted. 'So the long and short of it is that I think maybe Hannah is the girl with the angry mouth, and she may be coming here. If Joe's hunch is correct, anyway.'

Edamine fiddled with the silver cross at her neck. She had stayed quiet as Beau had recounted as many details as she could; her face serious. If she had thought it far-fetched, she hadn't shown it outwardly. Now she finally spoke. 'Joe. He's known this woman for how long?'

'Almost twelve years.'

'Long enough.'

'Yes. And after the admission that he thinks she possibly murdered the friend before me, he's just wary, I suppose. I didn't think too much of it, she can get pissed off as much as the next person but murder? I'm not sure, but with Daniel and Ophelia almost saying the same thing in a different context too... I don't know. I just don't know what to think.'

'Why don't we check out the picture?'

The rocking chair creaked - just once - and then it stilled again. Beau felt the nape of her neck tingle, and she swallowed hard. 'Do you... do you think he agrees?'

Edamine flapped a hand dismissively. 'I have no idea what the hell that means, probably just that he wants to rock. Get the laptop, that's scary shit, and I'm intrigued.'

Beau messaged Joe for the link to the newspaper article and went to get the laptop from the dining room. By the time she had started the machine up, Joe messaged to say he'd sent an email. Next to Edamine, Beau clicked the link, opened the article, and began to read aloud.

Tragic Boating Accident Leaves One Dead.

Tragedy struck yesterday when a pair of friends who had travelled to Earnshaw for a short break took a rented boat out onto the lake. Trouble hit when, against advice, the girls took off their provided life jackets because of the hot weather. This started a chain of events which would ultimately lead to the death of one of the girls, Cassandra Martin, who was just twenty-eight years old, couldn't swim, and couldn't get the help she needed in time, despite witnesses to the event.

One onlooker gave the following account. 'The girls were out in the middle of the lake. It was hard to tell what was happening at first, but one appeared to stand, and then fell. A few of us heard the splash. At first, we thought she had jumped in for a swim - it was hot, you know? - but when the other began yelling, we knew there was trouble. It's a terrible shame to hear she died, such a waste of a young life.'

The girl's friend, Hannah James, also twenty-eight, was distraught. She says that Cassandra had simply wanted to swap
seats and had stood, but as Hannah also stood, the boat had
rocked, and Cassandra fell overboard. Hannah, a fully qualified
pool lifeguard, tried to pull Cassandra back into the boat, but
had trouble when the boat began to drift. In panic she too
jumped overboard in order to perform a lifesaving swim hold
to get her friend to shore, but the panic of a real open water
situation overwhelmed her, and she too found herself in trouble
as the boat drifted further from the pair leaving them stranded
in the water. Rescue and the emergency services got to the
pair within just four minutes, but it was too late for Cassandra
Martin, who was pronounced dead at the scene.

Beau sat back from the screen, her heart pounding. The main
picture featured Hannah and Cassandra, arms around each
other's shoulders, their smiles wide. They were standing in
front of a lake, with a backdrop of mountains behind. Hannah's
hair was shorter, chin length, the same as Cassandra's, and had
been dyed jet black to match. With their heads tilted in together,
they looked the picture of happiness.

'They look like sisters.' Beau whispered.

'Interesting assumption, considering what's going on here
tonight.'

Beau blinked and turned to Edamine. 'Sorry, I didn't mean to say
that out loud.'

'The statement stands. Would you look the same if you were
standing together?'

'Like sisters?'

'Appearance wise. Look,' Edamine pointed at the picture. 'She
has the same haircut, the same colour t-shirt, and the same
shoes. They're even wearing the same necklaces.'

Beau felt her stomach roll over as she zoomed in.

'Shit.'

Edamine peered closer. 'Shit?'

Beau pulled the necklace from under her shirt to show Edamine.
The half heart with the small diamond at the bottom.

'Tell me she has the other half.'

Beau nodded. 'Except hers has the diamond at the top. Two halves of the same heart.'

Edamine looked back at the screen. 'Well, at least you got a new one. This one is all filled in, not open like yours. You didn't get a dead girl's necklace.'

Beau felt bile rise from her stomach and placed a hand over her mouth. 'That's... well...'

'Good is your answer. So now back to the question. Does she look like you now? Could you be passed off as sisters?'

Beau thought about the length of their hair, which was almost the same, and how Hannah sometimes curled hers to match. How Hannah had many of the same clothes and the same boots. She nodded.

'She brought contact lenses once so that her eyes looked like mine. Same shade of green, but she couldn't quite match it. She got really upset, but she has gorgeous blue eyes. I didn't know what she was getting upset about.'

Edamine reached for her coffee cup with a sigh. 'If this were nursery school, I'd let it go, but seriously, how old is this woman?'

'Same age as me, forty-five.'

Edamine shook her head. 'Hmm. Is this the picture he wanted you to look at? Because although it's not unheard of to presume she's mad from clothes, necklace, and hair length, it's not really conclusive evidence now, is it?'

Beau blew out a breath and scrolled down to the next picture. 'I think it was this one.'

The caption was chilling 'A bystander's phone captures Hannah James in trouble in the water moments before rescue.'

The picture was as Joe had said. An image taken on a phone of the girls out in the water, the boat quite a way off to the left. Hannah had her head back, one hand in the air, and appeared to be signalling, but Cassandra couldn't be seen at all. Beau shivered and tried to calm her thumping heart, which wanted to bump right out of her chest and get as far away from this place as possible.

This was minutes before Cassandra died, either that or she was already dead, and that thought is chilling.

Edamine peered over her shoulder.

'So aside from her wanting to morph into her friends, what makes him think it wasn't an accident, as the paper says?'

'The picture. He says to enlarge the picture.'

Edamine leaned toward the screen, her eyes narrowed. 'Well then, what are you waiting for? Go ahead.'

Beau felt nauseous as she clicked the picture to save it to her desktop and then opened it in a photo viewer. She zoomed in as far as the image allowed before it got too pixelated, just as Joe had said, and then looked again.

She shivered as a chill ran down her spine.

Cassandra *could* be seen, just about. The top of her black hair was just visible if you looked closely enough. There were a couple of odd beige strips that couldn't be defined. She looked closer. Cassandra had no coloured strips in her hair in the picture above. Beau frowned, puzzled, and then it came to her what they probably were. Fingers. Just at the side of Cassandra's dark hair. Hannah had her other hand, the one she wasn't signalling with on top of Cassandra's head.

'Am I seeing what I think I'm seeing?' Beau asked, sitting back, and trying to breathe air that didn't feel stale and sickly. She was half ready to run for the front door and gulp good clean ocean air until Edamine spoke.

'I see her face. That's a smile. That's not someone in trouble, and no matter whether she has her hand raised, she's certainly not shouting for help. Not right in that moment, anyway.'

Beau's breath caught. She turned her attention back to the picture and Hannah's half pixelated face and immediately saw what Edamine - and Joe - meant. She was smiling... wasn't she?

Was that a smile?

She squinted and then pulled away and looked at Edamine with horror. 'You're right, that seems to be a smile, and that's what Joe said, too. I mean, it may be a flicker of a moment, that instant where she was going to shout and her mouth was making the motions of a smile, possibly, but look at this. I hadn't even noticed the smile.'

Beau pointed out the strips of pink on the top of Cassandra's hair, and Edamine gasped.

'Oh! I was going to say you may be right about the timing of the photo, but why on earth would she have her free hand on *top* of the of the other girl's head? This changes everything, doesn't it? One may be a coincidence, but both? And why would she smile, knowing that her friend is underwater, and she has her hand on top of her head? Is there a situation where that would ever accidentally be the case?'

'I don't think so.' Beau swallowed hard and shook her head. 'I don't know. This isn't the Hannah I know. She wouldn't do something like this, I'm certain.'

Edamine looked at Beau. 'Is this Hannah?'

'Yes, of course it is.'

'Then she's right there, in full colour, doing what you believe she wouldn't do. She has her hand on that poor girl's head, holding her down, and even as she signals, she has a smile on her face.'

'The picture is all pixels now though. We can't be a hundred percent certain that's what's been captured in that split second.'

Edamine shrugged and counted on her fingers. 'She's angry. Her husband confirmed she has attachment issues. The way she is dressed almost confirms it - she's not a child- and to top it off, there's photographic evidence that she's smiling as she drowns her friend.'

Beau rubbed her palms against the legs of her jeans and shook her head.

'You want to hear something worse?' Edamine said, her hand finding Beau's arm.

Beau closed her eyes. 'What could possibly be worse?'

'If she did choose to kill poor Cassandra, she was confident enough in her own abilities to do it at a boating lake in broad daylight.'

Beau nodded, and hope lit her chest. 'Yes, and that's exactly why it can't have happened. She would have been stupid to even try it. It must have been an accident, after all. I think we're all making a little too much of one photo when the next half-second may have shown something completely different.'

Edamine shrugged and nodded. 'Maybe so. Time will tell.'

Beau frowned as there was a series of taps over by the door, which almost sounded like footsteps leaving the room. Beau's stomach shrivelled as Edamine looked out into the hallway.

There was a beat on uneasy silence, and then the most horrific sound, one that Beau thought she would trade even for the record player's blast.

The doorbell.

Its cheery ding-dong announcing someone at the door. In the worst storm that Beau had ever seen, and in a cottage miles from anywhere.

As Beau and Edamine froze in their seats, the sound chimed again, and again, and again.

Chapter 41

H ANNAH LOOKED LIKE A drowned rat, which reminded Beau of every horror film ever made. To make matters worse, lightning lit the sky behind her, and Beau just knew that she was doomed.

Completely doomed.

But when Hannah spoke, she didn't sound like a killer. She sounded like Hannah. She sounded like her best friend.

'Beau!' she said, a smile cracking lips that were almost blue with cold. 'I'm so fucking glad I found you. You can't begin to imagine. I got so lost out there, and this weather is fucking awful.'

Despite the jolt of uneasiness, Beau felt her mouth stretch into a smile at the sight of her friend.

'I'd noticed. You chose the wrong day to visit.'

Hannah laughed, actually *laughed*, and then she launched her-self at Beau. Beau almost screamed until she realised that Han-nah was just coming in for a hug. Fierce, tight and wet.

'I'm sorry, Beau, I'm so sorry. I had to come and see you. I've been away for work, see? It's been so busy, or I'd have contacted earlier, but I've been up here with you all this time, so I thought I'd come and visit instead of messaging. Surprise! Oh, who's this?'

Beau unwrapped herself from Hannah's arms and turned to see Edamine in the living area doorway.

'I'm Edamine Locket. Owner of Bluebell Cottage,' she said, her face neutral. No warmth, no chilliness. Edamine was playing it a whole lot cooler than Beau, whose heart wanted to scream how happy she was to see Hannah, while her head wanted to push her friend back out of the door and lock it behind her.

'I'm Hannah, Beau's friend.' Hannah heaved a rucksack onto her shoulder, stepped forward and held out a hand that Beau didn't think Edamine would take, but they shook as Beau closed the door on the weather outside.

She wanted to lock it, but as she looked at the dripping rucksack on Hannah's back, she wondered if they may need a quick escape.

Better to be safe, there's no one else around here.

She left the door unlocked, and turned to Hannah and Edamine, wondering if they'd noticed.

'I thought this was a house-sitting job. You didn't say that you lived *with* the owner, Beau.'

'Is that a problem?' Beau said, realising that Hannah had been caught off guard and that this may be a good thing. She wouldn't be expecting a third party for her reunion. It may change her plans a little.

Depending on just what her intent is here, anyway.

Hannah shrugged and dropped the soaking bag on the runner. Beau saw Edamine wince and Beau moved the bag to the door-mat instead.

Hannah, whose eyes were travelling around the hallway and stairs, shrugged.

'Whatever floats your boat.'

A chill ran down Beau's spine.

Is that to assure me that she knows I know? Or just for her own amusement?

Beau paused, but only Edamine seemed to notice. She raised an eyebrow as she looked Hannah up and down.

'I should go and take a hot shower, Hannah, get out of those wet things, and I'm sure Beau will make us all a hot drink.'

'Sounds like heaven. I'm frozen.' Hannah gestured to her bag. 'I did have a spare change of clothes as I knew I'd be walking in the weather, but I suppose they're all wet now.'

She bit her lip, and Beau gave her what she wanted to hear.

'Use some of mine. I have a suitcase in the green room. There are clothes still unpacked in there.'

'You haven't unpacked yet?' Hannah said as she ran her hands down her long dark hair and squeezed. 'Wow, you are a slow mover, Beau.' She looked back at Edamine, who was raising another eyebrow at the water pooling at Hannah's feet. 'Don't take it personally, I'm sure she still had clothes in a suitcase at mine too, and she lived with me for nine months!'

Hannah let out a peel of laughter, and Edamine smiled. 'I'm sure Beau can put her clothes where she likes. It's no business of mine.'

'You don't sound very Scottish,' Hannah said, flipping her hair back over her shoulder.

'My parents were English, that's probably why. We didn't get many playmates or chance to mix out here. Other than Sundays at church, of course.'

Hannah wrinkled her nose. 'You're religious?'

Beau felt her cheeks redden at the comment. 'Her father was rector of the church, Han, this place was a rectory. Come on, let's get you in the shower. You're dripping everywhere.'

Beau tried for casual but wasn't sure she hit the mark. If Hannah noticed, she didn't let on.

'Rector? is that like a priest? I suppose you had no choice then. Sucks to have no choice what you believe.'

Beau noticed Edamine's face darken. 'I had a choice, and a rector is a rector.'

Sensing brewing tension, Beau pulled at Hannah's arm.

'Shower.'

Hannah laughed. 'Okay, okay, I'm coming. God, I missed this bossiness.'

———————

Beau wondered if Hannah would try anything while they were alone upstairs, but Hannah was chatty and apologised over and over that she hadn't been in contact, listing the reasons on her fingers.

'I was being stupid. I wasn't thinking. I was angry. I was working. I was sad. I didn't understand. I was upset. I'm so sorry. I really want to make it up to you.'

Beau said very little. She focused on trying to act normal, and trying to keep Hannah in front of her, in case she attempted to make any moves. In all honesty, she was glad when she heard the latch of the bathroom door, and the shower turn on.

Downstairs, she took over from Edamine, who was giving the puddle a rudimentary wipe with a cloth underneath her foot, and then gestured her into the kitchen.

'What do you think?' She whispered, flicking the kettle on.

Edamine leaned on her stick in the doorway.

'I think you should watch your back, and I should watch mine. If I'm in the way, then my fate is as assured as yours. Mine would be a relief, but yours would be untimely.'

Beau felt her stomach plummet. 'Oh.'

'What did you want me to say? She's come here for butterflies and rainbows and tea parties? She's crossed the land in a storm, and you saw the look on her face in that picture. Three people have warned you she was coming here, one has warned you of possible ill intent, and you know that she may have done this kind of thing before. We're alone out here, Beau. No one will hear us scream, I can assure you.'

Beau's heart thundered as she closed her eyes and chewed on her lip. 'I shouldn't have let her in, it's just... she caught me unawares.'

'She's your friend. She's familiar. I get that Beau, but it changes nothing, unfortunately. You could look at the positive. If you hadn't let her in, she would be out there now, prowling round, working up her anger because she would know you had been tipped off. We have the advantage here... well, *you* have the advantage, I have MGLD, I'm dying before we even begin.'

Edamine forced a mirthless chuckle, but Beau was horrified.

'Don't say that Edamine, bloody hell.'

'It's the truth, no point in leaving it out of the equation. It makes a difference.'

'How can it possibly make a difference?'

'Because if I can put myself in her way, then you need to run. I don't want you to save me, I'm beyond getting away from the clutches of a madwoman, but you are not. You have a life to lead, Beau, and books to write. I have only long days of pain and pills and nurses, and that only goes downhill from here. It's ironic, but I only saw the doctor yesterday. It's in my chest. It won't be long now. I don't mind choosing a quicker route.'

Beau felt her mouth drop open and a surge of protection rise up her chest.

'There's no way I will be leaving you in her hands, Edamine, not a chance.'

'It's not a request, Beau, it's an order. And if anything happens and you join me up there, I shall give you more to worry about than opening doors and footsteps in the attic, believe me.'

Beau felt tears gather behind her eyes and tried to blink them back as she shook her head.

'No. That's not going to happen.'

Edamine smiled as Beau poured three cups of tea. 'Then you'd better hope she's being genuine.'

The wind gusted and pulled outside, and a flash of light lit the kitchen as upstairs the shower squeaked off. With looks that soldiers must give each other when they know they're going into battle, Beau took the tea into the living room with Edamine following close behind.

'I mean it, Beau. Every word,' Edamine whispered behind her, and then Hannah skipped down the stairs, and it was all Beau could do not to balk.

Hannah wore the blue jeans and jumper that Beau had picked out for her, but she had obviously been back into the bedroom, where she had found boots and Beau's brown leather jacket. She had even left her wet hair in loose curls, which she never did at home.

'I hope you don't mind. We're the same shoe size and I'm cold. Hey!' she said, her face lit up as she pulled her necklace from under the jumper. 'You're still wearing your side of the heart. I didn't know if you'd dump it after all I've done. Aw, we look like twins, don't we, Elladean?'

'Edamine.' Edamine smiled before giving Beau a look as Hannah flounced past and sat on the settee. 'Yes, you look just like sisters.'

The word sent chills down Beau's spine. She wished Hannah would just get to the damn point. If her intent was to harm her, she would rather get it out of the way. The tension coiled in her stomach was almost unbearable.

She sat next to Edamine on the opposite settee to Hannah, watching as her head swivelled around the room. 'This place is like a time warp, right? A regular scary movie set. A murder would go unnoticed here for quite a while, don't you think?'

Thunder crashed outside and a howl of wind raged against the window.

Here we go, Beau thought, her stomach in knots, here we go.

'...so, I think we're going to move to the coast. Joe has always wanted to be by the sea. It was me who needed to be in the city, but to be honest - and be honest, Beau - how much do I actually leave the house for work?'

Beau blinked.

Is this part of her psychopathic build up, or is she actually just telling me what's going on? If this is part of the game, I don't understand.

Maybe she's trying to throw you off the scent, to really take you by surprise?

'Well?'

Beau blinked. 'Um... barely ever.'

'Exactly, and most of the meetings can held online now. There's absolutely no need to be in the city anymore. I've done some thinking while I've been away. A lot, actually.'

Here it comes.

But it didn't come. Hannah just kept rattling off what she had learned and how she wanted to change and what had brought her across the land on this dark and stormy night.

'I have to get home to Joe and Leila, I miss them so much, but I'm in the country, and I couldn't go without reaching out to you first, could I? I owe you, Beau. I owe you lots! And I had to tell you in person, this is something that couldn't be messaged.'

Now?

But no, Hannah just kept talking, and Edamine and Beau could do nothing but listen and wait, until it seemed that the moment finally arrived.

'Oh, I forgot! I brought a gift for you, Beau. You're going to love it. Give me a sec.'

Hannah disappeared into the hallway to get something from her backpack and strolled back into the room wielding a large knife.

Darkness shrouded her smile as thunder rumbled across the sky outside, long, and loud.

Chapter 42

D ANIEL HEARD THE SCREAMS from inside the cottage and fled as fast as his legs would carry him back up the hill toward the church. The clouds were dense and the rain heavy. There was no moonlight to light the way, only his sense of treading the path many times before and hoping that what was in his mind was right.

There was no phone signal down in the dip, but he knew the mast wasn't far from the church, and he only hoped he could get something up there.

He also hoped that too much blood wouldn't have been spilled by the time help could get to the Cottage.

Please, please let everyone be okay.

His insides didn't think everything was going to be. That scream had been bloodcurdling. Not the kind you hear in horror movies, but genuine terror.

Daniel's shoe hit something on the path, and he was falling. He landed hard on his stomach, and lay for a while, winded, wondering what the hell had just happened, and then his mind came back together like a magnet finding its broken pieces, and he was on his feet again, heading for the ruins.

His arms pumped, his legs screamed, and his lungs burned, and just when he thought he had no more in him, the slope began to level out and he saw the ruins loom above him.

'Not far. Not far. Not far,' he chanted as each foot struck the ground, hoping that no rocks would appear under them and send him sprawling again, and then he was at the wall of the church, panting hard, wondering if his lungs would ever recover, and if his heart would ever slow.

Had he just witnessed a murder? Was that scream a scream of pain or shock?

How would he know the difference?

His shaking hands fumbled with his phone, causing him to drop it twice in the slickness of the rain before he managed to get the screen lit.

No signal.

'Shit! No, no, no!'

He ran around to the church doorway, tried inside, tried the west wall, tried further out.

No luck.

'Fuck, no! This can't be fucking happening. I had signal here just fucking yesterday. Work you piece of shit!'

He ran in circles with his phone held in the air and then looked at his phone incredulously, at the little circle with the line through which stated emergency calls only.

Emergency calls only.

'Emergency calls only! Daniel, you utter nob.'

He half laughed, half cried, as he dialled 999 and the call connected instantly.

Chapter 43

ANNA FLINCHED IN THE hallway, the door swinging closed be-hind her as a woman she had never seen before let out a scream worthy of an Oscar. She raised an eyebrow as the woman covered her mouth with a hand, the scream cutting off into silence – not that anyone would have heard her out here even if she had carried on.

'Jesus! You scared me to death!' The woman turned to look back into the living area. 'You could have told me you were expecting more visitors.' Then, looking back at Anna. 'Who the fuck are you?'

Unruffled, Anna shook a hand through her long dark hair; itchy, messy, and wet where the rain had got under the wig, which was now stowed safely in her rucksack. No need for anyone here to know about it. Anna locked eyes with the woman and saw a startling blue, almost like her own.

'I could ask you the same question. You're in *my* cottage.'

She took in the woman, who looked a little wild, her blue eyes large and round, her long black hair hanging in wet strings, and a knife clutched in her right hand. Anna felt no fear, just a flash of strangeness, like she had entered an alternate universe.

Is this me? Am I watching myself? Do I do it already? I had things to share first, I wanted to be there for that. Did I wig out?

'Your cottage? I thought it was hers.'

The woman hitched a thumb backward as another lady with red hair and a further with white appeared in the hallway. Everyone seemed to be as confused as she felt. There was a moment where all four women simply stared at each other.

'It's not hers,' the dark-haired woman continued, pointing to the redhead with the tip of the knife, 'She's just house sitting.'

Anna blinked.

Well, this isn't going quite the way I expected. Interesting.

It was a good rage diffuser, all of this unexpected activity, and she *had* been in a rage. She was tired, muddy, wet, and fucked off. She had intended to kick the door in and just unleash her anger, get in and get out, but the door had been unlocked, and this scene had thrown her completely. Now she was glad that she had a chance to calm herself and assess the situation properly.

First reunion, then terror, remember? That was the plan. Keep it calm, Anna. This could be real good fun if I can keep the upper hand. No way I'm going back out there now. I've started, So I'll finish.

Anna put on her most charming smile. 'I'm glad we cleared that up. Whew, it's absolutely awful out there. I wonder-'

But the white-haired woman cut her off.

'Excuse me, but this is *my* cottage, and *you* are trespassing.' She put a hand to her head and rolled her eyes. 'Good Lord, I can't keep up with what's going on tonight. No one visits the cottage in the daylight, but now two people late on a dark and stormy night? Enlighten me, please, what are you doing here?'

Anna took in the jut of the chin, the authoritative stance, the tilt of the mouth, the pale blue eyes - never as blue as hers - and a flare of recognition ignited in her brain.

Well, well, after thirty-odd years, here we are. Daniel came up good. Now play it cool, Anna.

She narrowed her eyes and let a small smile play on her lips. 'Edamine?'

The white-haired lady shifted. She was steely and tough. This should be a lot of fun.

'Who are you?'

Anna pasted a huge smile on her face. She'd been rehearsing this moment for a long time, and the motion came easily. She patted a hand to her soaked chest.

'It's me, Anna! I've come home.'

Edamine held firm, looking her up and down in that same fucking way she always had – the way that said she was better than everybody here. Anna seethed under her smile as Edamine jutted her chin.

'I don't know anybody called Anna, and this certainly isn't your home. Are you lost?'

Anna struggled to keep the smile in place and tried hard to let the comment slip. Lost? She'd show her fucking lost.

'No, I'm not lost. I'm sorry, I've just been called Anna for so long now. I forget. It's Constance, Edamine. Constance, your sister.'

Anna - she hated the name Constance - saw Edamine pale, the woman with the red hair flinch and shake her head, and the dark-haired girl gogging between the three of them as though she hadn't a clue what was going on, the knife down at her side.

Interesting.

Edamine shook her head and stepped in front of the other two women, showing Anna just how frail she was. The walking stick was ornate, and probably paid for with Anna's inheritance, but it was still just a walking aid for an infirm lady.

At fifty, wow! Someone didn't look after herself, too much partying with my money no doubt. Serves her fucking right.

'Listen,' Edamine said, her face pale but hard. 'I don't know who the hell you are, but that's a cruel trick. I don't have a sister, and you well know it. Who are you?'

Anna rolled her eyes and shook her head. 'Edamine, look at me. It's Constance. I know I'm a mess from the weather and it's been a long time, almost thirty-odd years-'

'Thirty-eight. Almost forty.' Edamine said, cutting her off, her mouth a stern line.

'Okay, almost forty, but even so, I recognise little bits of you that haven't changed, and I remember so much. I remember the way your eyes used to light up when mother said that we could go down the beach alone. I remember the way you used to hide under the bed when father was angry. I remember the way you'd jut your chin when I got to the bathroom first, or when I got to wash, and you had to dry and put everything away.'

'Double duties,' they said together, and Anna saw a slight smile on Edamine's lips before she covered it with that hard exterior.

You need more? I've got bags of it, darling.

'I still remember the set of your shoulders, the one you're doing now, the one you used to show father when he was shouting at me, and you were trying to warn him off - not that it ever worked. My way was so much better, you just had to be more flamboyant, Edamine, stop reigning in that temper and let it ride free. I scared him, did you know that? Scared them both.'

Edamine shook her head slowly as the red-haired lady moved forward and slipped a hand around her arm. Edamine seemed to wobble, and Anna thought she'd cash in on the break in composure. More personal, let's hit home now.

'I remember Elf, the reindeer with the tartan antlers? The one that you got for helping with the holy communion that Sunday. I was so jealous that I cut off its legs, remember?'

Edamine made a small noise and slumped against the wall, the red-head now the only thing holding her up. 'How do you know all of this?'

'I know even more. I know we had a collie called Beanie who loved to be in the sea. He used to round us up if we were too far apart on the beach, remember? Remember that day we were writing the message for gran in the sand? I was so mad that you got to write it, I just wanted to be as far from you as possible, and yet Beanie kept trying to herd us together. So annoying.'

Anna let out a laugh that didn't feel so fake. It hadn't been funny on the day. Back then she had wanted to cut Beanie's legs off like she had the reindeer. In fact, she had tried, but the dog had growled and yelped, and their mother had been horrified as she bandaged the top of his leg, but there hadn't been *that* much blood, not really.

For the next week Anna had been kept in the dining room, polishing silver, polishing photo frames, polishing the table, anything that their mother could get her hands on so that her 'idle hands' were kept busy, and for the rest of their time together Constance and Beanie never really made amends.

'You hurt him,' Edamine said, but there was the edge of a smile, and the hardness was almost gone.

'I tried to cut his legs off, like the deer. He wasn't too happy about that.'

'You were so silly,' Edamine said with a shake of her head, 'so young. I remember you were in awful trouble and mother was almost at her wits end when Beanie chewed his bandage off every half an hour. I don't think the cut was as bad as you were punished for.'

Anna huffed a laugh. 'No, it was barely a nick.'

There were tears in Edamine's eyes, and Anna felt a strange rush of emotion. It hadn't been called for, but Anna actually shed the first tear. Afterward, she would look back in amazement at how good she actually was. She should have been an actress, really.

'Is it really you?' Edamine said, and Anna thought it was funny how people could change within seconds. This steely woman was now slumped up the wall, tears flowing down her cheeks, looking like she could be taken out with a flick of a finger. Anna really hoped this wouldn't be true. 'But it can't be. I thought... they said...'

Anna nodded. She could only imagine what lies had been woven over her departure. It was all lies, their entire childhood, well until Anna was seven, anyway. Then she got the truth. Hard and cold, and time had done nothing to erase any of it. It was time to really hammer the nail home.

'I have something to show you, something I kept. I stole it because I knew I would find you one day. I always knew that I would come back, and I didn't know what they told you, but I needed you to believe me... I *need* you to believe me.'

Anna dropped the rucksack on the floor and opened the zip, cursing herself for putting the damn wig on top of everything else. She rummaged around and finally found the envelope at the bottom, under her wet shoes. She wanted the knife too, but she couldn't seem to find it.

Fuck, good going Anna. If you sit here too long, they'll get suspicious.

Anna pulled out the envelope. It was wet and dirty, and she only hoped that the contents inside had survived. She wanted to prove that she was authentic. It was important that Edamine knew - *really* knew - that she was her sister, and just how deep blood ran - when the grand finale came.

She patted around the inside of the bag, hoping to feel sharp steel, but finding nothing.

Anna blinked.

Where the fuck is the knife?

Plenty of time. Focus, Anna. Focus.

Anna straightened with a smile and flattened the soggy envelope against her coat.

'I hope the rain hasn't damaged too much.' She handed the envelope to Edamine. 'Take a look. I sneaked them out just before I was taken away.'

Edamine patted the tears on her cheeks. 'Taken away? I don't understand any of this. What is going on? My sister is dead, she's been dead for thirty-eight years. She's dead, isn't she?'

Edamine looked at the red-haired woman, who looked at Anna.

'I'm not at all sure. Look, I think Edamine needs to sit down. Shall we go into the living room?'

Anna almost rolled her eyes.

About fucking time, my legs are caked, and a drink would be nice too. Manners are hard to come by here, but then I suppose they always were.

'Sure,' she said with a shrug as she hung her coat on the same old coat rack that she had used almost forty years earlier. 'Is the living room wall still blue and covered in the same white flowers?'

Chapter 44

BEAU MADE WHAT SHE felt was the fiftieth drink of the day, and the cups were strangely multiplying each time, even out here in isolation. It was surreal, and she was still on edge. It had been bad enough when Hannah had produced the knife and waved it around, telling her it was a ceremonial knife called a *sgian dubh*. Apparently, Hannah had thought it a great gift, not only because it would remind Beau of her time here, but because she could use it to defend herself in the great outdoors.

'Never can be too careful, Beau.'

Beau had found herself searching every sentence Hannah uttered for ulterior motives and meanings, but up to yet, she hadn't shown an ounce of bitterness. She had even tried to give the knife to Beau and laughed when it caused her to flinch and shy away.

'Jeez, Beau, it's just a knife!'

Hannah had continued to look amused as she unsheathed the knife and turned it over so that it glinted in the low light. It was decorative, with a Celtic symbol on the handle which Hannah

went into detail about, but Beau was more worried about the
sharp-looking blade.

Only two things ran through her mind.

Is she going to kill me with this knife? Or is she being genuine?

It was killing her waiting to find out. She hadn't realised just how
long it could take for the bad guys to get to the point and just
do what they came for, and at this point Beau was almost ready
to start the fight herself so that they could just get to the finale.
It was excruciating.

Now, as she twirled a spoon in the cups, she listened to the
chatter from the living room and felt like the world had com-
pleted a three-sixty before she had strapped herself in. God
knew how Edamine felt. Only a handful of hours after telling
Beau her sister had died and her father may have done it, the
very same sister turns up on the doorstep in a storm like she
was delivered from the heavens themselves?

It was bizarre to say the least, but the strange events certainly
didn't make her feel any safer, especially after Ophelia's earlier
warning. All Beau really wanted was to send them all back out
into the storm and get her quiet cottage back to normal. She
would even take the eerie noises over the tension.

With a sigh, she found a small tray in the cupboard and took the
cups back to a living room full of relaxed and chatty women,
two of them emotional - after looking at some photos, a small
badge, and a child's heart necklace that proved Anna's identity
without a doubt - and one who may very well be psychotic.

Lightning flashed, highlighting the women, who were hunched
over the coffee table like the contestants of a game show. Beau
paused in the doorway and her breath caught.

Ladies and gentlemen, it's tonight's episode of Guess the Psycho!

Is it Hannah, full of jealous rage because her friend moves to
Scotland? Is it Anna, who is actually Constance, risen from the
dead? Or in a cruel twist of fate, is it Edamine, whose fake
knocks and bangs from her father reeled Beau in?

Beau tried to smile as she put the tray on the coffee table, but
no one looked up, not breaking the chatter even for a thank
you. She wondered if she could turn the tables with enough
conviction.

Surprise! It's me, I'm the psycho, I'm the horror writer, now fuck off out of my cottage!

She almost let out a nervous laugh, which accelerated a pain that had begun to nudge the side of her skull. She sat next to Hannah, keeping the gap between them as large as possible. Now that Edamine was beyond being alert, she had to look out for herself.

It's just nerves and tension. Maybe nothing will happen, maybe things have just been put in your head. Or maybe because there are more of us now, Hannah won't bother at all. Maybe Edamine and the stranger have saved your life? Not that witnesses bothered her last time, but they weren't so close. Maybe she won't try anything until Edamine and Anna have left?

Beau's heart banged in her chest, and she glanced at Hannah, who was hanging onto Anna's every word.

How psychotic is she?

Beau flinched as Hannah scooted forward, her butt almost hanging off the edge of the chair. 'So you were *dead* just minutes ago, for thirty-eight years?'

Something winked in the light between them, and Beau saw the ceremonial knife sheathed on the seat between them. Her heart gave a quick flip.

Had Hannah put it there for quick access?

Should I take it?

Could the outcome be any worse? If I put it out in the open, there's less chance of a sneak attack.

Beau snatched the knife, which was heavier than she thought and put it on the coffee table, using her fingers to push it out of reach. It was now nearer to Edamine than Hannah, and that made Beau feel that little safer. Hannah didn't notice, and Beau felt a trickle of sweat run down her back.

Let's hope that luck holds out.

She tried to focus on the room, struggling to keep her mind flitting from one scenario to another - all of them horror stories. The room felt heavy under the weather, damp. Rain pushed against the glass, which creaked under the pressure of the wind. The storm outside seemed to have been going on for hours with the same fury, the thunder still grumbling its annoyance.

Then lightening flashed, and what Beau saw outside terrified her.

The land was running with water. Streams of it all running toward the ocean, which smashed it back to land as though rejecting the rains offering. It would be a quagmire out there.

Her heart banged as she remembered the bogginess of the dry land that she had walked over just days before. Peat bog, Gerard had said, dangerous in dry conditions, lethal in wet. 'But don't worry, Beau,' he'd said. 'Just look carefully for the path and follow it, never step where you're unsure and if the ground seems wet and spongy, move around it until it's firm again. Take your time and take care until you get back on track.'

But there was no path, not really, and now it's a river who knows how I'd ever get to the car. I'm trapped here until this storm runs through.

Well, we are.

Together.

For better or worse.

Beau swallowed hard and forced herself to look at Anna, trying to focus on the conversation rather than the doom that was in her mind.

'It's deranged that Edamine was told I had died. What kind of parents tell a child that? I hated that Edamine never came to find me. She had been my best friend in the world, and I really thought that she didn't care. I knew they may have told her what happened, of course... but I mean, I was young, and I was angry.' Anna said, her lips pinched. 'What I did was wrong, but I was sorry, and I knew I had stepped over the line. I tried to apologise, but they were adamant I should leave. Father was furious, but let's face it, he was a monster, so I wasn't too bothered about him. I knew that mother was scared and that she would do anything father said, so I didn't hold out any hope there, but you, Edamine, I had thought that you would understand. That you would find me and help me. I spent years wondering why you'd deserted me and wondering why I wasn't good enough.'

'I didn't know,' Edamine said through a sob, holding the little collie dog badge that Anna had kept all this time. 'You were dead, that's what they told me, fallen from the cliffs.'

'Didn't anybody question that when they didn't see my body?'

'Well, of course not. It was assumed that you had been washed out to sea and would turn up on another shore at some point... maybe. I was told to get on with it. You were gone, and there was nothing to be done. You know what mother was like, no point crying over spilled milk.'

'Spilled milk,' Anna spat with a shake of her head.

'I'm sorry,' Edamine said. 'That was insensitive.'

'She said it. I can hear her even now.'

Edamine nodded. 'Yes, but your 'death' hit her hard, you know, she tried so hard to keep it all together afterward, especially when people speculated that father had pushed you. We were targeted viciously until he hung himself two years later in 1985.'

Beau watched Anna raise her eyebrows in shock. 'He hung himself?'

Edamine shrugged and dabbed her eyes with a tissue. 'Mother thought he couldn't deal with the loss, but to be honest, as time went by and the rumours didn't die down, I wondered whether he had pushed you after all, and that it was guilt. I'm sorry about that now. I should have known. He was strict, but he was never a murderer, and that evidence is clear to see.'

'He was an evil man,' Anna said, dropping her gaze to the table - and was it Beau's eyes or did she double check that Edamine was watching?

'He was strict,' Edamine said, taking her hand. Anna kept her gaze low, and Beau saw her working her jaw. 'But he wasn't bad, Constance.'

'Not bad? Not only did he send me away and tell you I was dead - like that wasn't bad enough - but he did some awful things to me. Things I'll never forget. I hope he's rotting down there in hell, and she's just as bad. Mother. Fucking spilled milk! She knew exactly what happened to me. They both did! Sending me away was discussed at length the morning I 'died". She punctuated the air with her fingers. 'And the speed they set the wheels in motion would have made the Mercedes racing team proud. I was gone before you even came back from school, and if I was supposed to be dead, Edamine, you know very well what that meant.'

Edamine dropped her gaze and reached for a tissue. If she did know, it seemed Anna was going to spell it out anyway.

'It meant they were intending never to see me again, and that you were never to see me again, either. They sent me away forever, and if I ever thought any different, it's clear to see now, isn't it? I know father was a priest, but how the hell would he ever explain me rising from the dead? It's so final, and I was just a child.' Anna sniffed and let out a sob. Edamine passed her a tissue, and she dabbed her eyes gently. 'What parents do that to their child? To their own flesh and blood?'

Hannah snuck a wide-eyed look at Beau, who shrugged lightly and turned her gaze back to the sisters. One grey, one brown. One light, one dark...one good, one evil? Like snow white and rose red.

This is hardly a fairy tale Beau, and you don't know what she did that led to those circumstances.

Beau pulled her bottom lip under her teeth and rubbed her temples as she listened to the conversation with growing horror. How did two small children deal with what had happened to these women, each of them having their own story of the devastation of their family?

Edamine shook her head. 'I don't understand. I don't know why they would do that, although I know now that it's true. What happened that day, Constance? Help me understand-'

'It's Anna now, Edamine, please respect that.'

Sorry. Anna. I was told that you had faked illness to be collected from school, and that had led to an argument that sent you running up to the church. They said that you ran around the back and slipped as father tried to get you back to safety.'

Anna's face curled into a nasty smile. 'And you believed them? How gullible you are, Edamine. Does that sound like something I would do? Does that even sound feasible? Why would I run to the edge of the cliffs and trap myself? I wasn't stupid.'

'No. No, and the more I've thought of it over the years, the more I questioned it, and that's why I began to believe that father pushed you. You have to remember that I was at school, and when father came to collect me, he was crying. He told me what had happened on the way home, and I never saw you again. I was eleven years old. What was I supposed to believe?'

Anna shrugged and turned to the window. Her face was dark as she shook her head. Edamine placed a hand on her shoulder, and she seemed to soften as she turned back.

'You were supposed to believe in me. To know that I wouldn't have done that, to feel my... my... spirit out there somewhere. We're sisters. I was counting on you to save me!'

Edamine's face contorted with pain. 'I didn't know I had to, Constance-'

Anna's face flashed with anger. 'Anna! It's Anna now. I hate Constance, and I won't have anything to do with her. She *did* die back then, maybe that wasn't such a lie, but it wasn't because I'd fallen, it was because my family had rejected me so harshly for something I couldn't control, and I needed help, Edamine, I did, and I understand that, but they weren't blameless. Neither of them!'

Beau felt her stomach roll as she took on Anna's words.

What the hell did she do?

What the hell did Hannah do?

Why is everything so messed up here right now?

What is going on?

Edamine seemed calm as she reached for Anna's hand. 'I understand that Co...Anna, I do, but I don't know the details. If you weren't sick that day, what happened?'

Anna took a breath and said the words that would change the tone of the evening. Words that struck more fear into Beau's heart than sitting next to Hannah. Better the devil you know.

'I stabbed someone in class, with scissors, and I wasn't sorry. I'm not sorry, because all that anger has to be released somewhere and the beatings here weren't half of my problem, Edamine. The abuse was. Did you know he used to take me up to the church to help clean and set up just so that he could stick his hand under my skirt?'

Edamine sat back with a small 'oh' and a shake of her head. 'No.'

Hannah gasped and grabbed Beau's hand, but Beau hardly noticed.

Anna sat forward, moving in. 'Yes. In fact, sometimes there was no reason to be at the church. He simply made one up and took me up there solely for the purpose of undressing me. He used to make me stand before Jesus and confess my sins before he did what 'Jesus' whispered into his ear would make me atone. You thought I was the favourite, always going up there to help out, always coming back with a pack of sweets, but you know nothing, Edamine. The sweets were just hush money, that's all. And as he did his thing, do you know what I was concerned about? That he never did the same to you. I was constantly watching him, constantly watching you, and anytime he tried to be alone with you, I would put myself in his way. I don't know whether you ever noticed that. Did you notice, Edamine?'

Edamine was now hunched over her hands, her body wracking with sobs. Anna stared at her. 'Did you?'

Beau could feel the tension weighting the room. Her head was pounding, and she wished she could wake from this nightmare.

'Anna,' she said, 'Edamine is upset, and she's not well. Give her a chance to process the information because this isn't the father she knew.'

'Are you calling me a liar?'

Beau felt her heart pounding under her jumper.

'No. Not at all. I'm just saying that this isn't her experience.'

'And? I didn't have a chance to process being taken from my family and thrown into a system that deals with loony delinquents either. Locked up with other dangerous kids. I hated father. Hated him, but he was still my family, and I still thought he would protect me. I didn't expect to be pushed out. I was a child. A fucking child!'

Anna's face was red now, and Hannah stood, her hands out in front of her. 'Anna, calm down. We're not the enemy, and neither is Edamine.'

Anna sighed and closed her eyes as she rolled her head. One full slow revolution, and then she smiled.

'That's where you're wrong, you see, because Edamine has everything, doesn't she? A privileged life, all the money, all of the inheritance, a nice childhood in a pretty house by the sea. I went through hell and don't receive a dime? I was crying out for help the day I stabbed that girl - who didn't die, just so you know - and all I got was shunned. Pushed out of society away from everything I've ever known. I was treated like a criminal.'

'Well, you stabbed someone,' Beau said, her eyes widening. 'And Edamine has had her own issues to deal with, not least losing you. She hasn't had it easy.'

'Oh, she had it a whole lot easier than me, that I guarantee. Why, here we are in the cosy little cottage that was our childhood home, all playing happy families again. She had family to help her cope with her hardships, and she had friends and a continuing life. She had stability. I had none. I lost every familiar face I ever knew.'

Edamine looked up, her face pale and contorted, one hand at her chest.

'No Constance, no, please-'

Anna leaned down into her face until their noses were an inch apart. 'It's fucking Anna! *Anna*, you selfish bitch. You think you can take everything and get away with it? You think you can call me that name and bring back all of me that used to be her? You think you can rub my nose in what I had to deal with? I hate Constance and I hate what was her life. I hate everything in this fucking house and all of the fucking memories that are being dredged up. Most of all.' She leaned in further until their noses were squashed together and grasped a fist of Edamine's blouse, almost pulling her up and out of the chair. 'I hate you.'

Edamine cried out and Hannah reached to pull Anna away as Beau jumped to her feet, her heart rushing up into her throat. 'Leave her alone! She doesn't need this. Please.'

Anna shrugged off Hannah's hands and pushed her backwards onto the chair. Hannah looked stunned as Beau felt the situation sliding. Things were changing fast.

Now Anna turned to Beau, red faced over the table. 'I think she does need this, because I don't believe she would have come looking for me even if she'd known I was alive.' She turned to Edamine, who was now sprawled across the chair, a shaky arm reaching for her stick. 'I saw the way you looked at me when I told you what I'd done. I saw the disgust, and I saw the filth in your eyes when I told you what he did to me. He was a fucking monster, Edamine, and you're still defending him!'

Edamine shook her head, and Beau moved to help her to rise, to try to get a distance from this lady who appeared to be boiling over.

'You are!' Anna raged. 'you're just like *her*! You even have that stupid way she used to shake her head and plead innocence with that pathetic little look on her face–'

There was a scratch and a shriek from the corner and the record player started up, full volume.

'Forget about me... don't you...'

Anna whirled round as Hannah and Beau threw their hands over their ears. The music pumped and Beau saw Edamine slump back to the chair as her mouth murmured one word. 'Father.' And then there was a crash, and she howled.

Beau turned to see Anna slam a fist into the machine, hard enough to break not only the Perspex lid, but the arm, the record, and the turntable.

'You bastard! You fucking bastard, don't you fucking dare!'

'Anna! Don't!' Beau yelled, horrified for Edamine and her house and what was left of her father, but also for the old record player.

Edamine was gasping for breath on the chair and Beau felt anger surge up her chest.

'Anna, that's enough! There's no need to break things–'

'No need? You know that song? That was his favourite. You know who he'd sing it to? Me! And you know where he'd sing it? At the church. Afterward. In a voice that used to raise the hair at the back of my neck and make me want to vomit. Does that sound like loving father behaviour to you? I felt sick, fucking sick, but I barely knew what the hell was going on. I didn't realise anything but the pain and frustration until much later. Only then did it hit me what he'd done. After that? I wanted to kill him. I so wanted to kill him, but I didn't know how and I couldn't keep the anger in. I lost it at school instead and everything fucking changed. Then I couldn't get out. They wouldn't let me out.'

There was a bang from the kitchen, and a swirl of cold air pulsed into the room. Beau held out a hand as Anna stormed past her to Edamine, but withdrew it as she saw the manic look on Anna's face. Her blue eyes were bloodshot and as wild as her hair, and her mouth resembled a snarl.

'All of these years, that pain and anger has been simmering. It's been kept under wraps because I needed to be released to do what I need to do, and that took so much fucking longer than I wanted it to. Years, and *years* of waiting, so much fucking WAITING!' Anna shook her head and Beau gasped when she saw Anna holding the knife out in front of her. Beau's knife. The one she had put on the table, in plain sight. There was a sinking feeling in Beau's pounding chest as the evening seemed to unravel further down a rabbit hole.

'Anna... Edamine...no,' she tried, but the room felt fluid and surreal, her words eaten by the roar of the storm.

Is this even happening? I should really wake up if this is a dream.

But she didn't. There was a shout amongst a small wailing that Beau thought was the wind, but then realised was coming from Edamine. Anna pointed the knife at her sister, and Beau thought she could almost taste her own fear. Beside her, Hannah vaulted the settee and searched frantically on the chair they had been sitting.

'Hey! Is that Beau's knife? That cost me a fortune!'

Anna ignored Hannah and leaned forward. The knife glinted in the low light as she flicked it toward Edamine, who made an animal like shriek and tried to grab her stick. Her fingers caught the end and it tumbled away and onto the floor with a clatter.

'But I'm out now, Edamine, and I'm here. Are you glad to see me? I hope so because I'm so glad to see you. It's taken so long to track you down, and now you have to pay, because who the hell else can I make pay? The coward took his own fucking life. I couldn't even do that for him. I'm owed an inheritance, I fucking deserve one, and I can't get my hands on anything until you're out of the way.'

'You won't get your hands on anything,' Edamine said, her hands splayed across the chair as she pushed herself back.

'Oh, I will, you see, I've been a good girl, and many officials can verify that. You know why? Because I've been watched, tracked, and had my behaviour checked both physically and psychologically my whole life. So, when I miraculously turn up at the reading of the will and say who I am, there will be no question where the money will go. I am family, and you've loved

me all of these years, even though you thought I was dead. I am
next of kin, your only next of kin'

'I have a will.' Edamine said, her face white.

'And I will contest it.' Anna shrugged. 'We'll see who's right
either way, won't we? Oh... well, I mean I will. You won't be here.'

Anna smiled as she drew back the knife.

'No!' Hannah shouted as she spun from the chair, a cushion
flying across to the fireplace.

As she realised what was happening - *really* happening - Beau
gave a shriek of her own and lunged for the back of the settee
as Edamine twisted and tried to crawl over the backrest. Beau
grabbed her arms and pulled, but the light glinted funny and
there was a small, thick, thu...ck sound.

Edamine screamed and Beau yelled as she pulled at Edamine's
arms, and the knife came down again.

Thu...ck.

There was a scrape and a bang as Beau saw Hannah run into the
coffee table and send both it and her sprawling with a yell. Anna
didn't seem to notice the commotion behind her.

'Come on!' Beau yelled as she tugged Edamine's dead weight
from under her arms and Anna plunged the knife again.

Thu...ck.

'Stop!' Beau shrieked. 'Just stop this!' but in the surreal landscape of this living room Beau realised Anna wasn't there. Her
face was placid, a small smile playing at her mouth, almost like
she was giving Edamine a gift.

There's a *real* psychotic look for you to write about, Beau
thought as her mind whirled and Edamine finally came, the
momentum sending Beau sprawling backwards onto the floor
with Edamine landing on top of her with a thump.

Confused and crying tears she hadn't known were waiting, Beau
clutched her arms around Edamine, holding her tight.

Did she get her? Has she been stabbed?

'You're going to be okay, Edamine. You'll be fine. You'll be fine. I'm going to get you out of here. I promise.'

Edamine moaned and spluttered and coughed blood. Beau's heart banged hard as Anna rounded the settee, the knife now red tipped and dripping.

Edamine turned her face weakly toward Beau and gurgled one word.

'Run.'

Beau shook her head and clutched tighter, but Edamine had fallen limp.

'No! Get up, I won't leave you!' Beau screamed. 'No!'

In the hallway, the grandfather clock began to chime.

It's 12.02, Beau thought stupidly, and then Hannah lunged for Anna.

Chapter 45

ANNA FELT A SURGE of power and satisfaction. It had been so long coming, so long waiting and planning that the sweet release was delicious. The knife slid in and out easily, like it was meant for her hand and meant for the job, and the red blooms spreading across Edamine's cream blouse were mesmerizing, almost poetic...

'Stop! Get away from her!'

Anna was jolted from behind as someone jumped on her back, knocking her forward onto the settee. She felt her own power as she pushed back off the chair and the pair stumbled back into the wall behind. A photograph crashed to the ground and smashed, and the hands let go. Anna spun to her feet, panting, and turned to see the woman with the dark hair retreating into the hallway backwards to sit against the staircase with a hand at her chest.

'Beau, we need to get out of here,' she called, but her voice was weak as she kept her eyes on Anna, and she was making no movement to run.

Her heart pounding with the thrill of adrenaline coursing through her body, Anna swung to find the red-haired woman sitting dumbly with Edamine's body, crying like they had lived a thousand lives together.

Hell, maybe they had, but no longer, Edamine was soon to be out of the picture.

Lights out, power off.

It didn't seem that these two would be much of a handful. Still in shock, which would give Anna the advantage. No rush yet, it seemed, and Anna was going to enjoy every minute she could for as long as this took to get critical.

She tilted her head on one side as she looked at Edamine's slack body.

'Has she gone yet? Or is she clinging valiantly on to those last breaths?'

The red-haired woman looked up at her incredulous. No fear, not yet, but that would change.

'Are you serious?' she yelled, her cheeks red, 'we need an ambulance, she's dying. Someone call for an ambulance.'

'Dying was kind of the point,' Anna said, stooping beside her with a small shrug. 'Didn't you hear a word I said earlier?'

There was movement from the hallway and Anna swung round to find the dark-haired girl tapping quickly at her phone. Her heart catapulted. That wouldn't be ideal, not at all.

Rising quickly, Anna strode into the hallway and snatched the phone from the woman's hands, giving her no time to react.

'Hey!'

'Sorry, no phones allowed,' Anna stated, while smiling through gritted teeth. A look at the screen told her there was no signal. Sweet relief filled her. This was turning out perfectly. 'And would you look at that? No signal. A real shame.'

'Oh God, someone needs to call an ambulance!' the red-haired woman called frantically from the living room, obviously not taking note of anything going on around her. Anna rolled her eyes.

'And I *said*, there's no phone signal, which is kind of the icing on the cake, to be honest.'

She pocketed the phone and moved back into the dim living room where the blue of the wallpaper looked a sickly green in the yellow light. She had never liked it in here after dark; it made her feel like hurling.

She stooped beside the pair again and placed a hand on Edamine's pulse. Still there, but barely, and from the rasp of her breath, she wouldn't be here much longer.

'Well, I'm pretty sure an ambulance wouldn't make it in time anyway, so no harm done, eh? Don't beat yourself up.'

She patted Beau's shoulder, and the woman flinched back from her touch. She seemed to see her for the first time since the stabbing, and finally, her eyes held fear.

Better. Much better.

Anna stood. 'Right, well, I think you should both be in here where I can keep an eye on you. We have unfinished business.' The red-haired lady swallowed so hard that Anna heard it over the noise of the wind and rain. She smiled. 'Oh, don't worry. It'll all be over soon.'

Beau's eyes flicked to the hallway and Anna looked back over her shoulder to find the dark-haired girl gone. Her heart staggered, and she rushed into the hallway as Beau called out behind her.

'She's coming Hannah! Hurry!'

Anna stalled in confusion, thinking that someone was coming for her, until she realised the red-haired lady had said Hannah, which must be the other woman's name. The two women hadn't been near each other, and the red-haired lady had been in shock, concerned only for Edamine, but now they were working together?

Anna was thrown a little off balance, but anger rose from her gut. Did they really think they had her?

She rushed into the hallway to see the front door shut and the keys swinging in the lock. She threw the door open and checked outside. The weather screamed and water ran in rivers toward the sea, but the woman was nowhere to be seen.

No way she could have got that far, she hasn't left the house.

Feeling the thudding of her heart, Anna shut and locked the door and pocketed the keys before turning to the kitchen, where the back door stood open.

No, no, no!

Anna ran into the empty kitchen, through the open door and out into the lean-to. The outer door was closed, but that didn't mean anything. She ran to the door and tugged at the handle.

Locked.

Anna battered a fist at the door in anger. Why had she not checked these before she had stabbed Edamine, before the other two knew what was going on? If she had known they were locked, she could have saved herself both time and a heart attack. She wasn't out the front, so the dark-haired girl – Hannah – she was inside somewhere.

Fuck. You idiot. This should have been planned better.

As she turned to go back into the house the kitchen door slammed shut, locking her inside the small extension.

'Hey!' she roared.

If you're fucking locked out now, Anna... Christ, this is a fucking disaster.

Anna reached the door and heard movement in the kitchen beyond. She yelled and pounded on the wood, kicking and punching until the door suddenly seemed to give way and swung gently open in front of her. Anna raised an eyebrow, marched across the threshold, and came to a halt.

The front door ahead was still closed. There hadn't been time to leave, and besides, they would have had to kick the door down to do it. She narrowed her eyes and listened. There was noise, whispering, coming from the living room if her senses were anything to go by, and Anna knew they were usually pretty accurate.

She crept forward to the threshold of the kitchen and the hallway, and the frantic whispers were louder. Anna let a smile creep on to her lips.

'She's back inside, Beau, we have to move. Now.'

'I'm not leaving Edamine. She's still alive, Han.'

'Beau, none of us will be alive if we don't move. This may be our only chance.'

'No, I can't leave her.'

'She's planning to fucking kill us. We need to go.'

There was a pause in the whispering and Anna felt the smile widen. No shock now, at least for Hannah. She was fully aware of their situation. Anna hardly breathed while she listened.

'Why would she do that? She doesn't know us?'

Anna actually had to cover her mouth to stop the giggles from escaping. How was this woman so dumb?

'We're witnesses, Beau. You think she's going to say thank you and walk away?'

'We haven't done anything. I haven't done anything, I don't understand!'

Anna rolled her eyes, fingered the knife in her hand, and moved to the threshold of the living room. She took in the pair, sat on the floor with Edamine, who hadn't moved an inch.

'Let me spell it out for you, Beau. May I call you Beau?'

Both women spun to the doorway, their fear almost palpable now, and Anna's adrenaline spiked again. This would be fun. A bit of a chase, a struggle, some screaming. It would be everything that Edamine's death hadn't been. Double what her death hadn't been. She felt a tingle of excitement zip through her.

There was no response from Beau, so Anna presumed it was fine to be on first name terms and continued.

'You witnessed a murder. I stabbed my sister in cold blood, and I *loved* it. It gave me such a rush-'

Hannah rose and tried to pull Beau up with her.

'Beau, we have to go.'

'But Edamine is still alive. We can't just leave her.'

Anna raised an eyebrow, anger boiling just below the surface.

Don't lose it, not just yet.

She watched as Hannah tugged Beau harder. 'Edamine is past saving. Look at the blood and listen to the rattle of her breaths. There's blood in her lungs, it's coming out of her mouth for god's sake. We-'

Anna banged the knife against the door frame, hard, silencing both women.

'Won't be going anywhere,' she said, forcing a smile as she twirled the knife in her hand. 'I can't have witnesses now, can I? It's a shame you were here, but you're involved now and there can be no way out. I'm afraid I have no choice.'

Beau looked up at Anna, breathing hard, as she clung to Edamine.

Fear. It was so lovely to watch.

'No choice? What do you mean?' Beau asked in a much more timid and pleasing tone, not that she thought Beau would be going anywhere. She was still fawning over Edamine with genuinely no idea that she was next on the list.

'I mean what I said. Let's play a game-'

Hannah, who was standing beside the settee in front of Beau and Edamine, turned to face Anna fully, her fists clenched at her sides.

'It's not a game, and that is not even your fucking knife. It was a gift that cost a bloody fortune and now it's ruined. Just stop this, it's stupid. You're outnumbered. Just let us go.'

Anna pouted. 'It's all a bit of fun revenge. Don't you like games?'

'She's gone,' Beau said, her voice cracking as she lay Edamine's body to one side carefully. She was deathly pale and covered in blood, and Anna had the strange urge to lick her clothes. Beau was now looking at her like she was an insect. 'You. You killed her.'

Anna shrugged and rolled her eyes. 'As I said, kind of the point.'

'She was your *sister*.'

Anna tapped the knife against the doorframe as irritation wound up her spine.

'She left me in that god-awful place while she got everything. How's that for sisterly love?'

Anna took a step into the room, but Beau stood her ground beautifully, her lip curling. 'She thought you were dead. Why would she look for you? None of this was her fault, she suffered so much, and now she's dead!'

Anna made a show of looking at the ceiling and narrowing her eyes in thought, and then she flicked her gaze back to Beau. 'Nope, she didn't suffer like I did, not by half.'

'Why should she need to? You're the one who stabbed someone. You have an issue with your parents, or with your father. Why would you take that out on Edamine after all these years?'

Anna blinked. Was she really having this discussion? Who the hell did this woman think she was? She felt her anger bolt and there was no reining it back.

'Don't you dare tell me who or what I have an issue with. There are things in my life which will never be forgotten and never be settled. Edamine's death makes it a little easier, that's all. It's none of your business.'

'You made it our business, both of us,' Hannah said, taking Anna by surprise.

How had she got so close?

Then there was hot sharp pain, and she couldn't breathe as Hannah dragged the knife down her thigh and she screamed with both rage and pain.

'Beau...' she heard Hannah say, and then there was a loud bang which resounded in her skull and all she could hear was a high-pitched whine as she fell to the floor, and everything went black.

Chapter 46

'GOOD FREAKING SHOT!' HANNAH said, her mouth dropping open as Anna fell to the floor and the cast iron frying pan reverberated in Beau's hands. 'She'll have an egg there for certain. Now we just need to get out of here before she's up.'

Beau stooped to search Anna's pockets for the front door keys and Hannah's phone. Her hands were shaking, and she felt like she was going to vomit.

'I didn't think it would work. I was dying just sitting there whispering. I thought she had us for sure.'

'Nah, too narcissistic. I told you to trust me. Let's go.'

Beau found the keys, expecting Anna's eyes to open at any moment as they ran to the front door and unlocked it.

The noise was the first thing that hit Beau, the roar of the weather was intense and then the soaking rain followed closely on its heels.

'Wait!' Hannah called.

Beau was at the end of the porch and stepping into an an-kle deep river of water when she turned back to see Hannah locking the door and pocketing the keys. 'There, it'll take her a little longer now. Let's go. To the boat, Run.'

The darkness outside was complete and terrifying after the light in the cottage. Water surged around her ankles as Beau ran for the beach, splashing up to her knees. What that didn't wet, the rain soaked within an instant, lashing into her face. It was disorienting, the only thing she could focus on was the roar and crash of the waves, which sent a further dimension of terror through her.

Beau felt an unreal sensation cross her stomach as she headed for the sea, for the water, and the small boat she had mentioned to Hannah in a hushed whisper inside, and at the last minute she caught herself.

What are you doing? You fell into her trap, she's herding you toward the water, she's taking you the only way she knows how, she knows your phobia, she knows your fear.

'Run!' Hannah yelled from behind as Beau felt her legs coming to a stop at the edge of the beach, then Hannah's hand was at her arm tugging her forward, heading for the small boat tied to the cliff.

'No!' Beau cried, pulling her arm back, tugging so hard that Hannah was almost pulled off her feet. Hannah turned to Beau, her wet hair flying wildly around her face, rain running from them both in streams.

'Beau, we have to get on the boat. It's the only place she can't reach us. As you said, the land is boggy. If we don't get caught, we'll get lost or sucked into the bog, both of which would be fatal out here. It would be stupid to run, and besides, we don't have time. You agreed!'

There was a loud bang over the noise of the storm, and Beau turned to see a figure on the porch of the house. Anna was up.

Shit, shit, shit.

Beau's thoughts were muddled and mixed. She feared Anna like nothing she had ever feared before, but now Hannah was asking her to get in a boat, which not only terrified her, but was the way she had possibly drowned her friend? Was this just Hannah taking advantage?

Hannah. Anna. Anna. Hannah.

Both dark hair and blue eyes. Was this a trick? Were they both out to get her, or were they one?

'I see you!'

Anna's voice carried down the land from the house and Beau felt like curling up and crying. She wasn't safe with either of these women, was she? Joe had warned her about Hannah, and this was a perfect opportunity to jump on the bandwagon, and even to pass off Beau's murder as someone else's. Anna got them both.

In a surge of terror, Beau lunged to the left and began running away from the beach and Hannah, and toward the rushing water that hurled down the steep path from the church.

'Beau, no! What are you doing? The path is a river. We'll be swept back down, or over the cliff edge, and cutting through the forest will only slow us down. We need the boat. It's our best chance.'

Hannah ran after her, caught her arm, and swung her to a stop. Beau's heart hammered madly.

'I can't, Hannah. The boat is small and look at the waves.'

Her breath caught as she realised Hannah would already have clocked that, wouldn't she? Perfect drowning weather.

'If we go up there, we're only going further into the wilderness. It will be a death sentence.' Hannah shouted over the wind.

'If we go out there, it will be a death sentence!'

'We won't drown. I know how to handle a boat, and I'm a life saver, remember? I can get you safely to shore if anything happens. Beau, I know you're scared, but there is a woman now not a hundred meters from us who has just murdered her sister. She won't have any qualms about doing the same to a couple of strangers. We need to get in the boat.'

Beau floundered for an excuse without angering Hannah.

'What if she's a good swimmer? We'll be trapped!'

Hannah shook her head, glancing in the direction Anna was approaching from.

'We have oars. Once we get past the breaking waves, we'll be fine. There's no way she can swim through them and get to us without being drowned. It'll be too tiring, and besides, she has an open wound to contend with.'

Then another voice cut through the darkness. One that chilled Beau to her very core.

'Nice to see you hanging around for your fate. Makes this so much easier.'

Anna had left the porch and was somewhere in the darkness between them and the house, and although her eyes were adjusting to the darkness, Beau still couldn't see her. Closer though, she could tell that by her voice. She felt stuck, quivering in the sand, her whole body shaking, as Hannah pulled at her sleeve.

'Beau! Please, we have to move or there will be no time.'

'I can't go in there, Han. You know I can't!'

'Please, we have to. It's our only chance. I don't want you to die, Beau. It's our best chance. Please.'

Beau looked at Hannah's face, her eyes frantic and pleading, and then she caught sight of something across the land.

'Lights,' she said with a frown. 'There are lights.'

Hannah looked toward the cottage, even as she tried to pull Beau back across the sand.

There *were* lights, small, several of them bobbing across the land.

'They must be coming here. Someone is coming, Han, we're going to be okay. We can just hide in the forest. Please.'

'Not the best idea. I know every inch of that forest, and I'm not sure they're going to save you. It looks to me like they're a good mile away yet, and the boggy land will slow them, plenty of time.' Anna's voice said off to her left.

Hannah screamed and pulled Beau down the beach as Anna limped toward them. Her silhouette now visible in the darkness.

Only a few meters away now. Run Beau, run.

She tugged against Hannah, who was pulling her toward the boat, but then realised that she had no choice. Anna was to their left, cutting off the path to the church, and to run past the cottage to the lights would be suicide.

With no more options, she ran, allowing Hannah to pull her the only way that she felt safe enough to go. Toward the boat.

Chapter 47

Anna chuckled to herself as she watched the women run to the other side of the beach, to the other cliff. She wasn't too bothered, let themselves get tired out. There was nowhere to go except the sea. If they backtracked toward the house and help - which she expected they would do - she was far enough back to block them off.

And there's still plenty of time, she thought as she looked at the low bobbing lights in the distance. Police. It had to be. Seven of them? Maybe eight? Maybe more to come?

She wasn't concerned they were on their way. She would be long gone by the time they had traversed the boggy land to get here, especially after this rain, but she was concerned about how they knew. Who had alerted them? Who knew enough to know her plans? It was perplexing.

She shook her head, winced at the pain that shot through it, and turned her attention back to the women who were almost at the cliff. Anna smiled. Right about now, they would realise they were cut off and run right back towards the house.

Anna limped back away from the beach, intending to put herself back in the shadow of the grassland. If she was clever, they would run right into her.

Wouldn't that be a delight?

Her head throbbed, which was a minor annoyance, but the leg was the worst. The pain in her leg was good, it burned and throbbed, giving her the drive and the fire to continue, but she couldn't move as fast as she wanted, that would open the wound too much, and she knew from experience that a bad enough cut to the thigh could kill. For the moment, a shred of Edamine's shirt was acting as a tourniquet and a bandage.

She felt a stab of anger that she had lost focus and let Hannah get near enough, and with a goddamn bread knife too, possibly the very bread knife her mother had used to cut sandwiches for them when they were young. Hilarious.

If I keel over and die now, before I've had the chance to finish this, get away, and be sipping wine to celebrate? I'll be majorly pissed off.

Majorly.

There was just one thing that was stopping her from letting her anger rage right now, one thing that stopped her from going all out to get these women at the expense of her own life.

It wouldn't be such a big deal if she didn't catch them. She would be blonde again by the time she got back to the hotel and left, and if anyone had seen a mad woman with dark hair and blue eyes? Well, hadn't she thought she was looking at herself as she entered the house? She and Hannah were so alike, it had been surreal.

The other plan she thought she could pull off if it was necessary was to get back to the house and collect her wig before pleading the victim and running to the police herself. She had been stabbed after all, and Hannah didn't have a scratch. She could convincingly turn the tables if she had to.

The only problem with that would be what happened afterward, that wouldn't end so well. She would end up on the run again, and her real identity was known by both of these women, and although she was no longer known by that name, she was almost sure they would trace her eventually. She would have to leave the will, take her family and start over, new identities, and possibly in a new country, It would suck, and probably buy her time, but nothing more.

Too risky.

Anna stumbled on an uneven wedge of grass, and pain shot through her leg. She felt new warm trickle underneath her trousers mingling with the cold of the rain.

Fuck.

Stopping by a patch of gorse, she swung her gaze to the women as she pressed a hand to the wound. She hissed with the pain and felt a fresh surge of anger.

But the bitch does deserve to die for what she has done. My own mother's fucking bread knife, how dare she.

The lightening showed the women were at the cliff now, probably discussing their next move and wondering where the hell Anna had gone. She grinned and straightened, and then she stiffened as there was movement *toward* the sea, not away.

What in the hell...

It was a strange feeling that hit her when she saw the small rowing boat being dragged down the sand. Only one woman pulled, the other seemed to be looking around nervously. Probably for Anna.

The boat! How could I forget about the boat?

Anna blinked and frowned. She looked at the sea, the height of the waves and the force of them as they crashed to the shore.

They'll be killed before they even start, and if they get past the breakers, they'll die of hypothermia in this weather.

She tilted her head in wonder that they would think this was a clever idea, and then she chuckled before wincing again at the pain in her head.

Well, the threat of bumping into you is obviously worse than the treat of a swollen ocean in a storm. I'd say that's a compliment, Anna, and a job very well done.

She watched as the one lady pulled the other into the boat, almost by force, and then she tried to use the oars to push off the beach.

Don't they know how to use a boat? Seriously?

The waves pushed them back to shore even when they managed to head out a little, and then they changed tactics and one woman got out and towed the other into the waves, holding the rope of the boat behind her.

Anna thought she should either go down and finish them while they were struggling, or just leave it and get the hell out of here before the police arrived, but she couldn't stop watching the act of stupidity before her, and her rage was dwindling as her curiosity piqued.

How surreal.

The entire night had been surreal really, from entering the house to find extra people, to finding out she had been dead all these years, that father had hung himself, and that Edamine had still been living here all this time. In a house of pain and misery and death. How could she?

Deliciously, Edamine's death hadn't been surreal. It had been real and raw and beautiful. She would have liked more screaming, more struggle, but the deed had been done either way. The way the knife had entered the flesh had surprised her. Although she had only been seven, she had remembered the push that the scissors had taken, the effort, the way the skin sank and the pressure before it had seemed to pop open, leaving a red gash. She remembered the body's shock response 'oh, I'm burst open!' before the blood actually began to flow. This time, the knife had slipped in almost easily, like a knife into butter, and it had felt good in her hand, weighty, like it was ready to help her do the job. And this time, the slice through flesh had almost contained a quiet acceptance from the body, there was no yield, no waiting for the blood, and then when the blood had hit the blouse, those wonderful flowers of red, small and light, and then turning large and dark as life-force flowed out.

Life-force that I took.

Her heart skipped in thrill as she remembered, and she clutched the knife tighter.

'Next time will be even better, and I'll take this with me. No point leaving evidence around now, is there?'

She turned her attention back to the ocean and saw that the women had already got further than she thought they would. There was still only one woman in the boat, so the other must be a damn strong swimmer because they were almost out of the breaking waves. Once they reached the swell, they would be much better off.

Anna watched in fascination as they did indeed pass the breakers and the woman inside rowed out a little into the darkness. It was amazing what a little fear could propel the human body to achieve.

She wished she'd had a cigarette to watch the show, especially when she saw the boat almost topple as the second lady tried to get in. Was it Beau? Or Hannah? She thought she heard the delightful screams from all the way out here, but that could have been wishful thinking.

She grinned, checked the bobbing lights behind her - still miles away - and then looked back to the boat. It was still now, aside from the swell. One woman in with a long night ahead, the other surely on her way to death already if she hadn't made it inside.

They're dead. Nothing more to see here. Time to make my escape.

Anna turned back toward the house and limped through the streams of water that flooded the boggy grassland back to the porch. On her way, she made a simple plan.

Get her stuff and anything she may have touched - no gloves, which was stupid - put on her wig, leave through the back door, get back to the hotel before daylight, leave as fast as possible. Head at least two hundred miles north before tending to her leg and deciding what to do from there.

Back at the cottage, she stepped inside the broken front door and quickly located her backpack and anything else that would incriminate her, gathering up the envelope and mementos that she had brought to convince Edamine that she was who she said she was.

She stepped over Edamine's body, giving it a small kick for good measure as she moved back to the doorway.

Anything else?

She pocketed the knife and looked around, unconvinced.

Fuck, I touched too much stuff.

Too late now, it won't be long before the police get here. Go Anna, just go.

She moved back into the room and took the wig out of the backpack. Something landed behind her with a thud, but she ignored it as she used the mirror over the fireplace to quickly rearrange the soaked wig into some sort of style. Grunts of agony left her throat as she brushed the bump that was still rising on her head. When she had finished, covered in sweat from the pain, she zipped the backpack and saw what had dropped.

Her lighter.

She thought of her cigarettes for a moment, but then an even better thought entered her mind.

No body, no evidence, nothing to investigate.

Will I have time?

She flicked the lighter to a flame and moved around the settee, placing it first against the remains of Edamine's shirt.

Get rid of the body first, just in case.

Her clothes went up quickly and Hannah moved just as quickly upstairs, ignoring the throb in her thigh and the warmth that seeped from the wound.

She set fire to the curtains in both bedrooms and the bathroom before moving back down. Covering her nose with the arm of her coat, she moved back into the living area where Edamine was roasting nicely like she was on a spit, her skin already blackened and split, and the settee already set alight. The heat must have been warping the floor because the rocking chair was rocking slowly in the corner, which was an altogether unnerving thing to see.

'Nice to have caught up with you again, Edamine.' Anna said with a small salute. Then she moved to the dining room and set light to the curtains in there before moving to the kitchen.

As if by magic, the back door swung slowly open. Anna stood a while unnerved at the cold that entered the kitchen and circled her legs, and then she shook her throbbing head, and put her lighter to the kitchen blind. It went up with a satisfying 'whup' and she smiled and turned to the door... which slammed shut in front of her, the sound reverberating around the cottage.

Anna blinked, momentarily on edge

Draft, Anna, it's just the draft from the storm in this shitty old cottage. Now get the hell out of here.

She tugged the handle of the door, but it was stuck tight, and even the key didn't want to turn. It was as though it had been sealed shut, which wouldn't have been so bad if the door hadn't been wide open just moments ago.

'It must stick,' she muttered, kicking at the panel as smoke filled her lungs. 'This just isn't a good fucking time.'

She coughed and kicked harder but the door wouldn't budge and heat from the flames was now filling the small space.

'Fuck!'

Her heart thumping, she turned back to the hallway and eyed the smoke-filled space, the flames licking around the walls as wood cracked and splintered.

The dining room doorway next to her was the same, and Anna knew that there was no other choice, the front door was her only option, both the dining and living rooms were all but consumed, and the kitchen was close on its heels.

Sweat running down her face and her eyes half closed against the sting of smoke, Anna covered the lower half of her face and ran through the scorching heat, her lungs protesting against the searing smoke, and her thigh protesting against the activity. She reached the door as the blazing coat stand fell across her path and she jumped back. Her thigh screamed and she screamed with it. The front door set alight more quickly than she would have thought possible, and she knew it wouldn't be a means of escape now. There was nothing else she could do but get upstairs and try to jump from the landing window onto the porch.

She scaled the stairs as quickly as she could, holding her leaking thigh. The smoke was thicker up here, and the flames just as hot. There was no way she would make it down the landing, she thought, frantic as flames licked the ceiling from the bedroom doors.

Shit, I'm stuck! I'm trapped!

Her heart clattered as there was a bang downstairs and she saw the entire floor at the bottom of the stairs was now impassable. There was nowhere to go.

Nowhere to go.

And then she screamed as the roof appeared to fall in around her with a crash that she knew must be the end of her, but when she peered between her fingers, she saw salvation... of a sort, anyway.

The attic!

The ladders had fallen from the attic, which should be safe from fire enough for her to get out of the attic window. If she could hang low enough, she could slide herself to drop over the porch below and hopefully deal with no more injury than a couple of broken bones, which she would have to sort later.

Seeing no other choice Anna limped to the ladder and climbed, realising her first mistake instantly. She could barely see her hands in front of her face with the smoke that filled the roof space. Coughing and heaving, her eyes streaming from the sting of the smoke, she crawled across the floor in the direction of the window, and finally found the small round glass.

Now she realised her second mistake. The window was tiny, much smaller than she remembered.

Well, you are forty years older, what the fuck did you expect?

With no other option, she smashed the glass anyway and wound the shutters open hoping for the relief of fresh air, but the smoke simply poured out around her, there was no escape, and no air to be had.

With all options, and almost all hope cut off Anna did the only thing that she could. As the grandfather clock began to chime downstairs, Anna tried to yell and wave amid the smoke pouring from the small attic window upstairs.

It was ironic, she thought as her strength ebbed, that the very thing that had made her plan so perfect would now be her demise. No one would hear her or the clock as they both chimed their last in a disaster of her own making.

Too many mistakes, she thought, as she struggled for breath, burning air searing her lungs. Too many mistakes.

Fuck.

Chapter 48

'LET'S TRY AGAIN. I'LL put my weight on the other side.'

Beau shifted to the right of the boat, wind and rain in her eyes, fear gripping her heart in a vice as the swell took the boat up and down like a roller coaster.

'No, it's no good, it'll t...tip on the swell. I'm okay h...here. Just remember to s...signal the lights with your phone t...torch when they get nearer. We need to g...get out of here asap. Do you...you... have signal yet?'

Beau checked her phone and saw the no calls sign still printed at the top. 'No.'

She looked back toward the shore, but from here the lights were barely visible. Too soon to signal yet. She wanted to cry as the boat tipped and pitched, and although she said nothing, Hannah seemed to sense her fear.

'It'll be okay Beau, the b...boat won't tip over out here, you'll be fine. We're safe.'

Beau continued to watch the lights as the horizon rose and fell, taking her stomach with it.

'I wish I'd trusted you from the start,' Beau said, her lips chattering in the cold, wet air.

Hannah was quiet for a moment and Beau felt her heart jolt to a start as she scrambled up, rocking the boat with a small scream.

'Woah, Beau, what are you doing? S...stay still, just stay still.'

'You didn't answer, and I...'

'I'll be f... fine, Beau. I'm used to the water now. I w... was just thinking.'

Hannah brought her chin up to the side of the boat to show pale skin and dark lips. Beau didn't think that was all right, not at all, but Hannah sounded fine, other than the shaking.

'Thinking?'

'Wondering why you wouldn't trust m...me. I'm your best friend, Beau, I... I love you. I'd never hurt you.'

Beau nodded and felt a tug of emotion rise from the pit of her stomach.

'It was something Joe said about your old friend Cassandra. I see now that it was stupid, all you've done tonight is try to save me. I was the one that jeopardised everything. I'm sorry.'

'Nothing to b... be sorry about.'

There was a period where Hannah looked out at the ocean. Her whole head was shaking above the water, her teeth clashed, and her eyes looked drooped. Beau took a freezing hand in her own and held it tight.

'There is. I should have known.'

'I... I've never told anyone th...this, but I k...killed her, Beau. I did. I w... was angry. I wanted to k... keep her with me, b... but I didn't know how. I l...loved her so much, I... I just wanted to...'

Hannah broke off as her head ducked under the water and she came up gasping.

'Hannah.' Beau reached her arms down and held her friend up out of the water. Hannah shook violently as Beau placed her friend's hands back on the edge of the boat and held them there.

'I know it...it was wrong. I d...did bad. I was frightened th...they would find out, I was so s...scared. I went... therapy. I never f...forgave myself. W...would do anything t...to bring her back.'

'It doesn't matter, Han, it's over. Don't worry.'

'I don't w... want you and J...Joe to think bad o...of me. I did w...wrong. I know. I... I love you... all. You, J...Joe, Leila. Oh g...God Leila, I h...hope she has m...more of J...Joe's good genes.'

Beau nodded, her teeth clattering against each other.

'Leila has the best parts of both of you, and we love you too, Han. We all do.'

Hannah shook. 'You...you said...'

'I know, but I didn't understand. I didn't.'

Beau felt tears fall from her eyes and down into the water, because whether Hannah had done that to her friend in the past or not, she had saved Beau's life tonight in more ways than one. What that meant if they ever got out of this situation, Beau didn't know, but she certainly wouldn't desert her friend. They would work through it and decide how to proceed, just as Joe would have to. The confession changed everything, and now it was said it couldn't be unsaid.

'I... I love t...too hard.' Hannah said, proving that she understood that, too.

Beau nodded at Hannah's pale face. 'You do, but if you're aware of that, that's the start. It's going to be okay. It was a long time ago, and you've proved you're better than that person tonight.'

'D...don't be afraid of m... me.'

'I'm not.' Beau said and realised that it was the truth. She had been afraid earlier, and maybe she would be afraid in the future, but right now, all she felt for Hannah was love and admiration. 'We're going to get out of here, and we're going to work it all out. It's going to be all right.'

There was a period of silence and then something caught Beau's eye, bright in the darkness. She looked up from Hannah to the shoreline and saw the burning walls of the cottage. Part of her heart wanted to burn with it. Edamine was in there, lifeless, burning in the remains of her childhood mess.

'She's burning the cottage.'

Hannah turned herself so that she could see to the shore, her hands shaking on the wooden edge of the boat.

'No ev...evidence.'

'She shouldn't be able to get away with it. Why can't those people move faster?'

'T...too dangerous, you know that.'

'I know it just annoys me. I'm freezing and I'm scared, and we've been attacked, and I'm terrified just lying here. What if they never find us? What if we drift out to sea?'

Hannah turned herself back round to face Beau. Her eyes looked dark in her ghostly pale face, and Beau felt her heart stumble.

'Too many I...islands h...here.'

Beau nodded and looked back toward the shore. It seemed that the fire had spurred the people – police? But how would they know? – into action. The lights were dipping rhythmically and were much closer than they had been just minutes ago.

Fire had a way of turning up the heat and intensity, and right now Beau was glad Anna had burned the place, maybe it could help them out.

She tried to smile, but her lips didn't seem to want to stretch over her chattering teeth.

'Huh! They're here, Han. Hold on a little longer. We're going to be okay.'

'T...torch.' Hannah said, her voice barely audible.

Beau thought she meant the people's torches and then she realised what Hannah meant. Out here in the black of the ocean with the swell of the waves they wouldn't be seen.

'Yes, I'm getting it. I'll yell at them too.'

Hannah just nodded, or maybe that was the shaking of her head. Either way, Beau thought, it meant that she was alive... for now. She didn't know how long they had been in the water and didn't know how much longer Hannah could last. Even her nails were blue, and the ends of her fingers looked dark, too.

Beau struggled against the slowness of her own brain as she tugged the phone from her pocket.

'H...hurry, Beau.'

'I am. We're going to be okay.'

Beau tapped the screen with shaking hands and flicked the torch on. It took a few attempts to make her voice loud enough to be heard, but once she had warmed it up, she screamed until she was hoarse.

She screamed until she thought there was nothing left and then finally, thankfully, one light turned their way, and then another, and then movement as some of the lights dipped and rose toward the ocean.

Beau continued to shout and wave, tears streaming down her face, mixing with the salt from the sea and the splash of the waves. Relief slid from her shoulders. They were safe, they would be okay.

'We did it, Han. They've found us. We're going to be okay. We're okay.'

Beau looked to where Hannah should have been grasping the boat, but she was gone.

'Han? Hannah!' Beau screamed and threw herself to the other side of the boat, thinking that her friend had somehow moved around while Beau was waving, but she wasn't there. She wasn't anywhere. 'Hannah!'

The boat rocked violently, and Beau felt terror grip her again as her voice echoed around the vast space. She sat herself in the middle of the boat, breathing hard, and gripped the sides, her frozen fingers shooting pain up her arms, her phone dropping to the floor of the boat.

'Hannah!'

Beau's head swivelled, but there was simply no sight of her friend, and no answer from the dark.

'Han! Hannah!' Beau's voice cracked, 'Han, they're here, we're safe! We're safe.'

Beau let out a sob and sat with her hands over her face, and then she sniffed and chastised herself.

Whoever these people were on the shore, if they could get help quickly enough, then they may be able to locate Hannah too. She may just have let go and couldn't get back. She was a strong swimmer. She may be swimming somewhere out there alive. If the oars hadn't gone over when Hannah had tried to get in earlier, she could have checked herself, but it still may not be too late.

'Hey! Over here! We're over here!' Beau shouted, waving the phone at the lights on the shore.

Miraculously she heard a male voice holler something back, and Beau let out a sob.

They knew they were here; they had been found.

Beau slumped forward, placed her head in her hands and sobbed as thunder rumbled far off into the distance, leaving only the hiss of rain to accompany her.

Epilogue

AUGUST

1 year later

Beau pulled on a jumper and relaxed back on the picnic blanket as she watched Leila paddle and Joe flip burgers on a small disposable barbecue next to her. The sun was warm, but the breeze was cool, nothing like the heat of the year before. Last year would have been perfect for Joe's 'barbie on the beach', but she supposed last year had been a lot of things.

'Is everything packed now?' she said, laughing as Leila screeched at the cold.

'All packed and ready for adventure.' Joe smiled. 'Do I sound confident? Because I don't feel it.'

'Ah, we'll all be there to help, and your brother isn't far away, is he?'

'No, that's one of the reasons I chose Frome. He's only a couple of miles away, by the golf course. I'm sure he'll be bugging me lots. We're closer now than we've ever been. Plus, I'm nearer the sea. The place is perfect, Beau. The school seems nice for Leila and she's happy to start her own adventure while I work and start mine. We're right across from the woods, which open out onto the nature reserve and the beach. All the amenities are within walking distance. I'm ready for a complete change. I just don't know whether I'm capable.'

Beau nodded. She certainly understood that feeling. She had felt lost after Patrick left and the divorce, almost cast out to sea with...

Nope. Not going there today.

She shivered and sat up.

'You've handled everything that's come your way so far, Joe, and this last year has been particularly hard, what with selling up and trying to sort Hannah's affairs and the business.'

'I feel wrecked.'

'You look it.'

Joe grinned, and then he laughed. 'At least I won't have to work in the local shop. I'm a businessman now.'

'Businessman!' she leaned over and slapped Joe's arm playfully. 'They carry you, and I love the shop!'

Joe grinned over at her, his brown hair flopping in his eyes, and she felt a tug of affection for this man who had been through so much, not just in the last year it seemed, but in the many years before, and all for falling in love.

'I'm glad, and of course they do, but I like to show willing, and I'm learning a lot.'

Joe had tried to wrap the business up, but Hannah's accountant and her second in command had persuaded him to let it run. The business was making a lot of money, and the deal that had been done in Scotland last year had been risky but had paid off massively. It was a shame that Hannah wasn't here to see it unfold, and it was a credit to her that she had such loyal and capable staff. Now Joe was at the wheel, and with no clue about what was going on, and the help of the accountant, he had upped everybody's wages and told the manager to do what he had to. A year later, he had a lot more of a clue and was getting more involved with Hannah's vision.

'You are learning a lot. Last time I saw you, you were talking plans and projections.'

'Yes.' Joe side-eyed her, reaching for a beer and handing Beau a can of her own. 'Did it sound good? I love to repeat what they say. It's like learning a whole new language.'

Beau laughed as she popped the can and took a sip of cold fizz. 'I'd have believed you if I didn't know you. Don't worry, you're getting there.'

Joe smiled, taking a much more unfiltered swig of his own beer. 'And what about you? Are you getting there?'

Beau looked across the loch and the area that now felt like home.

'I think I'm there already. I wouldn't want anything to change right now. I just want time to keep everything the same.'

After the night of Edamine's death, the attack and subsequent rescue from the boat, Beau's life had fallen apart for the second time in just two years. Everything was gone, everything except the clothes on her back, her phone, and luckily, the money in her bank account. If she thought she had stripped her life of excess after Patrick, it was nothing compared to this. She had nothing. Not even a best friend to stay with.

For a while, she had stayed with Ophelia and Gill in their spare room. They had grieved together and begun to heal together, all of them for Edamine, but Beau more for Hannah. The guilt was the worst. The guilt that she had doubted Hannah, that she had tried to twist her words and look for the negatives, even when she gave her the gift she had brought down from her stay in the highlands. The doubt that even after they had worked together to get out of the cottage and away from Anna - which was all Hannah's plan - that she was still looking for ways to get her revenge by getting Beau into the boat.

The grief and the loss of Edamine she could share with Ophelia and Gill, but the guilt and loss of Hannah she shared with Joe. He had been in contact almost daily since the attack, and he too had beaten himself up for both thinking that Hannah was psychotic, and that he had put doubt into Beau's head. He had sobbed for hours after Beau had said that some of her last words were of how much she loved Joe and Leila, and Beau had sobbed with him.

It had taken her three months to realise that having so little gave her a massive opportunity to start over. Homelessness hadn't hit her as hard this time, she felt more prepared, more able to cope, and after some consideration, and some reassurance that she would be back to visit Gerard and Ophelia and Gill, she had decided to cut ties and move to a small village further north and significantly more inland, albeit at the side of a large loch.

She didn't know the area, and hadn't heard of the village, but the house that had been up for rent was perfect. Small enough to be cosy, large enough for her to dedicate a whole room to her writing - a real office. Not only that, but the scenery was stunning. Mountains surrounding the small hamlet, and the loch, complete with sandy beach, across the road, just a small way down the track.

There was no seventies decor, no shutters, no ruined church on the cliff, no roar of the ocean, and most of all no unexplained noises from a dead rector, and Beau couldn't have been more grateful. What there was, however, was a robin, small and rotund, with a perfect red breast, that visited Beau every day, tapping on the window of her office if she hadn't been out to chat with it and throw seed by ten am. Beau loved the moments of perfect solitude and yet perfect companionship of simply sitting with the bird and watching it eat at her feet. It reminded her of a time not too far back when she had met the bird man in the park and her life had changed almost overnight. He had said that the swan reminded him of his wife, greedy and bossy, and Beau thought that she understood. This robin reminded her of Hannah; it had the same chatty, insistent manner. If loved ones could come back as birds she wondered, maybe she and the bird man had hit upon theirs by chance. She chatted to the robin every day, minding the bird man's advice of leaving the phone behind and being present in the moment, and strangely, she really did feel better for it.

It wasn't long after she moved in that she had rescued a small wire-haired terrier from an elderly neighbour who could no longer look after her properly. It was the perfect deal, giving Beau companionship and an excuse to get out when not writing, and the gentleman next door, Ned, the chance to continue to see his very excitable little Poppet. When an opportunity to work part time had arisen in the local shop, Beau had seen it as an opportunity to get to know her neighbours and make some friends. She had found the village welcoming, made friends, joined a book club, and even met a man, Troy.

Things were still new in that area, and Beau wasn't up for a whirlwind romance, she was content to let things play out slowly, and Troy, a victim of his own divorce, coincidentally at the same time as Patrick had been telling Beau that he was filing for divorce, was on exactly the same page. So far, the last two months had been sweet courtship and plenty of laughter, and that had been all she needed.

Writing in this house had come fast and sharp, with ideas and creativity flowing freely as Poppet slept at her feet. At the time of the fire, losing over a fifty thousand words of story about a possessed girl had seemed catastrophic, but now she understood the story was never meant to be told. The events in the cottage were all simply there to teach her she could. After a call from her publisher telling her they would extend a further six months after her ordeal, Beau had simply, and gratefully, restarted.

Strangely, she had finished putting the last words to this new story within the old six-month deadline, and had submitted the story early, surprising everyone, not least herself. Now that the pressure was off to make the kind of money that she had needed to live in Chester, the words flowed so much more easily, and the story had to be the tightest she had ever written.

Who was it that said that to me once? Or did I make it up?

The robin came to mind, and Beau thought of the bird man.

Yes, it was him! He was full of advice that came to pass. I wonder where he is now.

Then she checked herself.

He's at the park lake the same as always, feeding the swan. Maybe I'll go back and visit one day, tell him how right he was, and how he changed my life... maybe.

Beau smiled as she looked across the scenic bay surrounded by pines, and rolling hills, and listened to the gentle lap of water at the edge of the loch. It was a large body of water and not something that Beau would be diving into anytime soon, but it was calm and predictable. Even on stormy days, there was just a half hearted lap at the shore. On calm days, the water was like glass. Today it was an even middle of the road, with ripples travelling across the surface.

A scream jolted Beau's gaze to the left, and she looked to see Poppet streaking across the waterline, showering Leila with water as he passed.

'I know someone who's going to have a cold, wet, little girl.'

'I know someone who's going to have a filthy, wet, dog,' Joe countered.

'Glad he's not sleeping on my bed tonight, then.'

Joe and Leila had been staying in her spare room for the last couple of days, and Leila and Poppet had been almost inseparable since they had met.

'Nor mine. Glad I'm not sheet washing either.'

Beau chuckled and Joe joined her, knocking her shoulder with his before tending to the burgers and placing them in buns.

'I'll help wash,' he said.

'No, you won't. This is your holiday.'

Joe winked. 'I always knew there was a reason I liked you, Beau.'

'Sheet washer extraordinaire.'

Joe snorted and then both he and Beau were laughing as he yelled for Leila and both girl and dog, each as wet as the other, came running to the smell of food.

'So, what happened with that American guy? Did you meet up in the end?' Joe asked when the small picnic was put away and they were both sitting with another beer on the mat.

'Hmm,' Beau said, swallowing beer that was making her colder in the already cool air, 'Daniel. We did meet up, he's a really nice guy. I met him once before, though, did I tell you that?'

Joe shook his head. 'No, you only said that he called the police, and you wanted to meet him and thank him.'

'I'd be dead if it wasn't for him, of that much, I'm certain. But it's funny. I saw him on the cliff that morning. I was up there alone and he's a strapping young lad, I thought he was going to murder me, but he seemed to hang back and give me space before we got chatting. He asked if I lived at the cottage, and I realised I had seen him down there before. I accused him of watching me, and he confessed he had been staking me out, for my sister, who was looking for me.'

'For Anna, who was looking for Edamine?'

Beau nodded. 'But obviously, I didn't know that at the time. I said that I didn't have a sister, and we parted ways. It was only after the conversation with you that I began to put two and two together. I thought it would be a plausible story for Hannah to use.'

Joe frowned. 'So, you thought it was Hannah?'

'I couldn't be sure, but this guy seemed sure that I was who she was looking for, and he mentioned a feud between us, and then, of course, that night, Hannah turns up at the door in a storm.'

'Creepy shit.'

Beau shivered. 'Unbelievably. So anyway, it turns out that Anna – the real star of the show – had been staying at the Antler hotel, where Daniel worked. Both he and his boss had their doubts about Anna. His boss had seen huge mood swings, and knew that she had taken a steak knife from the dining area a few nights before the attack, but Daniel who had been... well, closer to her, had not only seen hidden plans for an attack at Bluebell Cottage, but that Anna was really dark haired after her blonde wig slipped.'

'He was sleeping with her?'

'Apparently.'

'Poor kid, that'll haunt his nightmares for a while.'

'Well, not only that. She set up the sob story about her sister, who we now know was Edamine, and he said that he would help find her. He staked out the cottage, found I was there, and put two and two together. Luckily for me, he didn't automatically assume. When I met with him last month, he said he wanted to make sure and that's why I kept seeing him around the cottage, and that he also had his reservations about what he was doing. When I said I lived there, he believed I was the person she was looking for and finally gave her the info she needed.'

Joe winced. 'Crap.'

'Meanwhile, coincidentally, I'm inviting Edamine down to the cottage for tea in the storm of the century. So she didn't know that I wasn't Edamine, and I didn't know she wasn't Hannah. If I just hadn't invited her that day, Edamine may still be alive, and so may Hannah.'

Joe took her cold hand in his and squeezed.

'Not your fault, I've told you.'

Beau nodded with a sigh. 'I still wonder if Anna would have stayed at all if Edamine hadn't been there. Maybe she would have moved on, and Hannah and I would have made amends, and everything would have worked out.'

'Maybe it would have been worse. Maybe you would have believed her story too and given her Edamine's address. Same fate, different day.'

Beau would like to have thought not, but in reality, she was a sucker for happy endings. If Anna said that they had been estranged and she was back to make peace? Yeah, she probably would have been delighted to show her where Edamine was.

'It could have happened, I agree.'

'Don't beat yourself up. So how did this kid know to call the police at the right time? It was pretty uncanny how they got there in time to rescue you.'

'He followed her, on a hunch, no less. He had seen the plans on her computer, outlining ways she could attack, and whether she would wear her disguise. Then he saw Anna go out to her car in the storm with her suitcase. He said he just knew that he should check on the cottage and make sure she was really leaving and not carrying out her plan. As it happened, he followed her right to the cottage door, and when he heard screaming, he called the police. But get this for uncanny, Joe.'

Joe sipped his beer and looked at her, his free hand still entwined in hers.

'The scream at that point was *Hannah*. None of us heard the door open, and then Hannah looked into the Hallway and this dripping wet woman was just standing there. If Daniel had stayed to hear more, he would have heard us all laughing and making tea. Luckily, he ran, thinking the scream was enough proof.'

'Which gave the police time to get to you over the land by the time Anna really was up to no good.'

'Exactly. They had officers speak to him before the night was over, and he showed the police her car, telling them she had stowed her suitcase in there before leaving. They were staking it out, but she never came back, obviously. He helped them with all he knew about her clothes and wig and what she had with her, but then they found her body in the rubble of the cottage with Edamine's the next day.'

Joe huffed. 'The kid should be on the force.'

'Well, funnily enough, he's travelling the next six months in Scotland and then going back home. He's training to be a lawyer. Starts college next year.'

'With that eye for detail, he's going to be one of the most sought-after lawyers in America, if not the world.'

'Absolutely. I was so grateful to him I couldn't even express, because if I'd have been stuck in that boat just five minutes longer, I'd probably have been dead too. I don't even remember the rescue. By the time they got to me, they said I was slurring and confused and stripping my coat off because I thought I was burning up when my body temperature was dangerously low. Isn't that weird?'

'It's terrifying, Beau, that's what it is. It was touch and go. They even had to warm your blood, did you know that? It was a remarkably close call.' Joe looked out across the loch and ran a hand over his face with a sigh. 'I could have lost you both.'

Beau cast her gaze down at the blanket, under no illusion how much Joe had been through since that night too. 'I thank you every day for being at the hospital with me. You didn't have to do that, and it must have been so hard to watch.'

He nodded. 'It was, but I wanted to be there. I was terrified for you... I also didn't want you to wake up alone, you know.'

Beau nodded. She had no family, and Patrick had been sunning it up in the Maldives with Laura as Beau had been recovering in hospital. He had sent his best wishes but made no move to be at her side. It had been the lack of care, and the lack of action that had pushed the final nail into the coffin. If she hadn't fully known she was nothing to him before, she did now. Beau had sent him no messages to say she was okay after release, and he had sent no further messages either, their last contact simply 'best wishes' like she had been moving away, not dying in hospital.

Last year it had hurt like hell. This year Patrick was a distant memory, and someone she knew she was better off without. His release had allowed her to stand on her own two feet, to be somewhere she loved, with people she loved. The last two years had given her more insight into herself and what she could handle than anything else she had ever done in her life.

'He's an idiot, Beau. You did nothing wrong. Don't think about it.'

Beau smiled. 'I'm not. I didn't need him. I needed you, and I needed Hannah. You did all you could even though you were hurting too. I really appreciate that, Joe. I only wish Hannah could have been at your side, or even in the next hospital bed, you know?'

Joe's eyes filled with tears, and he quickly scrubbed them away with a sniff. He watched Leila splash with Poppet at the edge of the loch for a while, and then he turned back to Beau with a sigh.

'I was so sure they'd find her alive. I'd have put money on it. She was such a strong swimmer. I just presumed that she would be okay. I had hope, even when they knew better than I did.'

'I had hope too,' Beau said, scooting to squeeze an arm around his shoulders, her own tears not too far behind Joe's.

Their hope hadn't been enough though, and when they found Hannah's body in the next bay nine days after the attack, it had hit both of them hard.

Joe squeezed his own arm around Beau's shoulders, and she rested her head on his shoulder.

'She was amazing that night, you know? I'm not sure I'd be sitting here if it wasn't for Han. I was a mess, trying to save Edamine when she was beyond saving, and when there was someone who was going to murder us, too. I just couldn't get my head around why Anna would bother killing us. It's obvious now, but I just couldn't understand, it's like my brain was running through treacle.'

'Shock, probably.' Joe said.

'Yeah, thankfully Han got it, she thought quickly, and moved quickly. She got the knife and the pan from the kitchen without Anna knowing, and she said that after she had stabbed her thigh, I was to hit her hard. I remember her saying it was important because Anna would be focused on her, not me, and that when she was down, we would grab the front door keys and run. I don't know whether she thought I would even follow through, but she never left me, Joe, and she had so many opportunities. She was sitting in the hallway alongside the open front door for a good many minutes while Anna played her narcissistic game. She could have run, she could have left me, but she didn't.'

Beau felt a tear leave her eye and run down her cheek. Joe was now crying openly, as he always seemed to be able to do.

'I'm sorry I gave you cause to think anything else. My head was all over the place. I'm just so sorry, and I wish I had a chance to tell her how sorry I am that I misjudged her.'

Beau nodded and stared at the water, a funny sensation arriving in the pit of her stomach as something Ophelia said came back to her.

'Karma.'

'What?' Joe sniffed, his tears drying on his face.

'Ophelia said something to me about karma when I lived with her and Gill afterwards. She was talking about Edamine's family at the time, but I think it relates to Hannah too.'

'Doesn't karma relate to all of us?'

'Yes.' Beau nodded. 'But mostly we can't see it, can we? Hannah drowned in the sea, Joe, right next to a boat that could have saved her. If I hadn't been so scared of the ocean, she would have tried harder to get in, and I would have tried harder too. I was so terrified that the boat would tip on the swell and that I would end up in the sea that she chose to stay in the water, honouring my fear more than her own life.'

Joe looked blankly at her.

'I don't get it.'

'If I'd have gone into the water, there is no doubt that I would have drowned, Joe. I could barely breathe *inside* the boat. I was so scared that my thoughts weren't rational. If I'd have fallen in, I'd have panicked and probably drowned us both.'

'Well, you've always been scared of the open water. She knew that.'

Beau knew that he still wasn't getting it, and she felt as though she could barely grasp it, either. The thread swinging away in the breeze and then coming back with a little insight before blowing away again. Beau frowned.

'She drowned, just like Cassandra. Back then, Hannah was safe, Cassandra wasn't, by her own hand. This time I was safe, and she wasn't, again, by her own hand. It was like a karmic situation, like she was turning the situation around, and making amends, even if she didn't know it.'

'Ah,' Joe said. 'I see where you're coming from, but we don't know that actually happened, do we? I mean, more than probably it didn't. I just wasn't in a good place for a lot of years, and I was looking for... something. I don't know, but Hannah wasn't a killer, that I'm sure of. She just loved too hard.'

The statement hit Beau in the stomach.

She loved too hard.

The exact words Hannah had said by the boat, back when she was freezing in the water.

Then Beau remembered that she had never told Joe of Hannah's confession in the water. He wasn't aware that she had killed Cassandra at all, even probably thinking that his own scrutiny of the photograph in the media was wrong.

Well, why does he need to know any different? Why taint the memory? She came good in the end, and she tragically paid for what she did. She'll always be a hero to me.

'You're right, it was just the tragic similarities that hit me,' Beau said, squeezing Joe as she watched Leila, now running with a stick, poppet running behind her on the sand. 'She'll never be anything less than a hero to me.'

'And now I've seen what it takes to run her business, she'll never be anything less to me either.'

Beau wondered if she'd heard right and pulled away to look at him. His mouth twitched as he stared back.

'I'm not joking, I'm glad I'm being carried,' he said, and suddenly they were both laughing. Joe raised his can and Beau raised hers to clink it with.

'Hannah the hero,' he said.

'Hannah the hero.'

As they were drinking a Robin flew down onto the mat, small and rotund. It chattered, picked at crumbs a while, and then flew away into a nearby tree.

Love you, Han, Beau thought with a smile as she watched it. There'll never be a better friend in the world.

THE END

Review

If you enjoyed this book it would be fantastic if you could leave a review.

Reviews help to bring my books to the attention of other readers who may enjoy them too.

Help spread the joy... or indeed, the fear!

Thank you!

Chapter One

T HE KEY TURNED EASILY in the lock, clicking the barrel over with a dull thud. Willow Townsend felt the cold metal under her fingers as the world seemed to tilt beneath her feet. Blood pulsed frantically in her ears and her vision doubled. She placed a hand on the doorjamb, closed her eyes, and began to count.

Breathe in for four, hold, out for six. In for four, hold, out for six.

It's okay. Breathe. Calm down. Stay present. Feel the wood under your hand. The paving under your feet, the smell of pine. Notice the breath in your chest, the beating of your heart...

Ah, well, maybe that was a bad one - her heart seemed to be racing a million miles an hour.

With a small huff she opened her eyes, and after a few more steadying breaths, the world seemed to come right again. She pushed a strand of mousy hair from her cheek where it had stuck with sweat.

Sweat.

Although it was a cool September day, and the temperature in the car had read just ten degrees.

She turned, pressing her back to the door, and released a long breath.

'Anxiety stems from thinking about the future, but I don't live in the future,' she whispered. 'What's here, right now?'

She inhaled the scent of the pine forest which wrapped the cottage and driveway with just enough open space to not feel claustrophobic, and just enough cosiness to feel like a hug. A gap in the trees gave way to a single-track tarmacked lane, which led down over the river Bree and into the village of Clover Nook below. Ahead, in the centre of the dusty stone and gravel packed drive, was her car, still cooling after the long journey.

'See, it's okay, the car is there, you can leave. There's always a choice. Always. You don't have to do this,' she whispered.

Although that wasn't strictly true. It was just a way of tricking herself out of the instinct to fight, or flee from, an old stone cottage in Central Scotland. A pretty cottage that she had rented on impulse after many urges from her concerned mum, and an understanding that things needed to change for her to feel okay again.

At least look around the place, even if you don't stay. The village is pretty and quiet. It would be a shame to run without even looking, especially as you've come so far... and you did promise Mum you would give it a go.

Willow chewed her lip as her mind began to settle into an uncomfortable compromise.

Clover Nook *had* been pretty in the sunshine. Along the single track lane she had passed a handful of grey stone houses with slate roofs, two small shops, a post office, community centre, and the Wild Pheasant pub. Just below her, at the bottom of the lane, was the only large house on this side of the village. A beautiful black and white building with a thatched roof, leaded windows, and large beams that trailed though it like a picture book cottage. On the outskirts of the village, there had been more houses dotted into the forest and hillside, but up here on this lane, she was alone. Ivy Cottage was the only house this side of the river, and that suited Willow just fine.

So, let's at least have a look around before you start back, eh?

As she felt herself backing down, there was a buzzing in her pocket, and her mouth stretched into a smile as she unlocked her phone. It was a message from Carlton.

Hope you're okay, babe. Missing you like hell. I don't understand this madness, but I do understand that you need to be given a chance to make your own mistakes. It's part of your healing. Anytime you need to, you can come home. There will always be a place for you here. Did I say I miss you?

Love always, C.

PS. don't forget we upped the Prozac to 40mg. If you struggle, it's okay to take 60mg, but no more. I have your prescription on file, just let me know when you need more, and I'll bring them to you. I know, I know, you're apparently hundreds of miles away, but... any excuse to see you.

Warmth spread through Willow. She missed him, too. Carlton had been her rock, the only one to have understood since the terror of that day, and he had been the right person to be with in more ways than one. Not only her long-term partner, but a psychiatrist by profession, he had taken care of her completely, inside and out. She was utterly grateful... but there was no way she would disclose her location. That would defeat the purpose of doing this at all, because he would make up all manner of excuses and end up staying here with her, or worse, taking her home.

She had promised Mum she would give this time alone, and she had promised herself. It was a promise she wanted to keep, no matter how much it hurt.

She messaged back, ignoring his urges to see her.

I'm good, missing you too. Just about to move in. Hopefully the year will go quickly, it seems such a long time right now!

Willow pocketed the phone, forcing herself not to immediately answer his reply. That was another thing she had to stop. She loved him, but she relied on him too much, and leaned on him for everything. She knew he didn't mind, but this was her time now, her own experiment in healing, because she'd discovered over the last four years that even a therapist didn't seem to hold all the answers.

Willow inhaled and blew out a long breath, pulling her attention back to the driveway. Now that her anxiety was subsiding, so was the impulse to get back in the car and flee.

And that's good, just go easy. No rush.

She turned to face the front door. The burgundy wood was sturdy and solid and adorned with nothing but a small round keyhole. It may have been stark and imposing, if the two large bay windows, with their colourful flower boxes, and a decorative free standing letterbox hadn't flanked it. As it was, the cottage was chocolate-box pretty, and the swathe of ivy enveloping the right-hand side only added to its appeal. She reached out a hand, felt her heart begin to thump, and paused.

Am I really going to do this?

Her hand was inches from the wood, and her breath caught in her throat. The door seemed to grow in size, like a strong sentinel, gatekeeper to all that is unknown, and all that is terrifying.

Stop it, Willow. It's just a bloody door. A normal door to a normal cottage.

Before she could think any further, she pushed the door open, grabbed her suitcase, and stepped inside.

She stood in a small porch area with a coat hook and a shoe stand to her left. Ahead was an entire wall of privacy glass, etched with thick swirls, and a central glass door. To capture the light in this small space, she supposed, but what she liked was that she could see shapes in the hallway beyond. The glass screen acting like a filter before she was exposed to the full 3D reality of the world inside.

Unlocking this second door - an added security measure that she liked - she stepped into a much wider hallway than she had expected. Plain brown carpet lined the floor, but it was a pleasant contrast to the freshly painted magnolia walls. A sideboard sat to her left, while a door to her right revealed a large storage cupboard. Beyond that, the cottage split in two.

To the right was a long corridor with three bedrooms, two smaller doubles at the back of the cottage, and one large bedroom with a bay window to the front. This room held a king-sized bed, flanked by a bookshelf and a small side table. Across the room by the window there was a dressing table, and to her right there was an enormous wardrobe, but even with the abundance of furniture, there was still space in here to perform her morning yoga routine.

Absolutely my room, Willow thought, feeling a tiny flicker of excitement light her stomach.

She left her suitcase in the bedroom and went back into the corridor. Past the bedrooms and back into the central hallway there was another glass door ahead. She pushed it open to reveal a bright living area, with a large bay window to the front and a smaller window to the side. A small dining table sat dead across from the door, flanked by four chairs. To its left, In front of the large bay, two small settees sat at right angles to each other by the fireplace. A blue rug divided the seating and the television, which sat on a stand in the corner.

Cosy, Willow thought, a smile lifting her mouth.

To her right, next to the dining table, a further glass door led to a small but functional kitchen at the back of the cottage. Above the sink was a window adorned with a red check blind, and next to it, another solid burgundy wooden door which led out to the back garden. To her left, after a stretch of worktop, was a further door, this one painted white. Inspection revealed the bathroom, which flanked the kitchen along the back of the house. Again, small but functional.

Shutting the bathroom door behind her, Willow walked back into the living area with a grin.

I like it. It's warm and cosy here. The place has a good flow, and a nice feel.

It was also a nice size for her alone, well protected, and secluded enough that the outside world wouldn't know she was here unless they ventured up the lane to Clover Nook woods. She had it on good authority from the owner that people didn't often trespass beyond the private lane sign at the driveway's end. The path into the woods took them away from the lane at the sign and up beside the cottage, but few people walked this side of the village. Access from the other side was much easier, and the walking more open with rising hills and incredible views.

It was more than enough for her to hide for a while. To be anonymous and invisible for as long as it took for her to understand who she was again and how to overcome her own paralysis of life.

I think I'm going to like it here.

She reassessed the small living room with a nod. She liked the low, uneven ceiling, and the neutral walls which seemed to give the room space it didn't have. Her eyes dropped to the fireplace, which was as ancient as it was charming, but she knew she'd never have to use it. The owner had renovated the cottage a few years ago. Oil-fired central heating had been added throughout, and the windows had all been replaced. The cottage would be more than warm enough.

Chocolate box, she thought, but without the hassle of being poky and chilly, as ancient houses often were.

Secure, as ancient houses often weren't.

Invisible, for as long as she needed to be.

'It couldn't be more perfect,' she whispered.

Want six free chapters of **HAUNTED?**

Sign up to my mailing list to read the first six chapters for FREE!

You also get access to exclusive behind the scenes content and extra's, and you'll be the first to hear about promotions, discounts, forthcoming titles and competitions!

Signing up is completely free and you will never receive spam from me.

To sign up visit - www.rebeccaguy.co.uk

You can opt out easily at any time.

DECEPTION. GREED. VENGEANCE. BETRAYAL.

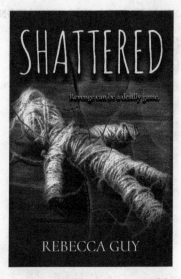

A secret envelopes Fortwind House, years old, covered in dust and locked up tight. Rumours surround the formidible woman who lives there, rumours that terrify Charley, but it is the secret that will blow her life apart.

Visit www.rebeccaguy.co.uk for more information.

DARKNESS. PARANOIA. ISOLATION.

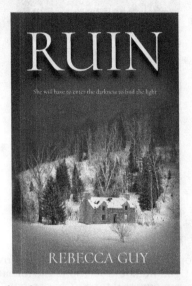

What do you do when your dream home becomes your worst nightmare? Emmie Landers is about to find out!

Visit www.rebeccaguy.co.uk for more information.

Printed in the USA
CPSIA information can be obtained
at www.ICGtesting.com
CBHW021206231124
17916CB00012B/440

9 781913 241100